The

# Violet Fox

## CLARE C. MARSHALL

*Enjoy!*

*Clare Marshall*

Other books by Clare C. Marshall

*Within*

# One

RUN. THAT'S WHAT instinct told me. It whispered to every Freetor, warning us of the danger the surface people could bring. The Marlenians would try to strike us down if we were seen in public, or worse, if our thieving hands touched their market goods.

They would never strike me down.

"I count three men to the left, on the street corner. There are four more on the other side of the market." My brother Rordan adjusted his hood, revealing his grey eyes. "Are you ready to do this?"

I grinned. "Whenever the others are in position."

Rordan shook his head, gliding his teeth over his bottom lip. "Sis, sometimes I wonder if you have a death wish."

"There are only seven guards. I've been up against more."

"We only *see* seven guards. There are always more around the corner."

"Stop ruining my fun."

"This isn't supposed to be fun. You're taking it too far with this . . . getup."

Rordan gestured to the worn violet cloak that enveloped my thin form. I pulled the hood down over my eyes to hide my mask. Every time we came up to the surface together, he got annoyed at me for "making a public display." I was always getting in trouble with him for something or other, mostly because I had a short temper. But it didn't matter what he thought. What mattered was keeping our stomachs full.

I peeked from behind the barrels where we were crouched. A stone wall ran parallel to us five stone-throws away, separating the streets into perfect lines that met at the castle far to our left. Carriages ploughed through the peasants and beggars that dotted the streets. Small blue lights hung from the second-storey windows and encircled the Marlenian royal family crest: a sceptre topped with a white orb, shining the way through the stitched, pointy mountains on the violet fabric. Over the past few months, I'd stolen dozens of stitched crests just to create my cape.

Wrinkling my nose, I lowered my eyes to the vendors. Merchants who hoped for a few coins to feed their families called to the Marlenian peasants, brandishing their wares. To my people, their apples and bread loafs were worth more than metal dug from the ground. We lived among the metal. It was everywhere and easy to get. But when you live underground, far from the sun, food is a rare treasure. I thought about the thick slice of bread and the tiny crab apple I had eaten that morning. My breakfast could've fed a family of three, but I was allowed to have it for myself—one of the privileges of risking my life every day on the surface.

A small vendor selling baked goods and fruits had the most crowded stand in sight. I gestured to the merchant and Rordan nodded. This vendor was not sympathetic to the Freetors, so he was a fair target.

The seven Marlenian guards patrolled the area like a pride of large cats stalking its prey. I'd only seen a picture of a wildcat once, when I was small. It was a special treat from my father, who had found it during one of his trips to the surface. According to him, the Marlenians had hunted them almost to extinction, except in the North, where they lived in the mountains and preyed on travellers.

Sometimes I wished the Marlenians didn't know about us. It would be easier to live that way. Every day our numbers got thinner. Maybe someday, someone would draw a picture of me to bring home to his family, and he'd say, "Those Freetors, whatever happened to them?"

It was a little hard to see with my hood blocking my vision, but a small space in the crowd cleared. My eyes were on a giant basket filled with fresh bread. The aroma tickled my nostrils and reminded me of my near-empty stomach. The basket sat on the ground next to the stand because it was too big. Approaching it from an angle, I glanced at the price tag dangling from a piece of string. For the same price as the bread, we could get enough food to feed a third of the Freetors in the Undercity. This made the unsympathetic merchants almost as bad as the Marlenian guards.

My friend Laoise was one of the runners today. She was disguised as a Marlenian middle-class errand boy. It was common for the nobles to have them—they were more reliable than Freetor slaves and they were fast, because if they displeased their masters, they would be disciplined. No one would question her as she escaped the streets with stolen goods, especially if she ran towards the castle. I nodded twice in her direction. With that signal, she casually strutted to the same merchant table.

The merchant was busy exchanging coins for goods and didn't notice as I slipped around the side of his counter. My hand hovered over the bread basket.

One of the merchant's customers, a burly man with a three-day-old beard, was gossiping beside me. " . . . and at the last address, could you see his eyes? They never left the sceptre. Every good Marlenian knows that he is not to be trusted. To think that the Holy One puts his faith in him . . ."

"Now, now, there's no need to question the Holy One's faith," the merchant replied as he reached under his counter for a bundle of apples and passed them to another customer, a lady on his right. "But I have heard rumours of the Advisor's . . . persistent behaviour lately. You'd think he was after the sceptre!"

Marlenian gossip. I knew I shouldn't care. All I had to do was close my hand around the basket handle and pass it off to Laoise—she would do the rest. But I was frozen, listening.

"Well, may his hands burn if he touches the Holy One's sceptre." The Marlenian scratched his head. "Then again, if the rumours are true, and he's as anti-Freetor as they say, maybe he should be holding the sceptre and ruling the lands. Damn Freetors, poisoning our children, stealing our food. I don't even trust the ones we have as slaves."

I gritted my teeth and wrapped my hand around the basket, slipping it between the folds of my large cloak. Marlenian lies were the only poison in the four provinces, and they infected everyone. Obviously he had never had to live underground for his entire life. I jutted my chin to Laoise, and she sauntered towards me. There were a few bundles of apples out front within reach. If I could just . . .

"You! Halt!"

I froze. Part of me wanted to run. I didn't have to look to know that the merchant had his eyes on me. My hood obscured my face, and the violet mask that hid my eyes and marked me as the Violet Fox felt heavy on my skin.

"Uncover your face, or I'll call the guards," the merchant said.

Laoise slowed and pretended to be looking at something across the street. In a few moments, she would pass behind me, take the basket from my hands, and run. I only had to stall until then.

"Tees a 'orrid sight, Meester," I said in a crackly, old-woman voice. "Tees one will get out of Meester's way."

"I thought the Holy One banned violet and purple cloaks from the market," the gossiping Marlenian said. "Because of the—"

My breath caught in my throat. Damn it.

Before the man could finish his sentence and before the merchant could shout for the guards, I tossed the basket to Laoise and threw myself on top of the merchant's counter. Apples and oranges dropped to the ground, and bread crumbled underneath me. I had to buy enough time for Laoise to escape with the goods. The merchant grabbed at me, but I swung my legs around and caught him between my thighs. He and the Marlenian citizens on the other side of the counter grabbed my upper body and pulled. The guards weren't far away. I kicked the merchant. He flew back against the stone wall and sunk to the ground. Grabbing two apples, I threw them hard over my shoulders. I heard two of them hit foreheads, and the grips around me lessened.

I propelled myself forward, underneath the counter, and found an empty basket. I shoved everything I could inside it before two guards appeared on either side of me. They drew their knives, but I was faster.

I faked left and then dived right, dipping underneath and evading the guard's grasp.

Rordan was across the street, and so was my escape route, but the road was busy with frightened Marlenians and determined guards. With two guards at my heels, I leapt on top of the barrels beside the merchant tent and threw the basket full of fruit and other goods on top of the canopy. Some oranges fell out, but I grabbed them as I climbed. The merchant tents lined the stone walls, but I wasn't close enough to jump on the wall. Praying they wouldn't collapse, I leapt from tent-top to tent-top, looking for another runner to take the basket. Marlenian guards shook the poles that held the tents upright, but I was always one step ahead of them, onto the next top.

Finally, I spotted a runner: a lanky boy with a gaunt but determined face, wearing a violet strip of fabric around his head. He was looking up at me, watching my every move just like the guards. I leapt from the tent-tops and, in mid-air, threw the basket to the runner. The guards reached for it, but the Freetor runner was quicker. He jumped and caught it with both hands, and ran. I ignored the stabbing pain in my ankles as I landed on the worn gravel street. There was no time to pause. The basket was tossed to a few different Freetor hands before disappearing into the narrow Marlenian streets. A few guards broke off to chase the runners, but the majority stayed with me, the prize, the Violet Fox.

I probably wouldn't get away with another basket of fruit, not today, not until I shook the guards. One of them grabbed my cloak— Rordan was always telling me this would happen, that I should not leave things dangling for them to catch hold of—but I undid the ties at my neck and let the fabric billow over the guard's face. I slipped away with my smaller violet cape still wrapped around me. My survival instincts told me to leave the cape behind too, that it labelled me as the Violet Fox, but I couldn't bear to part with it. The large cloak fell beyond the guard and tripped up the horses. One of them whinnied and reared, blocking the other three guards chasing me. Struggling to stay on the horse, the guard shot me a death stare as I disappeared into an alleyway.

The Marlenian streets were a maze, filled with tall, narrow buildings and even narrower alleyways. I wove between them like a master seamstress, the map of the city burned into my mind so fiercely that even the more experienced guards began to question their whereabouts. They would bring my cloak to their superior, and that would be their accomplishment for the day—but the real prize would remain elusive.

I had to get to the safe point, but I got distracted just as I was leaving the merchant district. On a narrow street, a carriage was parked outside a pub—no driver in sight, but the pub was surrounded by houses and businesses. The sun was barely at its highest point in the sky, and the driver was already having his first pint. The horses smelled like they hadn't been taken care of in days. This carriage was probably bound for the slave trade market, further north.

I flipped my cape around to hide the violet fabric and darted for the back of the carriage. No guards in sight, not yet. A few Marlenians strolled down the street but paid me no mind. Even so, I knew they'd squeal as soon as the guards showed up. A barred gate kept my people from escaping the carriage. As I approached, I counted at least twelve. Children cried for their mothers and fathers, while the older ones—some old enough to be Elders—slumped against the walls, defeated.

I couldn't let them give up. I would not see my people enslaved.

The gate was locked, of course. I wished that I had the Elders' magic. Then melting the lock would be easy.

"Look," the woman whispered. "The Violet Fox."

My face flushed as they all scurried to the back of the carriage. I had to focus. I didn't look like a driver or a guard, so I'd have to hurry. I plucked a pin from my hair and worked the lock as a child wrapped his tiny fingers around the bar.

"Are you here to save us?"

"Yes," I said.

The boy wiped his nose with the back of his hand. "I knew you were real. My brother Pat said you were just some story, but he works in the South caves, and he don't know nothin'."

I cracked a smile just as the lock snapped open. "There." A carriage was heading towards us, and I could feel Marlenians watching from their windows. We had to hurry. "Everyone out. Quick."

The Freetors tumbled out of the carriage as the driver emerged from the pub. One of the Marlenians watching from the window above, too frightened to say anything before, spoke up.

"The slaves! They are escaping!"

"They aren't slaves anymore!" I shouted. "Freedom for all, under the sun!"

I took off down the street as the freed Freetors scattered. They'd have to find their own way back underground. I hoped that Laoise or one of the other runners would intercept them, because right now, I had to make sure I didn't get caught.

Even so, I flipped my cloak again. The chase wouldn't be any fun if they couldn't spot me.

I headed for today's safe point. Safe points were chosen by the Fighters each morning. The Fighters guarded these entrances extra carefully—you needed that day's password to get back in. People who tried to enter the Freetor underground through a non-safe point entrance were treated as hostile. Bad news for the Marlenians trying to find us and for any uninformed Freetor stuck on the surface.

Today's safe point was in the eastern district of the city, which was home to the less-than-wealthy merchants, the blacksmiths, the bakers, and other Marlenians who made their living with their hands. The houses were two or three storeys tall with brightly painted shutters. Some of them even had plants hanging from windowsill pots. My stomach grumbled. I was almost hungry enough to climb up and snatch some flower petals. The guards were still teeming behind me somewhere, but I slipped into the darkness of an alleyway. The stones were smooth and cool against my body and offered a momentary respite from the chase. I closed my eyes and counted the seconds. I was not safe, not yet, but each second I counted was one second that they did not have me.

He was a whisper of wind on my cheek. I knew he was beside me, but I chose to ignore him until he spoke.

"What were you doing? You could've gotten caught!" Rordan scolded.

"Did Laoise get away?" I asked.

"Yes, she's safe, and so is everyone else. Now c'mon, let's get back before you stir up any more trouble."

Horses trotted down the road beside us. A carriage decorated in deep blues and purples and gold with a large royal crest on the door caught my attention. They swiftly passed, heading towards the castle. My eyes jumped to the stone wall running parallel to all Marlenian roads. There was a ladder lying against it, beckoning me.

"Kiera!" Rordan hissed. "That is the prince's carriage. We have to leave!"

The prince's carriage. I wouldn't dare pass up the opportunity. I scampered towards the ladder.

"What are you doing?" Rordan shouted.

"There might be something valuable in there!" Something that we could sell or trade on the underground market for silver, or food. My mouth watered.

"I doubt it! Get back—"

He trailed off. Sounds of horses galloping on the gravel and angry guards fast approaching drove me to hurry up the rungs. I snuck a glance over my shoulder. Rordan had disappeared. Fine, if he wouldn't help me, I'd do this myself, and he'd thank me later.

Guards piled into the alleyway, pointing at me and shouting my street name. They started up the ladder. With the Marlenian guards nipping at my heels, I gripped the wall and balanced myself. The wall was barely wider than my foot. On the other side of the wall, the carriage wheeled through the commotion. More guards and concerned citizens gathered. Up ahead was another street that crossed this one, where the wall turned.

It was a narrow window, but I had no choice. I concentrated on the moving carriage as I ran on top of the wall. There was a canopy beside the fork where the wall ended. Without a second thought, I leapt onto the canopy and bounced off, flying through the air and landing on top of the carriage just as it whisked by.

"Stop the carriage!" the guards shouted.

The carriage veered hard to the left. I grasped the gold trimming as my legs flew out from under me. A footman riding on the back drew his short sword. I dove into a summersault to avoid his sharp blade. While the footman struggled to catch me, I scrambled to the front. The driver looked up and saw me and tugged on the horses' reins. It was too late. I jumped on top of him. I wasn't heavy enough to throw him off. Instead, I tore off a piece of my cape and blindfolded him. While he tried to free his eyes, he released the reins. I grabbed them and whipped the horses. They rode faster. The driver pulled off his blindfold, and I drew my knife and held it to his neck.

"Help! Freetor!" he cried.

"Who is in this carriage?" I demanded.

"Prince Keegan and his servants."

"What about supplies?"

"This is a transport carriage. There is nothing of value."

I hated when Rordan was right. The driver reached for me, and I scratched his face. He yelped, and I pushed him off the carriage.

More galloping sounds came from behind. The guards were catching up. I tied the reins to the edge of the seat and climbed back on top of the carriage. Ten guards on horseback were chasing us. I waved. They spurred their horses to ride faster. I flopped down on my belly and peeked through the carriage window. A manservant gasped in surprise. Before he could draw a weapon, I rolled over and dove feet-first into the carriage.

I landed in between two servants. The prince faced me. I'd seen him a bunch of times in the square, but never this close up. My heart was pounding in my rib cage. He couldn't have been much older than me. Curly black hair framed his face in an almost feminine way. I could smell the soap he had washed with. It almost drowned my own stench. Recognition and fear crossed his yellow-green eyes. At the same time, we drew knives and pointed them at each other.

"How dare you attack my carriage, Freetor," the prince said. His voice was thick with the regional accent: long *a*'s and hard *c*'s.

I laughed. "You Marlenians like to pretend to be brave and dashing." My knife toyed with a gold chain around his neck, but I had my eye on a shiny brooch over his left breast. "Really, you're just scared meat hiding underneath silk and gold."

"And you're just a filthy Freetor playing dress-up!"

I pressed the knife against his neck and felt the cold blade of his knife dig into mine. All I had to do was press a little harder, and the prince of Marlenia would bleed like my people had bled and join them, rotting in the ground.

"It seems we are in a stalemate," the prince said. "Release me and leave, and I will forget this ever happened."

"Give me everything of value that you're wearing, and I'll consider it."

"You're in no position to bargain."

The two servants leaned away from me and shared looks of extreme terror. Balled into fists, it seemed like they wanted to fight, but were too scared to move. I twisted the blade pointed at Prince Keegan's neck. "Neither are you."

The carriage slowed to a stop. The guards shouted outside. I looked to the window, knowing I only had seconds to escape.

"My family will eat tonight," I said.

I released the knife from his neck. The prince followed suit. The carriage door opened, and an angry, sweaty guard appeared. Smiling at him, I grabbed the prince's brooch and tore it off his jacket. The servants seized my legs as I reached for the opposite door. I kicked free but lost my balance, and the guard sliced my arm. The brooch flew out the window. I screamed and fell forward. My weight pushed the door open, and I landed in the dirt.

"Seize her!" the prince ordered.

I was dizzy with shock. Something dug into my side. Thinking it was a rock, I rolled to avoid it, but the gold glint in the sun caught my eye. With my good hand, I tucked the brooch into my pocket.

"Well, well, the Fox is at it again."

Guards pulled me to my feet. I still had the mask around my eyes, but I doubted they would let me keep that for long. The prince stepped out of his carriage, and the guards parted to make way for him.

"Give it back, thief," the prince said.

"I don't know what you're talking about."

The guard yanked my head backwards and held a knife to my throat. "Perhaps this will refresh your memory."

"I wouldn't try anything if I were you," I said. "There're a bunch of Freetors watching us right now with crossbows. If you so much as scratch me, they will open fire on your precious prince."

The guards exchanged glances. I kept my expression blank. Of course there was no one waiting to rescue me. In the underground, everyone helped their neighbours get by if they were trouble. Even when I joined the Fighters, I took the vow to put my personal needs second to the needs of the Freetor people. On the surface, that vow didn't always apply. It was every man for himself to avoid getting captured. Because getting captured meant death, or worse, torture. And giving up the names of our fellow Fighters and information about our safe points meant we'd all die. Heroics were something only Marlenian women read about in their weekly gossip stories. I prayed that the guards were ignorant of Freetor customs.

"If you return the brooch, we will let you go free," the prince said.

I couldn't help raising my eyebrows. Let me go free? The guards mirrored my reaction. Wasn't I the most wanted Freetor on the streets? Wasn't the price on my head enough to feed ten starving Freetor families for a year? As if to prove his good faith, the prince held out his hand. The guards loosened their grip on my head but still held my arms tightly.

My eyes darted back and forth between his open palm and his face. If I gave up the brooch, everyone within three caverns of mine would starve. But I would be free to steal again tomorrow. Unless the prince was lying. His eyes didn't waver from mine. They were different from the guards'. Less hardened. Sheltered. Green, speckled with flecks of gold. My teeth gritted as I realized that he probably didn't worry about where his next meal was coming from.

One of the guards holding my arms kicked me in the shins. I couldn't hold back a scream.

"You have nothing to say to the prince?" the guard said. "She stares at you with such disrespect, Your Highness. I take it that she is declining your generous offer?"

"She was quite talkative in the carriage," the prince remarked.

I ignored the pain in my leg. "This brooch, when sold, will feed twenty people, maybe more. I won't give it up."

"Any merchant showing sympathy to the Freetors is breaking the law. Perhaps you could enlighten us as to which merchants are helping you, and we might be lenient."

Right. As if I would betray the few decent Marlenians sympathetic to our cause. All we wanted was to be free of Marlenian tyranny and have our own lands on the surface.

"I didn't think she'd talk," the guard said. "I would say that's a no to your deal, Your Highness."

"It would seem so," the prince replied, heaving a heavy, sarcastic sigh. "Take her to the dungeons, then. I imagine she'll feel right at home there, in the cold, damp underground."

Marlenian dungeons hadn't existed until fifty years ago. The prince's grandfather—the previous Holy One—had decreed that if the Freetors wanted to hide in their filthy holes, he would dig one for them in the castle. The dungeons were said to be twice as deep as the Freetor caves and three times as cold. Light could not survive down there. It was also said that the whole underground was reinforced with half a league's worth of stone, so a prisoner wouldn't be able to dig himself out. No Freetor had ever lived to report what was really down there, and I certainly wasn't going to volunteer for that mission.

I had another knife hidden in my boot. If I could only . . .

"Find the brooch," the prince ordered.

Their hands slipped into my pockets, and out came the brooch. Twenty people's meals in the centre of his palm. The guard handed it to his liege. My heart sank.

"Take her to the dungeons," the prince said. "Alert the authorities and the business councils that we have apprehended the Violet Fox and that she will terrorize our streets no more."

"Yes, Your Grace," the guard to my right said as he tightened his grip on my arms.

I resisted. There was no way that I was going to live the rest of my life in a dark dungeon. If I was going to die, it would be with a knife in my hand and a smile on my face—and I'd take as many Marlenian guards as I could with me. The prince, too, if I could.

One of the guards slammed me in the stomach. I doubled over again, but this time I took advantage of the opportunity. Grabbing the knife from the hidden compartment in my boot, I whipped up with a steady swing and slashed Prince Keegan across the lips. Like two fat worms, they split in two and oozed red. He screamed and fell to his knees in agony. Part of me wanted to watch him suffer, as he had made my people suffer, but Rordan's voice shouted from a distance, and it would be foolish not to heed his call. I slipped by the guards, rushing to help their prince, and followed my brother down a side street.

"You came back for me," I remarked.

"You're my sister," was all he said.

The Marlenian side streets had only foot traffic, so it was easy to lose ourselves in the bustle. More people were out than usual buying things from vendors that were tucked away beside and inside the buildings. Probably because of some Marlenian holiday that I didn't care about.

Rordan nodded to one of the vendors. Without looking down, he tilted his head to an alleyway off to the right. It wasn't wide enough for the two of us to walk side by side, so we slid between buildings with our noses scraping the opposite brick wall until the alleyway widened enough to accommodate a wooden door beneath our feet.

My brother bent over and rapped on the trap door. He muttered the day's password. After a few moments, the door popped open a crack. Two nervous eyes looked us over, and then two hands pushed the door open to its fullest. There was only enough room for one person to climb down at a time, and so I waited as Rordan slipped into the underground. Taking one last look at the sun as it shined precious rays into the small corner of Marlenia that I could tolerate, I gripped the ladder and descended into my home.

"Welcome back," said a Fighter as we reached the bottom. Fighters were our version of Marlenian guards, but they did more than just protect the people. They made sure everyone had his or her share of rations and sometimes went on secret missions to the surface. That was why I had joined, at least. The Fighter gripped Rordan by the shoulder and smiled, and then nodded to me. "The goods you took were delivered to the Freetor families in need. Well done."

"It was easy," I replied.

I grinned, but inside I knew it wasn't enough. Even if you combined the fruit and the bread I had taken, it would only feed about three Freetor families, if rationed correctly. I could've had the prince's brooch. Another Freetor guard approached the first and whispered something into his ear. I took off my violet cape and rolled it up.

"Kiera," said the second Fighter, "The Council of Elders has requested your presence in the Central Cavern."

My eyes popped. My fingernails dug deep into the cape's smelly fabric. Were they going to punish me for what I had done to the prince? Or reward me?

"Right now?" I asked.

The first Fighter nodded. "Immediately."

ONE HUNDRED NINETY-NINE years ago, a man named Alastar rose up against the Holy One, starting the war that would forever change the land of Marlenia.

Alastar had a gift that the Marlenians both feared and coveted—he could wield magic. Alastar presented his talents to the Holy One and offered his services in the name of Dashiell, their man-god. In exchange, Alastar asked the Holy One for lower taxes for merchants and other common folk. Back then, the commoners were so poor that some sold their children into slavery just to get their next meal. But the Holy One refused him. Magic was an unholy curse, meant to lead us astray, away from Dashiell's grace and light, said the Holy One. He rallied the forces of Marlenia to strike Alastar down. But Alastar resisted, and others joined him: our ancestors.

While the Holy One wanted Alastar and his magic destroyed, some secretly wanted Alastar's gifts for themselves. Alastar only entrusted his closest friends with the secrets of magic, and he made these few his apprentices. He taught them how to make objects float in mid-air and how to conjure lightning from the sky, and other spectacular things that you could only imagine. Those who joined Alastar's cause only to learn his magic did not meet a happy fate. Our ancestors fought for one reason: to be free of the Holy One's tyranny. Anyone who fought for any other reason was considered an enemy.

Thousands from around Marlenia joined Alastar's cause. And thousands died. Among the dead were the Holy One and his family. With no heir, the throne of Marlenia was ripe for the taking. Just when it looked like Alastar's men were going to win—just when it looked like everyone would be free of tyranny—another man rose to take the Holy One's place. Captain Killan Tramore took the sceptre from the Cathedral of Dashiell in the Grand Square and rallied his men. A surprise attack. Even Alastar's magic couldn't stop Tramore's rage—some say he was guided by Dashiell himself. Those who weren't killed were driven underground. They built tunnels and learned how to survive. But the Marlenians never learned how to use magic.

And now, they never would.

The flames from the Fighter's torch danced and threatened to lick the cave walls. Green moss, glowing in the orange light, grew around us. The summer weather meant a warm underground, but it also prevented us from lighting torches on the walls in fear of burning the moss, our one stable food supply. The entrance tunnel was long and narrow, sloping downward, and we walked one by one, manoeuvring around the occasional moss picker. Even if the pickers worked all day and night, the moss wouldn't feed every Freetor. Nor would we want to eat it constantly: it had a bitter taste and stuck between our teeth.

After many twists and turns, we came to an opening in the tunnel. The Great Cavern was the largest cave in all of the underground. Its walls, worn smooth by thousands of Freetor hands, sloped in a concave fashion almost two hundred arm-lengths above me. The tiniest hole at the top let in a speck of sunlight. It shone down in a perfect straight line. A few Freetor merchants showed their wares on matted and mouldy blankets, but the Great Cavern was nowhere near as busy as the Marlenian streets. The poorest of Freetors squatted beneath the line of sunlight, craning their necks to the ceiling, hands clasped in deep prayer. Some of the Freetors believed that the underground was protected by our exiled ancestors. No doubt the words on the praying Freetors' lips were a plea to those dead and gone. One of the women among them held a crying baby. She sang a song about green hills and children with full tummies, but a melody can't satisfy a child's hunger.

Their gazes were full of hope. One of the hungry Freetors reached for me, as if to ask if I had any food.

"You'll get your share soon enough," the Fighter said, brushing the hungry Freetor's hand away.

They looked to me and saw my bunched-up violet cape. They knew who I was. I nodded, confirming the Fighter's words. Meekly, they retracted their dirt-stained hands and returned to their prayers.

Rordan and I followed the Fighters through one of the passageways, away from the Great Cavern. We passed by modest Freetor homes, one- or two-roomed caverns. Some had makeshift doors: cloth pinned to the dirt and stone. Some were open, showing the secret lives of my people. Nothing was a secret here. We passed by at least forty-nine; I lost count after that.

As we drew closer to the Central Cavern, the dirt on the walls became smooth stone and there were more and more cloths hanging from the walls, not just as doors, but as decoration. One was violet and gold and depicted a hand bursting from the ground, brandishing a spear. There was a story attached to the spear, and I could almost hear my father's voice whispering it to me, but stories were only words. A spear would be better for the Violet Fox.

We stopped before a set of doors, the only wooden doors in the entire underground. The Fighters turned to face us.

"You are about to enter the Central Cavern, the place of the Elders," the first Fighter said. "What is said in the presence of the Elders stays in their presence. Am I clear?"

"Crystal," I replied.

Rordan nudged me, hard. I cried out and rubbed my arm. "I mean, yes, clear."

"Good." His eyes turned to Rordan. "Because she is not of age, you may enter as her guardian."

I couldn't help but roll my eyes. Great. Now I had to share my glory with my brother. I then felt ashamed at the thought—he had just saved my life. Rordan nodded at the guard.

From a pouch on his belts, the Fighter produced a small silver key. I watched, fascinated as it slipped into a hole beneath the protruding door handles. He fiddled with it for a moment, and then there was a loud click. The Fighters each took a handle and pressed down firmly. The doors opened as they strode into the room.

It was a magnificent sight. The walls were made of smooth, carved stone like in the Great Cavern, but everything seemed to glow. Even the floors were smooth, and they were decorated in repeating tiles with violet circular patterns. I looked around for torches, but there were none.

But the greatest sights were the Elders themselves: seven Elders to make decisions on behalf of the Freetor people and to preserve and protect the magic that separated us from the Marlenians. But only six Elders were here today. They were suspended in the air on carved stone chairs. Each chair had a high back and was carved to look like an underground animal. Elder Mainchin sat upon the giant earth-worm chair. His salt-and-pepper hair grew in patches on his head, but maybe it was just styled that way. Next to him floated Elder Clancy, on the crouching badger chair, and his twin sister, Elder Cleena, on a chair shaped as an alert rabbit sniffing the air to the left. It was said that Elder Cleena had been chosen first to train with the Elders, but she had refused to be apart from her brother. Training to be an Elder was a lifelong commitment, and for half of that time, apprentice Elders were not allowed to speak. It made me think of what I would do if I was chosen to be an Elder. Be away from Rordan most of the time and not be allowed to speak? I didn't think I'd be able to do that.

To the right, Elder Trecia sat on a chair shaped like a fox—I smiled at this. Elder Trecia was younger than the other Elders, in the middle of her child-bearing years. Her face was round but her hands, sticking out from her oversized robe, suggested she had a smaller figure. Elder Garvan, with the groundhog chair, was thinner than a tree branch and looked twice as frail. He wheezed and hacked into his hand and breathed heavily through his mouth.

The chair at the end was empty and featured an oversized ant rearing on its back two legs. I stifled a laugh. Elder Raibeart was supposed to sit there. Perhaps he was busy training the younger Elders.

The centremost chair, and also the highest floating, was a large spider. It was the seat of the Great Elder Erskina, the oldest and the most powerful person in all of the underground. The stone arachnid's legs wrapped around her frail body in a tight embrace, as if they were the only thing holding her there. Erskina looked as old as the stone in the walls, but she was nowhere near as smooth. Wrinkles lined every part of her face like the tracks that worms made in the dirt. I knew that some of the lines were scars from when she used to battle Marlenians on the surface. It was said that she could pick out a disloyal Freetor with a look and kill a Marlenian by blinking. She laced her fingers, reminding me more and more of a black widow crushing its prey as her dark, beady eyes evaluated my presence.

"Welcome."

Her voice bounced off the cavern walls. It was gravelly but melodic. The two guards in front of us bowed. I was a little shocked to see Rordan bow too. I didn't know we bowed to the Elders. Then again, I had never been summoned by them before. I hastily followed suit.

"Rise," Erskina commanded.

We did. The Fighters parted to each side of Rordan and I. "We brought her," said the first.

There was a moment of silence. Not knowing if I was supposed to introduce myself, I stepped forward and forced a meek smile.

"You are Kiera Driscoll?" Erskina asked.

I gulped and nodded. "I am."

"How old are you?"

The question startled me, and it took me a few moments to remember. "Uh . . . I'm fifteen. But almost sixteen."

"She's not old enough yet, Erskina," said Elder Trecia. I tried to hide my grimace.

"We do not have a choice," Erskina replied, unlacing her fingers and gripping the armrests tightly. "We must take action."

"If the information hadn't leaked—"

Erskina raised a skeletal hand to silence Elder Mainchin.

"What is done is done, and cannot be undone," she said. "We must stop the Marlenians from destroying us before it's too late."

"What happened?" I asked.

The two Fighters stared daggers at me, as if it were forbidden to speak. I swallowed my fear. Nothing could be worse than facing the Marlenian prince like I already had earlier that day. "I have the right to know why I'm here."

Erskina's beady eyes bored into my skull once again, but I didn't dare look away. Instead of reprimanding me, a smile spread across her wrinkled, leathery face. "Yes, you do have that right."

I glanced at Rordan. He was staring at his feet. I knew he disapproved.

"Over the past few years," Erskina began, "the Marlenians have become more cunning and aggressive. They have denied us access to food, wood, and other supplies we need to survive. They've captured our people for slave labour. But nothing compares to what they have taken now."

"What did they take?" I asked.

Erskina breathed deeply, looking up at the top of the cave. A faint blue light wafted in and drifted down the walls. She followed it with her eyes. As if by some secret order, the two Fighters left the cavern. The door banged shut behind them, echoing throughout the space.

"The knowledge of the ancients," she said quietly. "Or, if you will, the origins of Freetor magic. When Alastar Allayway led our exiled ancestors to the underground, he vowed that the surface folk would never learn the secrets of our power." She rubbed her forefinger and her thumb together daintily, producing tiny sparks of green light. "But he did want to ensure it was preserved among us. He wrote down his knowledge in a tome in a code that has now become common for the Freetors to interpret.

"Upon his death and the creation of the Council of Elders, it was determined that one of our sacred duties would be to protect Alastar's Tome, as it is what every newly chosen Elder learns from in the Temple of the Elders." She gestured to her right to a cavern blocked by a thick tapestry, where the young Elder apprentices mastered the secret Freetor magic in silence. "Alastar's Tome is more sacred, more valuable than the life of any one Freetor.

"And the Marlenians have stolen it."

My throat tightened. Every Freetor alive today owed their lives to the Elders—it was their magic that kept the Marlenians afraid of us, and it was their magic that protected us from any large-scale attack. If the Marlenians deciphered the secret to the Elders' power, we would lose our only advantage.

"How is that possible?" I asked.

"Recently, a hunchbacked merchant entered the Great Cavern selling woven blankets and clothing. The patterns were full of bright colours, and his family name and colouring suggested he was from the Southern underground, and so the Great Cavern merchants welcomed him into their fold. Somehow he managed to sneak into the Temple of the Elders, undo the magic binds, and escape with the tome without being immediately detected." She paused. "Our information suggests that there was someone working on the inside. A Temple Fighter, perhaps. Or a Freetor paid off by a wealthy Marlenian with promises of surface freedom."

I was so angry I couldn't speak. All this time, I had been trying to make a difference on the surface, to help our people, and then to be stabbed in the back by one of our own?

The folktales said that each Freetor had a drop of magic in his or her blood, and because the Holy One snubbed Alastar's offer almost two hundred years ago, the Marlenians were cursed to always want but never have our magic. Magic was dangerous in the wrong hands, and that was why only those selected to be trained as Elders were allowed to know its secrets.

"Fortunately, we know the tome has not gone far," Erskina continued. "Its pages contain special magic bonds, known only to the Elders. We feel its presence at the castle."

"If you have special bonds to the knowledge, why didn't you know it was being stolen?" I asked.

"Kiera," Rordan hissed.

"That is what is most troubling," Erskina replied, ignoring Rordan. She exchanged solemn glances with the other Elders. "We should have felt it. Because we did not, we suspect someone with knowledge of Freetor magic has undermined us."

"Someone like . . . the Holy One?" I guessed. I'd always suspected that he knew more about Freetor magic than he should. The sceptre he carried had been kept in the mountain-embedded Cathedral of Dashiell long before the Tramore family reigned Western Marlenia—it was said that when Captain Tramore held it high above his troops, it was as if Dashiell spoke through him, inspiring the men to fight for their lands. That was the day we lost ours.

"His faith in Dashiell is foolish but strong, and his fear of magic is stronger. Some acolyte of the Holy One is responsible for this, perhaps. He is not to be underestimated," Erskina admitted. "That is why we must retrieve the ancient knowledge before he has a chance to decipher our secrets."

I pursed my lips. "And that's what you want me to do."

Erskina smiled once more. "Precisely."

I couldn't help but grin. This was the most important assignment in possibly all of Freetor history, and she was giving it to me. My gallivanting around the Marlenian streets in a violet cape had paid off. It took every ounce of willpower not to jump up and down with glee.

The Great Elder's smile disappeared. "There is one condition to your acceptance of the task, Kiera."

I held my breath. "What's that?"

"No matter how tempting it may be, you mustn't read the knowledge. For if you do, we will know." The other Elders nodded profusely. "You were taught to read?"

"Our father taught us both," I replied. Pride swam in my chest. Not many Freetors could make that claim. "And I agree to your . . . condition."

Anything to accept the task.

"Excellent. I hope this won't be a challenge for you, *Violet Fox*," Erskina said with a hint of amusement in her voice.

I bowed my head and smiled. This would be easy. Even a blind man could spot Freetor magic—if he was a Freetor.

"With your forgiveness, Great Elder, if I may ask," Rordan said quietly, lifting his head, "how can I assist my sister?"

"Ah, of course, Rordan," Erskina said, turning her dark eyes to him. "You will be her messenger."

"Messenger? What do I need a messenger for?" I asked. "I go to the castle, get the tome, and come back. One day tops."

The Elders chuckled.

"Such spirit you have, young Kiera," Erskina said. "But I'm afraid you misunderstand the mission. This is not a one-day affair. I cannot have the Violet Fox gallivanting through the halls of the Marlenian Castle, as entertaining as that may be for you. You will stay at the castle, in disguise, and retrieve the tome."

My mouth fell open. "In disguise . . . at the castle?"

"I hear you are quite the impressionist. And your knife skills, they are . . . accurate, as well?" Erskina's lips were thin and bloodless as she smiled. "Quite a feat, for someone so young."

I bowed my head in thanks as my cheeks heated. She had heard about today's events with the prince. The prince. Me, staying at the castle. The prince would be there, and I would have to look at what I had done to him and pretend that I was not the Violet Fox. I tried not to think about that. "No one can, of course, completely replace the Violet Fox in your absence," Erskina said as if she had just read my mind. "But there are plenty of willing hands to dip into Freetor pockets."

"When do we leave?" Rordan asked.

"After the training. Elder Trecia will oversee the preparations."

Elder Trecia stood and humbly bowed her head. "My apprentices will be glad to assist as well."

"We will instruct you in the details of your castle identity tomorrow," Erskina replied. "In the meantime, Kiera, do not return to the surface unless instructed. I cannot have you arrested."

I hid my disappointment and nodded. So I was trapped underground, for now. A good trade-off though, for how much time I would be spending on the surface.

"That is all we require of you today," Erskina said. "Safe travels, until we call upon you again."

She waved her hand, and the doors behind us creaked open. Rordan and I bowed once more and left the Central Cavern. The Fighters escorted us to where the smooth-stone walls and Elder tapestries met the dirt-rock walls splattered with glow moss and then left to deal with other business. From there, we made our way towards our home cavern. I bounced most of the way.

"Can you believe it, Rordan? Me, in disguise, in the Marlenian castle?"

Rordan snorted. I stopped bouncing.

"What's the matter with you? Jealous?" I taunted.

"Hardly," he muttered. He grabbed my hand. His eyes darted back and forth as he made sure no one else was listening. "I have something to tell you."

"What?"

He looked over his shoulder again. I had never seen him this nervous. He brought his lips to my ear and whispered, "I think I saw the intruder who stole Alastar's Tome."

# Three

My mouth fell open. "You saw what?"

Rordan pushed me against the cold, rocky wall. "I saw him."

"Who was he? What did he look like? Was he really a Marlenian?"

"Yes . . . yes, he was definitely a Marlenian."

"But the Elders said he acted like he was from the South."

"Well, it wasn't a good impression. His accent . . . it didn't have that up-and-down flow that the Southerners have. But that's not important. Kiera, he's . . ." He struggled with his words, like they were stuck in his throat. "He was definitely the one who stole Alastar's Tome."

"Why didn't you tell me?"

"Tell you!" His voice was a heated whisper. "You would have blabbed to everyone. Your voice echoes the loudest in these caves, don't I know it. And, you were busy on the surface. It was the day you almost had to stay overnight underneath a merchant's stall because the guards were so furious—"

Three Fighters turned the corner, and Rordan quickly started telling me how I shouldn't sleep under a Marlenian merchant's tent in case I was found there in the morning and in case the Marlenian turned out not to be sympathetic to our cause. The Fighters nodded and smiled thinly to acknowledge us, and when they were out of sight, Rordan trailed off.

"I wouldn't have blabbed," I insisted, crossing my arms.

My brother looked like he was going to pull his hair out. He grabbed my arm and led me down the corridor towards home. "It doesn't matter now. The point is that I saw him . . . and he saw me."

How could my brother be so careless? After our mother and father left, it was Rordan who taught me how to move unseen through the Marlenian crowds. Sure, the rest I learned by observing the surface dwellers and mimicking their habits, but it was Rordan who was always there, guiding me, protecting me when I couldn't protect myself. If a Marlenian could spot Rordan underground, there was no hope for me on the surface.

"He spoke to me too," Rordan continued. He glanced warily behind us.

"I would have killed him on sight," I said through my teeth. "The Fighters work day and night to keep all of our entrances a secret, and even if one Marlenian discovered—"

"No! Killing him is . . . was . . . look, just relax, Sis, or I won't tell you the rest of the story." We were getting close to the Great Cavern, and there were more people around. And since the intruder had dressed as a Freetor merchant, I looked upon their tattered robes with distrust. We took a right at an adjacent cavern to bypass the bustle.

"Fine. Tell me," I said when we were alone again.

Rordan's face was as still as the stone surrounding us. "I was heading back from the Central Cavern. I had just given them a report on a surveying mission I had done that day. Like I said, you were on the surface. I decided to take a different route than usual. I don't know, I guess I was in an exploring mood." He scratched the back of his head while another Fighter passed us. "I was lost in my own thoughts when I noticed something out of the corner of my eye. I looked and thought it was a shadow—I was carrying a torch at the time, and those flames can play tricks on the eye. So I ignored it and continued on.

"It was about two minutes later when I felt the steel at my throat."

I swallowed, remembering the Marlenian guard's knife against my vulnerable flesh. Just thinking about it made me angry. "He caught you off guard that easily?"

"He was silent. He was quick. Well-trained." Rordan shook his head. "You don't have to beat me up about it. I was angry. Ashamed."

"So then what happened?"

"He said that if I told anyone that I'd seen him, he'd find me and kill me. That part I didn't believe. He'd gotten past the Fighters, but we both knew I'd keep a sharper lookout next time. But . . ."

We were nearing our cavern now. Rordan had kept his voice low the entire way home, but there was no telling who had heard us. He coaxed some glow moss from the dirt wall and started chewing on it. I found a patch and did the same. It would muffle the sound and confuse the echoes, briefly.

"There was something else."

My stomach felt heavy, like I was eating rocks instead of moss. I didn't like where this was going. "Yeah . . . ?"

"He held out his hand in front of him, like this"—he held his palm face up and lowered his voice to barely a whisper—"and suddenly this . . . this flame burst out of it. I could feel the heat on my face, but it didn't burn him."

"But only the Elders know magic!"

"Because of Alastar's Tome."

I dropped the moss as little goosebumps prickled all over my arms and legs. "He had already stolen it . . . and deciphered it? That quickly?"

Rordan's nod was slow and his face was grim. "Yeah. I think so."

"And you let him get away?!"

*Get away . . . get away . . .*

My words bounced off the cavern walls and cut through the silence. Rordan shoved me against the wall again, and this time it hurt. Pointed edges dug into my back—the walls were rougher here, less worn. I gritted my teeth and bore the pain.

"Would the mouse try to steal from the hungry fox, Kiera?" His fingers squeezed around my arm like a coiling snake. I struggled to escape, but my brother was bigger, stronger, and angrier than me in that moment.

"You could have tried!"

He smirked. "Don't you think I did? I got this for my efforts."

Letting me go, he pulled down on the collar of his dirty shirt. A blazing red scar tore down the left side of his chest, stretching just under his collarbone to below his nipple. The skin around the wound looked tender and swollen. It could have happened yesterday, by the looks of it.

"Have you seen a healer about this?"

"And say what? I wasn't chased by Marlenians that day. The whole Fighter force knew I was on a surveying mission." He slid his shirt down again. "I treated it the best I could myself."

I paused, listening for the rustling sounds of people in nearby caverns, but all of the sounds were coming from the nearby Great Cavern. "So you didn't tell anyone about this Marlenian?"

"Just you, now."

"If you tell the Elders, they could stop him!"

"If the Elders find out I've withheld this information, they'll deliver me to the Marlenians, and they'll throw me in their dank dungeon."

"You . . . you could say that he used a memory spell or something and you're just remembering everything now!"

"They'll know I'm lying. Standing in front of them today was hard enough. If they find out, they will make me disappear in one way or another. And I'm not leaving you here alone."

My heart sank as I slumped against the wall. I had to be strong in front of my brother. We depended on each other, just like the moss depended on the rain from the surface to drip down into the earth and feed its roots. He was right: while the Elders protected our people with their magic, Freetors who openly spoke against the Elders or gave into Marlenian promises of riches and surface freedom seemed to evaporate like smoke into the air. I wouldn't let them take Rordan away. He was all I had left.

"You can't tell anyone about this, and I've only told you because I think it will help you with your mission," he said firmly, resting both hands on my shoulders. "Do you swear not to say anything to any living soul?"

I looked up at him. His eyes were filled with desperation and fear.

"I swear on my honour as a Freetor. As the Violet Fox, and on the Driscoll name, I swear," I said.

Rordan released me slowly, watching my every twitch. He drew in a deep breath, let it go, and started down the passageway again. "All right. Let's go home before we get into any more trouble."

"You should've waited to tell me all this at home. Where it's safer."

"I couldn't wait any longer," he said. He hung his head in defeat. "You don't know how hard it is for me to keep secrets from you."

Home was ten caverns away. Like many other residential caverns, it was separated from the hallway by a wool blanket hanging from the ceiling. Inside, our cavern was divided into three "rooms" by thinner fabric. Rordan and I had our own rooms for sleeping, and we shared a common area for eating and socializing. We were the lucky ones. Some families only had one room. It was because Rordan and I had both joined the Fighters at a young age—after our parents had fallen on the surface to the Marlenian soldiers. They were Fighters too, and Fighters were given more comforts than other Freetors because of the risks they took on the surface.

After the Fighters had told us that our parents were probably never going to come back, Rordan took our parents' bedroom. He was only ten when he joined the Fighters. I was six. There were no rules against children joining the Fighters. Every hand was needed, and sometimes the smallest hand could reach into places the Marlenians couldn't see.

Rordan retrieved our empty water bowls and placed them outside for tomorrow's ration. Each person received two bowls of water a day—one for drinking and one for washing. He retrieved a full one that was waiting outside—our washing water. Floating in the middle of it was an opened letter. I went to fish it out, but Rordan swung around so fast that some water splashed on the dirt floor.

"Careful!" I shouted. "I was just trying to—"

"I know what you were trying to do," he muttered, setting the bowl on the stone slab that served as our table. "I opened it this morning. It's another marriage proposal."

My eyes widened. "Another one? Isn't that . . . ?"

"Two in the last month? Yes."

"Rordan! And they even took the time to write it on paper."

He slumped down onto a large rock by our stone table and sighed. "Yes, yes, I know. It must have fallen out of my pocket when I was rushing this morning. Anyway, it doesn't matter. I'll dry it out and write a rejection tomorrow."

I drew back the blanket-door, feeling the fuzzy fabric on my rough hands, picked up the other full washing basin, and brought it back inside. "Who is it from?"

Rordan shook his head. "A merchant family on the other side of the Great Cavern. Heard of your exploits, praised how well I must have trained you, said how it was a tragedy about our parents, said how their daughter is strong—same as the last one."

I set the bowl next to Rordan. He winced as I helped him pull his shirt over his head. The wound looked even angrier in the torchlight that lit our tiny cavern. I hoped it wasn't too far gone to react to healing herbs. We stored a small herb kit in our belts because herbs were too valuable to be left lying around a cavern. I unbuttoned mine and took out a small, sharp needle and some thread and some dried-up nettles for the pain. Rordan clenched his teeth but made no sound as I applied the shrivelled leaves to his wound and sewed him up. There would be a scar, since he'd left it so long with so little treatment, but maybe his future wife would be happy to have a man who bares his scars proudly. Even if he couldn't say where he'd gotten it.

Freetor weddings were the opposite of Marlenian weddings, or so I had been told. They were small gatherings in either the bride's family's cavern or the groom's. The guests were expected to give something to the new couple as a present—usually food or a trinket snitched from the surface. Food—which was the most common gift—would be shared among the guests and the bride's and groom's families. Marlenians exchanged gold or silver rings as a sign of commitment, but they were too expensive for Freetors, and even if we found the precious metal in our underground world, the family would end up selling or exchanging it for food anyway. Instead, the bride and groom exchanged solemn vows of commitment and protection. This tradition came from the Freetor-Marlenian war almost two hundred years ago, when almost everyone was a Fighter. The vows were sworn in front of an Elder and were said to be magic. If the bride (or groom) saw one of her new family members in trouble, she was obligated to help. If she didn't, her heart would burst and blood would spew through her nose—or at least that was what Rordan had said when I was younger.

I bit the thread clean and knotted it. The area around the wound had swelled more as I had punctured it, but at least it didn't smell. When wounds began to smell, that's when you had to worry about infection. "That should hold it until it heals."

Rordan traced the wound gingerly. "Thanks. I would've done it, but—"

"Yeah, yeah. Too busy. It's all right, I needed the practice."

After putting my supplies back into my pouch, Rordan took his basin into his room to wash. Our rooms were on opposite ends of our cavern. I was grateful for the privacy. I stripped off my clothes and folded them neatly on my dirt-stained, straw-filled mattress—another luxury—and washed. The water dripped off me onto the floor and created pools of mud between the stone. I was anxious to be dry; I wiped my hands on my violet cloak and sat naked on my bed of straw.

I liked to think that my parents died saving each other. No one could tell me the details of their death—it had been a horrible slaughter, Rordan said. They were caught off-guard in a store they thought was safe with a bunch of other Fighters. Sometimes I imagined a guard approaching my mother, wielding a large, curved sword, and my father stepping gallantly in the way, pushing my mother to safety while he dealt with the Marlenian, not just because he was obligated by any magic bond, but because they loved each other. Sometimes I am that woman being saved, and the man is a faceless admirer.

That would never happen, though. I was the one who saved people. Every day. If I didn't, maybe someone else would take up the mantle I had created—the Violet Fox—to keep the Marlenians guessing.

After stuffing my legs into some trousers and changing into a raggedy brown tunic held together by a fraying thread at the chest, I collapsed on my bed again. Under my mattress lay the most valuable possession I owned. I pulled out the black book with ten years worn into the cracks in the spine. If food was hard to come by, and medicine rare, books were as scarce as sunlight in the underground. Not that most Freetors could read or write anyway. I opened the book in the middle, where a raven-feather quill marked my place. The writing end of the quill was permanently black with ink. I picked it up, and the ink dripped onto the page.

*The quill and the book are magic*, my father had told me. *You could write all of the tales of all of the Freetors and still its pages would hunger for more. Feed it every day that I am gone, so that it can have stories to tell your children and their children. Promise me you'll write in it.*

And I'd promised him. Where he had gotten it, he hadn't said. Sometimes Father had brought back things from the surface for us, but only the Elders had magic things. I assumed it was a gift from them for an act of bravery. It glowed a faint light blue, a sign of its inherent magic. His name, *Conal Driscoll*, was inscribed in Freetor runes on the interior cover. Regardless of where the book had come from, what mattered was that it was his last gift to me before he and my mother perished on the surface.

Every day, no matter how little or how much had happened, I wrote something in the journal. It was the last promise I'd made to him, and I would honour it until I died. I guess the younger me had also thought that maybe somehow my father could read it from the afterlife. Now I knew that it was a tool to help me through my grief—and to secretly chronicle my adventures as the Violet Fox.

My hand moved as if guided by another force as the quill spilt my secrets onto the page. I paused only to think whether or not I should include Rordan's confession—but then I wrote it down anyway. It wasn't like many people around here could read it anyway, and the book was magic—maybe it would protect my secrets from untrustworthy eyes. Rordan would probably be mad if he knew that I was writing about it.

A rustling in the kitchen disturbed my thoughts. I shoved the book and the quill under my straw mattress and froze, listening. Fighters? No, they would announce themselves. Scavengers? They would not steal from the Violet Fox. I crept out of my bedroom.

I relaxed when I saw her. Laoise's short hair looked freshly washed, something she'd recently taken to doing before visiting us. Rordan lifted the cloth that separated his room from the kitchen. Smiling shyly at him, Laoise didn't even seem to notice me. Rordan sauntered towards the water bowls, suddenly becoming very interested in arranging them exactly the same distance away from each other. I held back a laugh. If she and Rordan wed, Laoise and I would truly be sisters instead of best friends.

I cleared my throat. When Laoise saw me, she squealed and pulled me into a fierce embrace.

"When the guards chased you . . . I got so scared . . ."

"I'm all right," I said, grinning. "I even got to see Prince Keegan today."

Laoise gasped and stole a glance at my brother. "I hope you gave him what he deserves."

I folded my arms triumphantly. "Let's just say he won't be kissing any Marlenian girls any time soon."

She squeezed my hands. "Kiera, what did you do?"

"My knife may have accidentally met his flesh. Oh, I got him good!"

"The prince's guards would've gotten you better, if I hadn't have come along," Rordan added.

I wrinkled my nose. Rordan always had to ruin my fun. Laoise smiled and looked thoughtful. "The kiss of the Violet Fox. Maybe you should share the love with the other Marlenian guards."

"I don't think so," Rordan said soberly, making a face.

"Not literally, of course," she said, backtracking with a blush.

He seemed to melt a bit at Laoise's innocent gaze. "Yeah, no, of course not. It's just . . . not exactly a reputation that the Violet Fox should have. Kissing Marlenians."

Kissing anyone didn't really interest me. My eyes darted between my best friend and my brother. The only kiss I wanted to see was between the two of them.

Running his fingertips through his frizzy locks, Rordan ambled to our fabric door. "Well . . . uh . . . I'm meeting a couple of people soon, so I should get going."

Laoise looked disappointed. "Oh. All right then. See you."

I wasn't going to let him go that easily. "Where are you going?"

"Mind yourself, Kiera." The warning in his voice was edged with reassurance: *leave me be, I'll be fine.* "I'll. . . um . . . see you, Laoise. Watch yourself in the caverns."

I rolled my eyes. "I almost murdered the Marlenian prince today. I think we'll be fine."

"Someday you're going to say that and it's not going to be true," Rordan muttered as he slipped through the fabric and into the tunnel. Laoise giggled. I wanted to be annoyed with him, but I smiled because he had made Laoise laugh.

"Who do you think he's meeting?" she asked, staring after him.

I shrugged. "Sometimes Rordan and a few of the other runners think it's fun to sneak up to the surface and play cards with the Marlenians and pretend to be from another province. Gives Rordan a chance to practice his accents."

"Aren't you afraid that he'll get caught?"

"Nah. Half the time the Marlenians are too drunk. And sometimes Rordan brings home more silver, and sometimes he gives me that silver."

"Yeah? Why haven't you spent it on a new cape?"

"It wouldn't be the same. Have to make it from the Tramore tapestries."

"They're gonna stop putting those up soon because of you, I bet."

I grinned. The Violet Fox costume had been through a number of changes since I created it almost three years ago. I was just thirteen, and even though I'd been with the Fighters most of my life, Rordan would never let me go to the surface on a mission. It was too dangerous, he had said. At the time I thought it wasn't fair, but now I know he just didn't want to see me die like Mother and Father. So I spent most of my time sorting stolen supplies and delivering it to needy families. On my thirteenth name-day, his present to me was a trip to the surface—but not just any trip. He and three other Fighter runners were sent to hold up a fabric shop. Clothing without any rips, tears, or mould was highly valued in the Freetor market. Rordan gave me what he thought to be the least dangerous task: create a distraction so that he and the runners could move the goods quickly out of Marlenian sight.

What should have been the most innocent job turned into the most dangerous.

For some reason, to be successful on my first mission on the surface, I thought I'd have to be as loud and as ridiculous-looking as possible. I found an old rag, cut out holes for my eyes, and wrapped it around my head. Then I tied a musty old blanket around my neck. When Rordan and the others went around the back to the storage room, I burst through the front and started screaming nonsense. The looks on the shopkeepers' faces—complete shock! They didn't know what to think.

Obviously, I learned a lot about subtlety after that.

My shenanigans caused quite a stir. While they chased me around the shop, calling for the guards, Rordan was able to take all of the fabric they had come for, plus some extra. I knew he wasn't pleased when some of the other Freetors laughed and encouraged me to do it again. The name Violet Fox was coined by a Marlenian tabloid because violet is the colour favoured by both the Tramore family and the Freetor Elders, and I started wearing it to confuse people at a glance. No matter what happened, I was always able to scurry away from guards, shopkeepers, or anyone else who tried to follow me back to my lair.

Besides the Freetor Elders, I now had the highest bounty in the province. I'd even heard of Freetors in other provinces imitating me, but most were caught. The Violet Fox would never be caught. She would rather die.

After sharing some of my daily ration with Laoise—day-old bread, twelve grapes, and a half-eaten apple—we left my cavern and ventured through the outer tunnels of the Freetor underground. There were thousands of caverns and tunnels underneath the surface—some safer than others. You could tell which places were inhabited by the smell of sweat and feces. The smell got worse as we moved further from the Great Cavern. Some of the caves were used for sewage storage. We avoided those places—I was secretly glad that I'd joined the Fighters young enough to never be drafted into cleaning up after other people.

The caves beyond were virtually unexplored by most of the Freetor population. Many had been hand-dug as recently as ten years ago and had then been abandoned when tunnels collapsed or another, more profitable, mission surfaced. Laoise and I explored these forgotten passageways when we were feeling adventurous—or when we wanted to escape our duties. Torchlight became rare this far down, but whether it was due to almost two hundred years of living underground or the Elders' magic, our eyes adapted quickly to the darkness. Water from somewhere above us dripped down and echoed in the ever-narrowing tunnels. Our hands and our eyes worked together so that we could travel further into the unknown.

That's when I saw it. The only feared Freetor symbol—one that all Freetors understood. Two pointy brackets facing each other like open mouths waiting to devour a long, squiggly vertical line. My heart hammered against my chest, but I refused to be afraid. Beneath it was an inscription scratched with an unsteady hand: *We all burn.*

"Kiera . . . that's an Extremist symbol," Laoise whispered. Her eyes darted to the nearby caverns. "We should get out of here."

The Marlenians thought we were all dirty rats, but the Extremists were the dirtiest of all of us. They hated everyone, and everything. Our exile was one thing, but they believed that only a select few were meant to return to the surface—them. They demonstrated their worthiness by strapping explosives to their chests and setting them off in the middle of crowded markets. It didn't matter who got in the way. To them, death was preferable to living underground, or stealing for a living, or being a slave. Maybe, in some ways, they were right. But killing innocent children and merchants who were just trying to make a living was not the answer.

"It's just a symbol, Laoise," I said, rubbing it with my thumb. The rock was cold and grainy beneath my touch. "Anyone could've scratched it in here to keep people away. Maybe there's a secret stash of food or supplies here that someone's hiding from the Fighters."

"Or," she said, taking my hand, "there really are Extremists beyond here, and we're trespassing on their territory."

"I'm not afraid of them," I muttered, but I allowed Laoise to guide me away, back down the tunnel from where we'd come.

Her eyes were wide in the torchlight. "I am. I wish the Elders would do something about them, and soon."

"I think the Elders have bigger problems to worry about," I replied.

She frowned. "What could be more important than the deaths of hundreds of innocent people?"

I'd already said too much. Rordan wouldn't be too happy with me if I blabbed to Laoise about our secret mission, even if Laoise was good at keeping secrets.

Laoise examined my face more closely. I did my best to wipe it clean of any details from the meeting I'd had with the Elders, in case she could somehow extract my thoughts by just looking.

"You're hiding something," she said.

Innocently raised eyebrows. Defensive stance. "No, I'm not."

"No? Then why are your fingernails digging into your palms?"

I looked down. My hands were balled into fists, and sure enough, my nails were leaving half-moon imprints on my calloused palms. I felt no pain. "Oh."

"Yeah. 'Oh' is right. So what is going on?" Laoise crossed her arms.

I started walking again. "Sorry, Lee, but I can't tell you."

"Why? Did something happen today after you hurt the prince? Are you in trouble for that?"

"No . . . no . . . I just can't tell you, okay? Look, I'll tell you as soon as I'm allowed to."

"Allowed to . . . " She trailed off and broke into a sly grin. "All right. I get it. I won't bother you anymore. But I will say that I'm jealous."

"Why? You don't even know what's going on." But I shared the smile. She knew exactly what was going on, even if she didn't know the details. Word would've gotten around among the Fighters that I'd spoken with the Elders today. Either that meant you were in trouble, or you were about to do something important on the surface. And since I wasn't dead, it was reasonable to assume I was leaving the underground.

"I bet I'll find out soon, knowing your big mouth," she replied.

"I'll just watch my mouth then."

"Not likely, though you really should, if you're doing what I think you're doing." A touch of worry crept into her voice. "I really hope my mom is okay."

I drew her into a side hug as we continued our stroll. "I'm sure she's fine."

"It's been days since I've heard from her. I hate it when she doesn't contact me. I start thinking the worst."

"Maybe I'll get to see her, somehow."

"That would be amazing if you did. If you could talk to her, that would be even better."

"I'll tell her that someone who loves her very much says hello."

"You're the best," she said.

I shrugged. "I know."

She chased me down the tunnel until we came upon the Great Cavern again. Together, Laoise and I had four pieces of Marlenian silver. Unlike the Marlenian market, the Freetor market had a little bit of everything, from stolen blankets and scarves to candlesticks to sweets. Most food was distributed throughout the city evenly according to what families received what rations—more for the Fighters and Elders, obviously—but sweets were considered a novelty and sold for three times as much in the underground. We gravitated towards them, our mouths watering. The woman selling them was probably old enough to be an Elder, but she had no teeth and her bodily smell overpowered the honey-nut treats and the chocolate bonbons. Dropping the four silver coins into her grime-covered hand, Laoise and I chose a single gumdrop-shaped chocolate candy wrapped in thin parchment paper for freshness. I let her have the first bite, and as I devoured the second half, drooling, I looked forward to living in the castle, even if only for a short while.

# Four

THE NEXT MORNING, Rordan shook me awake.

"Get up, Kiera."

I moaned and curled up into a ball, burying my face in the straw-stuffed pillow. "Just a little while longer."

"The Elders have summoned us."

My eyes snapped open. Rordan stood over me, wearing his finest cotton-woven tunic and cleanest slacks. So it was true. I threw off my wool blanket and sat up.

"Right now?" I asked.

"Yes. Hurry up and dress."

"Okay, okay!"

Rordan left, and I quickly pulled on my shirt with the smallest number of holes in it (one in the right armpit, and another near my left hip) and my black trousers from yesterday. They were one or two sizes too big for me—they'd been Rordan's a long time ago—so the belt that held them up also housed my herb kit and my knife. I also had a smaller dagger, which I slipped in my shoe. It had saved my life yesterday, and I wasn't taking any chances today. I hesitated for a moment, looking longingly at the Violet Fox cape draped over my clothing chest, but then decided against taking it. The Elders had summoned me, not the Violet Fox.

My brother waited at the entrance to our cavern, chewing on a browning apple. He offered the half-eaten fruit to me, and I gratefully accepted. The sour taste exploded in my mouth. It might be the only thing we would eat today, unless I was able to sneak up to the surface later. As I followed Rordan through the twisty turns of the underground caverns, I ate the rest of the apple and pocketed the seeds. Sometimes seeds were like currency to the right people who could make them grow. I imagined a giant apple tree reaching for the sunlight in the Great Cavern. Then, no one would be hungry ever again—unless we got sick of apples.

My fantasy was interrupted when we met the Fighters standing guard outside the Central Cavern. Like yesterday, we were reminded that what was said in the Central Cavern was to remain a secret. We both swore to keep our mouths shut, and the Fighters produced the key to open the double doors.

Inside, Erskina sat suspended on her giant stone chair with the other Elders. One seat—the giant ant chair—was unoccupied again. The Fighters shut the door behind us with a loud, awkward slam. Rordan bowed deeply to the Elders, and I sunk to my knees beside him, but I couldn't take my eyes off the empty floating chair.

"Elder Raibeart is no longer with us. The Marlenians murdered him when he strayed into an unguarded tunnel." Erskina's voice was gravelly and echoed off the smooth-stone walls. The news carried a chill to my heart.

"We are sorry to hear that," Rordan said, rising to his feet. "May he know sunlight in the afterlife."

"Why was the tunnel unguarded?" I asked.

Rordan nudged me, trying to tell me to be quiet.

"Our numbers are dwindling. The tunnel was beneath the eastern side of the city, where one of the Marlenian barracks is situated," said Elder Mainchin. "The passages are narrow, but they are often populated with various underground plant life not seen here on the western side. He often liked to stroll in these passages with his apprentices to observe the plant life, but a group of Marlenian guards found the entrance to the tunnel and filled it in with an acidic substance as he was passing under." He shook his head. "The Marlenian scholars are unceasing in their efforts to come up with new, creative ways to pick us off. His remains were not found until several hours later by a group of Freetors coming back from the surface through a nearby tunnel entrance."

I bowed my head in reverence. "I'm sorry. I'm . . . sure the loss will be felt throughout the caverns."

"The Marlenians are finding more of our secret entrances and safe points each day," Erskina thundered. "And if they manage to decipher Alastar's Tome, they will only become more reckless. We must hurry. You will be briefed today on your mission."

My stomach churned with excited butterflies. The more quickly I was trained, the more quickly I could get to the surface and steal back what was rightfully ours.

"I'm ready," I said.

Erskina nodded once. "Rordan, take Kiera to the surface."

"The surface?" I questioned. "But I thought I wasn't supposed to--"

Rordan was already on his way out of the cavern. I turned back to the Elders for further explanation, but they had turned the backs of their chairs to me. I had no choice but to follow my brother.

He led me down a rocky tunnel, where several stones stuck out of the earth and threatened to trip us up. This passageway was not traversed often. I prided myself on knowing most of the caverns and passageways, but there were still many that I hadn't explored, especially this close to the Central Cavern.

Two Fighters stood beneath a wooden trap door. They held maces with both hands, but as we approached, I saw brown Marlenian merchant robes draped over their arms.

Rordan nodded curtly in greeting to the Fighters. They lowered their weapons—slightly—enough so that they could pass us the robes. I slipped mine over my head and breathed in the fresh smell of lemon and citrus.

"These are clean," I remarked.

"We don't want our smell giving us away," Rordan said. He turned to the Fighter. "Open the hatch."

One of the Fighters hoisted the other on his shoulders. There wasn't even a sound as the Fighter undid the hatch and cracked the door open. A stream of light burst through, and although it was barely the width of my finger, my eyes burned, and I snapped them shut. The first few seconds were always the worst.

"All clear," the Fighter whispered.

I forced my eyes open. The light still burned and my eyes watered, but I was provided with momentary relief when the trap door slid shut again; the Fighter nimbly slipped off the other's shoulders. Purple and green squares haunted my vision as the Fighter boosted Rordan up. He opened the door again and slipped onto the surface like a snake disappearing into the grass. I wiped my eyes and followed suit.

The foreign smells of the surface invaded my nostrils as my palms dug into the gritty sand that populated the alley. Almost all entrance points were outside, in the narrow crevices between buildings: this one was no exception. Besides some weeds and an abandoned garden, there was little to hide the door except a large patch of dead, brown grass that looked like it had been attached with magic to the wood. I stood up and pressed my back against the stone wall. The space between the buildings was so tight that I had to keep my head turned to the right. My left cheek almost scraped the other wall. To my left, was a gate three times taller than me; we could only go right.

We crept away from the trap door and towards what looked like a tall stone wall. I was about to say that it was probably a dead end and that we'd have better luck climbing the gate behind us when I saw that the wall was the side of a building and that there was a narrow opening that turned into a street.

"Follow me, and don't wander off," Rordan warned.

After sliding himself out from the narrow alleyway, he rounded the corner and disappeared. I pulled myself from the narrow space and looked around to see if the Fighters were coming with us, but they weren't. When I turned back around, there was no sign of my brother. Grumbling, I turned the corner and ran into the middle of the street . . .

. . . and found that it was almost completely empty. A few grumpy-looking merchants tended their stalls, and the beggars defended their corners, and a few wayward children chased each other in circles up and down the street and between the houses, but that was it. One of the merchants caught my gaze and held it squarely for a few seconds, examining me. I felt sorely out of place.

Someone grabbed my shoulder. I spun around and was about to reach for the knife hidden beneath my cloak when I saw it was Rordan.

"I said to follow me," he hissed. "C'mon."

I didn't let him out of my sight again. We stuck to the less-travelled streets, not that it really mattered since it seemed that everyone had evaporated. I even started thinking that maybe this would be the best time to attack, to take over Marlenia City! That would show them. If only I could tell the Elders! I thought about turning around and heading back to the Central Cavern. Once we conquered Marlenia City, the Freetors in the other three provinces would see how brave we were, and they'd be inspired to do the same, and—

Rordan's hand slammed me in the chest, bringing me back to the present. I'd almost run into a well-dressed couple and their three children. We averted our eyes and mumbled some apologies as they gave us rude looks and then continued on their way. When they were gone, Rordan's gaze was stern.

"Aren't you watching where you're going?"

"Maybe if you told me where—"

There was a thunderous roar not three stone-throws from me. I gasped and pressed myself against the wall. I scanned the area, waiting for some monster to leap out and rip me to shreds.

"What was that?" I whispered.

From beneath his hood, I saw Rordan smirk. "Look."

We rounded another corner and I found myself on the edge of the Grand Square. I'd never seen so many Marlenians in one place at once. There were thousands of them, all squishing up against each other, some trying to get closer so they could see and hear better. My eyes slid to the guards at the perimeter. My stomach tightened as Rordan led us into the crowd, grunting an "excuse me" as we struggled to get close to the pavilion in front of the Cathedral of Dashiell.

The Grand Square was the size of three Great Caverns—no, maybe four—the open sky confused my ability to size things up. The square was built at the foot of a massive cathedral. Up until about a hundred years ago, the Cathedral of Dashiell had been a big deal to the Marlenians—that was why their leader was always called the Holy One, because they used to believe that their man-god, Dashiell, spoke through him directly. During the war between Eastern and Northern Marlenia (something about fur trading and hunting animals—I wasn't really paying attention when Rordan had told me about it), everyone was too busy fighting to worry about saving their souls, so the popularity of Dashiell worship declined. Now there was a whole generation of Marlenians who hadn't really been brought up with Dashiell's teachings of the Church and didn't care about attending the services at the cathedral.

Even so, the exterior of the cathedral had not fallen into disrepair. One thousand years ago, the people of Marlenia City dug out the side of the mountain and built their cathedral within its rocky confines. It was supposed to be a holy place, but there had been more deaths in the square in the past two hundred years than in the entire history of the Western province. Freetors caught on the surface, slaves that disobeyed their masters, and sometimes even Freetor sympathizers were put to death at the foot of the cathedral. I knelt down and peered at the dark spot beneath hundreds of pairs of feet—the rain hadn't come yet this week, and so the spilt blood of the latest Freetor remained.

As we neared the middle of the square, slipping between the Marlenians (whose pockets Rordan slipped his fingers into! I wished I were as good a pickpocket), the stone statues protruding from the face of the cathedral glared down at me. There were two on each side of the doors—I think they were supposed to represent the four nameless saints who cared for Dashiell on his deathbed. The doors themselves had to be at least one hundred hands tall and were made of sturdy logs dyed blood-red. Above the doors, a stone mason had carved scenes of Dashiell's deeds and stacked them on top of each other. Wind and rain and time made the scenes difficult to decipher, but they were easy enough to guess: in one, Dashiell was passing out food to his faceless followers, and in another, his faceless followers were crashing into a sea of tiny monster people. On top of all of this was the biggest carving: Dashiell, depicted with four arms, carrying his four arte-facts of legend: a silk cloth, a sphere of all-knowing power, a walk-ing stick, and the slab he used to create magic. Or so the Freetors say—I remember my father saying that after the war, the Marlenians wanted to believe that Dashiell was as magicless as they were and changed the slab's power to something less divine. It didn't matter to me: they were just stories to interest Marlenian children in Dashiell's supposed all-knowing, all-seeing power. I stuck out my tongue at the carving. *Do you see that, Dashiell?* I wanted to shout. *I am a Freetor, descended from those who rebelled against the Marlenians who worshipped you, and I am standing in your court. You are dead a thousand times over. What are you going to do about it?*

The one hundred and twelve steps that led up to the cathedral doors were swept daily by Marlenian labourers (slaves were considered too filthy for the task). Courtiers and other noblemen and noblewomen graced the steps with their pristine, delicate gowns that hung so freely on their bodies it looked like the wind would blow the fabric away at any second. The men looked bored as they stared out at the crowd of peasants, but the women fanned themselves aggressively. A group of them feasted their eyes on Prince Keegan. The prince stood with his hands behind his back, and his eyes lifted to the statues, almost as if he were thinking of climbing them. I smirked.

Between the nobles and the prince stood the Holy One. I'd only seen him a few times this close up. He looked as ancient as our Elders, with a voice as deep and commanding. White hair hung down from beneath a heavy gold crown. His robes were also white, with a blue and gold strip down the middle. As he turned slightly, pointing up at the cathedral and droning on about Dashiell's good deeds, I glimpsed the Tramore family crest sewn on the back of his robes. I rolled my eyes.

To his left stood the Advisor, Ivor Ferguson. I'd seen even less of him than I had of the Holy One, but even so, hatred boiled within me. He was better known by reputation than by his smug, pompous face. Since he had been appointed to his position several years ago, more Freetors had been arrested, put into slavery, or murdered since the war. The words from the man at the market came back to me, and sure enough, the Advisor was staring at the sceptre in the Holy One's hands. The orb fixed to the top of the sceptre glinted in the sunlight. My fingernails dug deep into my palms. When I got to the castle, I'd find a way to make the Advisor pay for everything he'd done to my people.

Rordan pinched my arm. "Pay attention."

I scoffed. "I'm—"

"Shh!" The merchant in front of us gave us both dirty looks.

" . . . and as you can see, many have arrived already." The Holy One swept his sceptre in the direction of the noblemen and noblewomen. Some of the crowd clapped and cheered while the nobles gave dainty, mousy waves.

"What is he talking about?" I whispered to Rordan.

"You'd know if you were listening," he said.

Right. Typical Rordan.

"Prince Keegan will be eighteen on his name-day," the Holy One announced. "Nobles and merchants from every part of Marlenia will be arriving to celebrate this momentous occasion, and to prepare for this, we have issued a city-wide tax, effective immediately."

Some Marlenians booed this; others responded with confused whispers. I fidgeted, my legs eager to run.

The Holy One smiled. "A silver quid will be collected from wagons entering and exiting the city. This quid will not be extra bread on the table for the soldiers—I know some of you are thinking they are overpaid already. Nor will this go to the cathedral, or even into the Holy Treasury. This money will go to building basements in existing establishments."

This caught my attention. Basements? Many Freetor tunnels were already really close to the surface. If the Marlenians started building basements, they would cave in the tunnels. Caving in the tunnels would not only kill us, but would also separate us from other Freetors. My fingernails dug into my palms so tightly that my knuckles turned white. I thought about my violet cape and how I should've snagged it before I left. I could have gone up on the pavilion and finished them all off. It would've been a suicide mission, but it would've been worth it.

While the Holy One droned on more about taxes and basements and celebrations, I studied Prince Keegan. That brought a smile to my face, though a different kind of smile than the ones that all the noble ladies were hiding beneath their quivering fans. His mouth was almost completely obscured by a white bandage that went from beneath his chin, across his lips, and up under his left ear. There was no swelling or blood that I could see, but I bet that he had been taken to a healer pretty quickly. Couldn't have the future face of Marlenia looking ugly.

The Holy One paused mid-sentence, faltering on his words. The Advisor leaned in and whispered something in his ear. I was actually surprised that the Holy One was out of the castle talking to the crowd when the Advisor was available to speak. There were a lot of rumours that the Advisor kept the Holy One under his thumb by making him sick whenever it was time to make a big speech or announcement. There were also other rumours that he'd tried to assassinate him in the past. Then again, the Holy One was really old, maybe older than Erskina and the other Elders, and probably more prone to sickness. And it wasn't like you could put a lot of stock in Marlenian rumours anyway. The Advisor stood with his hands behind his back, his eyes scanning the crowd as if he was worried someone like me would jump out and attack.

The Holy One gestured again to the crowd of nobles standing behind him. "More esteemed ambassadors will arrive in the coming days. Join me now in the Holy Prayer to make them feel welcome and to see our people safely to their destination."

The Marlenians around us bowed their heads and began to mumble their holy words along with their leader. I kept my head low, but my eyes kept flying over the crowd. The prince couldn't speak because of the bandage, and the Advisor didn't even bother inclining his head.

When the words were done, the Holy One threw his hands up in the air and a great smile lit his face. "Go now, and rejoice!"

"We rejoice!" the crowd yelled, and another thunderous roar filled the square. Women near the front threw their handkerchiefs at Prince Keegan and screamed his name. Although half of his face was covered in white bandages, he smiled at them and waved. The Advisor helped the Holy One up the steep stairs to the cathedral. The ladies and court-iers surrounded them, almost like human shields, making it impossible to see them. I pursed my lips. Someday, I'd get him. But not today.

We drifted with the crowd as it dispersed. I kept a sharp eye on Rordan as he silently motioned for me to follow him again onto a side street.

"Do you get what you have to do now?" he asked.

"We have to stop them from digging basements in their build-ings?" I guessed.

Rordan sighed and rubbed his hands with his face, like I was being a nuisance. "Weren't you paying attention, Sis? Or did you only have eyes for the *handsome* Prince Keegan?"

I felt as though I'd been slapped. "I'm not a stupid Marlenian girl. I don't fawn over Marlenian men."

"So you're just plain stupid then."

"Rordan!" I balled my hands into fists, ready to punch him. Even though we were in a secluded alley, there were still Marlenian eyes everywhere. My fingernails dug half-moon prints into my palms as I gritted my teeth. "Stop playing games with me. Tell me what my mis-sion is, or I'll tell the Elders about what you *saw*."

His face clouded over and became very serious. "You wouldn't. Not over something as trivial as this."

"Tell me what I need to know."

Rordan looked me over with an uncertain gaze. "You wouldn't betray your own brother."

Guilt swam inside my stomach. No, he was right about that. Rordan was all I had in this world. That, and my Violet Fox cape. And my father's magical journal. But the cape and the journal were just things, and Rordan was my brother. We both knew that I wouldn't make good on the threat. I sighed and leaned up against the wall. "Can't you just tell me so we can go do other things today? I thought I wasn't even supposed to come to the surface."

"For a good reason. At least you kept your hood up the whole time." He crossed his arms. "You remember the ambassadors that the Holy One mentioned?"

"Yeah. From the other provinces. I don't have a memory problem."

Rordan gave me a look but let my sarcasm pass. "Well, when he says *ambassadors*, he really means, *young female noblewomen of marrying age*. The women from the South have arrived, and the Easterners are on their way . . . but the Marlenian lady from the North has had an unexpected . . . accident."

I lowered my voice to barely a whisper. "I'll be taking the place of some Marlenian lady?"

"Not just any Marlenian lady," Rordan whispered. "Her name is Lady Dominique Castillo. She's the daughter of the Northern province, the only daughter of King Matís Castillo. She is expected at the castle within the week."

"But . . ." It was too much information at once. I had so many questions that my hands were shaking. My stomach felt ill. "I don't know anything about the North, other than that it's cold up there and that there're more mountains there than in all the other provinces combined. How am I supposed to act like her? And get her accent right? And what if someone knows that I'm an impersonator? The guards, they'll kill me!"

"We've been lucky. The civil war that happened between the North and the East is still fresh in King Matís's mind. He's kept his children in isolation, mostly because he thought the Easterners would try to kidnap or kill them. No one from outside the North has seen Lady Dominique since she was three-years-old."

"But what if there are other Northerners there? They'll *know*."

"There won't be."

"But Rordan—"

"There won't be!" Rordan hissed. "They're all too poor to go anywhere. And even if there are some there, you won't have to worry about it. A bunch of us will be there with you, as your guards, pages, and escorts. You won't be alone, I promise."

"So . . . you really will be going with me into the castle."

Rordan tried to hide his smile. "Don't worry, I'll have your back, Sis. Like always."

A smile and a laugh escaped me. I covered my mouth before I could draw any unwanted attention. "We should go."

"There's one more thing," he said, leaning in close to make sure no one was listening. "We've only got a week to get you all sorted. Maybe less. So I need you to . . . you know . . . be on your best behaviour."

I raised an eyebrow. "Aren't I always?"

He snorted and gestured to the open street. "C'mon. I've got something else to show you."

"I thought that there were no more things, that that was the last thing."

"No, you're going to like this one. 'Cause by the end of the week, you're practically going to *be* Lady Dominique."

For some reason, that wasn't very reassuring.

# Five

It wasn't long after our feet touched the smooth, damp, soil-stone underground that the Fighters told me I was needed elsewhere. I looked to Rordan for guidance, but he just half smiled and said that he had other errands to run. So I was left to discover on my own what the Elders had in store for me—the key to becoming Lady Dominique.

The Fighters led me through a confusing set of tunnels. The usual sounds of laughter or any kind of human voice were completely absent. The only light came from the Fighters' torches, and the air was humid and smelled more earthy than usual. I stepped in a puddle and ended up splashing my good trousers. Droplets landed on the Fighter in front of me. I breathed an apology and it echoed in the walls around me. *Sorry . . . sorry . . . sorry . . .*

I felt the moss growing on the walls and ripped some off to ease my grumbling tummy. But when the smell of decay and feces hit my nostrils, I lost my appetite. I knew where I was now. This was where we kept the dead, the dying . . . and the prisoners.

After a few more turns, I saw a warm, yellow light coming from one of the caverns up ahead. One of the Fighters wheeled around to face me.

"Remember, she is restrained, but she still has a dirty tongue," he warned. Shadows from his torch danced across his face, making him look like an executioner.

I was about to ask whom I was going to see when it hit me. The daughter of the North had had an *unexpected accident* while on her way to Marlenia City. The Freetors had captured Lady Dominique.

Excitement and fear swirled in my stomach. It wasn't often that we stirred up big trouble for the Marlenians. I mean, as the Violet Fox, I taunted the city guards and ran around stealing food for my people, but I'd never really hurt anyone that badly. We only captured people who weren't really essential to the society, like servants or labourers if we wanted information or to take someone's place. I couldn't remember the last time we had actually captured someone of worth.

I followed the Fighters into the lit cavern and wished that Rordan were with me. Water dripped from the ceiling and pooled around the walls. Two Fighters stood guard at the entrance. It was the only way in or out. There was only one torch in the room, and it was burning low. The Fighter replaced it with his.

In the middle of the tiny cavern, my eyes came to a rest. Sitting on the chair—an actual, wooden chair—was whom I assumed to be Lady Dominique Castillo. She had long, dark curls that looked frizzled— probably from being captured and from her extended stay in the humid underground air. Thick, black eye-dye ran down her cheeks; some of it still encircled her cold green eyes. She had high cheekbones and a mole on her chin. She was not beautiful, or pretty, but she did wear a low-rise, tattered dress that accentuated her bosom. No doubt that attracted Marlenian male attentions.

Four Fighters surrounded her. She wrestled against the ropes that encircled her waist and wrists, binding her to the chair. The rope glowed a faint blue. Freetor magic. The Elders were taking no chances. She would never escape. When she saw me, her eyes narrowed into slits.

"J'ou are de scum dat is replacin' me?" she said.

Each word nicked the air like a dagger digging notches into a wooden wall. Lady Dominique's accent was sharp and quick with a hint of smoothness underneath, with her rolled r's, but the demeanour made her voice all the more prickly.

Somehow she'd figured out our plan. I hoped she was the only one who had. One of the Fighters slapped her across the face, and her black dye rubbed off on the Fighter's hand. A red mark appeared on her cheek. She cried out and cursed at him, and the Fighter hit her again.

I stepped closer to our prisoner. "I'm not the scum—you are!"

She struggled with the physical and magical bonds that held her to the chair. "Dey'll know j'ou're a Freetor de moment dey see j'ou."

I grinned. "No, they won't. I'll be you." I threw back my shoulders, straightening my posture. "I tink I'm so high and noble just because I'm a Marlenian and I live on de surface! I eat all de good food and kill Freetors because dey are evil and must be exterminated!"

Doubt clouded Dominique's eyes. I'd spent my whole life impersonating Marlenians to blend in and steal from them, and she knew I had done an impeccable job of sounding like her, even though I'd just met her. She sunk in her chair, steaming with hatred. "It is said dat de Advisor Ferguson knows a Freetor wit' only a glance. He will catch j'ou."

I refused to let her see my fear. She seemed like a fearless foreigner, and that was what I had to become. "The Advisor won't suspect me. He is too busy admiring the Holy One's sceptre. He wouldn't notice a Freetor if one was stealing the breeches right off his legs!"

She snorted. "Cheeky little rat, aren't j'ou?"

"I have questions for you, and you're going to answer them."

Lady Dominique said nothing. I took it as a cue to continue.

"What do you know about the Gathering?"

"J'ou mean j'ou weren't invited?"

My fingernails stabbed my palm. "Don't do this. You're trapped here, and you might as well answer my questions."

"I *might as well* keep my mout' shut. I don't take orders from Freetors."

"I already know your name, and where you're from. You know, any information that I can't get out of you, the Elders will. And their magic . . . you don't want to cross them."

Lady Dominique gave her invisible restraints the briefest of glances. The corners of her cracked, red lips twitched upward. "Fire ants are dangerous too, but dey are only insects. I *crush* dem beneat' my boot."

"You won't be saying that when the Elders are through with you."

She shook her head slowly, like I was a child who would never learn. "When I escape, de Nort' will hunt j'ou down and hang j'ou by j'our entrails."

I laughed. "I'm the Violet Fox. You'll never catch me."

"Den I will memorize j'our face." She leaned forward in her chair. Her irises were pools of fire, her pupils wide and feral, taking in every detail. "And when I escape, I will tell every Marlenian who will listen about j'ou. Where j'ou live, what j'ou look like. We will find dose dat sympat'ize wit' j'ou and ensure dey never see de sun again. J'ou kidnap a Marlenian princess, and j'ou will make wrat' inside de High King and de Holy One. Freetors will die. If not j'ou, den dose around j'ou."

"You won't escape," I said again, but her gaze made me pause. What would happen to her after the mission had been completed? Thinking about it made me nauseous. The stench of death was in the air, and Lady Dominique was neither the first nor the last Marlenian who would rot here. The Elders' magic was powerful and mysterious, and I was not to question their methods, or their plan.

I tried a different angle. "Tell me about the Freetors in the North. What are they like?"

She smirked. I wasn't sure if she'd answer my question. "Freetors in de Nort' are obedient slaves. Dere are one or two nests around—but raidin' dem is sport pour our soldiers."

"We would never be obedient to the Marlenians!"

"No? I esuppose j'ou have never had de pleasure of visitin' de Nort'. De ground is cold and hard, unlike here. Trees are scarce, and mountains surround us. Dere is nowhere pour j'ou to hide, and dose who want to run, we let dem. Dey would never survive de tigers livin' in de mountains. Dey feed on j'our kind."

I didn't know what to say. Marlenians were natural liars, but some of what she said rang true. The caverns beneath the ground ran far, some had even existed before our ancestors dug them out, but the Freetor underground was concentrated in the West, where Alastar the Hero had fought and lived. Besides the Freetors who camped in the forests to hunt and ambush travellers, no Freetor I knew of lived on the surface outside the city, because escaping the city was near impossible. Guards checked every wagon, every noble person—not even the Holy One or Prince Keegan was able to pass through inspection without being checked for Freetor stowaways. We were a contained disease.

Dominique saw this on my face and leaned back in her chair, fiddling with her bonds. "J'ou are animals, all of j'ou. Filt'y, and disgustin'. Did j'ou know dat my fat'er passed a law only a mont' ago? Any Freetors who speak directly to Marlenians—whet'er because dey are bein' defiant, or because dey are acknowledgin' a command—will have deir tongues cut out. Our blacksmit' forged a special pair of sharp, tick scissors pour de task. He showed dem to me. I'd do de task myself, but I can't stand de sight of blood, much less gettin' de filt'y estuff all over me."

She said all this with a smile. She was doing it to aggravate me, and it was working. I punched her in the stomach, hard, before the Fighters could stop me. She keeled over as far as her bonds would allow. Through her wheezing, though, she laughed, long and cruel. If I had a pair of scissors, I would cut out her tongue. And those scissors would not be sharp, but dull, so that she would suffer. She deserved it, not us. The thought of Laoise or Rordan or the Elders getting their tongues ripped out made me even angrier.

"My people, dey are lookin' pour me. My brot'er is young, and our army small, but each sworn man would die pour my family. One Nort'erner is wort' ten men from any ot'er province. My brot'er will lead his men here. He y'is a strong boy. His men will cave in j'our tunnels and put an end to j'our people. J'ou will be slaves pour de rest of time."

"I'm done here," I told the Fighters.

Lady Dominique's laughter died away, and she called after me. "When I y'am freed, not only will j'our tongue be ripped out, but I'll see dat j'ou are drawn, quartered, and hung. De crows will eat out j'our eyes and j'our insides and den I'll feed de rest of j'ou to my dogs. How do j'ou like dat, eslave? How do j'ou—?"

The smacking sound of flesh on flesh stopped her midsentence and continued as I wove through the tunnels, away from the death and the torture. I didn't look back, fearing and hoping at the same time that the Fighters had beat her into unconsciousness.

\* \* \*

I had only a week to prepare to take Lady Dominique's place, and each minute that slipped by meant I was one step closer to the castle.

I met with Elder Trecia in the Central Cavern. The Cavern felt cold and empty without the other Elders present, but part of me was glad that Elder Erskina wasn't around. I hoped she was interrogating Lady Dominique instead. Four Elder apprentices—maybe ten years older than me—had been selected to prepare me for the surface, under Elder Trecia's supervision. They stood like ducklings around Elder Trecia, hanging on to each word that flew from her mouth.

"You will learn everything a lady learns in years of training within days. I fear your sleep may suffer, but this is a small sacrifice you must make for your people. You will never be alone," she said. "We are only a whisper away."

That brought a smile to my lips. "Thank you."

What surprised me was how much Rordan was involved. He worked tirelessly with a few of the Elders to glean information from Lady Dominique. How they got as much as they did, I didn't know, nor did I want to know. Rordan came home each night exhausted and weary, like the weight of a thousand stones was resting on his shoulders. But no matter how tired he was, he sat down beside me at our weathered table and told me everything that he had learned that day. And I listened, and absorbed everything I could. When he collapsed on his mattress, I hurried to write it all down in my journal. If I didn't, I wouldn't remember it. And if I had to study it later, it would be there.

Lady Dominique was the eldest daughter of Matís Castillo, High King of the North, also known as the Pauper King. Her mother had died in childbirth while bearing her only brother, Marin, who was now nine-years-old. He was heir to the Northern seat of power. Because of the war between the North and the East and the High King's paranoia and his father's depletion of the treasury due to drug addiction, neither Dominique nor her brother had travelled much. Most roads were heavily guarded during the war, and because they weren't able to travel outside the province, many people were forced to marry their cousins. Dominique's mother was rumoured to be gaunt and sickly even before bearing children, as she was a product of such interbreeding.

Learning her history was one thing. Physically becoming her was another. I wrote Lady Dominique's name hundreds of times in the Elder apprentices' presence until they were satisfied that my chicken scratch cursive could pass for a lady's handwriting. My food rations doubled in a late attempt to make me look well fed. "It's not like I'm going to be parading around the castle naked," I told Rordan as I tried to share my rations. "They'll never be able to tell I'm Freetor-thin underneath the dresses I'll have to wear."

"Maybe. But we can't be too careful," Rordan replied. He refused every crumb.

I practiced Lady Dominique's accent when I was with Rordan until I felt comfortable switching between my normal way of speaking and hers. That was what really made me feel like I was slipping into her skin. Stealing her voice was like stealing her soul. I could command any Marlenian to do what I wanted under her name, and at the sound of her voice, they would do my bidding. It gave me chills to think about the potential power I held, and it wasn't even magic—it was just something I had spent hours and hours practicing.

Soon, I would be in the sun, and I would have free reign of the castle.

Halfway through the week, after I had finished reciting Lady Dominique's personal history to Elder Trecia and her pupils, Rordan asked me to meet him in one of the common caverns near the Great Cavern. There were several of them, and they formed a semicircle around the main tunnels that connected the Freetor underground. The walls and floors of these particular caverns were polished smooth, making it the perfect place to train Fighter recruits. Peeking my head into the various caverns, I finally found my brother. He was posing with his back to the entrance of the cavern, as if he were preparing for a fancy, assassin-like attack on an invisible enemy. Eerie, echoing violin music played from somewhere I couldn't determine, and Rordan was humming along. I wondered if we were both going crazy.

"What is that?" I asked.

Startled, Rordan whipped around. In his hand, he held a soft, glowing orb of light.

"What is *that*?" I repeated. Excitement pounded inside my stomach.

His face was stern, but he couldn't hide the boyish fire in his eyes. "The Elders gave it to me. They've captured *sound*."

I pursed my lips. It was almost as if the musicians were in the cavern with us, the high, shrill notes descending into a slow but melodious song that made my heart yearn for a place without conflict and war. I reached for it again. "Can I hold it?"

Rordan drew away. "No. Elder Trecia said I can't let anyone else touch it."

Grumbling, I resigned my efforts. Magic items were rarer than food and greatly sought by Marlenians. Merchants conned eager people every day with false magic artefacts. Bolder merchants claimed to have one of the four artefacts of Dashiell, but even that was a stretch for most Marlenians to believe. If they were to ever get their hands on anything with a real drop of magic in it, I had no doubt they would somehow figure out how to use it against us. "Why do you have it?"

Carefully, slowly, as if the artefact were an infant, Rordan set it down on a smooth stone-chair. "It's to teach you how to dance."

"Why do I have to know that?"

"Near the end of the Gathering, there's usually some sort of ball. This year, it's a masquerade." Rordan snorted and kicked some of the crumbling, soft dirt from the wall opposite the artefact. The song paused for a brief moment as bits of earth flew around the room but then resumed.

"What?" I demanded.

"Just thinking about you in a Marlenian ball gown. I mean, have you seen them? Seriously, Kiera, you'll be larger than a fat Marlenian noble after his three-day name-day feast."

I rushed to tackle him, but he grabbed me by the waist with one hand and started whirling me around the room in time to the song. His steps were practiced and controlled, like he had grown up dancing with the nobles. I was so surprised by his grace that I fell in line at once, trying to follow his moves.

"How do you know how to do this?"

Rordan's face was playful. "What? You know how to jump and climb and rob a man blind while pretending to be his friend. I'm quick on my feet too, just in a different way."

I rolled my eyes. "But I'm just reading their facial expressions and body cues. Dancing actually takes practice. What have you been doing, sneaking into the castle and attending the balls and dancing with all the Marlenian ladies?"

"Marlenian ladies? Please, Kiera. They'd smell me a mile away."

"Not if you washed beforehand." Rordan lifted his hand and I spun in a circle. "Freetor ladies, then. You've been seeing someone."

"Kiera . . ."

"Is it Laoise?"

Rordan stumbled, and we would have fallen had I not shifted my weight to my back leg, which shook as I held him steady until he regained control. He looked flustered and swept me into another twirl.

"You have seen her lately, haven't you?" I pressed.

He sighed. "It's none of your business."

He was lying. I had only seen Laoise once since my training had begun. She was hurrying to the surface and I'd stopped her. She said she'd just been talking to Rordan. Her face was all flushed, too—maybe they were doing more than just talking. I grinned.

"If Laoise is going to be my sister, it is my business. I want to make sure I'm there when the words are said and you're not going to whisk her away to some private cavern."

"You're jumping to conclusions. I'm not sure if she even likes me like that." But his expression said otherwise. He knew it just as well as I did that she hung on his every word as her bright eyes stared up at him. "I don't really want to talk about it anyway."

"Why not?"

He slowed our twirls to a stop, and his hands left mine as he drifted away towards the door. "It's . . . complicated, Kiera."

"You don't like her?" I guessed.

He shook his head in exasperation. "I like her fine. That's not the issue."

"Then what *is* the issue? The man you saw stealing Alastar's Tome? Maybe you feel guilty about it, and you can't stop thinking about it—"

Rordan's eyes contained a harsh warning. "I thought I told you to never bring that up again."

"Fine. But it sounds to me like you're creating excuses. Don't you want to get married and have a family?"

"And bring up children in *this* world? Down here, with the people up there capturing and killing more of us every day?" He scoffed and looked at me like I had a disease. "I'm surprised at you. You've seen first-hand how it is."

"Yes, but we're trying to make it better."

"Are we? We barely steal enough to feed ourselves. Whatever we take is distributed throughout the caverns, like pouring a cup of water over a desert. It's not enough."

"Well, maybe the Elders can help. If a bunch of us got together and asked them to use their magic to mount a large-scale attack, then the Marlenians would take us seriously. I don't even know why the Elders haven't taken over the surface already."

Rordan leaned against the wall and bit his lip, thinking. "The Elders prefer subtle attacks. Less casualties. Only Extremists think about large-scale attacks."

I crossed my arms. "I'm not an Extremist!"

He looked apologetic. "Don't get offended, Sis. I know you're not an Extremist."

"Good." I paused. "So? Will you think about Laoise, then, so we can get back to our lesson?"

But my brother was gone, lost in a greater world of strategy and politics and bigger things. He stared down at his feet. It had been whispered that the Elders guarded their magic more than they guarded themselves against attack, and the secrets were only granted to those who were invited to be on the council. Elder apprentices prepared their whole lives to be granted this magic. Even though I wasn't an Extremist, maybe now that some of the Marlenians were targeting the Elders directly, they would listen to the Freetor people and prepare a larger attack. Then Rordan might feel safer, and he would marry Laoise.

"I'll speak with Laoise," he said finally. His voice echoed in the silence.

"Do you want me to help you draft an intent letter? I could get some paper from the Great Cavern." I had saved a few silver pieces under my mattress for this occasion.

Shaking his head absently, he headed for the cavern entrance. "No, I'll speak with her directly."

"But . . . Rordan . . . that's not part of the tradition . . . "

"I'm making a new tradition," he said bluntly. There was a hint of frustration in his voice, but he hid it with a charming smile. "Work on the steps I just showed you. I'll be back later. I've got some things to do."

"You didn't even show me—"

He disappeared around the corner. I stormed after him but then thought better of it. If he was going to talk to Laoise, I would have to let him do it his way.

* * *

The day before my mission, it rained. The Elder apprentices collected buckets of water. It only rained once every two weeks or so, and rainwater was highly prized to Freetors. When it soaked into the earth and nourished the glow moss on the walls, we rejoiced, but there was no easy way to get drinking water. Hiding the buckets from the

Marlenian guards was a challenge, and we were extremely grateful to the sympathetic merchants and families who kept buckets outside their shops and homes for us. After it was collected, water was rationed and divided. The Elders decreed that there would be a portion rationed for my bath. Except for the spies and probably the Elders, Freetors almost never had real baths—it was a waste of precious water.

Three of the female Elder apprentices escorted me to a cavern near the Great Cavern and stripped me naked. I shivered as they lowered me into the basin filled with cold rainwater, but I didn't complain. The last bath I remembered having was when my mother was still alive—this memory was one of the only ones I had of her.

Unlike my mother, however, the apprentices were not gentle. They scrubbed me until my skin was raw. Two brushes and three combs: that's how many they broke trying to get through my tangled hair. My hair wasn't as curly as Lady Dominique's, and it seemed to have a will of its own, curling and twisting around my face until it ended just below my shoulders. The women lathered it with a special cream that they said would increase its thickness, curl, and shine.

After wrapping me in towels, the apprentices carried me to a bedrock layered with blankets while the tub was being refilled. I went through two more washes until they determined I was clean enough to pass as a Marlenian lady. If all bathing was this arduous, I was not looking forward to it at the castle. One woman brushed my hair as it dried and applied more scents and creams as she styled it while two more clipped my fingernails and toenails.

At least two hours passed. I had to be done soon, I decided. The three apprentices left and were replaced with different women—these were not apprentices, as they wore clean blue tunics and breeches rather than the simple white and purple robes. The Elders had special attendants who helped them bathe and dress—maybe that was who they were. They carried thin metal trays steaming with hot wax. Wax made candles, I knew. Maybe they needed to fashion some for the journey. Maybe Lady Dominique had to bring her own to the castle.

They set trays of hot wax upon flattened stones and took several strips of paper from the pockets of their robes. I was about to tell them that they should probably get the paper away from the water so that it wouldn't get wet when one of the attendants—an older woman with a weathered face that looked like it had seen many battles—grabbed a stick with a glob of the hot wax and lathered it onto my leg.

"What are you doing?" I shouted.

The other attendants surrounded me and held me down. Another woman was laying the paper strips on top of the wax. Why were they wasting—?

And then she yanked back the strip.

I screamed. The pain was intense, like someone had stuck my leg in hungry flames. The women held me down. This wasn't something I could leap away from. More waxed was slapped onto my leg. No, no, I wouldn't go through this again—

"Sis, are you okay?"

Rordan stood in the entrance, his chest heaving, as if he'd run a great distance.

"What are you doing here?" I wrenched my arms away from the women to cover whatever nakedness I could.

He averted his eyes. "I just . . . wanted to make sure you were okay."

"You've been out there the WHOLE TIME?"

"Well . . . no . . . " He looked frustrated. "What are you looking at me like that for?"

"What yourself! You expect me not to scream when I'm having all of my hair removed?" One of the women pressed another strip to my shin. I drew in a deep breath and prepared for the pain. "And stop staring. Get out!"

Rordan made a face and muttered something about having seen it all before anyway, while the women shared an amused chuckle. He went back outside. Didn't he have anything better to do? Maybe he was just being overprotective, I thought as the woman tore away more of my hair. I gritted my teeth—it hurt less this time. Maybe Rordan was afraid I would tell the women about the man who stole Alastar's Tome.

After my arms and legs were bare, they shaped my eyebrows. By that time I was so numb to the pain that I barely felt the tweezers pluck away what was left on my face.

"Just one more place we have to tackle," said the woman who had done the waxing. She raised her bushy eyebrows expectantly.

"What?" I asked.

The women exchanged awkward glances.

"Kiera, no Marlenian lady would ever have such a mess," she said, pointing between my legs.

I frowned and covered myself. "I don't think it's messy. Who cares about that, anyway? It's not like anyone's going to see."

"And you think all Marlenian ladies bathe themselves, do you?"

She had a point, so I reluctantly surrendered again to the waxing strips. It was another hour before they were finished with me, and by that time, I feared I could barely walk. They wrapped me in a long blue robe that felt like silk on my skin. Rordan returned, smirking, and asked if I needed any help getting back to the cavern.

"I'm fine," I said.

"You look awful, Sis."

"I didn't ask you. Remind me never to do this again."

The women tied clean leather around my feet so that dirt could not burrow beneath my toes. Rordan walked behind me the whole way back to our cavern, ensuring that I didn't touch the walls, fearing that I would dirty myself again.

In the middle of our cavern was a large black chest—two hands deep and two arms wide—covered in scratches and nicks like it had taken a beating. A creature with a bulbous head and eight splayed tentacle arms with two crossed spears in front of it—the Castillo crest—was etched on the face-up side. Even though it was a finer carving, it reminded me of the Extremist symbol scratched somewhere deep in the Freetor tunnels. This was not my property. This belonged to someone who hated everything I stood for. The chest was locked with several silver clasps, which the Freetors had been careful not to force open in case the Marlenian guards inspected it closely. I crept cautiously around it as I thought of what valuables might be inside.

"This is Lady Dominique's. Where . . . ?"

"From her hijacked carriage," Rordan answered. He inhaled sharply, and suddenly he looked twenty years older. I wondered if this was how Father had once looked, if he had been as brave and as patient as Rordan. He would be an Elder someday. The thought of being apart from him in the Freetor underground hurt more than knowing I'd be apart from him on the surface. I knew I should tell him that. But I didn't.

"Kiera, this is really important. No Freetor items," he said. "No trinkets that you've gotten at the market, and definitely nothing that would mark you as the Violet Fox. Understand?"

"Yeah, I know," I replied, defeated.

"This is one of the trunks filled with Dominique's clothes. The rest are with the wagon. Choose some undergarments to wear under your Freetor clothes tomorrow," Rordan said, his face twisting with disgust and exhaustion. He rubbed his weary eyes and headed for his bed. "I'm going to get a few hours of sleep before tomorrow. Do you need me to get you up?"

"I should be fine," I said, knowing that it didn't matter what I said—he'd wake me up regardless.

"Oh. One more thing." He dug into the pouch on his belt and pulled out a black drawstring bag the size of his palm. "Catch."

He tossed it underhand, and I caught it with my right hand. It was heavy with silver. The coins clinked inside the bag as I pulled it open to see how much. "Rordan . . . "

"I don't want to hear it. I'm too tired."

"But . . . this must be at least two hundred quid. Everything you own. Why?"

"I can't have you stealing things at the castle," he said with a mischievous smile. "Maybe I'll get lucky in the coming days when I play cards and win it all back. Just . . . take it and use it wisely, all right, Sis?"

"I promise," I said.

"Right, then."

Within minutes, his snores drifted into the kitchen area. I retrieved my Violet Fox costume and the magic tome my father had given me.

The cape was chilly in my hands—I hadn't worn it all week. I wrapped the cape around the coins, hoping that it would be enough to keep both items safe. The chest opened with a slight creak and revealed the rich, colourful dresses that would soon be mine.

I buried the tome beneath a sea of fabric, along with the quill and the Violet Fox cape and mask. If I was going to snoop around the castle, I was going to do it as the Violet Fox, no matter what anyone said. My people had worked too hard to steal Lady Dominique's identity, and if I was caught, they would suffer as well. I wouldn't let that happen.

No one catches the Violet Fox.

IT WAS TIME for me to become Lady Dominique.

I was so nervous that I'd barely slept. The undergarments Rordan had forced me to put on were tight on my skin, like leeches in cloth form. And the dreams that had found me when I did sleep were fragmented and too real to have been made in my mind. When I went to pen my fears, I remembered I'd already packed the magic tome in the suitcase; if I disturbed it, I'd probably rouse Rordan's suspicions.

Fighters arrived at our cavern during the early morning hours. It was impossible to tell time while underground, but my internal time-ticker said it was four hours past midnight. Rordan emerged from his bed-cavern with bags under his eyes and dishevelled hair. He hadn't slept either.

The Fighters waited as Rordan and I washed our faces. They gave us both our morning and afternoon rations: three brown, shrivelled apples, four slices of bread, and a handful of blueberries. Rordan let me eat most of it. Even after a week of doubled rations, I could still see my rib cage. The corset I'd have to wear would just be for show.

I wasn't allowed to carry or touch anything. Even the hay I'd slept on the previous night was fresh. "Lady Dominique's family might not be as rich as the nobles here in the West, but they do have their pride. If you have a speck of dirt on you, someone will comment on it," Rordan had said. My hair would be styled again, and I'd be helped into a dress from the suitcase the Fighters now

71

carried once we reached the carriage, hidden deep in Feenagh Forest outside the city.

The Fighters led us down a tunnel that looked to be largely unused. The only light came from a single torch in the Fighter's hand, and the ground hid nasty secret roots that popped up randomly and caught my boot. Rordan grabbed hold of me before I could fall and make myself dirty. In the darkness, his hand was never far, and kept me steady and focussed.

It was the longest underground trek ever. The ground slowly inclined, and there were places so narrow that we had to crouch to continue. Flecks of dirt nestled in my hair and rested on my skin like brown snowflakes. Above us, thousands of feet trampled, not knowing what was truly below them.

"Does it get narrower than this? Kiera's going to have to have another bath when we get there," Rordan said.

"It's just a bit further. The women at the camp will wash her down and spray some sort of perfume on her if they have to," one of the Fighters replied.

My leg muscles were cramping when we stopped. The Fighters set the large suitcase and the torch on the ground and rapped their knuckles on the tunnel ceiling. More dirt fell. Rordan scowled. I wrinkled my nose, but I grinned at the thought of Lady Dominique walking into the castle and reeking of the earth.

Moonlight poured into the tunnel with the creaking of the trap door. Even though it was not as bright as the sun, it burned my eyes momentarily. The Fighters went up first and made sure the area was clear: then the suitcase, then Rordan, and then me.

Marlenia City was walled off and was tens of thousands of stone-throws in the distance (about two leagues in Marlenian terms). I'd run alongside those city walls too many times to count, but they were always too high to climb without a ladder. Even if I would've somehow managed to climb to the top, my purple cloak would give me away, and I would have no way to escape the guards except to fall one-hundred-twenty hands or more to my death on the other side. It didn't seem worth the risk.

Now, outside the city, a wide dirt road stretched across the grass and branched off into other roads, some leading towards the thick trees and others towards the stone and thatched houses and red farm buildings. Horses whinnied in the distance as Rordan helped me out of the hole in the ground. Thick, lush greenery surrounded us, creating a protective barrier between open sightlines and hidden Freetor camps. We knelt in the bushes. Tall evergreen trees sheltered our heads from the dew water. I stuck out my tongue to catch the stray drops that fell. There was nothing quite like fresh rainwater.

"Where are we?" I asked.

"Somewhere in the less-thick part of Feenagh Forest," Rordan replied.

"We still have at least an hour's walk ahead of us," one of the Fighters said as he and his partner picked up the suitcase by the side handles once more. "This way."

No torchlight guided us this time: only the moon and the stars. Every tree and bush looked the same to me—how the Fighters could tell where we were going, I didn't know.

Hiding Freetor camps in Feenagh Forest was probably the most dangerous thing you could do, besides stealing from a busy market-place as the Violet Fox. Regular patrols of Marlenian guards kept the Forest Freetors on their toes. They changed camps often, sometimes multiple times in a day, and barely lit fires. It was worth it though. The information and the supplies they gathered were crucial to our fight for freedom. Whenever a carriage rolled up from the South carrying goods, they'd size it up, hold it up if necessary, and then flee. Runners transported the goods from the forest to the underground, where the Elder apprentices rationed the goods and the Fighters distributed them to merchants and families in need. Other times, the Forest Freetors would hunt down Marlenian camps and gather information or steal their armour.

By the time the Fighters made us stop again, my feet were sore—whatever shoes were waiting in Lady Dominique's case, I was not looking forward to wearing them. But I didn't complain. I looked up at Rordan. The bags under his eyes seemed more pronounced in the moonlight.

"What are we—?"

Rordan put a finger to his lips. I followed his gaze.

At first I didn't see them. The moonlight made their windblown, twig-infested hair one with the dark bushes until a woman peeked her head up: her face, her neck, and her hands were painted forest green and black to blend with the surroundings. Swords and knives scraped as the hidden Freetors drew them from their scabbards. My heart pounded. What if they didn't know it was us?

Rordan covered his mouth and hooted like an owl twice. I gripped his arm tightly and tried not to be afraid, but my nerves would not settle. So many people were involved in this. If something went wrong, if the Marlenians found us, we all could die.

We waited until there was a response: two long owl hoots, and then one short one. Rordan crept from our hiding place and skulked towards the sound. Even with the acknowledgement of the other Freetors' presence, we couldn't be sure that we weren't walking into a trap. I followed cautiously, giving the Forest Freetors in the trees a wide berth.

After a few more minutes, I noticed the smoke billowing through the trees. We cleared the thick brush and found the Freetor camp. It was surrounded by trees thicker than any pillar I'd ever seen. The ground was covered in light brown dirt flattened by several boots: they'd been here awhile, or this was a popular spot. That made me uneasy. I counted seven Freetors, not including us, but there could have been more. Five slept on makeshift beds made of moss and tree boughs; I wondered what it was like to sleep with the sky as your blanket instead of rock and clay. Another two Freetors sat close to a dying fire. The ashes glowed a dark orange. Sleeping or awake, the Freetors kept their knives close. The ones by the fire froze like mice cornered by cats and watched us rustle through the woods until we broke free of the foliage.

They didn't bother introducing themselves. The fewer names I knew the better.

"We'll leave at first light," said one of the Freetors—he had long, greasy hair and a large, bushy beard—the exact image of a Freetor who snuck around the thick forests, evading Marlenian patrols, living off the land, and bringing back what game he could to sell or distribute in the underground market. He faced me. "You're the one going in?"

"Yes," I replied. "Where's the carriage?"

Both Freetors pointed behind them, deeper into the forest. "We've got a few others watching it. Had a couple of close calls this week, but we haven't been discovered. Yet."

"You should move camp," Rordan said as the Fighters set down the trunk and cracked their sore backs and hands.

"We will, once you're on your way."

On my way. These were the final hours—the smell of the early morning dew couldn't have been sweeter. "Do I get to see the carriage?"

"You need to get dressed. And don't think about sitting down, or touching anything," Rordan replied.

I eyed the bits of dirt and clay on my arms and legs. "I could use another wash. Just a little one."

Rordan was going to protest when the Forest Freetor interrupted him. "We'll wake up the girls. They'll take care of whatever you need."

Three of the Forest Freetors at the camp were women. They yawned and stretched but were quick to their feet once they realized who we were. Soon they were rooting through Lady Dominique's belongings—not so deep that they could see my Freetor things, thank goodness—and they chose a gown. Rordan joined the men at the fire while I was whisked away from the camp. With each step, the Forest Freetors were careful not to leave a trace.

When we were far enough away from the men, the women helped me into the clothing they had chosen: a bright white chemise, three layers of petticoats, each thicker and warmer than the last, and finally, the gown. The gown was a faded emerald colour with lace around the sleeves and bosom and white fabric swirling around the skirt. I felt like a cake in one of the Marlenian bakers' displays. After I was laced into the dress, the ladies applied black dye to accentuate my eyes— not too much, I told them—I was supposed to be Lady Dominique, but I didn't want dye dripping all over my face. Two of the women spent some time arguing over what jewellery I should wear: the pair of teardrop earrings with a matching necklace, or the trendier, bulkier square earrings with beaded jangly bracelets. I had to stop them from tearing each other's throats out—I didn't care what gems were hanging off me, so long as it looked good. And to me, both of them looked good, but the teardrop ones made me think of blood, so I wore those to inspire confidence. The shoes weren't flat like my leather slippers. They had a heel the size of my fist. I'd put them on when we got to the carriage, to prevent them from getting soiled.

Moving in the dress was like dragging heavy stones tied to your waist. No wonder Marlenian noblewomen never lifted a finger. They could barely get from one place to another without taking a rest. By the time we returned to the camp, the sky was leaving darkness behind and showing light purples and deep reds to the east. When Rordan saw me, a wide smirk spread across his face.

"Nice dress, Sis."

I wagged a finger at him. "Don't you start."

His grin didn't disappear. "I'm not saying a word."

I was hoping for some real meat, a rabbit, or maybe a deer, but the Forest Freetors hadn't done any hunting in the last day, in case of a patrol. I stood away from the smoke and fire and munched on raw onion slices, radishes, and half of a potato that had been roasted over the remaining coals. My last meal as a Freetor. I wondered what Lady Dominique would say if she saw me eating a poor man's meal in her elegant gown. I snorted and then laughed, which got me a weird look from Rordan.

After finishing his meal, Rordan rose from his seat at the fire and grabbed a cloth bag next to his feet. He disappeared into the trees for a few moments and emerged a new man. Lady Dominique's clothes weren't the only ones that had been snagged from the carriage. He wore a forest-green, long-sleeved velvet tunic with the Castillo crest embroidered on the front. He'd licked his small curls back into place, giving him a somewhat distinguished look. Coarse, black fur leggings covered his bottom half, and his mud-splattered brown shoes with green buckles stuck out like a spring bloom from a pile of ash.

"Now who's the silly-looking one?" I said.

"Still you."

I scowled. He was right. "Your shoes. They're covered in mud."

"It'd be suspicious if they weren't. Pages run everywhere to deliver messages for their nobles." He bowed deeply.

A loud laugh escaped me and echoed through the trees, earning me glares from the Forest Freetors. I covered my mouth. "I guess I didn't really think you'd be around the castle that much."

"Elder Trecia's apprentices didn't tell you that?"

"No. Why would they talk about you?"

Rordan appeared to be giving that serious thought when the Forest Freetor who had greeted us spoke up. "We'd better get moving. We've been here too long. The horses should be fed and groomed and ready for you."

My heart leapt. This was really happening. I was sneaking into the castle in plain sight, and my people were helping me. I was overwhelmed with a sense of pride. I was a Freetor, and I was on an important mission to retrieve and protect what was rightfully ours. I grinned at Rordan. He smiled reassuringly.

Getting to the carriage took a little longer than expected. The women helped me through the dense wood, brushing aside tree branches and leading me around soggy, muddy sinkholes. Rordan was less careful. Tree boughs slapped his face and caught him in the back, but he spat out the pine needles and kept going.

I could smell the horses before I saw them. Three men dressed in tunics and furs identical to Rordan's were grooming the elegant beasts with thistle brushes as we arrived. I assumed they were our driver and footmen for the carriage: more Freetors in disguise. They had at least one or two days worth of stubble on their faces, and they exchanged comfortable banter in a Northern-inspired accent. I hoped they'd be able to maintain it.

The carriage itself was nothing special. The prince's carriage was more elegant with its gold trimming and vibrant violet banners, and in comparison, this looked like it had been constructed from crates and barrels and left unfinished. A single green banner with the Castillo crest hung from the back, torn in three places. This wouldn't make a great impression, but maybe it wouldn't be terrible, either: it was a long journey from Ninyanas, the capital of the Northern province, to Marlenia City.

One of the horses snorted. I'd always admired horses from afar, when there weren't Marlenian guards on top of them, and when they weren't being used to chase me around the city. They were powerful animals, but sadly obedient. I approached one warily, ensuring that she saw me. The horse snorted again and started munching on some grass. Wondering what would happen if I set her free, I stroked the horse's brown hide.

"Kiera," Rordan hissed. "C'mon. Don't get your hands dirty."

"The horses aren't dirty," I replied, scratching her behind the ears.

"Female horses pee on their tails. That's how dirty they are. Now get in the carriage."

I wiped my supposedly dirty hand on my dress. I hated when Rordan told me what to do, but especially now, when I was pretending to be royalty. He'd pay for it when we got to the castle. I'd find Alastar's Tome *and* have a bit of fun with Lady Dominique's authority.

Two Fighters stood next to the entrance of the carriage. Based on the size of my dress, I thought it would be impossible for me to get inside. The door was only an arm wide, maybe one and a half, and it wasn't even a real door. A heavy, black tiger pelt covered the entrance. Like home, I thought, but we didn't have man-eating tigers in the underground—just ratty, moth-eaten blankets. The two of them helped me squish the fabric to my side as they stuffed me inside the carriage.

Inside, it was not quite as spacious as I had imagined. Two seats faced each other that could fit maybe four Freetors, or two well-fed Marlenians. In my case, one seat fit me and my dress fine.

Rordan climbed nimbly into the carriage and took his seat across from me. "Your story?"

"The wagon was hijacked by Freetors in Carrigan Forest, two days north of here. There were only a few of them, and my guards were able to kill them quickly. We feared we were being followed, so we took a longer route around Carrigan Forest and into Feenagh Forest, where we are now."

"And?"

"My father extends his regards, but he was unable to attend the celebrations, as he has fallen unexpectedly ill."

"We hope that the intelligence we got about his bad stomach is true. What else?"

I rolled my eyes. "I have an older sibling who is annoying me so much that I make him run around and do errands for me."

Rordan gave me a look. "That's not funny."

I grinned. "Yes it is."

The carriage rocked slightly as the driver whipped the horses to life. It was a half-hour drive from here to Marlenia City, but we had to back-track through the forest and get onto a part of the main road that wasn't as populated. The fewer people that saw our carriage pop out of the woods, the better. It would be at least another hour or two before we'd enter the city.

Growing up underground, I was pretty comfortable with enclosed spaces, but sitting for hours in one place, knee to knee with someone, was not looking like a pleasant way to spend an afternoon, especially for a highborn lady. I wished that I had the magic journal my father had given me. At least that would have helped the time pass faster.

There were no windows, and the only glimpse of the changing land-scape came when the tiger pelt to my left lifted gently with the wind. The Northern Marlenians must have found it cold to travel without proper doors on their carriages, but maybe they were so used to the chill that they didn't mind. The air was crisp and fresh at least. I welcomed the breeze on my face.

Rordan was not much of a conversationalist either. He seemed preoccupied. I really hoped that he wasn't beating himself up over letting the tome thief get away. It was careless of him, and we might not have had to go through all this if he had been paying attention to his surroundings, but I just wanted him to feel like his old self again. He resisted any kind of conversation topic I came up with, especially when I hinted again that he should talk to Laoise. Eventually, I gave up. I knew I couldn't force him and Laoise to be together, but it would just be so perfect. Was it too much to ask for that one wonderful thing in our damp and dreary existence? If Rordan was taken care of—if Laoise could take care of him—maybe he wouldn't be on my back so much. Laoise would come live with us, or better yet, we'd get an even bigger cavern since the three of us were Fighters. I hoped that Rordan would see the advantages of having Laoise as part of the family.

What felt like hours passed on the bumpy road, and I was starting to get anxious. Sweat was dripping from my forehead, and Rordan wiped it wordlessly from my brow with his sleeve so that the black dye and whatever else was on my face wouldn't be disturbed. I hoped I still looked the part. Maybe it wouldn't matter. Maybe if I looked disgusting, people would leave me alone and I could find Alastar's Tome and then get out of there quickly. What if I found it before Prince Keegan's name-day celebrations were over? I'd be back on the Marlenian streets stealing apples before I knew it.

More time passed. I must have fallen asleep because the carriage halted abruptly, jolting me forward. Rordan caught me and pushed me back just as a Marlenian City guard pulled back the fur-curtain.

"State your business," he said quickly.

The gate search! I'd almost forgotten. I did my best to look in control—this was where my act truly began.

"I y'am Lady Dominique Castillo, daughter of de High King Matís of Nort'ern Marlenia," I said. "I demand to know why my carriage has been stopped."

The guard seemed taken aback. "My lady, this is a routine search. We must check every carriage entering or leaving the city for Freetors."

"Don't even talk to me about Freetors," I said, brushing a curl out of my eyes. I twirled my ankle absently to seem like I could care less. "Dey almos'took my carriage."

"Almost . . ." The guard's face reddened. "My lady . . . I hope you are not injured."

"I y'am fine. My'escort is very capable, and my carriage is durable. We had very little damage," I replied.

"I'm happy to hear that, my lady. A . . . fine carriage you have, my lady," the guard said pleasantly. "Your horses look very well looked after."

"We bred dem especial just pour de trip sout'." I smiled and pretended to be interested in my nails. "Are we almost done here?"

"Yes, my lady. Just let me talk to my commander. It will just be another moment's delay."

"I don't like delays," I said, but the guard had already closed the curtain. I exchanged a look with Rordan. "Do you think—?"

He silenced me with a curt shake of his head—he was right, I had to stay in character.

The clatter of the market called to me outside as the smell of bread and pies wafted through the curtains. My stomach let out a little gurgle, earning me a stern look from Rordan that said, *didn't you eat this morning?* But it was never enough. I sat up straighter and hoped that the layers of fabric around me would cover any embarrassing sounds.

The guard returned a few minutes later with an apology written on his face. "Sorry for the delay, my lady. Your carriage is free to proceed. I hope you enjoy your stay here in Marlenia City."

I averted my eyes. He was a low-born, a servant to Lady Dominique. "Tank j'ou."

The sudden jerk forward flooded me with relief—we were finally moving again. But with that relief came more anxiety. Every second brought me closer to the castle. Closer to the Holy One, and the stolen magic, and the prince. My head bumped against the carriage wall as we climbed the steep, winding road to the castle grounds. I heard the creaking of the gates as we were admitted into the inner sanctum of royalty. My nerves waged a war inside me. I was so consumed that I hadn't noticed that the carriage had stopped moving.

Rordan nudged me. I waited for him to get out first. He held the fur-curtain aside and took my hand lightly as he helped me from the carriage. It was like stepping into a dream. While the merchants and the Freetors scurried below within the expansive, winding streets, breathing in the smell of urine and feces from both people and horses intermingled with baking bread and pastries, the air up here was somehow fresher. Calmer. The castle bailey was not as busy as the merchant district, but there were blacksmiths and farmers selling their wares here all the same. Because the castle was on top of a mountain, it didn't make sense for the nobles or their servants and slaves to waste valuable time running all the way to the market to purchase food and weapons. The richest merchants sold in the bailey, which ran inside the castle walls but outside of the castle itself. There were only four booths, all tended by middle-aged men. Some called to me, "Fresh vegetables, my lady, from the green fields just outside Marlenia City!" and "Protect yourself, my lady, this necklace is embedded with Dashiell's blessing!" There were guards here and there, wearing their gold-and-silver cloaks and the Tramore crest, but they seemed to stroll at a leisurely pace. There were no Violet Foxes up here to chase. The gravel was gritty beneath my heels but the ground was flat and the grass was as green as it had been in the wild forest.

The Marlenian castle cast a large shadow over the bailey and half the city. Walls of stone stood thousands and thousands of hands high, and stone soldiers stood vigil at various points along the wall. From far away, I'd always thought they were real guards who were extremely committed to protecting the castle. I laughed. The Tramores were cleverer than I thought. The highest towers were laced with clouds. Arrow loops dotted the lower towers. I caught a glimpse of an archer— a real man—through one of the small holes, ready to fire in case of a surprise attack. Tramore flags and banners boasting the sceptre in front of the mountain we stood on draped over the castle walls. As if I would mistake who was in power here. In addition to the patrol, two Marlenian guards stood by the large arching entrance, thirty or forty hands high.

"Don't look up," my brother whispered from the side of his mouth as he shut the carriage door. "A Marlenian woman of noble birth looks up to no one, not even to the castle of her allies."

An entourage of young boys approached us. They wore the Tramore crest but carried no weapons. A few began to pet the horses. The driver slipped down to interact with them, and one of the boys jumped up on top of the carriage and stole the reins.

I gasped. "Hey, wait—"

Rordan grabbed my arm lightly, but didn't look at me. "Stable boys and pages. They're taking the carriage to the stable, around the other side of the bailey, where the horses will be kept."

"Oh," I said. I batted my brother's hand away from me. "I thought they were stealing back the carriage."

"Don't talk about it anymore," Rordan said stiffly. "Walk in front of me. Don't look at me. I'm a low-life compared to you."

I smiled smugly, but inside my nerves danced. I lifted my dress slightly, so that my shoes wouldn't trample it and the mud wouldn't stain it, and sauntered on the grit towards the door. A patrol of three guards passed—I drew in a deep breath. I felt their eyes on me, examining my dress, my face, my walk, my bosom, but they just acknowledged me with a quick nod and a smile, and then continued on. This was going to take some getting used to.

"This is strange," Rordan muttered. "No one has come to greet you."

I tried to remain calm, but he was right. The two guards at the door were staring at me, as if they were trying to figure out who I was. The tips of their spears glinted in the afternoon sun. Wouldn't the carriage inspection guards have told the castle guards I was coming? Unless their runner hadn't gotten here yet. Or, maybe they knew that we had captured the real Lady Dominique. Maybe they were just waiting for me to walk into a trap.

The two giant reinforced wooden doors towered over us. As Rordan and I approached, the guards barred the door with their spears.

"State your business," said one roughly.

My heart pounded. They had to know it was me. I was on the streets almost every day. The Violet Fox was on every poster in every shop, on every wall. The guards' eyes were black and empty. I remembered all the times when I feared them looking at me, feared them seeing my thievery. Now I stood before them, naked of my violet cloak, with only my wits to save me.

I cleared my throat. "I y'am here pour de Gat'erin' celebration of Prince Keegan's name-day. Let me pass."

"All guests have already been accounted for," the guard said.

I tried as hard as I could not to let my fingernails dig into my hands. I breathed deeply and increased Lady Dominique's accent. "What do j'ou mean, de guests have been accounted pour! I was invited specifically by de Holy One to attend Prince Keegan's name-day celebration! Perhaps if I went back to Nort'ern Marlenia to tell mine papa de King Matís—"

The guards perked up. "Northern Marlenia?"

"J'es, *de High* Nort'ern Marlenia. I y'am Lady Dominique Castillo, j'ou fool! Did I go trough de inspection at de gate pour not'in'? J'ou guards disgust me. I go home to my papa and tell him de West is unkind to de Nort', and—"

"Allow me to tell the Holy One of your presence, Lady Castillo," one guard said.

"Please accept our sincerest apologies, my lady!" said the second.

They uncrossed their spears. The first guard turned himself sideways—afraid to turn his back to me—and called up to the closest castle window.

"Open the doors!" he shouted. "Lady Dominique Castillo has arrived!"

I waited impatiently as the large wooden doors creaked open. As soon as they were wide enough to fit me and my dress through, I stormed into the castle.

My shoes touched a soft surface, and I was momentarily set off balance. I stopped and stared at the red surface, testing it gingerly with my pointed shoe.

"It's called carpet, Sis," Rordan muttered. "Let's keep going."

"It's like . . . grass," I whispered. "But it's inside."

Fascinated, and a little put off by the soft traversing, I continued on. The entrance hallway was tall and dimly lit: flags of the four Marlenian provinces draped over the stone walls. Besides the Tramores and their sceptre, and the Castillos and their tentacle-monster with spears, there was the Frostfire family from the East with their blue and red banner, and the Zaman family from the South with their bright spring pinks, yellows, and sky-blues. Four provinces, ruled by the Holy One in the West. Statues of former Holy Ones carved from marble lined the walls—some were at least a thousand years old and were crumbling to the floor. A servant was polishing one of them. I stayed on the carpet road, which led me further and further into the Marlenian castle.

Near the end of the long entrance was an entourage of men and women. They appeared from behind the corners of adjacent, narrower corridors and hurried towards me. They wore no weapons. Servants— from the look of their bland, cotton dresses and tunics—and pages. I waited for them to approach me, twiddling my toes within my shoes.

The crowd stopped, panting, and one page pushed his way through. He unrolled a thick piece of parchment and spoke between gasping breaths. "To Lady Dominique Castillo, daughter of the High King of Northern Marlenia," the page read. "Prince Keegan and the Holy One bid you welcome to our humble and holy castle. The Holy One herby invites you to attend the First Feast in honour of the name-day of his son, Prince Keegan, tonight when the moon shines high above the mountains."

The boy looked up from the parchment. Men and women, waiting with smiles and shaking their hands with excitement, turned their eyes to me.

All I could do was stare back.

Rordan nudged me. "My *lady*," he hissed.

"Oh . . . uh . . . " I cleared my throat and knitted my eyebrows. "I would be honoured to join de prince."

That seemed to satisfy them. Two servants, not much older than me, stepped forward while the crowd began to dissipate. "Allow me to show you to your guest quarters, my lady," said one.

"Tank j'ou," I replied.

"Will the messenger be accompanying you to your room as well, my lady?" the second servant asked, eying Rordan up and down.

I paused. The Elder apprentices hadn't prepared me for this. They were relying on my quick thinking to help me survive. I cleared my throat. "Has my baggage been unloaded from de carriage?"

The servant girls had blank looks on their faces. They wouldn't know. I realized that because I was the royalty in this situation, I was the one in control. I smiled and flicked my wrist towards the door. "No? Den you could see to it, page."

Rordan stifled a smile and bowed. "J'es, my lady."

"Please follow us, my lady," said one of the servant girls.

As the giant doors to the castle creaked open and then shut again behind me, I gathered my courage and followed the servants down a long, curved hallway off the main entranceway. Torches lined the stone walls, along with more Marlenian tapestries. They were longer than my arm-span and probably about three times my height. I wouldn't have normally paid much attention to them, but I drank them in because they depicted scenes from great battles between the Marlenians and the Freetors. The Marlenians in the tapestries were tall and noble. Halos encircled their heads and made their golden armour and long swords shine with heavenly light. The Freetors were twisted and ugly, with short knives and torn, navy blue rags. I could almost hear them hissing and screaming as the Marlenians cut them down. In another tapestry, the Marlenians dumped the Freetor bodies into a massive grave, while other Freetors dug their own holes to hide from the grave diggers.

In one of the scenes, a Marlenian stood on top of a mountain of Freetor bodies, sticking a Marlenian flag into them as if they were dirt. He had long, flowing blond hair, and a large nose that stuck proudly in the air.

As we continued down the hallway, the scenes became less violent and focussed on the development of Marlenia City. It showed the construction of the castle, and again, the golden-haired Marlenian appeared, but this time with a crown on his head and a woman by his side with a baby suckling from her breast.

The conflict between the Marlenians and the Freetors had gone on for almost two hundred years, but the tapestries made it seem longer, as if it had been going on for ages. Their hatred of us ran deep—so deep it seemed that their royalty had been founded on it. I shivered.

At last we left the hallway of tapestries through a large wooden door and continued up some stairs and into a much narrower hallway. The torches were sparser here, but I could see light at the end where it opened up into a larger, shorter corridor. There was a window with flowing golden curtains that looked out upon the courtyard, which was teeming with guards, as well as a hedge maze that made my head dizzy to look at.

"Your quarters, my lady," one of the servant girls said, bowing.

The other girl produced a key from her bosom, but the door opened swiftly before she could unlock it. The servant jumped back in surprise as a woman I knew well stepped out.

Laoise's mother wore a long, faded blue cotton dress that almost covered her steel-toe boots. Her hands were dry and wrinkled from years of servitude—only one of the sacrifices she had made to spy on the Marlenians. An off-white scarf covered most of her auburn hair, save a few curly strands that peeked out the top. Her name—her real name, Bidelia—almost fell out of my mouth. I knew that she worked at the castle, but I hadn't known that I would run into her this early during my mission. I was even more surprised when the servant girls did a quick curtsey and kept their heads bowed—as if she were royalty.

She turned her eyes to me. They were cold and hard, almost like the Marlenians'. She had had years of practice. I had to be sure to keep up my side of the charade not just to convince the servant girls, but to impress Bidelia as well.

"Mother Margaret . . . we did not know you were preparing Lady Dominique's room!" one of the servant girls exclaimed.

"Considering that the tardiness of her arrival could only be the fault of slow, untrained girls and fumbling footmen, it was the least I could do to keep everything on schedule," Bidelia replied.

"But it wasn't our fault! The lady arrived late, and we didn't even know if she was still—"

Bidelia slapped the girl across the cheek. I stiffened and then quickly regained my composure. Bidelia had never raised a hand against Laoise, not even when she and I had upset a barrel of soft peaches in the underground market. The Marlenians seemed to only respond to violence. I had to follow Bidelia's example. The real Lady Dominique wouldn't flinch at one servant hitting another. She'd probably be the one doing the hitting.

"You dare blame a lady for tardiness? There will be no supper for you tonight," Bidelia declared. "Now get out of my sight. Run to the kitchens and tell the cooks that we will need an extra barrel of Bluesberry Wine for tonight's feast. Bring back the lady some bread and cheese—she must be starving from her long journey."

The girls were quick to disappear, but Bidelia did not break character until she had escorted me into the guest chambers and shut the door. I threw my arms around her, and she squeezed me tightly, as if I were her own daughter.

"For the longest time I thought the guards had captured you," she whispered. "When I saw the prince, with his lip . . . "

"That was me," I said, keeping my voice low. "But I escaped. And now I'm here to—"

"I know why you're here. And we best not discuss it. There are many eyes and ears in this castle, and many of them do not belong to Freetors." She raised her voice and gestured around the room. "What do you think, my lady?"

The room was larger than my cavern, and so full of light and colour that it stung my eyes. Woven gold and navy rugs adorned the wooden floor like bright islands in a rustic muddy sea, while purple silks draped from the stone walls reached down to gently caress the floor. A large mirror sat on top of a dark, wooden dresser in the far right corner. And the bed—a real bed! The canopy was liquid silver and fell on both sides of the bed, providing shelter and privacy. Ignoring my dress's bulky layers of fabric, I bellyflopped onto the mattress and sunk my head into the fluffy white pillows. They smelled like lemons and lavender, the smells of luxury.

"You forget yourself, Kiera," Bidelia said, her grip tight on the bedpost. "Get up, before those stupid servants get back."

I sat up and straightened out my dress but remained on the bed and let my feet dangle to the floor.

Bidelia cleared her throat as she inspected my appearance. "These are Lady Dominique's clothes?"

"Yes, we took all of her trunks."

"I'll see they are delivered safely to this room. You didn't put anything Freetor in there, did you?"

I thought about my Violet Fox cape and mask as my fingertips made little half-moon indents in my palms. My guilt must have showed. The colour drained from Bidelia's cheeks.

"Kiera . . ."

The door creaked open, and the serving girls entered with two trays. They set them on the dresser beside one of the windows. The smell of bread made my mouth water. I leapt off the bed as ladylike as possible, and one of the servants lifted the tray lid. A whole loaf—steaming from the oven—sat on the silver plate, with a hunk of cheese and a slab of butter. The other tray, once revealed, contained fresh strawberries and blueberries and other berries that I hadn't even seen before. I turned to say thank you to the girls, but they had already left. Servants were supposed to be as invisible as thieves.

Bidelia made her way to the door. "Eat, and become familiar with your surroundings. The feast is in three hours. We will talk later."

She left me alone with the trays, which I promptly carried to the bed for my own private feast. After I had stuffed myself, I lay face up on the bed with one hand on my tummy, satisfied. When was the last time I had felt this full? Never. And this is what the Marlenians felt like every day. I didn't even know if I could eat again in three hours.

The sickening part was that I would be here until I located Alastar's Tome, or at least until the end of the Gathering. I could get used to being full. To being treated like royalty instead of like a rat. Like a Marlenian . . .

No.

I climbed off the bed and stared out the window. The bailey was crawling with Marlenian nobility fanning themselves in the afternoon heat. The tall, stone wall connected with a massive hedge maze that led to the stables. While I had studied every part of the castle through the information the Elder apprentices had given me, it was something else entirely to see it with my own eyes. Servants slipped between the ladies and offered them treats on silver platters while pages scurried around with messages rolled between their nimble fingers. I was in enemy territory, and all of those ladies and guards and pages and servants were against me. The thief was here, in this castle, and I was going to steal back what rightfully belonged to my people.

I wiped the crumbs off my dress and crossed the room to the door. Outside, two men stood guard. I froze as they stared at me.

"My lady?" one of them prompted.

I reprimanded myself for being so afraid. They didn't know who I was. The more I acted like a scared Freetor, the more suspicious I would seem. Confidence was the secret to my success. "J'ou are my personal guards?" I asked.

"We are, my lady. Would you like to walk the grounds?"

Yes, I would like to scout out the castle grounds, I thought, with Marlenian guards as my escorts instead of as my enemies.

"Take me out back," I said.

"Of course, my lady."

One of the guards took the lead and the other followed behind me. I was escorted down the hallway and down a flight of stairs, through another hallway, and out the postern into the bailey. The heat hit me, and I regretted not bringing a fan. I thought of all the times I had huddled freezing in my straw bed, of how I would have killed for real warmth.

The hedges looked more formidable now that I was on the ground than they had from my bedroom window. The ladies chatted in twos and threes. I was alone, standing there with two guards behind me like I was someone important. The other ladies and lords didn't have anyone hovering over them, so I dismissed the guards. They didn't seem to mind either way, and marched back through the postern.

I sauntered around the grounds and took note of other guests who had come to celebrate Prince Keegan's name-day. I counted thirty-six nobles in a variety of colours. If everyone was wearing his or her house colours, then I had a good idea of who was present. Dark blues and silvers—the Western colours—dominated the crowd, but the fiery reds and yellows of the East were a strong competitor. There were fewer Southerners—spring blues, pinks, and pale yellows—but that wasn't surprising, as Southerners liked to isolate themselves from outside contact.

I searched for other Northerners, knowing I wouldn't find them. Travel was restricted in the North because of the rocky roads, the animal attacks, the climate, and the general lack of wealth. Fur merchants and blacksmiths made up the Northern noble class, and none of them would be interested in sending their children away to compete for Prince Keegan's affections, especially when there was more important work to be done, and when they were competing with their High King's daughter, Lady Dominique.

A loud screech cut through the gentle conversations. At once I was on my toes, ready to act. Who was in trouble? Would I be willing to help a Marlenian? The other nobles looked around for the source when the screech came again—and this time, it descended into a high-pitched laugh speckled with snorts. I crept towards the offending lady, an Eastern girl who commanded the attention of two other ladies. Her dress was tight at the waist, but by the look of her bosom—spilling over her low-cut neckline—and her chubby, baby-faced cheeks, she enjoyed her food. Her sun-bleached hair was drawn back with hundreds of pins, and part of it curled down the side of her shoulder, like a freshly abandoned snakeskin. Scrunched up or puckered, it didn't matter—her lips were fat worms, and the annoying titter that emerged from them made me cringe. She seemed beautiful next to the other two ladies—I wondered if she surrounded herself with less attractive ladies so that she could benefit. One of them had the same white-blonde hair, and it was pulled back so tightly that she constantly looked like she had tasted a sour lemon. The other was not from the East—her soft sky-blue gown complimented her dark skin, but her eyes were so large they looked ready to pop out of her head at any second.

It was the emblem stitched into the large, screechy-lady's dress that caught my attention: a white hunting bird with a crooked beak hovering over twin flames—one blue, one red, both burning yellow. That could only mean one thing: she was part of the Frostfire family, the rulers of the East. The North and the East had a history of not getting along, thanks to the trade war thirty years ago. And the more I looked at this large Frostfire lady, the less I liked her, with her screechy, annoying voice and the way she was stuffing hors d'oeuvres into her face like she hadn't eaten in days. It wouldn't be too hard to pretend to hate her.

"... pleased we arrived yesterday. The carriage ride was beginning to make me nauseous," she was saying. She yawned and fanned herself with her splayed sausage fingers. "And I thought we'd be late."

"I think the prince was happy to see you," said the lemon-face blonde. She also wore a yellow-orange low-cut dress with the Frostfire symbol on her hip, but it was smaller, suggesting that she was a cousin rather than part of the direct Frostfire line.

The fat girl's cheeks widened as she smiled slyly. "I knooow. He's even more handsome than the last Gathering. Remember last year when he asked me to dance at the ball? No one even had to tell him to ask me. And I've got the best dress for this year's ball. I think this may be *the* year!"

The two other ladies giggled and issued a number of responses. "Really? Oh, I *hope* so! This is what we've been waiting for our whole *lives*!" I rolled my eyes and sauntered towards the hedge maze.

"Unless some *other* girl comes and ruins it. Especially a Northern girl," the lemon-face girl grumbled. "The chances of that happening are slim, though."

My ears perked up once more.

"I didn't see any Northern ladies here," said the lady from the South. Her voice was quiet and reserved in comparison to the two Eastern ladies and had only a trace of the melodic accent of the South.

"Count it as a blessing. We don't need those savages running around here with their spears and their loud, clunky boots," said the screechy, fat lady.

"Lady Sylvia!" the lemon-face lady exclaimed, trying to contain her amusement by hiding her face behind her fan. "What a horrid thing to say."

"Ladies. My father visited the North many times when he was negotiating peace during the trade war. He said that the Pauper King was living up to his name, dressed no better than the servants. They even ate together at one table. Can you imagine? Sharing your food with the people who sleep in the stables? It's a wonder my father didn't come back riddled with fleas."

"Perhaps it's better that the Northerners aren't here, in that case," said the Southern lady. "Doesn't the North have a daughter, though? Surely the North would want—"

"Yes. I can't remember her name. She's never attended a Gathering that I can remember, and I've been to them all. But I heard she's afflicted with a mediocre face and a violent temper."

I smirked at the flowers. They were right about the temper. But was my face as mediocre as Lady Dominique's?

"Wasn't she supposed to be here?"

"Yes! I had heard that as well."

"Well! I heard the guards whispering that her wagon was hijacked by Freetors!"

Enough listening. It was time to make myself known. "It was not'in' my guards could not take care of."

Their fans stopped wagging as they turned to look at me. The lemon-face lady and the Southern lady looked completely horrified. Served them right. Lady Sylvia's pink, wormy lips twisted into a smile.

"Lady Dominique, I presume?" she said. "We are glad that you were able to make it here safely."

"I y'am sure." She had known Dominique's name, I realized, and hadn't told the other ladies. This one knew more than she let on. I had to be careful around her. "My fat'er would have been terribly upset if I did not spread my fleas to de ot'er provinces. Especially de East."

Lady Sylvia's smile disappeared. "Careful, Lady Dominique. We wouldn't want another war to tear this nation apart."

"Is dat a t'reat?" I asked before I could stop myself.

She sneered and looked me over like I was an inconvenience. A Freetor. "You are too little too late. If you are the only thing the North has sent to try to claim the throne, then you have an impossible task before you."

"Maybe dat's not what I y'am here pour, and j'ou are de one makin' a fool of j'ourself," I replied.

A tiny bit of spittle flew in my direction as she laughed. "Please. Don't play ignorant. We all play this game. Your father has wanted control of the West for years, and for a while, the East was the only thing barring him from taking over completely."

"Dat may have been true four hundred years ago, before de provinces were y'even clearly defined. De only ting our provinces cannot agree on is de price of wool and silk."

Lady Sylvia's face turned a bright red as excitement surged through my blood. This was almost as good as being chased by the guards. I silently thanked the Elders for my thorough training in Marlenian history.

I looked to the other blonde lady with the sour face. "And j'ou are a Frostfire as well?"

"Lady Milda Seacream is my name," she said, but was quick to add, "I am descended from the Frostfires. My mother's father and Lady Sylvia's father's father were brothers. But everyone says I could be Sylvia's sister!" She grinned and clasped Sylvia by the arm, but Sylvia did not seem to share Milda's enthusiasm.

"Yes, a shame. But how would Prince Keegan be able to tell us apart otherwise?" She ran her fingers through her golden hair.

"The prince, he is clever," said the Southern girl. "He knows every girl's name, and every girl's face."

Terror seized my gut. Would he know my face? No, he only saw me with the mask. A piece of fabric with holes ripped out for eyes, accented with golden glitter.

"Oh, Lady Na'ima. We all know that some faces he knows more than others," Sylvia gushed.

I prayed that this was true.

The quick padding of soft shoes on grass reached my ears before it even registered with the ladies. I turned and saw Rordan. His page's outfit was already wrinkled. I wondered what he had had to do while I was socializing with the Marlenians. Maybe he was doing reconnaissance. A pang of homesickness hit me as I realized that I wouldn't be able to discuss my day with him tonight.

He brushed a stray lock from his eyes, and the ladies appraised him silently. The two of us favoured our mother's side, we were always told, as we shared the same cheekbones and prominent jaw. At least our eyes were different: his cloudy grey and mine a murky blue. I wondered if we should be seen together at the castle, in case someone smarter put two and two together. The Elders wouldn't have sent him here if they thought there would be a risk, I decided.

"My lady," Rordan said, making a point to bow deeply. "I have been sent to fetch j'ou pour de feast. Dey are seatin' people now."

Lady Sylvia smirked. "A personal servant to tell you when supper is ready? How quaint."

How else would you know when to go, I wanted to say, but I had to show Rordan that I was integrating with the ladies. "Tank j'ou, page. I will be in shortly."

"Will de lady need an escort?" he asked.

I tried not to laugh. "No, de lady y'is fine."

He nodded and ran off towards the castle. Apparently I wasn't the only one trying to contain my laughter; the ladies looked like they were ready to explode into a fit of giggles.

"Lady Dominique, you have male servants in your employ?" Lady Sylvia asked.

"Dey have deir uses," I replied.

At once I knew this was the wrong thing to say, as the Marlenian ladies tittered, covering their little pouty lips with their uncalloused hands.

I couldn't take it anymore. I stormed off after Rordan.

"Oh, Dominique, you *must* sit with us at dinner!" Lady Sylvia called after me, but her voice was lost in a fit of the ladies' laughter.

Stupid, stupid ladies. How was I supposed to fit in here if none of them liked me? I took a couple of deep breaths to calm myself down. It wasn't me they didn't like. It was Lady Dominique. She couldn't help that she was from the North. Maybe it wasn't as barbaric as they said. But Dominique herself had bragged to me about all of their inhumane practices. I had to take it in stride. I was here to blend in, but I wasn't here to make friends. I was here to find Alastar the Hero's Tome and leave before they noticed that there was a Freetor in their midst.

# Seven

THE GREAT HALL was at the centre of the castle and took up most of the ground level, which it shared with the twisting hallways of violent tapestries and the kitchen. Four tables created the outline of a square, with narrow spaces at the corners where servants and Freetor slaves (marked with a giant *s* burned into their cheeks) weaved in and out. Some set out the finest gold and silver dinnerware I'd ever seen, while others arranged purple roses with cut stems in square glasses, placed at every third table setting. There were at least forty place settings. The silver gleamed in the low-hanging chandelier. I shuddered, thinking how many Freetor slaves had died mining the tiny diamonds that hung threaded through hundreds of almost-invisible strings.

Outside, the merchants and the lower-class commoners would be celebrating as well. The Gathering meant more drunks wandering the streets, and drunks rarely took note of their coin purses until the next morning, when their silver was gone. Just looking at the gleaming silverware made me want to snatch the plates and run, but I kept my distance from the table. Lady Dominique wouldn't be interested in the table settings and the busy rush of servants and slaves. I couldn't even remember the last time I'd eaten at a table. Rordan and I took our meals whenever and wherever we had a spare moment.

Other nobles trickled into the room and stood idly, chatting with one another, but the servants and the slaves outnumbered the nobles three to one. Rordan had called me here early, I realized. Part of me wanted to thank him for an excuse to be rid of the horrible ladies, but maybe he was just checking up on me. Making sure I didn't get distracted. I was here to observe, not to make friends.

Bidelia appeared from an archway and started ordering some younger servants around, directing them to make the final touches on the table. The slaves melted into the exits (where did they go? I wanted them to know freedom again) while the servants took over the final preparations. Each place setting had a piece of tinted-grey paper folded neatly in half with a name written in the curly calligraphy I'd only seen on the signs for the women's dress shops. I sauntered around the table once more after finding Lady Dominique's name, searching for another name that looked more like my own so that I could take the card as a keepsake, if the Elders let me. I was seated closest to the west exit, which led back to my bedchamber—I wondered if this was deliberate on Bidelia's part. To my dismay, Lady Sylvia and several other ladies had been seated next to me. They would hate this more than I would. After this was all over, I'd never have to see them again. They did not matter.

Gripping the back of the chair gingerly, I pulled it out from the table. The legs scraped across the floor and suddenly two female servants were at my side, prying the chair from my grasp as if I'd touched something I wasn't supposed to. I recoiled, terrified that the guards would flank me next, but the girls gestured to the seat.

"Allow us, my lady," said one of the servant girls, bowing deeply.

I tried to appear calm and collected as the servant girls tucked me into my dinner place. A few lords sat at the other side of the table, but I was the only lady who was sitting. Awkward. The servant girls poured me water in a silver-plated goblet and red wine in a clear, thin glass. I thanked them before remembering that I didn't have to.

I needed to relax.

More guests flowed into the room. I recognized a few of them, including the captain of the guard—Captain Allan Murdock—a six-foot-two man with a portly stature. I hid a smile. Usually he sent his men to chase me, but if he was around, but he would never dismount his horse. He made it easy for me to escape into the many narrow alleyways and dark corners where his rich eating habits forbade him to go.

Lady Sylvia made her way into the hall, with Lady Milda and Lady Na'ima at her heels. They eagerly read the place cards. The servants saw them approach and, under Bidelia's watchful eye, escorted them to the seats next to me. Lady Sylvia's cheeks were flushed red, as if she'd already had a few glasses of wine.

"Lady Dominique," she said, trying to hold back a fit of giggles as she settled in next to me.

Maybe they weren't going to hate sitting next to me at all. They were going to love making fun of me. Again. "Lady Sylvia."

"Where did your manservant get to?" she asked, glancing around the room. "I do admit, he was very cute. I can see why you . . . keep him around."

The other girls descended into laughter. I dug my thumbnails into my palms and almost laughed myself. Rordan as my lover? I wished I could tell him so that we could laugh together about it.

Their laughter turned into excited, muffled squeals as Prince Keegan and his armed escort billowed into the hall. Servants and nobles alike stopped whatever they were doing and immediately bowed in his general direction. Those sitting rose to their feet in respect. I barely made it up before everyone was sitting back down again. Servant girls returned to our sides to keep our dresses from being caught under the chairs.

Prince Keegan was looking better since I'd seen him in the square a week ago. He no longer wore the bandage that covered half his face. From across the room, I couldn't see his scar, but his lip did look a little swollen. So he did have a good healer after all. I tried not to look too disappointed as he greeted the nearby noble ladies with a charming smile. So much for making a big impact. Maybe he would think twice before angering the Violet Fox or any other Freetor, though. He slicked back his coal-black hair, carefully minding the thin circlet resting on his head. The golden rings around his fingers sparkled like the chandelier and accented the gold trim on his velvet tunic. The man was a walking gold mine, and the ladies surrounded him, hoping to pick him clean. I rolled my eyes.

The room was filled with the laughter of people who wanted for nothing, the popping of champagne, and the smells of food that I had only before dreamed of tasting. My eyes swept the room, counting. Thirty-eight people including myself.

Last to arrive was the Advisor, Ivor Ferguson, the most dangerous man in Western Marlenia. A trimmed greying beard hugged his face, but it was the thin moustache growing on his upper lip that disturbed me the most—the way it twisted unnaturally away from his face, like antennae on an insect, listening in to every conversation in the room. His eyes sunk into his face like a dead man's and were shadowed by thick, caterpillar eyebrows. Next to Captain Murdock, the Advisor was a twig.

People were mostly seated now, sipping at their wines and their waters and making pleasant small talk. Prince Keegan sat in a large, decorated chair that looked too big for him off to the far left of the square table. The Advisor lingered to his left, his bejewelled hand resting on top of the chair.

He cleared his throat and raised his other hand. "Could I have everyone's attention, please?"

His voice was not as commanding as the Holy One's, and it had a sort of underlying slime to it, like overripe moss that had been left in the dark too long and had started oozing onto the dirt.

"I would officially like to welcome you all to the name-day feast of Prince Keegan Tramore, first of his name, son of Eamon Tramore, the High King of Western Marlenia, our Holy One, the always and future ruler of Marlenia."

Polite applause and the dinging of wine glasses filled the air. Lady Sylvia looked so excited that I thought she might explode.

"This Gathering is an historical moment," he continued as he surveyed the room. "Prince Keegan is leaving his childhood behind and facing manhood with only his courage and family name—and all that comes with being a moneyed prince, of course." Polite laughter. *Too* polite. "I think we can all agree that Marlenia's future is bright with Prince Keegan as its heir."

Murmurs of "well said" and "I agree" and a "Oh yes, of course!" from Sylvia ensued.

"There is one man missing from this table tonight. Unfortunately, the Holy One is not feeling his best," the Advisor said. His tone suggested that he was apologetic, but based on what I'd heard about the man, I couldn't help but wonder if that manner was forced. "He sends his regards and hopes to see you all tomorrow at court."

Polite condolences spread across the room, and I smiled and nodded like the rest of them. The Advisor exchanged private words with Prince Keegan, but his hand was in front of his mouth, so I couldn't even guess at what they were saying. I wondered if the prince knew the rumours about the Advisor wanting to take over the throne, and if he was going to do anything about it.

I took a deep breath and let it out slowly. Marlenian politics were none of my concern.

Those who remained standing found their place cards as the first course was brought out: steaming chicken soup with large chopped carrots, celery, and potatoes floating in the broth. Even though I'd stuffed myself earlier, my stomach rumbled. The ladies brought spoonfuls of the thick broth to their red, treated lips and blew gently, taking the tiniest sips, and then abandoned the bowl after three or four spoonfuls. The soup was like a fire in my mouth, but a good fire, one that warms you after being out in the rain. I wanted to have the entire bowl and more, all at once, but I ate slowly and deliberately, as Lady Dominique would have.

Lady Sylvia was loud beside me, and it was hard not to be part of her conversation. "*My* servants bathe once a week. A waste of water, my father says, but I can't have their filthy hands doing my hair and touching my skin. I'm sure Prince Keegan has a similar philosophy. Look at him. He's so . . . clean."

The thought of my formally dirty self wiping my hands all over Lady Sylvia made me giggle.

"What's so funny, Lady Dominique?" Lady Sylvia inquired.

"Dat's absolutely ridiculous," I said.

"What is so ridiculous? Or do you like letting the commoners and the slaves touch you with their disease-ridden hands?"

"Aren't j'ou listenin' to j'ourself? Fawnin' over de prince like dat.

100

Like he is a puppy instead of a man. Seems like j'ou do have a disease after all."

The look on Lady Sylvia's face brought me down a few notches, back to reality. I hadn't thought those words, as I'd meant to. I'd spoken them. Only a few sips of wine and already my tongue was being bold. This was not good. Fortunately the prince didn't seem to hear me over the other conversations, but the Advisor's eyes did flicker my way. I downed what was left in my glass, which was almost nothing.

Bidelia's servants brought around a wider selection of wine, but Bidelia herself came to serve me. Her shoulder brushed my arm as she leaned in to pour the dark liquid into the glass.

"Keep your mouth shut," she whispered. "And stop eating your entire course. No lady finishes a meal—it implies they've eaten nothing else that day."

I kept my face still as her words washed over me, knowing she was right.

The second course was ham treated with a pineapple glaze and mashed potatoes so soft they melted in my mouth. I'd been so busy concentrating on following Bidelia's advice and savouring the taste of my first real meal in my life that at first, I didn't notice Prince Keegan's stare. His gaze flickered from my end of the table, with the chattering ladies, to the Advisor.

I did not want to talk to the prince. What if he knew me? Somehow, he'd recognize me as the dirty Freetor woman who'd maimed him, and I would be put to death immediately.

Prince Keegan turned his gaze fully to my side of the table. I stuffed a large piece of ham in my mouth so that I wouldn't be obligated to answer any questions directed at me.

"Ladies. I trust your day was enjoyable?" he said.

Beside me, Lady Sylvia gushed and practically hovered in her chair. "Yes, Your Grace. We strolled through the markets and found the most wonderful dress shop!"

"I see," he replied with tilted eyebrows but his gaze returned to his wine. The prince would never be interested in some dumb dress shop. He placed a finely sliced piece of meat in his mouth, just as I had, to avoid conversation. That sly Marlenian bastard was doing exactly what I was doing. I hid my amusement in my wine glass.

The Advisor picked up the conversation thread. "May I ask which shop, my lady? I happened to own a number of successful businesses. Still do, though mostly only in name, now."

"Oh, I don't remember the name," Lady Sylvia said offhand-edly. "I'm terrible with names." She giggled nervously and glanced at her fellow ladies for help. "Laura's Lace, maybe? Linda's Lace? Something . . . "

I knew exactly what shop she was talking about. I'd never been inside, but I passed it often enough during my Violet Fox escapades. It carried the latest fashions from the West, as well as the South. "Lucinda's Luxuries and Lace," I supplied.

"Yes . . . that was the one . . . " She eyed me suspiciously. "You have visited it, Lady Dominique?"

There was a pang in my stomach. My face felt hot. I hadn't meant to draw attention to myself, but here I was, being loud and getting noticed. "De sign caught my eye on my way to de castle."

"Ah." The Advisor nodded and rubbed his chin with his forefin-ger and thumb. "Forgive me, my lady. I believe we have not been formally introduced."

"Dat . . . dat is correct," I replied. I cleared my throat and increased my accent, as if that could help me. I was already in the thick of things. "I y'am Lady Dominique Castillo, daughter of de High King Matís of de Nort'ern province of Marlenia."

"We are pleased that you could join us, my lady," Prince Keegan said with a slight incline of his head. "On behalf of my father, I wel-come you to the West."

I smiled politely and bowed my head. "Tank j'ou, J'our Grace. I y'am honoured to be here."

"And after so long an absence," the Advisor noted. He twirled his fork in the centre of his plate, and I dug my fingernails into my palm, counting the seconds. Did he know? He couldn't know, he had never seen me before. But it was his business to know everything that hap-pened in Marlenia City.

"But yes. I do hear that Lucinda's is the place to go if you are a young lady looking to have the latest in Western designs. Not that I would know, personally." He chuckled at his own joke, and the prince laughed politely, and so, the rest of the nobles followed suit. "It is a shame that their business has been so affected lately."

"Affected?" Lady Sylvia prompted.

"The Freetors," Captain Murdock piped up. "Don't ask me what it is. Some weeks it seems like they'll only attack the food shops. Other times, it's only the smiths. This week, it's been all about the clothes."

I hid my guilty face in my napkin. Was this about me? Did Freetors steal more fabric this week to make more clothes so that I wouldn't be naked? Lady Dominique only had so many trunks—could they even fit more clothes in there? A bead of sweat rolled down my face. It was getting hot, and I'd already drunk all of my wine, and it was only the second course. There were at least two more to go. Or was it three? No, that was not right! Rordan had told me to never drink too quickly! My head was swimming. I had to keep my tongue in check.

Lady Sylvia was talking again. "And who is this Violet Fox character gallivanting on the streets of Marlenia City? Surely he must be a laughing stock of this court."

There was a stiff silence at the table.

"It's a woman, actually," Prince Keegan said finally. "A Freetor woman who almost slit my throat during an outing the previous week. Instead, she left me with this rather unattractive scar, here." He pointed to his lips.

The ladies gasped and expressed their sympathies. A servant came by and poured more wine into my glass, and I took a long drink.

"The kiss of the Violet Fox, the folk are calling it," Captain Murdock said.

"The kiss of cold steel was all it was," Prince Keegan said bitterly. "Anyone capable with a knife could have done it. I . . . I was foolish to have let my guard down."

Ladies murmured more sympathies, with Lady Sylvia trumpeting above the rest. I moved my lips to make it look like I was saying something relevant.

The Advisor raised an eyebrow. "I was curious to ask the ladies from away what they thought of a woman leading the Freetor charge here in Marlenia City."

"She certainly has no knowledge of Marlenian fashion," said Lady Milda. "Violet was last spring's colour."

The ladies tittered and then men chuckled politely. I hid my disgruntled expression in my napkin as I dabbed my upper lip.

"I couldn't imagine running about the city all day. It would be very tiring," said another lady from across the table. She wore bright red—another Eastern lady.

"Imagine what her husband must think!" Lady Sylvia exclaimed.

"I highly doubt she has a husband," I murmured.

"Quite right, Lady Dominique. No man would ever want her," she replied, nodding emphatically.

I inhaled sharply and stuffed more potatoes into my mouth. I'd never thought about it that way before. Rordan was getting marriage proposals left and right, but I had had none. Was it because of my street fame? No—that was a Marlenian way to think. Maybe other Freetors didn't expect me to live long—I would not make a good wife because I would not be able to reproduce since I'd be on the surface stealing food and other goods all the time. Yes, that was the Freetor way to think.

"But she does keep the city guard on their toes," Captain Murdock said. "She's done more damage to the economy than anything else we've ever faced."

The corners of my lips tugged upward. Finally. Useful information.

"Really? How so?" I asked.

"Well, my lady, it is simple economics," the Advisor said. "Our farmers can only produce so much produce a year. When it is taken without adequate compensation, they cannot afford to plant as many seeds on as much land as they did the previous year. Our food supply has decreased by nearly twenty percent since last year."

Twenty percent. I thought back to the previous year. No wonder it seemed like the Freetor thieves were working twice as hard and yet yielding the same results.

"Beyond that, she has also become a symbol for the Freetors," he added. "She encourages them to take what isn't rightfully theirs. Reports have cropped up all over the West of Freetors trying to take land belonging to smaller lords and farmers."

It should be ours, I thought. But we couldn't have land because the Marlenians and their ancestors would not let us share the sun with them, just because of Alastar's magic.

"And not one of your fine men have caught this Violet Fox?" Lady Milda asked.

Captain Murdock cleared his throat. "Not yet, but we will."

I hid my true grin behind a polite smile. I was sitting at their table and they didn't even know it. They would never catch me, not in a thousand years.

"She's been strangely quiet in the last week, isn't that true, Captain?" the Advisor noted.

He hurraphed into his napkin and wiped stray crumbs from his moustache. "I suppose so."

"Is that unusual, Captain?" Lady Na'ima asked.

Captain Murdock shrugged. "The Freetors like to keep us on our toes. She could be planning something. Or, she could be waiting for us to become lazy with our watch. Regardless, we vary our patrols and keep on the lookout for any suspicious activity. Just because she's not out there doesn't mean there isn't some other filth that's acting in her name." He bit off a piece of bread and chewed with his mouth open. His eyes flickered to mine and for a dreadful, long moment, I thought he was going to command my arrest. Instead, he spoke, and bits of chewed bread flew across the table. "Tell me, Lady Dominique, do you have characters such as the Violet Fox in the North?"

I gritted my teeth and remembered Lady Dominique's words. "No, we do not."

"You're lucky, then. I remember from my correspondence with your castle's captain that you keep many Freetors for slaves, many more than we do here. Not necessarily a surprise, I told him, as the slave trade is mostly based up North."

I swallowed and nodded grimly. "We do keep slaves, j'es." The table was silent, as if waiting for me to say more. I took a deep breath and tried to capture some of that cruelty that the real Dominique had shown me. My grip on my wine glass tightened. "Dey're much more obedient when j'ou cut out deir tongues."

Captain Murdock snorted and laughed from his belly, and commanded that more wine be brought to the table. The Advisor remained expressionless, but Prince Keegan appeared concerned. Maybe I was being too forward. Would the real Lady Dominique act this way? I remembered the cruel fire in her eyes—she'd say anything to get a rise out of someone. Out of me.

"A clever tactic, if we could catch them first," Captain Murdock replied when he had recovered.

"Do not belittle your achievements, Captain. You have caught how many Freetors this year? Almost a hundred? That's at least twenty more than last season," the Advisor said.

"Doesn't matter. The more we catch, the fewer we seem to have— not once they're in the dungeons, but it seems like not every Freetor we catch makes it there. I thoroughly screen my guards to weed out the Freetor sympathizers, but those Freetor rats are slippery. Cutting out their tongues would do little. If we cut off their feet—"

"Dey wouldn' be y'able to work. Where will de eslaves come from?" I interjected.

"Lady Dominique does bring up a good point," the Advisor said. "Even servants must be paid something—but slave labour is free. The merchant's council has been whispering about some merchants who have considered keeping the Freetors caught digging in their coffers until they pay their debt to society—or in plain-speak, forever."

"My father would never allow that," Prince Keegan replied. "And I don't believe I would either. Our economy would cease to function if we gave jobs to the very people who are stealing from us."

"My prince, you put it so elephantly!" Lady Sylvia giggled, her face flush with drink. "Wine! Please, more wine!"

I was thankful that I wasn't as drunk as Lady Sylvia. Bidelia quickly scurried to Lady Sylvia's side and poured the delicious red-blue substance into her glass. The red dye on her lips had long since worn off on the glass and had been replaced by the dark colour of the wine.

"I don't understand these Freetors. I really don't," she said between sips. Bidelia was about to walk away when Sylvia gestured to her again and shook her dainty half-empty wine glass. "Why don't they just leave us alone? Or why don't we raid them and kill them all like the pests they are? Surely you must have thought of this, Your Grace." She smiled, her cheeks red and warm, and I didn't know whether I wanted to throw up or laugh.

The male nobles and less inebriated ladies exchanged gossipy whispers. Apparently Lady Sylvia was more airy when she was in her cups than when she was out. Keegan set his fork carefully on his plate and appeared to consider how to handle her. "My lady, although on the surface the Freetors are an annoyance, they are a serious threat to our economy. We don't know their true numbers, as Lady Dominique pointed out, and we mustn't forget that they are ruled by powerful Elders with access to a strange magic that we have only recently begun to understand."

My heart was pounding. "J'our Grace, I was under de impression dat j'our scholars have had a handle on de Freetor magic pour some time now."

Keegan's gaze fell to me once more. He smiled slightly as he reached for his wine. "One of the greatest mysteries of the world is the Freetor magic. Where did you get the impression that our scholars were so well versed?"

"Oh . . . just rumours from passin' travellers," I said.

The Advisor twirled the stem of his wine glass between his bejewelled fingers. "It is a fascinating field of research, even if it is filled with speculation."

"Magic. I'll believe it when I see it!" Sylvia exclaimed. She gestured to Bidelia again. "You, servant lady, give my friends more wine!"

"Oh, it has been seen, my lady. I do not know how the Freetors have organized themselves in the East, but here in the West, there have been public displays of their power over the last twenty years. That alone would make anyone wary of sending their men to the depths to fight."

The Advisor was right about that. Of the seven Elders, there were usually more than a few who weren't above showing off their power. Most if not all of the Elders had been Fighters before they had been selected to be Elder apprentices and had seen more horrors than most of the Freetors who spent their time underground. Some of the younger Elders, who had seen forty name-days, were more adventurous than the older Elders like Erskina, who had seen at least seventy name-days (almost unheard of among Freetors—though it could be the magic that had kept her alive). Upon learning the secrets of the Elders, some men and women wanted to show the Marlenians just who held the power in the land. In the last year alone, three Elders who had ventured to the surface had used their magic against the Marlenians.

One had blasted lightning at a guard who had cornered him. The guard baked in his armour and fell down dead.

The second attack had occurred just outside the city walls. A recently inducted apprentice and a team of Fighters were staking out a large carriage filled with silver quid coming towards Marlenia City. Hijack the carriage, that was the plan. When the Marlenians opposed them, the Elder apprentice called high winds from the mountains and swept them thousands of stone-throws away.

Perhaps the most chilling was the third account. A Marlenian child was playing with his brother on one of the streets near the merchant district when an Elder broke through the soil. A full Elder, not an apprentice. The child, afraid and yet fascinated at the display of magic, stopped playing and went to speak with the person who came from the underground. He never made it two steps before he was reduced to a pile of ash. The brother ran, but the ground swallowed him whole. Some report that it was Erskina's doing, but the children who could say for sure were both dead.

If the Marlenians figured out how to use magic against us . . . we were doomed.

"The Freetors wouldn't dare use magic against my father," Sylvia boasted. "He would spare no man hunting down anyone who dared to attack him or any of our blood in that manner."

I didn't know about the use of Freetor magic in the East. Maybe Sylvia was speaking the truth. "Deir magic is powerful and dangerous."

"We are right to fear it," Prince Keegan said.

The Advisor shook his head. "I envision our fear of this magic soon being a thing of the past."

The other conversations quieted as the nobles turned their attention to the Advisor. We waited for him to say more, but he simply smiled and took another sip of his wine. Servants descended upon the table and cleared away our plates, whether we were finished or not, and brought the next course, but I didn't take my gaze off the Advisor.

There was a very good chance that he had stolen Alastar's Tome. My stomach felt like it was being eaten by worms.

Sylvia slowed down her wine consumption and inhaled the third course—slices of lamb chops laid delicately over creamy mashed potatoes swimming in spicy gravy and encircled by peas as green as the emeralds sparkling on the prince's ring. I nibbled and pushed around the food, wondering if I could tell Bidelia to give it to a needy Freetor family instead.

"The Freetors are fast little buggers, though. Cowards, most of them. Running back to their tunnels to 'fight' another day. Ha!" Captain Murdock slammed a meaty fist on the table. It trembled under his weight. "Whatever it is they're planning, they're not likely to get it soon if they keep running away from my sword!"

"Dey say dat dey want deir freedom," I said quietly.

"Freedom, hah!" said Captain Murdock. "They aren't caged. We didn't send them to live wherever they do. There's no room for them to live on the surface, so someone's got to live underground. We don't have any control over them whatsoever. If they're complaining about that, someone should tell them that we don't care what they do, as long as they stop stealing our resources!"

There was a chorus of agreement around the table. My insides boiled.

"What if we gave them a plot of land and left them alone?" Prince Keegan suggested. "Wouldn't they be grateful for our generosity and resort to peaceful interactions with us and the surrounding provinces?"

A hint of sympathy from the prince? He did have the power to grant and take away land anywhere in Marlenia. I couldn't get my hopes up, but if I could sway the prince to our cause, that would be a major victory for the Freetors. A peaceful victory.

"Their freedom is not ours to give, young majesty," the Advisor said. "Even if such a thing were to happen, there are almost two hundred years of war weighing between us. One cannot simply erase that and expect them to be peaceful. If anything, their population will grow to numbers we cannot control, and they will eradicate us all."

"Deir numbers could already be greater dan what we imagine," I said slowly, conscious not to make it sound like a threat—since it wasn't true.

"Potentially. We can only perform a census on the slaves and Freetor criminals we have captured and use what little information we obtain from them."

"It's too bad they're so feral," Keegan said. "But I still stand by my idea, no matter how dangerous it may seem. Let them work the land for a day, and maybe they will learn the errors of their ways."

We weren't the ones in the wrong, I thought. If the Holy One of two hundred years ago hadn't spurned Alastar's gift, everyone would be happy and free.

"Well, it is your name-day," said the Advisor. "I yield this argument to you. However, we must remember whom we are talking about—Freetors. They're so feral they might as well be animals. And like any other animal, they can be caught and trained to respect their betters, or put down."

My fingers wrapped so tightly around the wine glass I thought it might break. Nothing would have pleased me more than to leap up, tear off my dress, reach across the table, and strangle them all. Instead, I buried my face in the wine as I took a long sip.

Keegan stood. "I suppose it is time for me to retire. Men?"

Chairs squeaked as the men rose, stretching and cracking their knuckles. It was not a question, but a formality. Traditionally the men left before the women to continue their combat training, back thousands of years ago when the Marlenians fought over the provincial borders. My eyes slid to the other women. They stayed put.

The prince's gaze swept over the table. "Good night, ladies. It was a pleasure to see all of you tonight. I hope I get to chat with you more tomorrow."

The noblewomen replied with their good nights and formal addresses. I took another sip of wine. All this formality was sickening.

"It was nice to hear a woman's perspective on the current affairs, Lady Dominique," Keegan said.

It took me a moment to realize he was talking to me. I forced a smile and bowed my head. Hidden in my shirts, my fingernails drove into the palm of my hand.

"I tank j'ou pour de opportunity to speak, J'our Grace," I replied.

"You are free to speak whenever you wish, my lady, as long as you continue to have something worthy to say," Keegan said.

"Then it seems, from her extensive schooling, she may never shut up!" said one of the nobles.

The men clutched their tummies and laughed heartily over this. The women stifled their twitters in their gloved hands.

*It would be a change from your uneducated opinions and snobbery*, I wanted to say. Instead, I kept my lips sealed.

"Good night, ladies," Keegan said again.

With that, he and the other nobles headed out of the Great Hall with their escorts and pages. The large wooden doors echoed in the high ceilings as they closed. Once the men were gone, servants flocked once more to the tables and began clearing plates. I waited for the ladies to slouch in their chairs or take off their gloves, but none of them relaxed. The party wasn't over yet. Their gossip only got louder.

"Did you see Lord Gilroy Foster's moustache? A dab of cream got stuck in it during the second course, and no one ever pointed it out!"

"Lord Shantanu Aman looked dashing in his bright pink. Even though it was last season's fashion," said a Southern lady, sitting at the far end of the table.

"Prince Keegan seemed quite friendly to you, Lady Dominique."

Lady Sylvia's comment caught me off-guard. "Friendly? He was friendly to everyone." I knew it was a weak defence.

"You of course know the rumour that he has been courting Lady Jameela from the South," said Lady Milda.

"Yes!" Lady Na'ima chimed in. "I was seeing her before I came here. Very happy, she was, with Prince Keegan's last letter. They write each other often." Her smile was wistful.

"A shame she's not here," Lady Sylvia said with a hint of sarcasm. "She and Prince Keegan got on rather well at the last Gathering."

"Rumours are for people who are too lazy to find de trut'," I replied.

"So you admit it!" she squealed. "You are seeing him."

"No!"

The ladies fell silent. My outburst had echoed loudly through the room. There was a clash of dishes. Bidelia had dropped her tray. I straightened, almost rising to help her clean it up. I had to hold onto my chair to keep myself down. The women merely glanced at her and then returned their hungry attention to me.

I cleared my throat. "I y'am not courtin' Prince Keegan, nor do I have any interest in doing so. I y'am seein' someone else."

"Oh? I hear that Lord Gerold Essayé has expressed interest in you, but that was some time ago."

I didn't know who that was. His name suggested he was from the East, maybe from the North-East border. "We tryst in secret, actually," I said. "I would rat'er not talk about it."

This sent the ladies into a fit of laughter. It was too late to take it back—I'd have to find out who this Lord Gerold Essayé was, because he was now part of Lady Dominique's story.

"Evading the truth," said Lady Sylvia, wiping a tear from her eye as the laughter died. "Wouldn't that make you prone to starting a rumour?"

I hated when people turned my own words against me. "I y'am not evadin' anyt'in'. I y'am preservin' my dignity and de honour of my man by keepin' it a secret." I stood. "Now, before anyt'in' else I say can be misconstrued, I y'am goin' to sleep."

I stood. A Marlenian servant quickly pulled the chair back to leave me room to move in the ginormous layered dress. I couldn't just storm out of the hall, not with the high shoes and the billowing, puffy dress. The Marlenian women whispered their opinions of me as I clunked across the shiny, echoing floor. The servant followed closely behind, fluttering like a small child who wanted something from its mother.

"My lady, is there anything I can do for you?"

"I just want to go to bed. Which way to my room?"

The servant pointed nervously down a corridor. "That way, my lady."

"Tank j'ou."

After navigating the narrow hallways for about ten minutes and climbing a flight of stairs, I finally found my quarters. I nodded curtly to the guard posted in the hallway and stormed into my room—only to realize that I wasn't alone.

Bidelia sat beside the desk, her eyes half open, her fingers massaging her temples. She looked tired.

"Won't they miss you at the table?" I asked.

She lifted her dress so that she wouldn't trample the hem when she stood, but she kept her cold eyes on me the whole time. "The servants are whispering words that are filthier than the sewage caverns."

"I don't know what you mean."

She straightened my bed sheets absently. "Lord Keegan has his eye on you."

My heart fell into my chest. "You think he knows I'm a Freetor?"

"I think he thinks you're a hot-blooded, Northern Marlenian girl who would be willing to warm his bed."

I sat on the bed, my ears and face red. The thought of Keegan touching me in any way made my stomach turn. It was common knowledge that Marlenians took Freetor slaves to bed when there was no one else to satisfy their lust—and some went willingly. Whatever was produced from that union was shunned by both races. Usually the babes were killed at birth, or sometimes, when the Elders were feeling sympathetic, such as in an instance of rape, the child was allowed to live. A terrible existence, though, knowing that half of you was barely human.

"I would rather slit my wrists and watch myself die than allow that to happen," I said quietly.

Bidelia's heels crunched on the wooden floor but softened on the rug as she came around to my side.

"You remember one thing, Kiera," she said. "Remember your place. You're a Freetor, and he—his people—have stolen ancient secrets we've worked so hard to guard."

"I know," I replied. "I know what I have to do, okay? I don't have any interest in him."

"You had better keep it that way," she said. "The Elders are never kind to women who devote themselves to Marlenian men."

The world was never kind to Freetors, no matter what they did, I thought as Bidelia took her leave. Only the Elders seemed to have real freedom, with their magic. Someday, I would be an Elder, and I would know their secrets.

If I lived that long.

# Eight

THE CASTLE WAS asleep, but I was wide awake.

The room was coated in moonlight. Red and yellow light from the torches in the hallway lit the floor. I knew that I needed sleep for the busy day of activities in the morning, but I was so used to the hard stone bed that I considered sleeping on the floor. If the servant girls came in to wake me, however, that would be hard to explain, unless I made up a story about Lady Dominique being prone to falling out of bed.

I sighed and sat up, throwing the thick, down comforter from my legs. Who I was kidding? The night was mine. If sleep would not find me, then I had to make use of the darkness.

Under my bed, that's where Bidelia and her servants had stored Lady Dominique's things. *My* things. The stiff rug dug into my bare knees as I knelt and yanked as hard as I could on the old case. It skidded on the soft floor, but scraped on the wood. I opened it wide enough to stick my arm in and feel around. Yes. My cape, my dagger, my mask, my roughspun pants and shirt: I knew them by touch alone.

I stole them away to the vanity. The air was cold, and for a moment, I considered snuggling back under the covers. There was always tomorrow . . .

"No," I whispered to myself, throwing my nightgown on the bed and slipping into my Freetor rags. It would only take one night of Marlenian comforts for me to grow accustomed to them—I had to watch that I didn't surrender everything I'd suffered through for a warm bed and a full belly.

I wrapped the violet cape around my cool shoulders, and its familiar musty, earthy smell overwhelmed my nostrils. Home. I tied the mask behind my head and stared at myself in the mirror. It was strange enough seeing myself as it was—sometimes I would snitch mirrors in the market just to see what I looked like, since murky reflections in underground streams weren't really reliable. My dark, curly hair fell below my shoulders and enveloped my heart-shaped face. I never considered myself pretty, because no one could really be pretty when they were constantly dirty. I was clean now, though. My looks were good enough to charm, I decided, but my breasts weren't as large as Lady Dominique's. The Violet Fox mask brought out the blue in my eyes, but I had to lean close to the mirror to see it in the dark. Seeing myself as the Violet Fox in the castle— it was like I was dreaming. If only Mother and Father could see me now.

I pinched myself to make sure everything was still real. I winced and rubbed the skin tenderly.

A sudden snort erupted from across the room.

Goose prickles rose on my arms as I spun and drew my dagger. "Show yourself."

The floorboards creaked as I crept closer to the sound. Sweat pooled in my palm as I held the knife steady. I could make out a figure in the shadows, less than a head taller than me. I'd never killed anyone before, not even as the Violet Fox, but I had to be ready to do some serious damage if the guards caught me.

Whoever it was, it looked like he had fallen asleep standing up against the wall, by the door. As my knife drew closer to his neck, he stirred and snorted again, waking himself up. "Kiera, don't—"

"Rordan?"

He moved into the moonlight. Dark bags weighed heavily under his eyes. "What are you doing dressed like that? You're not going around the castle at this time of night, are you?"

"What are you doing in my room?" I hissed, ignoring his questions. "The ladies already think you're my . . ." I blushed and couldn't continue the thought. "Get out of here before we both get caught."

"Are you going to take that knife out of my face?"

I scowled and placed the dagger in my belt. "I sure hope you were sleeping while I was changing."

"Look, I'm sorry," Rordan whispered. "I just wanted to make sure you were okay. And I was wondering if you learned anything useful at dinner."

"Yes, I did." I told him my suspicions about the Advisor. "I'm going to check out his tower. What do you think? Does he look anything like the man you saw in the caverns?"

Rordan looked uncomfortable. "I . . . I don't know. The Advisor . . . he's a dangerous man, Kiera."

"Yeah. Especially if he has Alastar's Tome. Which is why I have to go." I started for the window ledge—going out the bedroom door would be out of the question dressed up like this, especially if that was how Rordan was getting out of here. "So get out of here, okay? I promise I'll be careful."

"Kiera . . ."

"What? You want to go out this way too?" I opened the window, and a cool breeze swept through the room.

"No. I . . ." He had that pained expression on his face again. Like he was hiding something from me.

"Tell me," I said. "What is going on? Is this about Laoise again?"

"No. Not Laoise." He shook his head and leaned his forehead against the bedpost. "It's just . . . I'm just worried about you. About this whole mission. I don't think I should have come."

"Because the ladies think that we're . . . you know, together?"

Rordan shook his head again. "I wish . . ." He stared past me into the moon that hung heavily in the sky. "I wish I'd never run into that man. Just try and find the tome as fast as possible, okay? Then maybe, we can go South."

"Go South? Are you crazy? What about the Violet Fox? Laoise? The Elders? People here depend on us, Rordan!"

He sighed and headed for the door. "I wish you'd hurry up and grow up, Kiera."

That stung. Grow up? I was retrieving an important relic for the Elders, and he was talking about running away. Everything I'd done, it was for our people. He was being selfish. He couldn't take the pressure. I could. Before I could say so, the door creaked gently open, and then he was gone.

"I *will* find Alastar's Tome," I whispered. "With or without your help."

Still, my stomach cramped with worry. Something was bothering my brother. He'd tell me when he was ready, I decided, but whatever it was, it was affecting his judgment.

I put Rordan out of my mind and focussed on the plan to infiltrate the Advisor's tower. I peered out the window. About one foot below the window was a ledge, wide enough for my foot, I guessed. Or I hoped it was wide enough for my foot.

Well, if I guessed wrong, I'd soon find out.

I slipped out the window and sat on the sill, testing the ledge with half my weight and then my full weight on one foot. The stone looked old and was covered with bits of dirt, but it held.

The Advisor's quarters were traditionally in the east wing of the castle, on the second-to-highest floor beneath what used to be a bell tower. Hundreds of years ago, the Advisor had apprentice scholars who would use the tower to watch for incoming enemy attacks and shipments. The apprentices would ring the bells to alert the castle— repetitive, deep rings for danger and a slow ring for incoming trade goods. Rusted and worn from disuse, the bell had been removed a few years back. No one needed bells to warn about Freetor attacks any- more. We were already in the city, beneath them. Waiting to make our move.

Because the Advisor's chamber didn't have a window that I could access directly, I'd have to brave the ledge here, slip in through a window somewhere on that floor, and continue up the servants' stairs.

My cape flapped violently around my knees as I stepped completely onto the ledge. I was not afraid of heights—if I were, I wouldn't have survived as the Violet Fox. Still, I was higher up than I'd ever been, and there were no awnings or tunnels to leap into if I fell. Don't look down, I told myself. But I did anyway. The hedge maze was lit with soft candlelights. I traced it with my eyes until I started to feel dizzy. Breathe—focus. I was here to get the tome, nothing else.

One step at a time, with my back to the castle wall and the wind whistling fiercely around the building, I sidestepped my way around the castle. I tried to make into a game, to keep myself focussed. There would be approximately two hundred sidesteps until I reached my destination. Every tenth spot I rewarded myself with thoughts of victory—me returning the tome to the Elders, them praising me, maybe even making me an apprentice once I was old enough.

I was nearing the east wing. Just a few more steps.

But as I rounded the corner, my stomach sank. There were a number of windows on this side of the castle. What I wanted was a window to a hallway or an abandoned room, but what if they were all closed? What if I accidentally snuck into a room where people were sleeping— or worse, what if they were awake?

I hadn't thought this far ahead. I'd just assumed that everyone would keep their windows open. The season was warm, and the night air held a pleasant, grassy smell, even if it was punctuated with cool breezes. The wind whistled and licked my clothing like a sweet treat it couldn't get enough of. There were only three more windows along this ledge before it ended in a large, stone angel protruding from the stonework—then I'd have to turn back, and I would have wasted an hour on this.

I approached the first window and chanced a glance down. Locked shut.

The next window was ten sidesteps away. I pressed my cheek against the stone as I went, but its rough caress reminded me that Lady Dominique would have a hard time explaining how one cheek had gotten scraped through the night, so I was stuck staring ahead into the trees and to the city below.

Fortunately for me, the second window was ajar. Slowly, care- fully, pushing my weight back against the wall and keeping my legs an equal distance apart, I squatted low enough to reach the window and bring it up higher. It gave an awful squeak as it lifted. I sucked in my breath and waited. No sounds but my breathing and the fierce wind wishing my death.

I brought it up far enough to stick the lower half of my body through and then slithered the rest of the way in like a snake into its burrow. My heart raced. I sighed in relief as I allowed myself to rest a moment beside the window. I'd have to find another way back to my room—there was no way I was doing *that* again.

I quickly surveyed my surroundings and compared it to the mental map burned into my memory. I was just down the corridor from the servants' staircase.

It was time to move again. Crawling to my feet, I tiptoed down the corridor and headed for the stairs. My every sense was on high alert, my hand poised, ready to draw my knife if I was caught at the last moment unaware. Not that they could catch me.

I was the Violet Fox.

I was in the belly of Marlenian territory, and no one had noticed me.

I was invincible.

Each step was an effort not to be heard as I climbed the winding backstairs to the second level of the castle. The backstairs were used mostly by the servant staff and the Freetor slaves. At every far-off snore, creak, or footstep, I froze against the cold stone wall. The steps were coated in dark shadows and about two stone-throws wide, but if someone were to venture too close, he would feel me, and then I would be dead. No one could be trusted—Freetors in slavery for too long were known to develop fond relationships with their masters and the servants. Their loyalty could not be assured.

At the top of the stairs were two long, narrow corridors arched at the top, one before me and one to my right. The ceilings were low here—I could touch their grit by standing on my tiptoes. Listening for breathing, footsteps—no, it was safe here, for the moment, but shadows danced at the end of the corridor before me. Not knowing if it was a torch mounted on the wall or clutched in the hand of a guard, I darted quickly to my right, out of sight.

I counted the doors as I went. They were made from a dark, stained wood, and almost all of them were doubled with circular pull handles as large as my head. Nobility lived here—ladies-in-waiting, children boarding from other provinces, rich families from away that came to the castle on business might stay here. Even though I knew this from the floor plan I'd studied, because of the scattering of dirt and mouse droppings on the floor, I probably wouldn't have guessed that the wealthy stayed here. It seemed like this part of the castle was no cleaner than the Freetor underground. I smirked.

If any of the nobles opened their doors, I would be dead.

If the floor plan the Freetors had was current—and I hoped that it was, since they had probably gone to a lot of trouble to get it for this mission—the Advisor's quarters were at the opposite corner from the stairs. There were at least two other ways to flee this level of the castle. It was that, or fight and die.

Rounding the corner, my eyes were prepared for darkness and pale yellow torchlight from the wall. That was not what I saw.

The Advisor's chamber was where I had expected it, and the door slanted to accommodate the diagonal wall. There were no guards, only the sound of my quickened breathing. I rubbed my eyes and looked again.

Something was glowing inside the Advisor's room.

My heart thumped hard in my chest. That had to be Alastar's Tome. There was nothing more unmistakeable than the soft blue glow of Freetor magic. It hovered around every Freetor artefact, visible only to the descendants of Alastar and his followers.

Before I could get any closer, I heard the loud rustle and muffled voices of the Marlenian guards just around the corner from the Advisor's room. I didn't have to see the glow of their torches to know that there were two of them. I felt like a mouse cornered by a cat. Fear crushed my stomach and almost overpowered every other thought.

I scurried further into the darkness, praying to the Elders and our ancestors that I wouldn't come face to face with a guard. The level was square, so I could easily run around and catch them by surprise, but I had to avoid confrontation. Waking up tomorrow with bruises and cuts would be hard to explain away, and Bidelia would have my head. Rordan, too.

When the guards seemed to stop, I timidly peeked around the corner. They were stationed beside the Advisor's door. Great. I would never get in there now. If only I had been a few minutes earlier . . .

They weren't stationary for long. They were coming down the hall. Straight for me. My legs quivered at the thought of being caught, but I had to know what was in the Advisor's room.

I was about to escape further when the Advisor's door opened. A torch hung on the wall above his room so I could clearly see him clutching what looked like a package wrapped in brown paper. But it wasn't just any package. It was glowing. Just like the walls of the Elder Caverns, it gave off an eerie blue light—that package was definitely of Freetor origin.

Two guards marched around the corner and were coming straight for me. I held my breath and was about to flee even further down the hall, but then they stopped to speak with the Advisor.

"Is there something we can help you with?" one asked.

"I was just returning something to the private collection in the library," the Advisor replied, holding up the package. Its light and the yellow of the torch mixed and cast a heavenly forest green onto the stone wall.

"Would you care for an escort?"

The Advisor waved them off. "I'll be fine, gentlemen. I'll just be in and out."

"If you insist. Have a good evening."

The guards started to walk away, and I had only moments to make my escape. As I ran down the hall, my feet barely touched the ground. I kept to the darkness as my mind raced. So he was hiding the Freetor magic in the library. Such an obvious place! I thought about wandering the castle to find it, but my legs ached and I knew I had to rise early tomorrow. I couldn't be tired when I was Lady Dominique. I had to be just as alert, maybe even more so than I was right now. Yes, tomorrow I would find the library, and retrieve the Freetor magic. Then maybe I could get out of this stinking castle and go back underground, where I belonged.

# Nine

I THOUGHT I'D have a hard time adjusting to the softness of the bed, after a lifetime of sleeping on something so hard, but after stowing away my Freetor clothes in the trunk, I collapsed on the mattress and went straight to sleep. The light streamed into the bedroom only hours later, waking me instantly. Waking in the sun. My heart swelled. I could get used to that.

Bidelia brought me breakfast on a tray: a bowl of ripe blueberries topped with a whipped cheese, two thick slices of bread dripping with melted butter and a sweet strawberry jam, and a tower of fruit fashioned into an evergreen tree, made of orange, pineapple, and apple slices. It was all so much that I didn't know what to eat first, and I thought of hiding some in my room for later. Then I remembered that that might attract ants and rats, which were not looked upon fondly on the surface.

I devoured the fruit tree and the blueberries, but the whipped cheese proved to be too filling for my stomach. I nibbled on the bread until Bidelia pointed out that I didn't have to eat everything. Reluctantly, I allowed her to take away the remains of my breakfast and crawled out of bed like a bloated snake after swallowing three mice whole.

I barely had a moment to myself. Bidelia's servants were all around me, dressing me and pulling my hair this way and that to tame it into an appropriate up-do. It was back into the slim-at-the-waist but wide-skirted style that Marlenia was so fond of. The stiffness of the dress weighed heavily on my lower back, and it was then I realized I had at least another week or so of this.

When I was presentable for court and the servants had gone, I remembered my knife. I retrieved it quickly from beneath the mattress, wrapped it in silk, and tied it around my left thigh, beneath the many folds of the heavy dress. It would be a bit of a hassle to retrieve in an emergency—my dress turned me into a large cream puff—but at least it was better than not being armed at all. I also tucked the coin purse Rordan had given me into my bosom—there was nowhere else to put it, and I didn't want to be without it, just in case.

There was nothing formally scheduled for that morning, Bidelia told me, besides attending court. I didn't know what that entailed, but if the Advisor was going to be there, it was another opportunity to observe his behaviour. Because it was the first day of the Gathering, the court was filled with dressed-up ladies and lords showing off their jewels and polite upbringings. I concentrated on putting one foot in front of the other. Court was held in the Great Hall, where we'd feasted the night before, but the tables were gone. Two large gold-and-silver thrones sat on a wooden stage at the back before a heavy curtain. Ladies fanned themselves vivaciously in a circle off to the right of the thrones. I meandered towards them, halting close enough to look like I was part of their circle but far enough to keep away from Lady Sylvia and her annoying Prince Keegan worship.

The court engaged in lively chatter until the curtains hanging behind the thrones parted. The Holy One hobbled through, followed by the Advisor and Prince Keegan. The Holy One's steps were careful and measured, but the Advisor offered no help, his eyes resting solely on the Holy One's sceptre. As the Holy One lowered himself onto the throne, his sceptre seemed more like a cane than an instrument of power. There were some who said that it was full of Freetor magic. I wondered if that were true. I dismissed the thought. If it were, the Elders would have done something about it long ago—and besides, it didn't glow.

Prince Keegan shadowed his father, sitting only after he was comfortable in his throne. What started as excited cheering and clapping erupted into a generous applause. The prince seemed startled by this sudden affection. He gave a curt nod and a slight wave to acknowledge the crowd. Some of the older nobles did not join the applause—mostly it was the guests, those who wore Eastern and Southern crests and colours, who whooped and cheered. Lady Sylvia clapped with her hands above her head, practically jumping up and down like a Freetor child who had been told she was getting an extra apple that day.

With a deafening thump, the Holy One brought the sceptre down on the hardwood and regained the court's attention. "Thank you for your support for my son. I hear last night's feast went pleasantly, and I officially welcome you all to this year's Gathering celebrations. Let us hear the petitions of the people quickly so that we can get on with the festivities."

Petitions of the people? I looked around the room again. Amid the vibrant colours of the wealthy were the drabber, worn fabrics of the poorer classes. One was a farmer. He and his wife stepped forward, bowed before their Holy One, and respectfully made their case about Freetor outlaws who were supposedly raiding their crops every night. The Holy One curled his lips in thought while the Advisor questioned them: How do you know the Freetors are to blame? The footprints in the mud suggest that it is so. The Holy One decreed that they would send a guard outside the city proper to investigate. Satisfied, the farmer and his wife bowed again and the crowd parted, allowing them to leave.

I stifled a yawn. We had to stand here and watch him make decisions about what was going to happen to everyone in the realm? I ached to feel the sun on my skin, to be out of my robes and have my cloak and my belt and my knife, but all I had were my wits, and they kept me still as the Marlenian citizens came forward, one by one, with their problems.

It was nearing noon. A Western lady standing next to me stretched her neck. Her stomach grumbled loudly. I was still full from breakfast, and from last night's feast. I wasn't the only restless lady. It seemed like every lady was chatting with her neighbour and throwing awkward glances to the exits and hopeful smiles up at Prince Keegan.

The last man to petition the court was a wealthy merchant. My ears perked up when his many beaded necklaces jingled together as he approached the thrones. Each necklace would be worth at least two meals per family if taken to the underground market. In tow, escorted by a guard on each side, was a Freetor, or so I assumed based on his shabby dress, the dirt on his skin, and his gaunt face. His hands were chained in front of him, and the merchant led him, as if he were some animal about to be put on display. Or punished. The latter seemed more likely.

The merchant bowed deeply and then yanked the chain so hard that the Freetor man fell onto the marble floor on his bare, scabby knees.

"You will bow before your rightful ruler," the merchant said in a slight Southern accent. Unlike the Northerners, who stressed each word equally, the Southerners talked like they were going up and down a musical scale. I wouldn't have guessed that this man was from the South—his skin wasn't dark enough—but maybe he had grown up there.

I flinched and fought to stay still as the Freetor man slowly found his feet. His legs were thin and trembled like twigs trying to hold up a stone.

"Please state your name for the court," the Advisor said, waving his hand like an Elder casting magic. His rings gleamed, and my stomach burned in frustration. He had the magic. I knew it. I would find a way to prove he was guilty.

"Your Graces, my name is William Hashim, owner of Righteous Rubies and Pearly Mountain Rocks, the jewellery shops in the merchant district here in Marlenia City. I am here because this filthy rodent was caught rifling through my inventory last night."

If the Freetor man felt guilt, he didn't show it. He was probably twice Rordan's age, his forehead creased with three heavy worry lines. His nose was long and wide and his cheekbones low, but his eyes were deep brown and showed only courage. I hoped that if I was ever brought before the Holy One as the Violet Fox, I could be as fearless.

The Advisor frowned. "I know that name. This is not the first time you have complained of Freetor theft, Mr. Hashim."

"This is true, Advisor." There was a touch of resentment in his voice as he stared up at the Advisor. "Gems worth hundreds of silver quid, even the ones I had locked in my safe, have gone missing over the last three months. But finally. Finally! I have caught the rat responsible." He smacked the Freetor upside the head, catching him off-guard. The Advisor and some of the other nobles laughed. Only the Holy One remained stern, while Prince Keegan looked bored with the whole affair.

"Do you confess your crimes before the holy court of Marlenia City, Freetor?" the Holy One demanded.

The Freetor remained silent and stoic.

"Speak, filth!" the merchant commanded, and he struck the Freetor again—harder, this time, and the nobles didn't laugh. Bright red blood oozed out of his nose, but it wasn't broken.

"You have nothing to say for yourself?" the Holy One questioned, leaning forward slightly in his throne.

"Your Grace, silence from a Freetor is considered an admission of guilt in a Marlenian court," the Advisor said.

"I am . . . well aware of that, Advisor Ferguson," the Holy One replied slowly, as if he were learning it for the first time, or forgetting it from a time past. "So be it, then. This man stole goods of countless worth, and now he will pay his debt as a servant of the Marlenian Empire. As Holy One, that is my command, and my voice is the word of Dashiell. Amen."

The amen was a formality, and it puttered out of everyone's lips but mine. Servant. That was just a nice way of saying slave if you were talking about Freetors. We had always assumed that Freetors who committed crimes against the Marlenians and were caught rotted in the dungeons of the castle. But now I understood. Why let an able-bodied man go to waste?

I had to stop this. But the Freetor spoke first. "I would rather die than clean up Marlenian filth."

A guard punched the Freetor in the stomach. The Freetor doubled over, but the guards pulled him upright again. His face scrunched up in pain, but he bit his lip to hide it. A smile tugged at the Holy One's lips. I felt like vomiting. They enjoyed preying on my people.

"Then you will get your wish," the Holy One declared. "This man will hang tonight in the square."

"No!"

The words had escaped me before I had a chance to contain them. All the eyes in the court slid to mine. I drew a sharp breath inward. There was no turning back now.

"You would like to speak for this man, Lady . . . uh . . . ?" The Advisor whispered in the Holy One's ear. "Lady Dominique Castillo?" He twirled the sceptre in his hand. The sphere at the top swirled round and round, catching the rays of sun from the skylight above.

"I . . . " My voice echoed in the throne room, just like in the Central Cavern, but this place held no sacred significance for me. I felt small and weak, but I had committed to this and I couldn't back down now. "I do not tink he deserves to die."

My heart pounded as the ladies around me exchanged gossipy whispers. The men across the room chuckled, probably at what they thought to be feminine innocence regarding political matters. Confused, the Freetor craned his neck to look at me. I wasn't sure if he recognized me or not, but he looked at me with a mix of surprise and relief.

"My lady, if this man prefers to die than be sold as a servant, that is his choice," the Holy One said.

"Have j'ou any proof dat dis was de man stealin' j'our gems?" I asked.

"When I suspected it was Freetor theft, I called in the guards, and we left the back door of my shop unlocked. We caught him in the act," Mr. Hashim said, eying me cautiously.

"Save your breath, Marlenian," the Freetor spat at me. "I don't want your pity, or your tears on your silk handkerchief. I don't regret anything I've done. It's put food on the table for my wife and children, and I will die knowing they had full stomachs for a little while."

But they'd starve without you, I wanted to point out. Then your wife and your children will have to go to the surface and would possibly die trying to find food. Or they'd be forced to pick moss off the walls for the rest of their lives, the saddest position for any Freetor, besides cleaning the sewage caverns. Or they'd end up like the families in the Great Cavern, praying for a miracle that never came.

I remembered the coins Rordan had given me. They jingled as I snatched the purse from its hiding place in my bosom. "How much is dis man wort'?"

More whispers. I cautiously took a few more steps towards the man, hoping that he would somehow recognize my face without the violet cape and mask, or at least realize that beneath these Marlenian clothes, I was still one of his people.

"My lady, male servants of his physique usually sell at fifty silver pieces, minimum," the Holy One replied. "But what use would you have for him? He would kill you in your sleep."

"Have j'ou dat little fait' in de Marlenian Guard, J'our Grace?" A smile tugged at my lips—maybe I was taking it a bit too far, but it was the cheekiest thing I could say while still sounding Marlenian. "I'm sure dere y'is plenty of work pour him to do, or else, I will have him shipped home to de Nort'."

"My lady, he's a thief—doesn't that earn him an execution up North?" Captain Murdock asked.

I bit down on my tongue as I remembered Lady Dominique describing the sharp scissors they used to cut out their slaves' tongues. And Captain Murdock was right. Punishments for Freetors were harsher in the North. But I didn't want to frighten the Freetor man.

"I do not believe in killin' a man pour a petty crime like teft," I replied. "I will make sure he y'is not harmed."

This caused more stir in the court. There were whispers that I "preferred" Freetor men to "visit" me at night, and that perhaps the tongues of Freetors were pulled out to stifle their lovemaking noises. Out of the corner of my eye, I saw Bidelia weaving through the nobles offering refreshments, pretending not to listen, but hearing my every echoing word.

"Your heart is soft, Lady Dominique, unlike the land you hail from," the Holy One said. "But if I spare this man's life, how will the other Freetors learn to fear us?"

"Dey will never learn," I said, with more conviction than I should have. "Every year de Freetors grow stronger. More resourceful. J'ou may kill many Freetors every year, but it only fuels deir anger." It was a struggle not to say "we" and "us" and "our."

The Holy One seemed to consider this. The Advisor leaned in to whisper something in the old ruler's ear, but the Holy One waved him away.

"Showing mercy to an animal will not teach it anything, especially since mercy is something that it does not understand," the Holy One said firmly.

I balled my hands into fists as a great rage welled inside me. "De Freetors understand—"

"My lady, Your Grace," the Advisor interrupted. "Perhaps we should view this as an experiment. Allow the lady to have the Freetor. Let him do what tasks please her. If he escapes, either he will die of starvation on the streets or the guards will kill him. If he does not escape, we know that he does understand mercy, and the lady will have one more man in her service."

"At great risk to the lady," Keegan said. He looked concerned, which made the ladies around me swoon even more.

I stepped forward, ignoring Keegan's gaze. "Like I said, J'our Grace, as long as I y'am in dis castle, surrounded by guards, no harm may come to me from any Freetor. I y'am confident in j'our abilities to catch him if he escapes."

But you will never catch me, I thought.

"Very well," the Holy One agreed. "Then I decree that this man shall be placed in servitude to Lady Dominique Castillo, of Northern Marlenia."

I curtsied and bowed my head so that they couldn't see me smile. "Tank j'ou, J'our Grace."

When there was no more business for the court, the Holy One took his leave. The Advisor helped him off the platform and behind the curtain that led down a private hallway that connected to the Holy One's chamber. Keegan leapt to his feet, stretching, but was soon surrounded by ladies seeking his favour. At the forefront was Lady Sylvia, waving her handkerchief to get his attention. Keegan searched the crowd and our eyes met briefly. He held my gaze. One second. Two seconds. His playfully curly hair covered his ears and looked so thick today that I could barely see the silver circlet that marked him as the prince. A smile tugged his lips. My cheeks flushed and I looked away. Alastar's Tome. I was here for Alastar's Tome. Do not get involved.

The nobles and the commoners dissipated. I spotted Bidelia with an empty tray heading out of the Great Hall, towards the servant staircase. I called her by her Marlenian name, and she turned. "Yes, my lady?"

"Please, take my new servant and set him to work in de stable," I said.

She narrowed her eyes and peered at him. He was still in chains, flanked by Marlenian guards who were waiting for orders.

"Tell your page to take care of that matter. I will not lay my hands on his Freetor filth," she replied, quite loudly. A few ladies caught her words and tittered.

Fine, I would tell Rordan, whenever he came back from his page duties. I hadn't seen him all morning, and after last night, I wasn't sure if he was eager to talk to me. I approached the guards—there were four of them surrounding the Freetor man. The Freetor snarled and spat at my feet. I nimbly sidestepped to avoid his slobber.

"J'ou will work in de stable until I see it fit to ship j'ou back to my homeland," I told the man. "J'ou should consider j'ourself lucky."

"I would rather die than serve a Marlenian," he said.

I ground my teeth and tried not to let my frustration show. Were we always this insolent? How could I make him see that I was not a Marlenian, but a Freetor, one of his blood?

"Take him back to his cell pour de afternoon, until my page arrives. I will not have him escape until he fills him in on his duties," I told the guards.

After their chorus of "yes, my lady," I left them to their task. Most of the noblemen had disappeared, possibly outside to enjoy the weather, or to dine with friends. There were a few hours until horseback riding, so I had some time to snoop around. The library was waiting for me.

Two guards lifted a blue velvet curtain as I exited the Great Hall through a side passageway. My shoes scoffed and clicked on the stone walkway. Clasping my sweaty hands, I walked briskly, going over the castle's layout in my head. Along with the library, the east wing housed the scholars and the healers. The scholars, although many were of common birth, wore clean, brown, cotton robes and trousers lined with the royal blue trim to mark them as castle dwellers. I saw two of them walking together, having a lively discussion about whatever books they were holding, and they barely managed a polite hello. The rest walked alone, noses in their books. My thoughts went to my father and the bound volume hiding under the feathered mattress. I prayed Bidelia hadn't disturbed it.

The history tapestries of the west wing were replaced with maps in the east wing. I knew I should keep moving, but I stopped in front of one. It must have been as tall as a two-storey building, and half as wide. Tiny ornate stitches held together the land of Marlenia. We were but one puzzle piece in the centre of the map, coloured in sky-blue, while the other Marlenian provinces were outlined in green. Dark blue fabric surrounded the provinces, representing the Forever Sea. I'd never seen the sea. It was blocked by a stretch of mountains impossible to pass. Alastar the Hero had climbed them on one of his adventures, but that was just a story. Besides, the Forever Sea was probably just a myth. That much water could not exist in one place—it would rise up and flood the land. Rordan had told me that once.

"It's hard to believe, isn't it."

The voice sent fear rushing through my veins. I hadn't even heard anyone sneaking up on me—being in this damned castle was dulling my senses. I wheeled around only to find Prince Keegan, with his hands in his pockets, staring up at the map towering above us. The sun from the two thin windows above lent a mystical innocence to his yellow-green eyes, like a child's eyes seeing the surface and the sun for the first time. It also highlighted his scar, which was looking slightly less inflamed today.

"J'our Grace," I said, curtsying to hide my surprise.

A smile touched his lips. "I didn't expect to find you in the east wing."

I swallowed my fear of being discovered and forced myself to smile back at him. "Y'am I expected elsewhere?"

"No, of course not. Unless you wanted to take care of your new slave yourself."

"I have my servants dealin' wit' dat."

"I see."

I held Keegan's gaze, but inside I felt like fleeing. My face was flush with the heat and here I was, stuck with the prince with nothing to say. I racked my mind for some pleasantries that the Elder apprentices had taught me, but his eyes were so distracting. All I could think about was being back in that carriage with him, where he had glared at me with such hatred. How could he not know that that filthy young girl stood in front of him now?

"You know, I could give you a tour of the castle, if you're interested," he offered. "It is a large place, and it probably wouldn't be good for diplomatic relations between our provinces if you got lost."

"Um . . ." I cleared my throat, and the sound echoed in the hallway. "I tink I would prefer to explore on my'own, tank j'ou . . . J'our Grace."

I bowed my head politely and sauntered down the corridor, but the prince wasn't far behind me.

"Really? Without an escort?" he asked.

I raised an eyebrow. "Dis is de t'ird or fourt' time today dat someone has implied dat de castle isn't safe. Don't j'ou trust j'our guards? Or is dere some secret assassin who y'is going to jump out and get me?" I laughed. The only dangerous person around here was me.

"My lady, the castle has hundreds of guards to keep us safe from the Freetors, but it was only last week that I was attacked. Here." He pointed to his scar. "I wouldn't want something to happen to your beautiful face."

He called me beautiful. The words melted into me like warm butter. I slowed my stroll. No one had ever called me beautiful before. I was always dirty, or Freetor scum, or a burden to someone or another. My cheeks glowed hot.

And yet, I was the one who had tainted his otherwise perfect face.

"J'our Grace y'is . . . too kind." I struggled to keep my voice steady. I had to focus. I had to remember what Bidelia had told me. He was the enemy.

"Are you . . . blushing?" Keegan asked.

This only made my face redder. I couldn't look up at him. I had to get rid of him and go about my mission.

"I'm . . . sorry if something I said offended you."

He sounded genuinely sorry. I almost felt bad for him. Almost. He was just trying to be nice to the Marlenian princess. Charm her, even. But I couldn't be charmed. I wouldn't end up in his bed. I would find Alastar's Tome and kill any Marlenian who got in my way.

Keegan was still talking. "Are you betrothed to someone? Is that why you are angry with me? I didn't mean to overstep my bounds, my lady, I was simply giving you a compliment that—"

"I y'am not betrot'ed to anyone."

He frowned. "You're not?"

"No, I y'am not." It was my turn to make a face. "Why do j'ou look so surprised?"

Now it was his face that coloured. "I . . . it was only a question, my lady."

I knew I should've let it end there, but I couldn't. If he knew something about Lady Dominique that the Freetors didn't know, then my cover would be blown. "Sounds like more dan a question."

"It was a rumour, is all."

"What kind of rumour?"

"Well . . . I really shouldn't say."

"If it's about me, den I tink I have de right to know."

He paused, and for the first time, I saw the prince of Marlenia looking uncomfortable. Human. "It was from some of the other ladies. A few of them broke their fast with me this morning. There's a rumour you are engaged to Lord Gerold Essayé."

I rolled my eyes. "Dat isn't true."

"Really. The ladies insist that you yourself said it one night at dinner."

Deeper and deeper I sunk into my own lie. I tried to dig myself out. "Dere y'is a pressure wit' de women to have juicy information to share. When I had not'in', I made it up to satisfy deir needs."

"It is a brave woman to admit that she has lied."

"It's a brave man to ask about a woman's love interest, especially when he has no intention of courtin' her."

"How do you know I don't have that intention?"

My heart skipped a beat. I started walking again. "I have to go."

"Riding isn't for another two hours."

"I . . . I was goin' to de library."

"I will walk you there."

Couldn't he take a hint and leave? I couldn't simply dismiss him—he was the prince. But he wasn't *my* prince.

"I y'am fine, J'our Grace."

Walking was slow in my shoes and the massive dress, and Keegan quickly caught up with me. "I don't take no as an answer very easily."

"I'm sure that's how you were brought up," I muttered.

"What does that mean?"

I dug my fingernails into my hand. I had to be careful with my accent. "My . . . apologies, J'our Grace. Dat slipped out wit'out me tinkin' about it."

Keegan laughed. "Not to worry, my lady. You're right, I have been brought up in a world of plenty, as have you."

I swallowed and said nothing for a little while. Keegan didn't seem to mind the silence between us as we sauntered down the corridor. Servants passed and greeted us with kind words and bowed heads.

"I've been thinking," Keegan said, once we neared the library.

"We all tink, J'our Grace."

"Very true. But I have been thinking about something you said today, and what we talked about last night at the feast."

The library doors were in sight. There were no guards around, no one around but him and me. My heart beat a little faster.

"What you said, about freedom," Keegan continued. "I should like to continue that conversation."

"Perhaps anot'er time, J'our Grace." I bowed my head, hoping to appear gracious in my rejection.

I tried to walk around him, but he slammed his hand against the wall, blocking the library entrance. He forced his face into mine. "Do you believe you're free?"

I stared into his eyes and decided for once to tell the truth. "No, I y'am not free."

"Tell me what I can do to help you."

I was about to reply with something disarming when the meaning of his words hit me. It was the first time anyone besides Rordan had extended a hand to me without asking for something in return. For once, words escaped me.

"My lady?"

"I...I...have not'in' to say."

"You defended a man's life today. Your mouth was full of words then."

"I guess I've spent my daily limit."

"You want to know what I think?"

"No, not really, J'our Grace."

He smirked. "I think you're used to helping yourself, and that you have become trapped because everyone thinks that you can be your own defender."

"I y'am my own defender," I replied. "I have to be."

"You see? Trapped, and you won't let anyone help you."

"I did not say I needed help, or dat I wanted it, especially from j'ou!"

"Now you're yelling. There's definitely something you're not telling me."

"J'ou are not my confidant," I said coolly. "I don't have to tell you anyt'in'."

Pulling on my skirts, I sidestepped him. He had a big smirk on his face, but he didn't try to stop me.

The door to the library opened with a loud creak that disturbed the hush within. The room was as tall as the Great Cavern and twice as large. Two long columns filled with rows of bookshelves stood proudly ten stone-throws away from me, behind a desk shaped like the crescent moon. A man dressed in a light silver cloak with the Tramore crest sewn on his breast sorted a tall pile of books on the desk that almost obscured him. The only sounds were pages turning and the thumping of covers on wood. I approached cautiously and peered between the stacks of books at the librarian; the desk was almost as high as my chin.

"I would like access to de private collection, please."

"Do you have written permission from Advisor Ferguson or the Holy One?"

I hesitated. "No, I don't."

"Then I'm sorry, my lady, I can't let you in."

Rats. I had to get in there—that's where the Advisor was hiding Alastar's Tome! I felt like I was so close to going home that I could smell the damp air, but that was probably just the musty, old books. Getting permission from the Advisor would be too suspicious, and I would never get an audience alone with the Holy One without going through the Advisor. I would have to return after midnight as the Violet Fox. I thanked the librarian for his time and went to leave.

"Excuse me, but I can also grant the lady permission to see the tomes."

Wouldn't he ever leave me alone? As I turned, Keegan crossed his arms and gave me a triumphant look.

"If it pleases you, Your Grace," the librarian said, bowing his head. He took a piece of parchment and a quill from somewhere beneath the stacks of books and placed it in front of us.

I didn't know whether to feel annoyed or grateful. Perhaps this was the real price for seeing the private collection. No doubt he'd want to come with me. He'd come this far. At least he wasn't out to hurt me in any way. As long as I continued pretending to be Lady Dominique. Bidelia's words hung sourly above my head. He might be an annoying Marlenian spoiled brat, but he was somewhat charming. If I gave in to him, I was doomed.

After Keegan had scrawled his royal signature on the document, the librarian stamped it, rolled it up, and sealed it with wax. He placed it in a drawer out of my sight. "Thank you, my prince. I presume you will be escorting the lady?"

"Yes, I will."

The librarian's eyes danced between us for a brief moment before he set a candle and its holder on the desk. "Light it on the pyre before you enter, and watch that you don't hold it too close to the tomes. One spark is all that it would take to send the whole collection up in flames."

Keegan took the candle and thanked the librarian. He gestured to his left and smiled at me. "This way, my lady."

"Tank j'ou," I said.

"It was the least I could do," he replied, shrugging his royal shoulders.

As I walked further into the library, the more I noticed its magnificence. I touched the bookshelves as I passed. The dark wood felt smooth beneath my hands, and smelled like Feenagh Forest. Some well-dressed peasants sauntered through the rows, choosing random books and studying them. I hadn't realized that the library was free for all.

Behind the rows of books was a gigantic mural that served as a false window. The scene was of sunny green fields and a flock of maidens dancing and twirling with floating flowers around them. Two maidens, one on each side, sat reading with their feet in the air and their bodices loosened. I shyly averted my eyes.

The door to the private collection was up a spiralling staircase, blocked by a rope and a sign that marked it as private. Keegan stepped over the rope and unlatched the chain from its place, throwing it to one side. I was grateful but also envious that I couldn't leap over it as he had. At the top was a small pyre that held fire. Prince Keegan dipped the candle in and it quickly blazed; he covered one side with his hand to tame the flame. I opened the door while he prepared the light.

Like most Freetors' eyes, mine adjusted quickly to the darkness. It was a cramped room, maybe ten stone-throws by twenty stone-throws. The books were not only piled on the shelves, but also stacked on the floor. I carefully stepped over a pile of loose pages as Keegan shut the door behind us.

"There's not much up here, my lady, save musty old books that haven't been read by anyone for ages."

With the door shut, I became aware of our closeness. The heat I felt was not just from the candle, either. My nerves fluttered as I ventured down one of the rows. "Maybe y'it is time someone read dem."

He followed, keeping the light in one hand and examining an old manuscript with the other. "I'm not sure what the Advisor would say to that."

"De Advisor seems to have a lot of control in de castle."

A dust cloud flew out of one of the tomes and caught Keegan's nose. He coughed and sneezed violently. The candle flickered, but he held tightly onto it. When he recovered, he said, "Sometimes my father can't be bothered with the lesser happenings in the castle and in the city. So the Advisor deals with those things that need the Holy One's attention. Isn't it so at your castle?"

"Castle," I muttered. As if everyone grew up in one.

"What was that?" he asked.

I coughed. "I said, no. My fat'er handles most of de necessary business. Advisors are pointless and unnecessary in de Nort'." At least that much was true, from Lady Dominique's perspective. "I do what I want, when I want, J'our Grace."

"That must be nice."

"It is, J'our Grace."

There was a pause. I could feel his eyes on me. The candle he held was so bright that it hurt my eyes and gave me an excuse not to look at him. Growing up in the darkness had suddenly come in handy.

"You don't have to call me Your Grace, you know."

I swallowed. "Den what should I call j'ou? Should I call j'ou *my prince*?" It sounded vaguely romantic to me.

"Well, yes, but . . . I'd prefer it if . . . at least, in present company . . . you called me Keegan."

My heart skipped a beat. "Keegan." The name tasted intimate in my mouth, but my tongue found the sounds agreeable.

"And it would sound awfully strange if you were calling me by my proper name and I were calling you "my lady," my lady."

"It does sound strange," I agreed. But I left it at that, and he didn't press the conversation further. I turned my face away from the light and smirked. He was *flirting* with me. The Marlenian prince was flirting with the Violet Fox. As entertaining as the thought was, it scared me to the bone. If only he knew who I really was.

I looked up, and that's when I saw it. A faint blue hazy glow around a book that looked like it had been hurriedly shoved onto the top shelf. It had the glow I had seen last night—I couldn't mistake Freetor magic when I saw it. It looked about the same size and shape as the package the Advisor had been carrying last night. A ladder was propped precariously against the leaning shelf. Whoever had been in here last could have used it to place the book high up, where no one else would think to take it—no one who didn't know about Freetor magic, at least. And the Advisor knew plenty about Freetor magic, it seemed. Perhaps my search for Alastar's Tome was over—maybe this was what I was looking for! If that was the case, then this would be easier than I had thought, and I would be out of the castle in no time.

"What is it?" Keegan asked.

I stood on my tiptoes, but even with my heels, I wouldn't be able to reach it. I pointed. "See dat book up dere?"

Keegan squinted. "There're a lot of them, my lady."

"Um . . . hold up de candle, please."

He did. The blue haze surrounding the book was faint, but unmistakeable. I smiled at the prince. "I'd like to look at dat one."

"Of course she wants the one I can't reach," Keegan muttered.

"Who said I wanted j'ou to get it pour me?" I challenged.

He chuckled. "Doesn't that dress inhibit any kind of . . . upward movement?"

"Try movement of any kind," I remarked. "And dere's only one way to fix dat."

A little voice in my mind told me I shouldn't be undressing in front of the prince—the person who had threatened to put me in the dungeon only a week before—but I paid it no heed. My heels were the first thing to go. They clattered to the floor with a guilty thump. The gown was done up tightly in the back, but I was able to reach around and loosen the ties on the bodice without asking for Keegan's help. Layer by layer, my dress fell to the floor. The knife hidden under the folds thudded softly as it landed on the fabric. I snuck a glance at the prince. Keegan had averted his eyes, but he was smiling. Good. He hadn't heard.

The bookshelves were made of splintery, dry wood. The ladder felt frail under my calloused hands. In only my petticoat and my undergarments, I started the climb. The rungs creaked as I tested my weight on them, but they held. Books and treatises held together with string and a spot of glue trembled as I moved.

I was nearly halfway up when Keegan said, "You climb well."

I looked down. There he was, grinning at me. I flushed red. The real Dominique wouldn't be so nimble, so I slowed my pace.

"I . . . like de climbin'. Keeps my arms strong," I said.

"Once, when I was small, my father took me to the North to scale part of a mountain. Mount Boudreau, maybe? One of the smaller mountains. I think I made it ten feet before my nurses got scared and demanded that I be brought down before I broke my royal neck. I always wondered what was at the top, but the top was far above the clouds."

Ten feet. Marlenian measurements. What was that, thirty, maybe forty hands high? I'd climbed higher. But the only mountain I'd ever been close to was the one that housed this castle. "Did j'ou ever go back to finish de climb? Now dat j'ou are older?"

"No, I didn't. I suppose I'll have to come visit, and maybe you could show me a thing or two."

I pictured Prince Keegan visiting Lady Dominique's castle only to find a different girl with a different face and no memory of this conversation. My stomach panged with guilt.

The glowing book was within my grasp. My toes perched on the edge of the rung as I lifted myself a hair higher—just high enough for my fingers to coax the book into my palm.

"Got it," I said.

Keegan's boots scraped against the floor. "If my father could see you now . . . or gods forbid, the Advisor . . . "

My grin was wicked. Too wicked. "Good ting it's just us, den."

"Yes, it is good."

I hoped that he couldn't see my face; it was as hot as a flame. I needed to focus. I was about twenty hands high, maybe twenty-five. As I stepped down a rung, I misjudged the distance and my toes slipped. The ladder shook. The books rattled and some fell to the floor as I tried to regain my footing, but failed.

"Careful!" he warned.

The ladder swayed and the bookshelf teetered. If I held on any longer, the whole bookshelf would come down on the two of us, and then we'd be no further ahead. I let go. Keegan reached out to brace my fall, but like an alley cat, I landed gracefully on my feet. I looked up, and his face almost touched mine. The space seemed narrower, and the warm swell of the candle enveloped my body like a heat wave. And yet, goose prickles rose on my arms as he stared at me, searching. Wondering.

Waiting.

My voice stuttered and crawled through the silence. "I should put my dress back on."

He broke his gaze. "Right."

The candlestick was burning down quickly—how long had I been in this room with the prince? Couldn't have been more than twenty minutes. Looking at the size of the candle, it could have been an hour or more. That was ridiculous, though.

He turned to give me privacy again as I slipped back into my dress. I had to tread carefully. I thought of the knife hidden beneath the folds. If I had to, I could reach under there, unsheathe it, and slit his throat before his dim eyes could register what was happening. But then I would have to get out of the castle. No, killing the prince within the castle would be a nightmare, and it was not part of the mission. Somehow, that made me feel safer.

"Do you need any help?" Keegan asked.

"Uh . . ." I reached around, but it seemed that doing up the tens of buttons and laces in the back was not something I could do alone. "I esuppose."

He chuckled, and then he was behind me. His face was so close to my ear that a shiver ran up my spine.

I inhaled sharply and peered down at the book. The Elders made me promise not to read it, but curiosity overwhelmed me. Would they know if I opened it, when they were underground and I was on top of a mountain?

"What kind of book is it?" he asked.

I couldn't just stand there and not open the book, not when the prince was asking what I'd risked my life to get. The Elders would understand. I hoped. My skin tingled as his finger brushed my neck.

I cracked open the book, as if it could save me from the rush of confusing emotions that swept over my body. My eyes flew hungrily over the page. I squinted to see the faded, black symbols that looked like they'd been written forever ago on the fading parchment. "It says somet'in' about legends. *Ancient Legends and Myths of the Second Age.*"

"I can't believe you can see that. It's so dark in here."

My stomach sank. This wasn't Alastar's Tome. There was something magical about this book—but maybe it had been written by an Elder. The words were in Freetor runes.

I laughed nervously. "Uh . . . my eyes adjust quickly to de darkness, I guess."

I flipped through the tome nevertheless. It might have been the tome that I saw last night with the Advisor. Maybe he was trying to decipher the Freetor code. The text glowed more softly than the tome itself, but the words stood out to me like glowing mushrooms in a dark cave. The words called to me. Wanting to be read.

Snapping the book shut before Keegan could see, I held it to my chest as if it were a newborn babe. If nothing else, this book belonged with the Freetors. I smiled sweetly at him. "I would like to take out dis book."

"You mean *I'll* take out the book. This is my father's personal collection. I don't think he'd be very happy if he knew I let you in here."

"No? Den why did j'ou give me permission?"

"Because, my lady . . . you are . . . intriguing."

It was like he'd called me beautiful again. I smiled shyly. All this attention was going to my head, but while I was in Dominique's skin, I had to play the part of an interested lady. But not *too* interested. If a friendship with Prince Keegan was what it took to make my mission easier, then maybe I could afford to be nice to him and respond to his charms.

After I put the outer layers of my dress back on and slipped my shoes onto my aching feet, we left the private library. Keegan checked out the book with no problems, and as soon as we were out of the library, he handed it to me. "Just be careful with it."

"I will," I said, hugging it to my chest. "I . . . have a fondness pour old books."

"Then maybe we could do this again, Dominique."

That brought a smile to my face. "Maybe."

"You didn't mind it."

"Mind what?"

"That I called you by your first name. You didn't chastise me. I must be getting through to you."

I looked away, blushing furiously. But I forced my eyes to return to his. "Don't tell dem I've gone soft."

"Who is there to tell?"

We shared a nervous laugh as we strolled down the corridor. He walked a few paces behind me, maybe to mind my large, poofy dress. His eyes never left mine as we chatted. It was like I was the most interesting person in the world to him. If only he knew how interesting I really was.

I rounded a corner and almost bumped into Rordan. I gasped in surprise and hid the book behind my back. There was no need for him to know about my adventure with Keegan in the library.

"Kier—my lady. J'our Grace." Rordan caught himself quickly as Keegan rounded the corner behind me. He fell to his knee, his hair drooping over his face.

"Rise," Keegan said shortly.

Rordan slowly came to his feet, keeping his eyes cast downward. His face was blood-red. He had almost blown my cover in front of the Marlenian prince. "My lady, I have returned from my ot'er duties. I hear we have a new man in our . . . eservice?"

"J'es. Tell de guards in de cell dat he is to be released and assigned to stable duties. Make sure he y'is watched at all times."

"J'es, my lady." He stole a glance at Keegan through his strands of thick, greasy hair. "Is dere anyt'ing else, my lady?"

"No, tank j'ou. J'ou may go," I said quickly.

"A male page," Keegan commented as Rordan scooted down the passageway. "I don't think I've met a lady with a personal male servant."

I shot him a sideways glance. "Are j'ou suggestin' what I tink j'ou are suggestin'?"

"No, I was just curious."

"A little too curious. Dat's de second time today j'ou've tried to find out whet'er or not I y'am . . . seein' . . . anyone."

Amusement flickered across his face. "You don't miss very much, do you."

I would die if I wasn't watchful, I wanted to say. My stomach was all aflutter. "A lady must always be on her toes."

It was then I noticed I hadn't been very watchful at all. He was standing so close that he brushed against my poofy dress. The fabric touched his leg, and his shoes were almost hidden beneath it. But I hadn't felt him invade my space. He was further away than he had been in the library, and still it felt like he was as close.

A flock of ladies came down the hallway, tittering and whispering as they neared. Lady Milda, Lady Na'ima, and Lady Sylvia were with them. The jealousy that lit up Lady Sylvia's face was as unmistakeable as dirt on a pristine tiled floor. I took a step back from Keegan and greeted her with a small smile. Anything to send the signal that I wasn't interested, that they could sweep in and take him for themselves.

"Prince Keegan. A pleasant surprise," Lady Sylvia said, curtseying. The other ladies bounced instead of curtseying, apparently too excited for anything else. Their smiles were wider than their dresses.

Keegan smiled and said a polite hello to Lady Sylvia and the other ladies, but his body remained facing me. "How are you ladies enjoying the day?"

"Very much, thank you," Lady Sylvia said. Her reply came out in a high-pitched squeak. "And you, Your Grace?"

"Splendid, so far." He glanced at me and smiled. "I was finishing my studies in the library when I ran into Lady Dominique."

"How . . . coincidental," she said. She shared a secret glance with her lady friends. "Will Your Grace be joining us for the afternoon ride?"

"Well, that's what Lady Dominique was just telling me about. I was considering it. I suppose I shouldn't let the ladies have all the fun."

Lady Sylvia and the other three laughed politely, and I allowed myself to smile. The small talk made me want to puke. The way Lady Sylvia was looking at Keegan—*just take him*, I wanted to scream. And the way he was smiling at her, his face full of charm. I wondered if it was all fake. Was he throwing charm at me too, just so he could bed all of us?

Did he really think I was beautiful?

"We will see you there, my prince," Lady Sylvia cooed, and with another curtsey, she and her entourage were off down the other corridor again. Watching them go, taking up the whole corridor like they owned the place, made me want to shed my dress, run after them, and pull every hair from their scalps.

"Dominique?"

Blood rushed to my face as my attention returned to Keegan. "J'es?"

"You looked like you were about to murder those ladies! I wouldn't want to cross you." He laughed. "I'll see you in a few hours? You are going riding, right?"

Did I have a choice? I clutched the book close to my chest. His scar looked like it was almost gone, but I knew that I would always be able to see it, no matter how much Marlenian medicine tried to cover it up. "I'll be dere."

# Ten

HORSEBACK RIDING WAS the last thing I wanted to do. I wanted to know why the Advisor was so interested in Freetor magic, and why he had taken that book from the library. If the rumours held a grain of truth, maybe he was trying to learn the Elders' secrets, so that he could usurp the throne. But *Ancient Legends and Myths of the Second Age* had nothing to do with Freetor magic, not directly. The Second Age was before the Marlenians had provinces, and before the scholars who recorded history. I stole another glance at the runes as I approached my room. Stories of men who had become heroes, women who had defied their husbands and battled monsters—that's what this book was about. Nothing about Alastar the Hero or the Freetor uprising. It wasn't my mission to investigate the Advisor, but curiosity swam deep inside me. I had to know.

Bidelia was in my room when I got back. Her eyes went right to the book. "Is that it?"

I sighed, flipping through it. "No. It's just some other old tome that the Advisor was looking at."

She chewed on that for a moment before taking and hiding it under my mattress. "You can look at it later. It's time to dress for riding."

At least the riding clothes were tolerable. Standing in front of the vanity mirror, I almost wished that I could go riding every day. I got to wear pants—sort of. They billowed out at the calf as if I had some weird growth there. So much for agility. The top was more to my taste—tightly fitted in the sleeves—even if it showed a little bit of skin above my breasts, as was the style. A brown leather vest covered the shirt, and it buttoned in the front and laced in the back.

"They taught you to ride, right?" she whispered as she tightened the vest's laces behind me.

"Unless you mean, 'did I sit on and almost steal Captain Murdock's horse one time while he was busy drinking in a tavern,' then the answer would be no."

Bidelia didn't seem amused. "Fortunately for you, the Northerners aren't prone to horse riding. It's too cold to keep them up there."

"Yeah, Rordan told me that."

When I was deemed suitable for a public appearance, Bidelia left me to attend to her other duties. I made my way through the castle, out the postern and across the bailey towards the stables. The stable weren't technically part of the castle. It was on the other side of the hedge maze. Fortunately I didn't have to walk through the maze—I could walk around the narrow perimeter, where the castle wall towered above me. The wall connected with the stable up ahead and had a guarded gate, where only familiar faces could pass through. I counted my steps to measure the length of the hedge fortress. I lost count after four hundred twenty-three.

Beyond the stable, the land sloped down steeply, and then stretched out into the horizon. Green fields, clumps of forests, open and ready to be explored—I think it was supposed to be the royal hunting grounds, and Marlenian guards patrolled it constantly for Freetors wishing to gain back entrance to the castle. In the distance, I could see part of the road, where it looped around and went north into the mountains, to Dominique's home. A swell of excitement rose in me as I sauntered closer to the stable. Maybe the ride wouldn't be so bad after all. I would get to see life outside the city walls, which was more than what most Freetors saw.

Guards swarmed around the stable like ants in their nests. The stable was a weak point, tactically. Anyone could attack the castle from behind, if he had enough men to get through the mass of soldiers stationed here. It seemed like all the guards in the city were there. The smell of manure and animals mixed in the air. There wasn't much of a breeze, either. I tried to breathe through my mouth until I got used to the smell.

The stable was long and jutted out about a stone-throw from the towering wall. In contrast to the wall, the stable was made of wood, but it was well kept. Two large doors were open, and I could see the horses' stalls, but most of them were empty. The sounds of their braying came from beyond the stable, outside the wall.

"Lady Dominique?" one of the guards said, approaching me.

"Yes?" I said.

"Follow me. The other ladies have been waiting for you to arrive."

I tried not to roll my eyes. Yeah, they were waiting for me to show up so they could make a fool out of me again. I followed the guard through the stable. I stepped carefully across the dirt floor, which was littered with stray pieces of hay. As I walked by, I peeked into the stalls. The horses were better off than we were. They spent most of their time in one place, in their own filth, but there were always people around to feed them, and to clean up after them. And when their masters got to take them out, they got to run in the open air. A controlled freedom.

Guards, pages and stable boys tended about twenty horses at the other end of the stable while the ladies and the nobles looked on, chatting excitedly about the upcoming ride. One thing immediately stood out to me: the ladies were still wearing their dresses. Not the big, layered, poofy ones, but the bodies of the dresses were still large enough that I didn't know how they were going to stay on their horses. I looked down at my riding clothes, and even though I was well-prepared for the ride, I felt embarrassed. Bidelia had dressed me in this. I was going to stick out worse than glow moss in a dark tunnel.

I took a deep breath and marched forward. I was going to have fun on this ride. I just had to keep telling myself that until I believed it.

I knew the nobles were watching me, but if anyone thought anything about my attire, they didn't mention it. Until I saw Lady Sylvia.

She was already atop her horse, a brown-and-white mare who seemed not to mind having an extra twenty pounds of dress on her back. The mare's tail swatted flies around her behind. Whenever she brought her tail too close to Sylvia's dress, Sylvia petted the hair affectionately. I tried to speed on past her, but she noticed me—how could she not.

"Lady Dominique! Did your servants make a mistake while dressing you? Or do you dress yourself?" Sylvia chided.

I grinned up at her. "Did j'ou know dat female horses pee on deir tails?"

The look of pure terror on her face made my day.

I found Rordan and the Freetor prisoner grooming my mare outside the stable. The prisoner was wearing shackles around his ankles, but the chain was long enough that he could walk without too much hindrance. He must have been advised of my true identity because when I approached, he almost tripped himself trying to bow. I tried not to laugh, because it really wasn't supposed to be funny—he would've died today if I hadn't been there.

Two stable hands flocked to my side and offered their assistance with the horse. I graciously accepted. At least they didn't care about what I was wearing. After the saddle was in place, they boosted me onto the magnificent beast. I tried to keep calm, to seem like I'd ridden a horse at least once before, but my heart was pounding. Rordan and the prisoner and the stable hands and everyone else not on a horse only came to my waist. So this was what it was like to ride above the rest.

"Stay wit' de ot'ers, my lady," Rordan muttered as he passed me the reins.

I didn't meet his eyes. The other nobles and ladies were all the way over there, and I was on top of a horse, ready to conquer the world. "Tank j'ou, page," I said loudly.

"I mean it," he hissed. "I don't know what you were doing with the prince, but I bet it was nothing good."

I had a retort on the tip of my tongue, but he quickly disappeared with the other pages and stable boys after gently patting the horse on its rump. She didn't seem to like that very much; she whinnied and trotted down the steep slope through the grass towards the open plains. I held onto the reins for dear life. Even though we weren't going that fast, the reins were made of thin leather and hardly reliable, and my suddenly weak thighs ached from squeezing the animal, desperate to hang on. I felt like I would fall with each leap forward. Terrifying, but exciting.

As my mare lead us in the general direction of the others—who were going at a slow enough pace out into the open plains—I adapted to the horse's rhythm and tried to relax. Maybe this wouldn't be so bad. As long as I stayed close, but not too close to the others, I could explore outside the castle walls to my heart's content.

I scanned the crowd of nobles. Keegan was nowhere in sight. I was content to ride alone, but I soon found myself surrounded by the irritating chatter of the ladies.

"Lady Dominique." Sylvia's words were lined with resentment. "We saw you were riding alone."

"J'ou saw correctly," I replied.

Her smile was thin. "Perhaps we got off on the wrong foot earlier. You know, I hate having this awful tension between us. As daughters of our respective provinces of Marlenia, we really should be more like sisters."

I struggled not to roll my eyes, or laugh, or groan in annoyance. I had to let this play out.

"J'es," I said slowly, forcing a smile. "Sometimes it's hard pour me to make friends."

"I forgive you," Sylvia said a little too quickly. Her grin widened as she exchanged sly glances with her lady friends. "I'm so glad that we patched this up. I hope that our friendship continues after the Gathering has ended."

"Dat would please me."

"It would please me as well."

There was a marked silence. There was nothing left to say to the fat privileged princess from the East. I gently squeezed my thighs around the horse, hoping that that was the correct way to tell her to move forward and away from the irritating sound of Sylvia's voice. Before

151

I could get even a half a step further, Sylvia snapped the reins and steered her horse in front of me. I tried to manoeuvre, but her lady friends were blocking my escape.

"You know that he is mine," she said.

"Who? Prince Keegan?" I almost forgot to say prince in front of his name.

"Yes, of course him. Who else? But maybe you didn't know. My father and his father are in *negotiations*."

I frowned. "Um . . . all right."

She looked from her ladies back to me. "You know what I'm getting at, then."

I lifted my chin and adopted a bored stance. "J'es, J'es, of course."

"Good. Then you know that it would be best if you stayed away from him."

"Dat sounds *wonderful* to me."

I laid the sarcasm on thick, but Sylvia either chose to ignore that, or she was really that stupid. She and her lady entourage left me for the larger group of lords up ahead.

Negotiations. Whatever that meant. Marriage, perhaps? I snorted. Queen Sylvia. *High* Queen Sylvia. That was someone I didn't want ruling over the Marlenians. It wasn't anything I had to worry about, though, not after I was done here. She could take the throne, and while she pumped out children, I would be back on the street, jumping from merchant stall awning to merchant stall awning, seeing how high my bounty could go.

A wash of shivers came over me as I thought about Keegan and Sylvia, standing together before the cathedral, while I crouched in the rooftops, watching . . . doing nothing . . .

I spurred my horse forward and tilted her towards a narrow opening through a patch of trees. It gradually sloped upward and disappeared beneath the hanging boughs. Perfect. Alone time would be welcomed right now.

"Dominique!"

My breath caught. It was not my name. He wasn't calling me, I told myself. But I looked around anyway.

Keegan's horse was a black stallion with a coat as shiny as a freshly minted silver coin. He spurred it into a light canter to reach me. The other lords and ladies were tiny dots near the horizon. No Advisor, and no Lady Sylvia. Her warning echoed in my mind as a sly grin crossed my face. It would make her furious if I made an effort to have a conversation with him again.

"What is that look for?" he asked as he approached.

Control. I had to maintain control of my face. Less cunning, more innocence in the smile. Upward-slanting eyebrows, more eyelash fluttering, shoulders back.

"I just didn't tink j'ou would find me," I replied.

"Well, I was beginning to think that you hadn't shown up at all, and that maybe you were back in your room, reading your new book."

The path was just wide enough for the both of us to ride side by side. My leg brushed against his, and my face coloured wildly. I coughed and wished that Bidelia hadn't tied back my hair.

"Tonight, maybe I'll get a chance to look at it."

We rode in silence for a moment. Each second was torture. What was I supposed to say? What would Lady Dominique say? She would probably be polite and ask him about the weather, or about whatever other manly pursuits he was into. Then he would return the favour and allow her to babble on about whatever it was that Lady Dominique did for fun. Torture Freetors, probably. I shuddered and curled my tongue, as if recoiling from a searing-hot knife.

I stole a glance at him. He was eyeing the road ahead, but his mind seemed to be elsewhere. He caught me looking and smiled. His gaze made me feel warm again.

"Yes, my lady?" He looked amused.

"Oh . . . not'in'." I thought quickly to come up with a conversation topic that did not involve me looking or talking like a fool. "I . . . I was just tinkin' about de man I saved today."

Keegan lifted an eyebrow. "Oh? More inspiring words to add? I thought you had spent your limit."

My lip twitched up into a smile. "Apparently not. I . . . I was just tinkin' about what his fate would have been, if I had not spoken pour him."

The Marlenian prince looked thoughtful. "He would have been thrown in the dungeons for a while, to remind him of his place." My insides went cold. "Then, he probably would've been fed and then sold as a slave to some merchant, or, if he had remained defiant, he would have been put down."

Like an animal, I thought. Our people were nothing but animals to him. "De Freetor laws are harsh here."

"From what I've heard, they seem to be harsher where you are. Cutting out tongues? Hanging bodies in the streets to warn against defiance? We just throw them in a dark prison."

"Well, maybe I'll be pushin' to change dose laws," I said.

Keegan raised an eyebrow. "How? You can't just change things with the wave of your hand, like . . . like some perverse Freetor magic. Passing a law takes time. You can't just listen to your own voice. You may not have an Advisor in the North, but your father must have a council to advise him. And of course, the people have voices too. You can say all you want, but if the Marlenian people don't agree with you, they'll revolt."

I laughed. "Dey wouldn't revolt. Dey do what de Holy One and de High Kings tell dem to do."

A dark look crossed Keegan's face. "Maybe in the North things are different, then, and people are more afraid of your father than I thought. Here, the people have the power. The Holy One is no longer a position of divine right—it's just that my family has been in power for so long. It's not uncommon for the common man to question the authority of the Church. I fear that it won't be long before they rise against us, and install a new government."

A new government, one that was Freetor friendly. But the image of Keegan being torn apart by the crowd that had once shouted its love for him, that scared me. He hadn't done anything hurtful towards me and my people, other than hating us for being born underground. And if the Marlenian people were in charge . . . some of them were sympathetic to our cause, but the majority of them were just as bad as the guards—hell, what was I thinking, they *were* the guards.

"But . . . dere hasn't been any talk of rebellion, right?" I asked.

Keegan sighed. "My father is so busy trying to develop a strategy to deal with the Freetors that he barely has time to meet the needs of his own people. Did you know that the farmers not twenty leagues from here refused to sell us their crops? We had to pay them triple what we paid last year so that Marlenia City wouldn't starve. Combine that with the increased theft from the Freetors, and, well, you see our problem."

I sat in silence, listening to the gentle clopping of the horses' hooves on the trail. I'd never thought that the castle would have problems getting food. I guess I never thought about the Marlenians having any sort of problems at all. And if the city was unable to get food, that meant we wouldn't have any to steal either, and we'd all starve.

"Usually Freetor sympathizers are thrown in the dungeons," Keegan said quietly.

"I didn't say I was a Freetor sympat'izer," I said, pronouncing each word like it was my last. "Dere must be a better way—a non-violent way, maybe—to treat dem."

"Dominique. I know your heart is in the right place, but the Freetors, they don't understand peace." He pointed to the scar on his lip. "The woman who gave me this. She was so desperate to steal my riches so that she could continue to live in her own filth that she resorted to violence. Is that the mark of a civilized—an advanced—culture?"

I gritted my teeth. "Maybe dat woman was so desperate to feed her family—and her friends' families—dat she wouldn't let anyt'in' get in her way."

"She was half-mad! She would have killed me over a piece of jewellery!"

I would have killed him now, over spoken words, and he still wouldn't have understood. I felt my temper rising within me like a violent windstorm. My hands shook the reins, desperate to release the anger within, and I was suddenly very aware of the knife in my boot. It would only take me a second to finish him off. Yes. No one would see me. In the middle of the Marlenian woods? Lady Dominique would have the blame, the poor crazy Northern girl, and I would slip unnoticed back into the underground.

Unnoticed. Forgotten.

"Dominique?" he prompted. "Are you all right?"

I pursed my lips. "I y'am fine."

"No, you're not. I've offended you. I apologize. I shouldn't be talking to you about politics, anyway. They're always telling me that ladies aren't interested in that sort of talk, but you seemed different, and . . . knowledgeable."

The irony. He calls my people stupid, and yet I am knowledgeable. If I were wearing the Violet Fox cape, he wouldn't have said that at all.

"I . . . apologize too," I said slowly. It hurt so much to say it, since I didn't mean it. "I get very worked up when I talk about dese tings. My brot'er says I overreact sometimes."

"You're lucky to have a brother who is honest with you," Keegan replied. "I have no siblings at all, only members of the court to tell me whether or not I'm being inappropriate."

"J'es, I y'am lucky."

And then his hand was on my shoulder. It was warm, and comforting. Even though I didn't want it to be. "Listen, Dominique. I am truly sorry. Tell me what I said to offend you. I cannot have you mad at me." He smiled. "I promise I won't even throw you in the dungeon."

That brought a little smile to my face. "It . . . it does not matter. J'ou were right. We shouldn't be talkin' about politics."

"Forget what I said. Forget what everyone tells us. Tell me as you would tell your brother. As you would tell . . . a friend."

His yellow-green eyes sparkled with sincerity. For a moment, I didn't know what to say. Every instinct told me to shut up and make a run for it.

"A friend?" I whispered.

"Yes," Keegan said.

I swallowed. There was no backing out now. "De woman who attacked you . . ."

*It was me.*

" . . . maybe she was not half-mad, as j'ou say. I don't imagine dat j'ou . . . or I . . . have ever felt so hungry dat we would do anyt'in' pour a piece of bread, or an apple. Maybe de jewellery she sought was not

just jewellery to her—pour what is gold to a hungry person? What if
. . . what if j'ou were in her place? What would j'ou have done?"

Keegan was silent for a few moments. Too silent. Maybe I had gone
too far. The trees were thick around me—too narrow to escape into.
His gaze never left mine.

"I don't suppose I really think about it that way too often," he said,
rubbing his chin. "I guess it would be pretty horrible to be hungry all the
time. When the farmers almost refused to sell us their crop, I was afraid
that we would starve. But to be afraid all the time, not knowing where
the next meal would come from . . . I suppose that would be excruciating."

"J'es, it would be," I agreed.

"Enough to drive one to commit theft, and perhaps murder. But
that doesn't make it right. What do you think?"

"I tink dat what j'ou said at de feast, it is true. If de Freetors had
deir own land, on de surface, a place to grow deir own food and live
freely, dere would be no need to steal anymore."

"Yes, that would be the ideal solution, Dominique," he said,
nodding. "But like the Advisor pointed out, that would never happen.
No lord would give up his land for Freetors. They would outnumber
and overrun us."

I parted my lips to suggest that maybe only some of the Freetors
could have land, and then I stopped. That wouldn't work either, of
course. That would only cause disharmony among us, and we needed
to save our strength for fighting the Marlenians, not other Freetors. "I
esuppose dat's true."

"My ancestors pushed them down there almost two hundred years
ago," Keegan said, caressing a tree branch that arched down in front
of his ride. He tore off a leaf and gripped it in his hand. "I don't know
if it was the right thing to do, but he did what he thought was right at
the time in order to survive."

"Just like . . . de woman who slashed j'our lip," I said.

Keegan allowed the crumpled leaf to drift slowly to the forest floor as
he touched his scar again. He smirked. "It seems that the Freetors are not
that different from the Marlenians after all."

A smile tugged at my lips. We were worlds apart, he and I.

Our horses came to a slow stop. We were at the bottom of a slow incline. I could hear the faint sound of water rushing somewhere up top. The trees were thicker up there, but the path had widened. We had ridden far, far away from the rest of the riding party while we were busy talking. I thought of plump Sylvia looking ridiculous on her mare and had no urge to rejoin the rest of the Marlenians.

Keegan looked up at the path ahead of us and then back to me. "There's a place I'd like to show you."

"Is it up dere?" I asked, pointing up the hill.

"Yes. Are you up for a bit of rough riding? I know Northerners aren't as well trained with horses, but—"

I'd show him. "Race j'ou!"

"Dominique, wait—"

I flicked the reins and spurred the horse with my heels, just like I'd seen the Marlenian guards in the streets do a thousand times when they were coming to chase me. The horse took off. A rush of excitement filled me. I bumped around the saddle as the horse galloped up the hill. I laughed and bent forward into the wind. I was flying.

I chanced a look back, and Keegan was gaining on me. His horse galloped in time with mine, and his was getting louder and louder by the second. I wouldn't let him catch me. The embarrassment of being beaten by the prince would be too much—I had to hold something over him as Lady Dominique, didn't I? The sharp wind dried my lips, and I bit them to keep them wet.

Before long, I reached the top of the incline. I slid down the side of the horse, mesmerized.

It was the most beautiful place I'd ever seen.

I'd only seen running water once before, when Rordan took me on a day trip to the Southern caves. We had gone on a long, underground hike that took most of the day, but it had been worth it at the time to see a two-hands wide, natural stream that gave the Southern Freetors fresh water.

The river in front of me was wide and made the stream I'd seen before look like droplets of water in the sand. I estimated it was at least ten stone-throws long, if not longer. The roar of the rushing water was exhilarating. Water from waves crashing on the rocks sprayed me gently, refreshing me after my harrowing ride to the top.

"It's something, isn't it?"

I gasped in surprise as I wheeled around. Between my fascination with the river and its loud roar, I hadn't heard Keegan sneak up behind me.

"It's . . . beautiful," I said.

He grinned. "I'm glad you like it."

"Do j'ou come here a lot?"

"I try to. When I was younger, the Advisor used to take me fishing here."

The Advisor. The stealer of Freetor magic, our new ultimate enemy. It was hard to think of him catching fish with a young Keegan.

"Seems like j'ou and de Advisor are close," I said casually, throwing my gaze to the water.

"I suppose. He didn't raise me, but I trust him like family." He paused. "Why?"

I shrugged. "I would have considered de Advisor to be more of a servant to de royal family dan a part of it."

"Advisor Ferguson has done a lot for the Marlenian people, especially in the past few years—my father has not been well. He'll continue to serve me when my father leaves this world."

"My fat'er's . . ." I caught myself. My father was dead. "My fat'er doesn't have an Advisor like yours. I tink he would be afraid dat he would betray his trust."

He frowned. "You're trying to ask me about the rumours about him, aren't you."

My eyes snapped to his again. He was cleverer than I gave him credit for. "I just heard some of de ladies talkin', is all . . ."

"Yes, they all talk." Keegan kicked a stone. It bounced into the water with a tiny *splosh*, the sound of its entrance drowned out by the roar of the river. "But he's a good man, with only the best interests of the people at heart."

Hmmph. The *Marlenian* people, maybe. "Den j'ou don't believe de rumours about him covetin' de sceptre? J'our fat'er's position?"

Keegan laughed bitterly. "He can *have* the sceptre if he wants it. An old stick with a big old gem is what that is." His voice softened somewhat. "A cane for an old man." He shook his head of it. "Ivor Ferguson does not want the throne. I think if he did, I would be dead already. Does that sate your curiosity, my lady?"

I half smiled. "Tank j'ou."

"And now it's my turn to ask a difficult question of you."

"Really? My answer about courtship hasn't changed since dis mornin'. I y'am not seein' anyone."

"That's not what I was going to ask, my lady, but that pleases me nonetheless."

My heart fluttered, and I turned away once again. "What is it?"

He paused again, and I snuck a glance at him. He seemed to be struggling with himself, stringing together words that would no doubt tease my ears and heart into submission. Catching my glance, his face reddened somewhat. "I . . . I was only going to ask . . . if you were enjoying your stay so far."

"Oh. Dat doesn't sound too difficult a question." And it wasn't a question about Lady Dominique's heritage either. I felt relieved. "Yes. I . . . esuppose I y'am enjoyin' myself."

His relief seemed to match mine. "I'm glad."

I crouched by the riverbed and slid my hand into the water. It trickled over my fingers like a soft caress but pushed on with the promise of something better. The water was cold and refreshing. I trapped a bit of it in my hand, and almost drank it, and then thought better of it. Lady Dominique wouldn't do something like that. The Violet Fox would.

But Lady Dominique wasn't here right now. And neither was the Holy One, or Rordan, or the Elders. It was just me and Keegan, the somewhat-charming Marlenian prince.

I could handle him.

A pile of rocks below the riverbed stuck out of the water high enough to step on. Water occasionally washed over them, leaving them smooth and wet. As quick as a stray cat, I leapt down onto them.

"Careful, Dominique. The water is deeper than it looks," Keegan said.

I rolled my eyes and smirked. "Oh c'mon. Where's j'our sense of adventure?"

"It's going to be in the river, floating belly-down, if you slip on those rocks."

I laughed. "Please. I climb on more dangerous tings dan slippery rocks."

"Oh really." Keegan folded his arms and looked amused. "And what would a lady have time to climb over?"

"Is amazin' what j'ou can find time to do when j'ou don't learn embroidery or sewing . . . or ot'er tings . . ." I trailed off, realizing that I didn't know exactly what "proper" ladies were supposed to do with their free time.

To my surprise, Keegan laughed. "You don't know how to sew? Even I know how to do that."

"Okay, okay. I know how to do dat. Bad example." I knew how to sew up wounds and patch my cape when it tore, but that was a thousand stone-throws from embroidering bloody battles onto larger-than-life blankets.

I teetered on the edge of one rock and leapt to the one adjacent. But it was slipperier than I had anticipated. My feet slid across the wet rock. For a moment I thought I would tumble into the icy waters and be swept away downstream, but before Keegan could reach out to save me, my hand caught a groove in the rock and I pulled myself up again. My feet hadn't gotten wet. I was fine.

"All right. You're starting to make me nervous." His voice was more serious now. Maybe he really did care about my well-being.

I sighed. He was probably right. One misstep and the Violet Fox would meet her untimely end, and the Freetor people would never recover Alastar's Tome. "Fine."

"Let me help you up." He offered his hand.

"Tank j'ou."

But as I reached to take it, I slipped once more, and this time I wasn't as lucky.

Things happened so quickly that I could barely tell what was going on. I fell backwards into the river just as Keegan bent to catch me—and an arrow whizzed over his head. Water filled my mouth before I could cry a warning, and I was swept under with the current. The cold seeped through my thin riding clothes and stiffened my limbs, dragging me down under further. My lungs screamed for air. I thrashed around, hitting rocks and getting tangled in underwater plants, but all I had to do was reach that light above me. It seemed so close, yet so far. The black spots on my vision grew bigger.

And then, bubbles. And darkness. But something was pulling on me towards the light. Maybe this was what the dying talked about—going to the place of Eternal Sunshine, where it was never night and we would never live in caves again.

The pressure lifted. I could hear again. Everything was so bright. And . . . a face. Keegan's yellow-green eyes pierced through my clouded vision. His lips were moving but my ears were waterlogged, and although his face was there in front of me, his voice sounded like it was a million yards away, trapped underground.

A flash of green. Rordan. Kneeling before me. That couldn't be right. Unless he had followed us, to make sure Keegan didn't try anything on me. He was saying something to the prince, his brow furrowed, and Keegan looked like he was defending himself. Was Rordan scolding him? His hand was a warm anchor, keeping me on land.

Keegan coughed and shook his head. His tunic had torn in the back, revealing a line of blood. Rordan slid his hands beneath me and tried to pick me up, but Keegan stayed him. *No*, I saw him say. My brother's lip curled, but he stepped back at the prince's command.

I closed my eyes for only a moment. When I opened them again, Keegan's lips were beside my cheek. The scar was closer to me now than when I had given it to him. He had raised the upper half of my body so that I rested in his arms. My body felt weightless, but my eyes were heavy.

As the world surrendered to the darkness, another form came racing towards us with heavy steel boots and leather gloves and a long, billowing coat . . . Advisor Ferguson. Where did he come from?

The arrow. It had knocked Keegan off balance. The blood on his back. If I hadn't been there, he wouldn't have been ducking, and the arrow would have hit its mark . . .

The Advisor was trying to kill Keegan.

As the distance between us closed, the thought bounced around inside my mind. It was as heavy as my eyes. Keegan saved my life. I had to tell him. Save . . . his . . .

Before I blacked out, I reached to touch the scar on his lips.

# Eleven

I WAS IN bed for the next day and a half. The good thing about that was that I got to miss a lot of boring Marlenian day-to-day court dealings, like watching the Holy One declare the law for everyone. The bad part was that I was wasting valuable investigating time. I *knew* the Advisor had something to do with the Alastar's Tome. Maybe he was trying to use its power to steal the Marlenian throne—I just needed more proof, and more time. I'd been at the castle nearly four days. At least another week remained. Each minute was precious, and I probably wouldn't get a second chance.

The magic Freetor text I'd gotten from the library was little help. I had read it cover to cover in bed once I started feeling better. Like I had suspected, it had nothing to do with Alastar or the Freetors. It talked about Dashiell, and the foolish Marlenian women and men who did heroic deeds to win his favour. Stories and myths. It talked a lot about his four artefacts, and those who sought them. There was a whole chapter on the Orb of Dashiell, which supposedly had the power to call lightning and control other violent forms of nature. I snorted and returned the book to its hiding place under the mattress. The Marlenians probably held on to these stories because they couldn't control *real* magic.

Something else weighed on my mind—everything that Keegan had told me about the Marlenians threatening to revolt and his future in the kingdom. If I took back the magic from the Advisor, I would really be helping Keegan and his father stay in power. But was that right? The Holy One had a bounty out for the Violet Fox that could feed ten Freetor families for life. Would the Advisor be a better ruler?

I sighed and leaned back into my fluffed-up pillows, nibbling on a biscuit that Bidelia had brought me. I was getting too comfortable here, and I only had a handful of days left before the Gathering ended and I'd be forced to return to my underground life. The Advisor was a power-hungry Marlenian like everyone else at court. There would be no difference between the two of them. It would continue to be the same, or worse, until the Freetors really took the battle to the surface and fought back.

The bedroom door squeaked open and Bidelia entered. She eyed me like a Freetor eyes a Marlenian: with suspicion and resentment. The breakfast tray was filled with grapes and buttered biscuits with a side of sliced strawberries. I remembered how hungry I used to feel when I looked at food. My mouth watered, and I felt guilty for wanting to fill my already content stomach.

"Your cheeks have colour in them again," she said. "You must be well enough to stand."

I thought about Keegan again, and felt sick to my stomach. "I don't think so."

"Then you will have to pretend. The masquerade ball is tomorrow night."

"Ugh." I hid under the blanket. "I'm not going."

Bidelia marched over to the bed and threw the blanket off onto the ground, spilling the biscuits and grapes and precious strawberries all over the mattress and the floor. "You are growing fat and lazy, Kiera. Just like that fat cow from the East, that Lady Sylvia. It's *easy* isn't it, to think that you might have a shot at being a Marlenian princess. You wouldn't have want for anything, ever again."

I went to grab her, but Bidelia leapt out of my reach.

"See? You have lost your edge." She gave me the once-over with a disgusted look on her face. "Remember what you stand for. The Violet Fox wouldn't allow herself to become a complacent slave to Marlenian life. You—"

There was a knock at the door. Our argument was forgotten as I scrambled to cover myself with the blankets and Bidelia rushed to answer the door. I recovered the abandoned tray and as many grapes as possible as a guard peeked his head through the crack.

"His Highness requests to see the Lady Dominique."

"I'm sorry, but she is not herself this morning. Perhaps this afternoon—"

"His Highness wants to ensure that the lady is well."

"She is," Bidelia said stiffly. "But she needs her rest."

I lowered my head onto the pillow. She wasn't going to let the prince see me, not after our argument, and not after the rumours that were flying around the castle. The conveniently clumsy Lady Dominique falls into the river so that Prince Keegan will rescue her and have no choice but to see her again. I saw the arrow again in my mind, whizzing towards Keegan, but this time the Advisor was standing a stone-throw away on the grass, drawing the bow.

"Yes, I will be sure she gets these," Bidelia said. She had to open the door a little wider, and I glimpsed Keegan and his guard. He was holding a large glass vase stuffed with blue roses. Their scent was faint from where I was, but they smelled like the river. Even though I'd almost drowned, I suddenly yearned to return there. Our eyes met, and his face lit up.

"I believe the lady is awake," he said.

"She is not receiving visitors," Bidelia said shortly.

"J'es, I y'am!" I called.

Bidelia couldn't contradict me, not in front of Keegan. He grinned and waited for Bidelia to step aside.

"These are to help you feel better," he said.

Bidelia offered to take them. "Allow me, Your Grace."

"Oh . . . of course," he said. He handed the vase to Bidelia as if he were handing her a sleeping infant. Curling her lip at the beauty of the gift, she set them on my dresser as Keegan sat down on a stool by my bedside. His bodyguard loomed over him, but he seemed not to notice. Bidelia wordlessly cleaned up the rest of my spoiled breakfast.

"J'ou seem . . . well," I offered.

A hint of a smile. "Yes. Well, I didn't try to breathe underwater. I suppose there isn't much opportunity to swim in the North with the weather."

"No, not really," I replied. My hands busied themselves with a loose thread on the flower-print quilt, but I held his face in my periphery. "Tank j'ou . . . pour savin' my life."

"Thank you for saving mine," he returned.

I tucked a stray lock of hair behind my ear. "What do j'ou mean?"

Keegan wrestled with his mouth, as if his tongue and his brain were fighting over what words should be spoken next. "I remember something whizzing by me. I thought it was nothing until I saw the blood on the back of my shoulder. I know that you were barely conscious at the time, but . . . do you remember something like that? Or am I speaking nonsense?"

Bidelia hovered over me like a dark cloud, commanding me to deny everything. I plucked the thread from the quilt and wrapped it around my finger.

"I . . . I tink I may have seen somet'in'," I admitted finally.

"Your Grace, she is still quite feverish," Bidelia said. "I doubt—"

"He would've had to be hiding in the woods, waiting for us. He probably followed us up from the path and waited for us to separate. I was sure we weren't followed . . ." He trailed off, but he was not thinking. I saw in his eyes that he knew exactly what he was going to say next. "There was a man whom I recognized as your page. He came to us rather quickly after I pulled you out of the river."

"J'es, I remember," I said quickly. "He's been in my service pour many years. I trust him."

"You know him well, then?"

I paused, and fought the urge to look to Bidelia. "As well as a noble knows any of her servants, J'our Grace."

"I see." He rubbed his chin. It looked like he hadn't shaved today; bits of black stubble dotted his face. It made him rugged. Feral. Handsome.

"I tink I remember someone else bein' dere," I said.

Keegan cocked an eyebrow. "Who? Oh yes, the Advisor. He often follows me on my adventures to ensure that no one nefarious is tracking my movements."

He didn't have any better things to do, like run the castle? I wanted to ask this, but I had to pretend to be sicker than I was or Bidelia would really have my head.

"And de Advisor didn't see y'anyone, did he?" I tried to make the question sound as innocent as possible.

"No. Only your page." Keegan frowned. "Maybe I'll talk to him. See if he saw anyone."

I couldn't disagree, so I nodded. My stomach was a bundle of nerves.

"Thank you, Dominique." His voice was soft now, like a cotton flower I'd stolen once at the market. "Sorry for disturbing you. Get your rest, and I will see you tomorrow night at the masquerade. That is, if you feel up to going."

"I will," I said, casting a glance at Bidelia.

He smiled. "It would not be the same without you."

The prince and his guard took their leave, and when they were out of earshot, Bidelia's hard stare returned. "Now you have turned the prince's eye to your brother."

"It's all part of the risk," I replied, rubbing my eyes.

"Indeed. But the more you associate with either Rordan or Keegan, the more the servants' tongues wag."

"I don't care about wagging tongues."

"Then best you focus on your mission and stop dabbling in Marlenian politics."

"I'm just trying to blend in."

"Hmmph. You're so blended in that you're sticking out, Kiera. Remember that."

My eyes strayed to the flowers Keegan had brought as Bidelia left the room. No one had ever cared when I was sick before, not in this way. To get sick was to die in the underground, and people died every day. Rordan had once given me his day's rations when I'd caught a sickness on the surface, but he had not dared to come near me in fear he'd get it too, and he'd been angry that I'd let my guard down. But Keegan had sat on my bed and shared my breath, and while I wasn't the same kind of sick that I was before, I was weak and he was strong. He could have stayed away.

If he knew who I was, he could make his move while I was down.

I leaned against the bedpost as my thoughts went to the masquerade. Maybe going wouldn't be such a bad idea after all. But I'd need something to wear. Something stunning. Keegan would be surrounded by women with beautiful, expensive dresses. He had to notice me. I was so blended in that I stuck out? Maybe I would wear the brightest colours I could find. Part of me wanted to just crash the party as the Violet Fox, but the thought of Keegan raising cold steel against me after we'd saved each other's lives . . .

Instead, I rooted through Dominique's suitcases. Compared to what I'd seen some of the other ladies wear, it seemed like Dominique's sense of colour was really drab. That, or someone had washed all the colour out of the fabric. That wouldn't do for the masquerade. The masquerade was all about colour, and using it to hide your identity. This was something I could do quite easily.

I did find a mask in her belongings. It was heavy, and metallic, like someone had blended silver and gold together to create a durable—yet elegant—piece of art. A black string threaded through two holes was supposed to wrap around my face. It barely looked strong enough. I tied it around my face and looked in the mirror. It felt heavy on the bridge of my nose. And I'd be expected to wear this thing all night. Maybe Bidelia was right. I was getting lazy.

There was nothing in her suitcases that was suitable for me to wear. But, that was a solvable problem, at least.

I took the rest of Rordan's coins and sent for him, telling him to have the carriage ready for me at the front bailey. He passed on the message and escorted me from my room. He seemed relieved that I was alive, and when I was sure no one was listening, I asked him about what had happened at the river.

"Yes, I followed you," he admitted in a low voice as he escorted me to the carriage. "I was . . . afraid that the prince would . . . you know."

I blushed. "But he didn't try anything. Where did the Advisor come from?"

Rordan didn't answer me immediately. The bags under his eyes were more noticeable today. I must have put him through a lot of stress.

"He was following you too," he said.

"Was he carrying any weapons? Like, a bow and arrow?"

Rordan frowned. "I...I don't remember. Maybe."

"Maybe? Rordan, I *saw* an arrow!" I lowered my voice to a whisper. "It almost hit Keegan, and he thinks that someone was trying to kill him. And you're his number one suspect."

Maybe I shouldn't have told him that. His face paled. "Maybe I should get out of the castle."

"But it wasn't you," I said, holding tightly to his arm and stopping him in the corridor. I heard far-off footfalls of servants, but the corridor was clear. "Right? There's no reason to kill Keegan."

"He's no longer Prince Keegan?" he asked stiffly.

"Stop it," I hissed. "Just tell me you're not going to kill him."

"I'm not going to kill him, as long as he doesn't get in the way."

I sighed and squeezed Rordan's hands. "He won't."

He allowed himself a smile. It didn't reach his eyes. "So, the Advisor . . . "

A flock of ladies entered our corridor, and I tore my hands quickly from Rordan's. I started towards them, with Rordan remaining a generous pace behind me. Their eyes flickered between us, but they resumed their normal chatter. Once they were gone, Rordan caught up with me again.

"I told you to be careful around the Advisor," Rordan whispered.

"Have you learned anything more about him? What are the servants saying?"

"Nothing. Just the usual." He looked a little distracted. "But you think that he's trying to murder the prince?"

I shrugged. "It makes sense, doesn't it?" I peeked around the corner, into a narrow passageway that led to the main entrance. "Keegan is the Holy One's only living heir. What man in Advisor Ferguson's position wouldn't want the throne?"

Rordan nodded. "He can't be trusted."

The carriage was waiting in the bailey. Rordan said he had other duties to tend to, and left me. He probably didn't want to go shopping with me anyway—that would be too suspicious.

Lucinda's Luxuries and Lace was located in the heart of the merchant district, where the Advisor had said it would be, and it hosted more dresses with more fabric than I thought existed. I couldn't dally and drink in the variety of dress colours: the sunny-yellow straight-lace gown hiding in the corner, or the moss-green skirt that ballooned from the wooden figure modelling it as if she were standing over a forceful gust of wind. I was immediately drawn to a dress at the back.

The gown had no sleeves, nothing on the shoulders at all. The back of the dress was criss-crossed with laces that held the dress tightly against the wooden figure. The slightly stooping bodice hinted at the figure's carved cleavage. Stitches so small they could only be the work of children or faeries formed an ornate chequered pattern across the bottom half.

The colour: a deep violet, similar to my cape, but richer. A hue that had not seen days running through the crowded merchant district, and nights fraying and freezing underground. This hue was innocent, and knew nothing of the struggles I had faced.

This was a dress fit for a princess.

"Can I help you?"

Lucinda's voice was high-pitched and shrill and sought to please. High, painted cheekbones, gaunt face, accentuated bosom where there was none—Lucinda was the picture of what I hated about Marlenian women. But she was the expert on Marlenian beauty, and that was what I needed.

"I'd like to try on dis dress," I said, pointing to the one I was admiring.

She looked over my attire and seemed to decide that I was worth her time. "I don't think I've had the pleasure of your acquaintance. Lady . . . ?" Lucinda waited expectantly, the paint on her face caking with sweat.

"Lady Dominique Castillo, daughter of de High King Matís in de Nort'," I said.

"Oh! I am honoured to serve a daughter of the North! I had heard you were coming to the Gathering. I understand this is your first visit in a long time to the West."

I simply nodded. Two of her assistants—women, painted and held together with tight-fitting dresses as well—undid the dress from the wooden figure and escorted it to a dressing room, built right into the wall. They draped it over a chair inside the miniature room and gestured for me to go inside.

The room was tight with three of us in there. The two assistants undid my gown and folded it neatly over the back of the chair. I hugged my chest. Normally tight spaces didn't bother me, but sharing the same breath with these women was making me nauseous.

"I can do de rest, tank j'ou," I said.

Inclining their heads, the two assistants opened the door and left. Just as it was closing, Lucinda called, "Are you sure you don't need any help, my lady?"

"I y'am fine, tank j'ou."

"You just let me know. We are more than happy to assist!"

I rolled my eyes and made sure the door was locked. I stole a glance at myself in the person-sized mirror. Such luxury. I held up the violet dress in front of me. The fabric was cool and soft against my skin. Dancing in this would feel like a dream.

Mission. I had to remember the mission.

I made a face at my reflection. Couldn't I just have fun, for one night? The only fun I had as the Violet Fox was when the guards chased me down for stealing bread for my starving people. And that wasn't supposed to be fun, not according to Rordan anyway. I wanted to have real fun, like a Marlenian princess would have.

Just as I was slipping into the garment, something rustled in the ceiling, like a large rat was scurrying across the panelling.

I pulled up the dress to conceal my undergarments and reached for my concealed knife just as the ceiling panel nudged open. I had to cover my mouth to keep from screaming. "Laoise."

"I have to talk to you," she whispered.

"Is everything all right in there, my lady? Allow one of my girls to come in and help you do up the back!" Lucinda said.

"I'll be outside," Laoise said. "It's important."

She had risked her life to come see me. I nodded quickly and gestured for her to leave.

"What's that sound? Lady Dominique, is everything . . . ?"

I threw open the door just as Laoise replaced the ceiling tile. I held the violet gown to my chest to keep it up. Lucinda's assistants and Lucinda herself stood less than a stone-throw from the dressing-room door. I prayed they hadn't heard my conversation.

"I swear I heard a rat," I exclaimed. "J'our establishment is not infested, is it? Because if it is . . . "

"No, no, my lady! I swear!" Terror struck Lucinda's face as she gestured to her hired help. "Search everywhere for this rat. I swear, my lady, we will not rest until—"

I couldn't have them looking for Laoise! I thought quickly. "No need, Lucinda. I will need all of j'ou to help me wit' dis dress."

Three of Lucinda's women surrounded me and yanked and pulled on the bodice laces until I was sure the dress itself was choking me to death. Another assistant brought over a full-sized mirror, even though there was one in the dressing room I could have used.

Yes. It was perfect. If only I could wear my Violet Fox mask, but I would have to be content with hiding in plain sight with the rich purple hues that shimmered as I swayed my hips slightly.

"I'll take it."

Delighted, Lucinda's ladies loosened the bodice and left me to change back into my other dress. I glanced at the ceiling to see if Laoise was still around, but there was nothing.

The dress was draped over the front counter when I came out of the dressing room. My change purse was burning a hole in my bosom, where I kept it. I dropped the rest of Rordan's silver on the counter, and Lucinda's eyes glittered at the clinking sound of silver in the bag.

"Yes, that should do nicely. I thank the gracious lady ever so much for her patronage."

"Take dis dress to my carriage outside," I said to one of the assistants.

The women tripped over themselves while fighting for the right to carry the dress, which was wrapped carefully in clean linens and hung on a wooden hanger. Two of them ended up carrying it together so it wouldn't drag on the ground. I showed them to my carriage, and after they had gone, I searched for the guards that had escorted me, and the carriage's driver. I spotted them across the street, having a pint at a tavern. I smirked. They probably figured I would be a while. Checking both sides of the street for onlookers, I tried to look inconspicuous as I slipped into the alley between Lucinda's shop and the bakery next door.

The alley was wider than most—not a place Freetors would frequent. There were no tunnel entrances that I could spot, either. I was about to return to the carriage when I heard a scraping sound above me. Laoise swooped down from the roof, crouching like a feral cat as she landed on her feet. In the bright waning sunlight, she looked even filthier than she had moments before. That was fine by me, though. I would take filth over face paint. I wanted to hug her, but between her griminess and my dress and blowing my cover, it was out of the question.

"What were you thinking? You could've been caught!" I whispered.

"I really had to talk to you."

"What's wrong?"

She kept her head low to the ground; I could barely see her lips moving. "Two more Elders have died in the past three days. Elder Clancy and Elder Cleena."

My stomach curled. "How?"

"Does it matter? Something is going on here," she hissed. Her eyes were like little hummingbirds, zipping back and forth across the crowded street.

"Well . . . what am I supposed to do about it? I'm trying to help the Elders the only way I can. By finding—" I slapped my hand over my mouth at the last second. "Sorry."

"I wish you could tell me."

"Me too." I glanced at my waiting carriage. "I should go."

Laoise inhaled sharply. "Just . . . keep your eyes out. Everyone's afraid. I'm . . . I'm afraid. What if there are no Elders? Who is going to protect us? What if the Extremists carry out bigger attacks, in more public areas?"

"That's not going to happen," I said.

"We don't know that!" Laoise was getting too loud now. I could feel curious eyes on us as people walked by the alley. "Without the Elders' magic to keep them in line, they could start killing everyone who doesn't side with them. A lot of innocent people could die."

"Laoise!" I risked saying her name to calm her down. "I promise you—the Elder magic will always be around to keep us safe." Even if I had to read every last book in that library, even if I had to confront Advisor Ferguson myself, I thought bitterly, I would find Alastar's Tome. "The Extremists will never gain enough traction. The Fighters would take them down. So would the Marlenian guard."

Something Freetor and Marlenian alike agreed on—the Extremists took things too far. If only the Marlenians could see that we weren't all Extremists.

If only Keegan could see.

"But Kiera . . ."

"I should go, before someone starts gossiping."

She hesitated, looking like she was going to say more, but she remained still against the gritty stone wall. "You'll be back soon, right?"

I nodded, even though my thoughts wandered to the intermingling colours of Keegan's eyes. "Yeah. Soon."

She grimaced but didn't meet my eye. "Please, hurry."

I'm trying, I wanted to say, but she was halfway up the back alley wall before I could say a proper goodbye. Her light footsteps faded gently into the sounds of the city streets as I stood at the edge of two worlds. There had to be an entrance to the underground around here somewhere. My dress might be poofy, but maybe somehow I could find out the password, and sneak back down home. Home, in the dark underground, where all I had to worry about was putting food in my neighbours' stomachs and staying one step ahead of the Marlenian city guard.

Putting one dainty foot in front of the other, I could feel every pebble on the road through my walking slippers as I sauntered back to the carriage. It couldn't be a coincidence that many Elders had died within such a short space of time. Yes, they had seen their fair share of endless nights underground, and battles on the surface, and access to food was scarce at the best of times, but they were always well cared for, and well guarded. Not to mention, they shared a magic that not even the learned Marlenian scholars could begin to understand.

But if this had to do with Alastar's Tome being stolen, then everything really did rest on my shoulders. Me, the Violet Fox, the one person preventing the Marlenians from knowing the secret magic of my people and destroying us. Elder Erskina had told me not to read Alastar's Tome when I found it, but if she and the other Elders were dead, then there would be no choice, would there? I saw myself standing on the cathedral steps, my purple cape flapping violently in the wind as I read aloud mystic words of power that made Marlenians freeze solid and shatter into a million pieces in the square. Then Keegan would see and . . .

And he would see what a horrible person I was. He would see the truth.

# Twelve

THE CASTLE WAS a flurry of activity. Servants skittered around the corridors and disappeared up their secret staircases, carrying trays of fruit and rolling barrels of fermented juices towards the ballroom. There was a hint of music in the ear that I could catch but never quite hear. I thought of Rordan and our dance lesson in the underground—hopefully I would not have to partake in any dancing.

In my chamber, Bidelia had gathered no less than six servant girls to help me prepare for the evening. Bathwater was drawn and poured in a basin they'd dragged in. Unlike my bathwater in the underground, this water was warm and filled with scented foam that made my skin smell like flowers and a fresh spring morning in the forest. At first I was afraid to remove all of my clothing in front of these young women, but Bidelia promptly stripped me without a word. Lady Dominique would have never bathed herself. There were servants for that, too.

The ladies removed what hair was growing back on my arms and legs with a one-bladed razor, similar to the men's facial razors I saw in the marketplace. I was afraid that they would see my scars—I hadn't many, but the badly healed lines on my arms where guards had nicked me with their blades would be enough to raise eyebrows. But they were silent as ever as they went about their work. No doubt Bidelia would have their tongues cut out if they ever started wagging.

The dress I had bought lay waiting on the bed. Bidelia threw me a disapproving glance as she picked it up by the shoulders and examined it. "You had many other dresses, my lady."

"I fear dat none of dem were pleasin' to my eye," I said.

After I was washed and dried, Bidelia and her servants sat me down in front of the vanity. The servant girls tousled my curls with a scent that smelled vaguely of lavender and roses. If any sweaty smell had remained from my life underground, it would be gone now.

Dinner was brought on a silver platter. A chicken leg, half a potato, and some baked carrots and peas—the meal was scant, Bidelia explained, because ladies don't want their stomachs to bulge in their gowns. Nerves filled my belly, and so I barely touched any of the food. My thoughts were on the mission: make a good impression. Find Alastar's Tome. Stay out of the Advisor's sight. So much to do, and so little time to do it.

When the sun disappeared beneath the horizon, I went to the ball-room. Ladies waited in line to enter. Most if not all of them had men on their arms. I stood behind Lady Na'ima as I peered further up the line. Lady Sylvia was closer to the front. She chatted loudly with the woman in front of her while her suitor looked bored on her arm—some noble from the East, who was just as plump if not more so than she was. She leaned away from him, her fingers only lightly grasping his velvet jacket. She happened to glance my way and caught me staring. Her piggish face sported a wicked grin when she noticed that I was standing alone.

The line moved slowly, and already my feet were starting to hurt from the heeled shoes. The mask weighed heavily on my face, but I kept my head up in fear of missing any useful details. The scribe announced each guest's arrival as he or she treaded down the staircase into the ballroom. It was a long staircase—almost a hundred steps, if I remembered correctly from the map I'd studied—and it seemed like the scribe was waiting until the ladies were at the bottom before proclaiming the next name because sometimes it was three to four minutes between announcements. I tapped my foot impatiently. This was a waste of time. I could've snuck into the Advisor's chamber instead.

By the time all of the ladies before me had gone, I had made up my mind. Fifteen minutes. That's all I'd stay. Then I would feign boredom—not that that would be hard—and get out of my shoes as quickly as possible. They were almost a hand high and arched my foot in a way that I didn't think was possible.

Maybe Keegan would see me in the dress first, and that would be enough.

"You are descending alone, my lady?" the scribe asked.

"Yes," I said sourly.

"Very well."

His voice echoed over the scraping of my heels and the royal music as he announced my arrival to the hall. Music that I had only heard at a distance and in the underground whispers came to life in that room; the musicians stroked their instruments like experienced lovers. Marlenians floated in circles around the room to the musicians' passion and revelled in their own budding romances.

The Holy One surveyed his subjects from a throne, with one hand holding his head and the other fingering some grapes in a golden dish sitting on the armrest. The sceptre leaned against the side of the throne. Two lesser thrones on his left and right were empty. The mask limited my vision, but I swept the room, searching—yes, there he was. In the corner, by the drapes. Ready to slip away at the slightest accusation. Advisor Ferguson stood demurely with his hands behind his back, his thin moustache waxed into sharp points like poised swords ready to strike. As if knowing that I was looking, his eyes snapped to mine. I dipped my head and feigned respect and looked away, but I knew he was still staring at me as I treaded down the flowing staircase.

Dishes of cheese piled high and carafes of wine decorated a table off to the right wall. How I wanted to go there and stuff every last morsel into every hidden fold in my dress, but I fought the urge. I dug my fingernails into my palm as I stood alone next to the dancing couples. The other ladies were engaged in conversations with various lords, but I had no one. Perhaps I would visit the food. I kept my head high as I sauntered towards the table, only to be stopped by the lightest touch of a man's hand on my bare, hairless arm.

"My lady." Advisor Ferguson smiled, lifting the points of his moustache to touch his nose. "You look lovely tonight."

My face reddened slightly as several excuses to escape rushed to my mind. "Tank j'ou."

"I see you lack a dance partner. Might you do me the honour?"

Terror seized my chest. "I'm . . . I y'am really not dat good at it . . ."

"Then we can make fools of ourselves together." He held out a hand.

The last thing I wanted to do was touch that man's hand. How many Freetors had he killed, or sentenced to death? I felt like I was going to be sick. I rested my fingers hesitantly on his palm as he led me onto the dance floor. If the Violet Fox could endure being chased by twenty guards and slip away unseen, then I could survive a three-minute dance with the most dangerous Marlenian in the city.

We bowed and curtsied as was the custom, and the music swung into a robust waltz. It wasn't at all like the music that Rordan and I had practiced with, but it had a similar tempo. He gripped my waist firmly and led me around the floor. My feet quickly grew accustomed to his steps and my dress swung around his legs as we paraded around the other dancers.

"You lied. You are extraordinary, my lady," he said.

"J'ou lead well," I replied.

He pulled me closer to him. "You are causing quite the stir with the ladies."

"How so?"

Spinning us around twice, he glanced over at Lady Milda and Lady Sylvia. They wore similar painted smiles as they gossiped together. Their dainty fingers held thin glasses of wine.

"I did not realize how different the North was than the South and the East. I doubt that any of the ladies here have visited Castle Castillo."

I frowned. "What do j'ou—?"

His grip tightened, and his lips were suddenly a kiss away from my ear. "*You think I don't know who you are?*"

I stiffened. The music and the joy in the atmosphere faded, and it was only me and him, and he had me close. My eyes darted around the room. Four of the Holy One's men at the entrance, up the stairs. Two more at the bottom. Five more standing by the Holy One, five or six mingling around the food, along with many other lords sworn to other Marlenian lords . . .

The Advisor released his grip to spin me around, and I pulled to get away, but he reined me back in for another few steps. This time his grip on my hand and waist was ironclad.

"A gutsy move, you coming here," he whispered, this time above my head.

"I . . . I y'am afraid I don't know what—"

"Do not feign innocence with me. Your moves of late have been careless. Saving the Freetor man, sneaking around at night and returning to your quarters in the early hours? The servants, they talk."

I felt like a cold hand was clutching my heart. I had to get out of here. Rordan, he was just outside the door, wasn't he? If I could just signal him that I was in danger. While I casually scanned the crowd for him or Bidelia, I had to stall. I kept up Lady Dominique's accent so he would not know my real voice. "What do j'ou plan to do wit' me?"

"That depends on you." He looked down at me. "Did you know you are outnumbered nearly seventy-five to one in this room alone?"

"I know j'ou're plannin' to usurp de t'rone. One word, and everyone would know. Den I would not be de only one outnumbered. And I can disappear quickly if I need to."

He chuckled and spun me again. The room whirled around me and all the faces blurred together.

"Then it seems we are at a stalemate."

"So j'ou admit to plottin' against de Holy One?"

"My plans are nothing to you. If you do not hurt the Holy One and his son, you may finish your mission and leave quietly. Unless you intend to leave with his son." His face was solemn.

While he didn't wear a mask this evening, his face was still hard to read. I frowned. Advisor Ferguson was going to let me go? No, it had to be a lie. He was trying to make me reveal my mission. He had to know that I was onto him. Stealing Freetor magic, trying to assassinate Keegan . . . I was in his way.

Rordan. There he was, at the top of the stairs, dressed in the green tunic with the Castillo crest on the front, the same one he wore the day we arrived at the castle. A knife gleamed at his waist. He was scanning the crowd, but he didn't see me. The Advisor spun me and danced us into the centre of the room, so that we were surrounded by a milliard of dancing couples.

"I have no interest in Keegan," I said.

Rordan descended the steps and for a few brief seconds, our eyes locked. The Advisor turned to see whom I was looking at, and then spun me to a different part of the floor, were there were twenty guards.

"You are on a first-name basis with him. Is your plan to seduce and kidnap him for ransom?"

"Stop playin' games wit' me. I know j'ou have what I want," I whispered. "And I know j'ou tried to *murder* him."

For the first time, uncertainty clouded the Advisor's eyes.

A flash of the Northern Marlenian garb. Rordan was coming for me. Two of us against seventy-five nobles and guards, plus the Advisor and the Holy One and . . .

"I'm sorry, can I cut in?"

Keegan.

The Advisor faltered in his step and let go of me to regain his balance. Keegan took that as a sign that he could steal me away for the rest of the dance. My hand rested on his tight-fitting red velvet coat, and my eyelashes brushed against his collar as he drew me in close. I would have struggled, but the look on the Advisor's face—a mix of rage and disgust—was too priceless. I smiled sweetly at my escape as Keegan twirled me away.

"Lady Dominique," he said briskly. "I didn't expect to see you on the dance floor."

"No?" My eyes flickered to Rordan. He was politely excusing himself through the dancers. When he caught my eye, I shook my head once and then looked away. I hoped he understood.

"I thought you more of a wallflower, to be honest."

A wallflower. That was a Marlenian saying. Meaning . . . no, I knew this. My heart was pounding so fast that I could barely think straight. "I . . . I was only dancin' because de Advisor asked me to."

"And you said yes to that prickly old man?"

"I said j'es to j'ou too."

A smile touched his lips, stretching his scar in a grisly reminder of what I had done to him. "I was grateful for that. If you had said no, I would have been forced to ask Lady Rosalin or Lady Nimat. One is so tall that my head would be in her bosom, and the other is large enough that she would eat all of the castle's stores, leaving us all starving. I'd be forced to steal my supper with the Freetors."

I looked for the Advisor, but he had disappeared. What if he had gone to tell the Holy One that he thought I was a Freetor? Or worse— what if he were rounding up a special force right now to flood the room and arrest me?

I had to leave the ballroom.

"I have offended you again, haven't I?" Keegan said softly.

The song came to an end. Couples bowed and laughed and dispersed, and I thought about losing myself in them, but he was holding my hands so tenderly that I couldn't leave. It wasn't that I couldn't slip out of his grip. I could have. It would have been easy. I counted to three and told myself to leave. *Go!* But my stomach was filled with stone butterflies that weighed me down.

I couldn't do this to myself. I had to get out of here before the Advisor found me. Before he revealed my real identity in front of everyone. In front of Keegan.

"No, j'ou haven't offended me," I said with a smile to reassure him. "Just . . . excuse me pour one moment."

"Oh . . . of course." He bowed slightly, and I curtsied as a flurry of ladies descended upon him, requesting and reserving the next dance with him.

Besides the entry at the top of the stairs, there was one other exit from the ballroom. I gravitated towards it, trying to look like I wasn't escaping the party. It was off to the left side of the room—a pair of giant oak doors that opened out into the garden on the east side of the castle. The garden was trapped within a large alleyway, at least ten stone-throws wide. Vines crept up the old masonry like rotting, spindly fingers and twisted around four pillars that created a square around the grounds. A variety of colourful flowers with pointed and starred leafs peppered the foot of the pillars. A water fountain with a winged dancing woman stood in the middle of the garden. Thirty stone-throws away, two guards chatted with each other, but they didn't seem to notice my presence.

A breeze filled with mountain air swirled around me. I had no coat. Would the guards think it strange to see a dressed-up lady heading for the stable? The surrounding walls were too steep to climb. I cursed the heels and the dress. My nails dug into the palms of my hands, and I cursed that too. What I needed was the Elders' magic to pick me up and carry me back underground.

Behind me, the giant oak doors squeaked open, bringing the music and the sound of the crowd outside momentarily before they were shut again. "Dominique? What are you doing out here?"

I whirled around so fast that I thought my dress was going to come undone. "Keegan."

His hair looked slightly frazzled. He must have weaved through dozens of ladies. "You left . . . I thought that . . ."

This was going to be harder than I thought. "I . . . just needed some fresh air. It was gettin' estuffy in dere."

He smiled and strolled towards me. The guards in the distance saluted him from afar; with the flick of his hand, Keegan acknowledged their gesture and waved them off. Part of me was relieved when they disappeared further into the garden. The other part of me wanted to sink into the ground.

"The musicians started to play something slower, and I wanted to see if you were up to the task," he said. His feet drifted through the grass like a slow, private dance meant to close the distance between us. The hair on my arm rose with goose prickles.

"I tink I've had enough dancin' pour tonight," I admitted. My feet agreed and ached for somewhere to sit down. The fountain had a ledge that circled it, but there was no way my dress would go for that, not without it tearing or getting wet.

I slipped one foot out of its heel and sunk my toes into the earth. The damp grass welcomed my skin. A small part of me was home again. My face coloured as I noticed him staring at my awkward lopsidedness.

"Sorry," I muttered. "I just . . ."

And then he was taking off his shoes too. He abandoned them in the flowers by the fountain. His toes were long and spindly, like little baby fingers. He wiggled them into the earth with mine. We were touching by proxy.

"You think my shoes aren't uncomfortable?" he said.

My smile turned into a grin as I expelled the other shoe out from under the canopy that was my dress. I flexed my toes and heaved a sigh of relief. If I had to run, I could do it now, but my feet were growing roots into the ground. Now I was at least a whole head shorter than him.

"You look exceptionally beautiful tonight," he ventured.

My heart fluttered, and I struggled to keep my face steady. "Tank j'ou."

It was a dance, but different than the one we had shared in the ballroom. Who could go the longest without saying what we wanted (and shouldn't, no I couldn't) to say. To stay or to go, to stay or to go? My bosom was heaving. The dress was too tight. I felt dizzy. Now I knew why the Marlenian girls carried fans.

"Dominique, there is something I have to say," Keegan said.

I froze. No, I couldn't let him, I couldn't let us happen.

"Never before have I met a girl . . . a woman . . . with such vigour, such life," he whispered. "Your spirit . . . it brings to life all the things that Marlenia truly—"

I shook my head. I could not let him go further with that thought. "We're . . . we're from two different worlds. I can't . . . I won't let it happen."

I started to move away, but he took my hand. "Dominique . . . please, don't leave . . ."

I couldn't let him see me cry. I squeezed my eyes shut. Remember the mission. Remember *my* mission.

"Stay with me," he whispered.

I refused to face him. "I y'am not who j'ou tink I y'am . . ."

"The court never allows a lady to reveal herself," Keegan replied. "Please . . . allow me to know you."

I didn't resist as he gently turned me around to face him. I opened my eyes. He moved my black locks of hair out of my face and brought his lips—the lips that I had once slashed—to mine. I took the scars into my mouth and moved my tongue gently over them, as if hoping to repair them and make them truly one with mine. They weren't Freetor, they weren't Marlenian, they were lips, and those lips belonged to me. And when we parted, it was like he had taken a piece of me with him.

"The Gathering is supposed to end in a few days," he said softly. "Please . . . stay longer."

My mind was mush. My lips moved without my consent. "Mhmm."

"Is that a yes?"

"J'es."

Keegan's eyes were sparkling fireflies that lit up his face. "Thank you," he whispered, taking my hands and kissing them. His lips sent shivers down my front.

I memorized every part of the moment—the gushing water of the fountain, the faint chirping of the crickets, the slight breeze from the south, the strings of the violins humming behind the giant oak doors behind Keegan, the feel of the cool earth beneath my toes, and the knowledge that beneath that was my home, and that together our toes were touching it. I sank into him and he wrapped his arms around me. Safe. I was safe.

I felt safe with a Marlenian.

"We've been gone a while," he said. "We should probably head back."

His words were warm on my ear, but I knew he was right. I nodded slowly and drew away from his comforting embrace.

The rest of the night was a blur. I remember putting my shoes back on, because the clacking sound of the heel on the granite floor was loud and I feared that somehow someone—the guards especially—would realize the treason the prince and I had committed just outside the hall. The music swept me into another dance with a Southern noble I didn't know, but my eyes always returned to Keegan. I was giddy. Advisor Ferguson had disappeared. Rordan was stuffing his face with food and appeared more relaxed when I flashed him a giant smile to let him know I was all right.

I was a sheep in the midst of tigers, and they didn't know the difference.

Slowly, effortlessly, the violins drew men and women together once more for a twirl around the room. The night would soon draw to a close, I sensed. Keegan's eyes found mine and we floated towards each other.

"Another dance, my lady?"

His voice was velvet.

"J'es, J'our Grace." The words tumbled out of me, and then I was in his arms again, swirling around the room . . .

. . . but looming above the dance floor, next to the Holy One's throne, the Advisor was surrounded by an entourage of guards, waiting to take me in with the slightest misstep. He hadn't left at all. He followed me around the room with his eyes. Watching.

"I should go," I whispered.

Before he could ask for an explanation, I slipped from Keegan's grasp and weaved between the happy couples. My heels barely touched the ground as I climbed the steps and fled through the ballroom door.

Several lords and ladies with lust in their eyes lingered in the corridor, fanning themselves. I pushed through them. I made a mental map in my head, thinking of the quickest and safest route back to my chamber, and followed it. My dress rustled, and I couldn't stop my shoes from making noise, so I tore them from my feet and padded the rest of the way back to the bed-chamber. There were more guards there than usual. The Advisor knew about me, that was why. Keegan's kiss was like armour, and because of that I kept walking. They nodded curtly in greeting, but they did not bar my path.

As my bedchamber door clicked shut, I slid down to the floor. Cold and hot flashes washed over me, like I was in a fever . . . maybe I was sick. I was sweating. I had to get out of this dress. Throwing my shoes in a dusty corner, I practically ripped open the bodice. Bidelia and the other servants weren't there to help me, and for once I was glad. If she were to see me like this, to know what I had done . . . what I had enjoyed doing . . .

When I was in my petticoat and undergarments alone, I climbed up onto the bed and retrieved my journal from its hiding place. If I could tell no soul the passion that had swept through me, then I would immortalize it forever in magic Freetor ink. Then, tomorrow, if I ever regained my senses, I could read it again and at least know that a part of me had known him.

I was so distracted that I barely heard the soft knock on the door. Then, suddenly, Keegan was there, opening the door, his face a tortured mirror of my own. My heart felt like it was going to explode out of my chest. I stuffed the journal under the mattress as he shut the door.

"What are j'ou doin' here?" I whispered, just as he said, "I'm sorry, Dominique, I had to see you."

My fingers wrapped around the bedpost. "If dey find j'ou here—"

"They won't," Keegan said. "The guards seem like they are swarming the castle, though. Three guarding your chamber alone. Do you want me to leave?"

"No," I breathed, even though all good sense screamed yes. Another hot flash washed over me, and tiny goose prickles appeared all over my skin. I realized that I was wearing almost nothing and shyly crossed my arms across my breasts. The Advisor had probably placed those guards there, to stop me from leaving. I bit my lip as my body warred with two strong, opposing emotions. "What did j'ou say to de guards? Are dey still dere?"

"I dismissed them. Their time would be better spent on the streets, or at the entrances, just in case the Freetors . . ." He trailed off, staring at me, as if my presence had caused him to forget his words. "It doesn't matter. If the ladies' whispers matter that much to you, I will dismiss everyone and anyone so that we can be alone."

To be alone with Keegan. My heart raced as he took my hands. Someone must have drugged me. I couldn't be feeling this way, but all I wanted was to be as close to him as possible, to take in the smell of his body and remain with him, to forget that he thought I was Dominique, daughter of the North, to forget that I was the Violet Fox, the reckless Freetor, and just have him know me, Kiera Driscoll.

"We are never alone," I whispered. "But . . .I don't tink it would matter, in any case."

And then the next thing I knew, his arms were around me again and he was kissing me. Softly at first, but then more urgently. I responded, my cheeks flushing. Some forgotten part of me knew I should stop, but she was lost in a sea of anxious passion. We fell together upon the bed, and the blankets tangled around us.

I fell asleep with his arm curled around my waist and his body curved with mine. In those precious moments I felt no regrets and surrendered to a sleep that already felt like a dream.

# Thirteen

I WOKE WITH a smile on my face. The memory of Keegan's lips on mine was fresh—it was as if he were kissing me now. I buried my face in the pillow, breathing in the smell of him.

"Good mornin'," I said.

There was no response. Maybe he was still sleeping. I rolled over and found myself on the other side of the bed.

He was gone.

I sat up and recalled the events of the previous evening. It had happened, hadn't it? Yes—my masquerade dress was lying in a heap on the floor, with the mask on top. But I was still wearing my petticoat—we hadn't done anything. If we had, I thought absently, that would've basically bound us together. Sleeping with someone made a real connection that Freetor families couldn't ignore, especially since it so commonly resulted in a child. It was easy for the Marlenians to have multiple lovers because of their access to medicines and remedies.

But he hadn't even tried anything. He hadn't even suggested it.

The bedroom door creaked open, and Bidelia slipped through. Her hair looked slightly frizzy, as if she'd been standing a long time in a place of high heat, a place like Keegan and I had been in when we were outside, wrapped in each other's arms . . .

"Kiera," she said.

I grinned. "Bidelia."

She slammed the door. "Good. You're here."

"Yeah. I am," I said, maybe too quickly.

She crossed the room and sat beside me on the bed. "I was worried. There were extra guards, you left the ball early . . ."

"Advisor Ferguson," I said quickly. "I think he knows that I'm a Freetor."

Bidelia's face turned a shade of grey. "Are you sure?"

I nodded. "We were dancing, and then he wouldn't let me go . . ."

And then Keegan had come . . . and he had kissed me . . .

She regarded me for a moment, as if gauging the truthfulness of my words. "Some of the servants saw you leave with Prince Keegan."

"I used him to get me out of there. Otherwise, I might be deep in the dungeons right now!"

The words hurt, but they were partially true. I fell into a day-dream where he was still here with me, and instead of in a bedroom, we were outside riding away from this place. Free. Bidelia might have been still talking, but she was moving towards the door again. Good. She was leaving.

She opened the door and Rordan burst in. He must have knocked. I hadn't heard a thing. I really had to pull myself together. All of our lives were at stake and I couldn't stop thinking about a boy! A Marlenian prince, no less.

"They want you at court," Rordan said while Bidelia shut the door.

"Me? Just me?" My voice felt small.

"Everyone. The Holy One is making some big announcement."

Moths fluttered in my stomach, beating their wings and unsettling my insides. "Do you know what it's about?"

Rordan shrugged. "Probably raising taxes or thanking everyone for attending the masquerade, some early wrap-up to the Gathering."

I was about to tell them how Keegan had asked me to stay longer when Bidelia said, "Kiera thinks that her position has been compromised."

My brother's eyes widened. "You were trying to tell me something last night when you were with the Advisor. That was it, wasn't it. But then—"

"Yes, that was it." I cut him off before Keegan's name could be mentioned so that I wouldn't become a smiling, dreaming fool. "He increased the guard. I almost didn't get away."

Rordan drew in a deep breath. His words seemed reluctant. "We should leave."

"We don't know what we're being gathered for," Bidelia replied. "We have to stay calm. If she's caught sneaking out, that only solidifies her guilt."

"She won't get caught. She is the Violet Fox."

"No. Right now she's Lady Dominique. And she isn't going anywhere, especially in these dresses."

I was torn. I wanted to agree with both of them for two conflicting reasons that were at war inside my heart.

"We'll attend court," I declared. "But near the back, in case we have to escape."

"If *you* have to escape. I am in too deep and have worked too hard to be compromised now," Bidelia said.

Rordan's face was grim, but he didn't protest. He wrapped his hand around the hilt of the blade. "I won't leave your side."

After he left, Bidelia helped me into court-worthy attire: a forest-green satin gown with a black-and-white bodice. She insisted my hair be up, but I argued that it should stay down. She didn't press it further—she just wanted to get me out. My hand glided over my curls, thinking of Keegan's touch. I wondered if I still smelled of him, and if she could smell him on me.

It was more than just the ladies and the lords and other nobles at court—the servants and the cooks and some well-dressed merchants were also in attendance. If the Advisor really was calling me out, it was going to be a public display for the rich elite. Rordan parted the crowd for me so that I could stand before the merchants but behind the rest of the nobles. He stepped into the rich satins and velvet coats, but he did not leave my line of sight—if he had to create a large distraction, he could do it in the middle of the crowd and give me time to escape. My hands were full of my dress, ready to lift my skirts and run if I had to.

On the raised platform that housed the thrones, Advisor Ferguson surveyed the crowd. I had escaped him last night, but today, he had the upper hand. When the Holy One crept from the curtain behind the thrones, Ferguson held out a hand. The Holy One waved him away, rejecting his help. I wondered if he suspected, as I did, that the Advisor had attempted to assassinate Keegan.

Keegan came next, and with him came the excitement of the ladies in the crowd. They cheered and whispered about how his formal, deep-blue tunic made his hair shine, about how baring his fresh stubble was a daring move for a seemingly important announcement but how it made him look even more handsome. Like a dashing rebel. His eyes swept the crowd, but he did not smile. My eyes begged for his attention. I didn't get it. Instead, he helped his father into his throne and then sat down in the smaller seat next to him.

The Holy One thumped his sceptre once on the wooden platform. The whispers and idle chatter ceased immediately. I was afraid to breathe it was so quiet.

"Ladies, gentlemen, nobles, and esteemed members of Marlenian society," the Holy One began in his powerful, melodic voice. "I thank you for gathering so early in the morning after so late a night. The masquerade was a roaring success, or so the Advisor has told me. Unlike you young people, I was unable to keep up and had to retire."

There were some polite, affectionate chuckles throughout the crowd.

"I have assembled you all here because I received some distressing news last night."

Wishing I could melt into the floor, I held my breath.

"It has come to the attention of the council that there has been increased Freetor activity around the castle," the Holy One continued. "Therefore, we will be doing random searches on the grounds to ensure that no Freetor is hiding in our midst." There was a rush of whispers from the foreign ladies, but the Holy One held up his sceptre. "Do not fear. If there is a Freetor in our midst, he or she will be caught quickly before any violence can come of it."

My heart thumped in my ears. No, I would not be caught quickly, like some animal. Your son kissed me and didn't know my lips from a Marlenian girl's.

Advisor Ferguson stared directly at me.

"Now that that unpleasantness has been dealt with . . ." His white moustache curled upward as he glanced at Keegan. "My son has an announcement."

The ladies around me burst into enthusiastic applause, but Keegan didn't stand up. He was shaking his head. "No, Father, I think it would be best if you made it."

Something wasn't right. I tried to catch Keegan's eye—*don't you remember what happened last night? We kissed and it was wonderful*—but his face was as unreadable as stone.

"Very well." The Holy One planted his sceptre on the wooden platform and used it to help him stand. Advisor Ferguson stood with his hands behind his back, watching him like a hawk watches his prey, waiting for that moment of weakness.

The Holy One cleared his throat. "We have been having the Gathering for many years now, and finally, my son is of marrying age."

Marrying age. Oh no.

"The future Holy One of Marlenia must have a strong wife. One who is devoted to the teachings of Dashiell, who represents the very pillars of our civilization. And I am happy to announce that this lady is here, in this room."

The ladies buzzed and squealed around me. My breath was catching. *Please be me. Please don't be me.*

"I am happy to announce the upcoming marriage of my son, Prince Keegan Tramore, to Lady Sylvia Frostfire, of Eastern Marlenia."

The heavy weight that was my heart fell to the floor. I couldn't pick it up in fear of giving myself away. The mission, everything I had worked for, seemed to spill, and I was the only one who noticed the mess. The ladies around Sylvia enveloped her with jealous congratulatory hugs and praise, but her eyes were on me. Smug. Satisfied. Like she'd *won*. Keegan's face revealed nothing. I had to pretend I was nothing again too.

"This union will unite the East and the West, forging a stronger bond within Marlenia so that we may fight our common foe," the Holy One continued. "The Freetors."

The crowd cheered and whooped. I clapped but inside I was scream-ing. He was with me last night. He said he wanted to be with me. And now, he was going to kill me.

"The Freetor population has increased, and even though they are rats, rats carry disease, and they continue to infect our people with their filth. High King Leszek Frostfire has agreed to send us troops to help rid us of this pestilence, in exchange for other goods we have acquired."

Other goods? What did they have—?

It hit me then. Alastar's Tome. They were going to trade Freetor magic for troops to exterminate us.

"Tonight, we will celebrate the engagement with a performance by our own city choir," the Holy One continued. "The marriage ceremony will take place in three days at the cathedral, as per tradition. We wait only for the arrival of High King Leszek Frostfire's caravan. Lords and ladies from afar are welcome to stay for the ceremony, and to celebrate afterwards. It will be the longest Gathering in the history of Marlenia!" He trailed off into a coughing fit. His breath was raspy, but he continued anyway. "We deeply apologize for the rushed nature of the wedding, but I am nothing if not a man of action. We will be able to celebrate more liberally when we are rid of the pestilence that plagues us."

Three days until the wedding. That was no time at all. No time to find Alastar's Tome. No time to reverse my feelings for Keegan. No time to reverse a wedding that could not, should not, take place.

People were dispersing. Some of the ladies gathered around the throne, dying to speak with Keegan. He nodded and thanked them for their congratulations but then disappeared behind the curtain. Bidelia and Rordan had vanished with the crowd. Maybe to deal with the increased Freetor activity. That was their mission—to deal with the details. My heart followed my feet as I crept by the ladies and down the corridor, following the castle walls, knowing the Keegan was just on the other side. If I did not talk to him soon, my knotted insides would burst.

A set of oak double doors met me a few minutes later. Captain Murdock stood guard. There were muffled voices on the other side—Keegan was in there, I knew it. Maybe the Advisor and the Holy One too. The council met in there. But Keegan would come out for me. After what happened last night, I would have done anything for him to leave that room. Part of me considered running back to my room and changing into my Violet Fox costume . . .

No. I was getting ahead of myself. My thumbnails created half-moons on my palm. The slight pain calmed me and kept me focussed on the task at hand.

Captain Murdock raised his eyebrows. "Something I can help you with, my lady?"

"I have to speak wit' de prince," I said. My voice felt uneven; unsteady. I felt like the world was spinning around me, yet I hadn't had any wine today.

"Afraid that's not possible, my lady," said Captain Murdock. "He is in a council meeting."

It was a struggle to keep my heart from leaping out of my chest. "When will he be out of de meetin'?"

"I don't know, my lady. I will tell the prince you wish an audience with him, and if he sees it fit, a page will send for you."

I wanted to say that no, Keegan could come to my room, but I made myself turn and walk away before I could get into any more trouble.

Maybe this marriage wasn't Keegan's idea. Lady Sylvia had bragged about "negotiations" days before, but I hadn't believed her. Obviously it was a strategic move, to unite the lands and fight the Freetors. Yes. This made me feel marginally better, but it complicated everything.

When I reached my quarters, there was a guard at my door. It wasn't the regular escort who had been assigned, and when he saw me approach, something lit up in his eyes—a look I recognized from the streets, meaning *you are not supposed to be here.*

"My lady," said the guard as he stepped in front of my door, barring my entry.

"What are j'ou doing? Let me pass," I demanded.

"I cannot do that, my lady."

"Why not?"

"Please, my lady, the search is routine. It will be over—"

Oh no. The thought of Advisor Ferguson dangling my Violet Fox mask as I burned in the public square turned my simmering rage into a furious fire. I pushed the guard aside and slammed into the door before he could recover. The door was unlocked, and I fell into a nightmare.

Guards—five of them—going through my suitcase. My drawers. The contents of the vanity were strewn about the floor like dead, crinkled autumn leaves, and my undergarments were littered on top of them. My breath caught. My mask. My cape! Nothing violet jumped out at me. My breath caught in my throat. Maybe Bidelia had beat them to it and hid it away, safe.

The Advisor looked almost surprised as I burst into the room. "Lady Dominique."

My hands balled into fists. I would fight him if I had to. "Get out of my room!"

"I will not play games with you, my lady. One of the books from my private collection is missing," he said. "And although the staff say it was checked out with the prince's permission, they also said you were with him. And I already know the prince doesn't have the tome."

I said nothing as my inner fear, shaped like hands with long fingers, tightened around my stomach.

"Might you know where it is?" he prompted.

But I had read that book, and it was nothing but myths and Marlenian fairy tales. It had been written by a Freetor Elder in magic Freetor runes, but other than that, what was so important about it? Frustration burned in my gut. I took a deep breath and spoke slowly. "Maybe if j'ou bot'er to clean de mess j'ou have made, j'ou may find it."

He scowled. "Then you admit it."

"I didn't admit anyt'in'."

"No? You did not take the book?"

I had to be careful here. Tons of people had already seen me with the book. "One of de servants must have seen it and returned it to de library. Perhaps de staff placed it in de wrong section. Is dat a crime? If so, it is not blood on my hands."

"That book was a Freetor artefact. Rare. It took me many years to track it down. I was . . . studying it," he said.

"Was it a Freetor artefact?" I asked, trying my best to replicate innocence—raised eyebrows, inclined like steep hills, parted lips, imploring eyes. "I only took it because it was de first book I saw when Prince Keegan invited me into de private collection."

The guards looked to Ferguson for confirmation, like obedient dogs to their masters, but the Advisor's eyes did not change. He could not be fooled like they could. He knew the truth about me.

As if my room were his territory, the Advisor sauntered to my bed-side. The hair on my arms stood on end. The journal my father had given me, the single most important thing I owned, lay exposed on the bed, as if someone had flipped through it and then abandoned it on the sheets. He grabbed it like it was any other book, and I found myself ready to tear into him.

"This looks old," he remarked, flipping it up and then down again. Cracking the spine, he laid it open flat on his palm.

"Dat's—!" *That is me, that is my father, my life.*

He flipped through the pages with a cocked eyebrow. Those sec-onds were the longest of my life. My fate seemed to hinge on how thoroughly he read the words meant only for my father's dead eyes.

"Your journal, it seems." His eyes flickered to mine.

I nodded slowly. Maybe I should have denied it. Could he tell that there was years of writing packed into such a small volume? Would the journal's magic prevent him from reading it? Would he be able to read the details of my adventures as the Violet Fox, of Rordan's encounter with the thief, of my mission here to retrieve the stolen tome? It was the proof he needed to convict me as the Violet Fox and have me burned.

My nerves were about to erupt inside me when there was an abrupt knock on my door. Both the Advisor and I said, "come in" at the same time. The door creaked open, revealing a timid page of about eight years. The Tramore crest was stitched onto his front.

"Advisor Ferguson. Your presence is requested outside at once!" the page said.

He let the book close and laid it on the bedspread. His fingers lingered on the worn leather cover. The page waited impatiently. Ferguson's eyes were angry fire as he crossed the room to leave.

"I will return, my lady," he said.

I remained frozen in the middle of the room until he and his guards were gone. He didn't take the journal, at least. Maybe he couldn't really read its true contents after all. Or maybe he wanted to lure me into thinking I was safe.

I stood there for another five minutes, just to be certain I was alone. The longer I stayed, though, the less time I had to escape. I could no longer stay in the castle. My name would not be cleared, not with what Advisor Ferguson suspected.

Rordan could get me out of the castle. He was the only one who knew our escape route, our safe points, and the current Freetor passwords to the Undercity. I tore off my gown, slipped into a more conservative dress, and looked around for my flat shoes. They were nowhere in sight.

Flipping over the mattress, I found my dagger wedged between the baseboards. The blade was cold, but it was still sharp and hungry for blood. I strapped it around my thigh. I had to be prepared to attack and run, but I had to get to Rordan quickly. My heels would have to do, since I couldn't find my flats. I would abandon them later, I decided. My feet were calloused enough to provide support if they had to.

I stepped out of my chamber. The guards that had been swarming the corridor before had vanished. As I made my way towards the servant staircase, towards the wing where the lesser nobles slept, I tried to recall Rordan's schedule for today and realized I had no idea where he would be. Rordan always came to me. He was always there when I needed him.

Except now.

I made my way to the southern part of the castle and climbed the twisting servants' staircase. A small window let sunlight into the dark staircase and revealed a large balcony, which overlooked the hedge maze and the stable, on the next floor. If I could get up there, I could look to see if he was outside and survey the area before exiting the castle.

My heels scraped against the stone as I climbed. There might not be time to see Keegan before I escaped. Maybe he didn't want to see me.

He said he wanted to know me.

Lies. They were lies.

But maybe I wanted to stay and know him.

"No," I whispered to my thoughts, as if hearing my own voice would calm them.

It wasn't fair. The one man who takes the time to respect me had no idea who I was. Had chosen another over me. Hated my true identity.

I shook my head. I had to stop thinking like this. I had to get Keegan out of my mind and focus my wits, or Rordan and I would end up dead.

At the top of the stairs I met two servant girls carrying fresh loads of laundry, followed by Bidelia. She stopped lecturing them about having clean hands when she saw me rushing past them.

"My lady!" Bidelia called after me.

Her shouts were like an annoying buzzing bee hovering around my ear. I didn't have time to explain—I'd have to get someone to relay the message to her later about sending my Freetor belongings back underground, especially my journal.

The double doors to the balcony were already open and chilled the short corridor. I shivered as I stepped into the clouded sunshine. A crowd of soldiers—including Captain Murdock, who was barking orders to the lot of them, gathered around something, no, some*one* . . .

"That's right, you wretched lot. You might've fooled the lady, but not us," the captain said, patting his belly triumphantly.

I carefully stepped closer and strained to see whom they had caught. I grasped the balcony railing for support as Rordan's grey eyes peered between the guards. He wasn't wearing his Northern Marlenia getup—he was dressed in Freetor rags. He locked his gaze on mine as he continued to struggle, but half-heartedly.

There was only one reason he would deliberately dress in Freetor rags in the castle.

He wanted to be caught.

He had surrendered to protect me.

"What is de meanin' of dis?" I demanded.

The guards whipped their heads around, and Captain Murdock looked startled. "My lady—"

"Dis man is in my employ," I said, pointing fervently to Rordan. "Release him at once!"

The captain looked apologetic. "Sorry to inform you, my lady, that this man is a Freetor."

I tried to act surprised. "Well, if dis is true, den I would like to purchase him. He can continue to work in de stable."

"I'm afraid that's not possible, my lady. We caught him sneaking a bag filled with stolen resources out of the castle. We chased him here. Tell me, my lady, did you ever suspect this man to be a Freetor?"

The balcony wrapped around this side of the castle. I noticed a strewn sown-together bag abandoned a few stone-throws away. Rordan must have entered the balcony at some other point, ran towards this spot and dropped the bag. There were apples and wrapped up pies and pastries rolling listlessly with the wind around the guards' feet, but there was something else sticking out from the bag. Bricks of clay, it looked like. Food, I could understand, but what would Rordan need red clay for?

I drew in a deep breath. Rordan's eyes were my strength. We'd practiced this scenario a dozen times last week. But to say the words, to disown my brother...

"He joined de caravan just as we were leavin' de Nort'," I said, keeping my tone even. "He had an official letter, wit' my fat'er's wax seal on it, indicatin' dat he was to join my party and keep an eye on me."

"And do you have this official letter?"

"No, I did not pay it mind. De rest of my escort checked him out, and dat was good enough pour me."

"We'll have to question them, too," Captain Murdock said. "But we've caught the Freetor scum, my lady. There's nothing to worry about. The castle's safe again."

Rordan chanced a glance at me. I knew my brother's face; I could read it as plainly as I could read the written word. *Don't do anything*, he said. *Pretend I am nothing.*

"Where will de prisoner be held?" I asked.

"The Advisor's orders are to take him to the dungeon," Captain Murdock replied. "He will be kept there until his fate is decided."

Until he rots and dies there, he meant. Or, until he was killed for his "crimes" against the Marlenians. On the Advisor's order. He knew to go directly for Rordan to cover for his failed assassination, and Rordan was willing to give himself up to protect my position, so that I could finish the mission. Rordan, how could you do this . . . ?

"I see." It was hard to feign disinterest when my mind churned with questions and my heart was ready to explode.

The guard who held Rordan twisted his arm so far behind his back I thought I heard a crack. I winced. Captain Murdock seemed to notice my discomfort. "There is nothing to fear, my lady. Come lads, let's take this one away so we don't spoil the good lady's eyes n'more."

I was about to speak up when familiar footsteps broke my conversation. A voice I both loathed and longed for cut through the silence. "My lady."

Keegan approached me and stood so close that I thought he might take me into his arms as he had the previous night. It would be so easy to forget everything that way. But I didn't take my gaze off Rordan as his pleading eyes told me to stay in character.

"You wanted to see me, Dominique?" Keegan asked.

My heart thumped hard against my rib cage as I watched them drag my brother away.

"Dominique?" Keegan prompted.

"J'es," I said. I forced my attention away from Rordan and the guards. Lady Dominique would not care about the fate of her brother. She would probably be happy if he died, because then she would inherit her father's seat in the North. The thought of me returning to our underground cavern alone made me feel sick to my stomach. I would not leave this castle without him.

Keegan and I were alone for the first time since last night. He reached for my hands, and I didn't resist as he brought them to his lips, squeezing tightly as if he were afraid that I would fly away. The emotionless young man that I had seen in the throne room was gone.

"I'm so sorry, Dominique." His voice was barely a whisper. "They only told me this morning that my father and Advisor Ferguson had finished the negotiations with the East. I didn't know that they were this far along. I would have intervened earlier, I swear it. When I told Advisor Ferguson this morning that I was going to refuse the offer in favour of you and the North, he wouldn't have it. Both he and my father think that Sylvia is a better match."

Marlenian politics were the last thing on my mind. All I wanted was to curl up with Keegan again and have my brother safe in the Undercity.

"What happened last night . . . I wish it could happen every day. Every night." His cheeks coloured. "I meant every word I said. Sylvia may be the best match politically, but I could never feel for her what I do for you. My father waited and married for love, and I knew that I would do the same. I am fortunate in that I did not have to wait long in life. I want to be with you, Dominique."

I closed my eyes to keep the tears in.

"I . . . I have somet'in' I need to ask of j'ou," I said.

"Anything. I'm going to tell Lady Sylvia that Advisor Ferguson and my father do not represent my wishes, and that it will be you in the cathedral, not her."

I shook my head. A small voice inside me said yes, this is the way it should be, but my forbidden, impossible dreams had to stay buried within me. Every word he spoke made it harder. "De man dat was just captured. I need j'ou to free him."

Keegan was taken aback. That wasn't what he was expecting to hear, that was clear. His hands slowly dropped mine. "Free him? Dominique . . ."

"Please, Keegan." I turned away and leaned against the balcony. My hands were shaking so badly that I gripped the railing to steady them.

I expected a reassuring hand around my waist, or in my hair, or at least the warmth of his body to comfort me, but there was only the stiff wind coming from the mountains in the distance.

"I thought so, but I didn't want it to be true. You love him."

The yes almost escaped me. To claim Rordan as my lover would be the easy way out. But it would make his looming death a horrible lie. Lady Dominique was not a Freetor sympathizer, though. Kiera Driscoll, the Violet Fox was.

"J'ou have to help him, Keegan," was all I could say.

He sauntered towards the railing, but he did not reach for me.

"This is why I didn't fight harder against my father's choice," he said quietly. "I cannot be involved with your . . . obsession with the Freetors. It is too dangerous. You could be killed, or disowned for this sort of treason."

"None of dat matters!" I shouted. My voice carried over the mountains and through the castle. My cheeks were wet with tears. "If he dies . . . he's de only . . ." My sobs obscured the rest of my truths.

"I thought what we shared was special," Keegan said.

It was, it was, it was. My lips formed these words but my voice would not betray me. "I have to do what is right in my heart."

My words were arrows, wounding him with each syllable. I could see the pain on his face as his brow wrinkled. He couldn't hide it from me, not from someone who had spent her whole life studying faces because her life depended on it.

He looked over the posterior bailey, over the hedge maze and the open plains and forests that touched the horizon of mountains. His knuckles hardened and grew white from gripping the banister. "What you ask of me is not right in my heart."

Then don't marry Sylvia, I thought.

"But I will do it . . . for you," he finished. "If I can. My father may not listen to me. Advisor Ferguson will think me foolish. So I will do what I can." His eyes were soft, like they had been on that night in the garden, but his face was hard like the castle walls. "And then we will be even."

I nodded curtly. I felt sick to my stomach. "Even."

He turned to leave. "Were you planning on staying for the wedding ceremony?"

Three days. That's all I had until the magic was handed over to the Eastern Marlenians. "J'es."

"I see." His tone implied I should leave. But if he actually said the words, if I was denied my invitation . . .

I couldn't be kicked out of the castle. Not before my brother was saved. Not before I could retrieve Alastar's Tome.

Not before this swirling lovesickness in my stomach was resolved.

"I'm stayin' because I do not want any hard feelin's between us," I said. It was hard to keep the desperation out of my voice. "I can't go home knowin' dat j'ou hate me."

The hesitation on his face was plain. For a moment I wondered if he would forget his engagement and sweep me off my feet, and carry me away. But no. He nodded slowly and then left me alone on the balcony with my lies and half-truths.

*\* \* \**

I didn't sleep that night. My thoughts were with Rordan in the dungeon. I lay in bed, desperately hoping for Keegan to burst into my chamber and declare that my brother had been released and that he had forsaken the throne to be with me.

The sun came up and slowly blinded me. My mind screamed for sleep but my eyes would not close. It was torture. I counted to three a hundred times before I had the will to sit up, and by that time Bidelia was already in the room.

"Any word?" I demanded. My voice felt dry.

"He is still locked away," she replied, setting the tray of breakfast fruits on the corner of my bed.

"I . . . I asked Keegan if he could do anything . . ."

Bidelia threw me a glance but said nothing.

"I hope he does. I hope—"

"You could stop hoping and put on that Violet Fox cape I know you have."

As if I hadn't thought of that a hundred times last night. When I'd returned to my room, everything that Advisor Ferguson had strewn around was back where it belonged. The Violet Fox cape and mask and a fresh pair of breeches and a white tunic were under my mattress. Bidelia only wanted to help me, I knew. I had turned over the entire scenario in my mind already, and every situation ended with either Rordan or me or both of us being slaughtered.

I propped up the pillows against the hard baseboard. Bidelia laid the tray across my lap, trapping me in bed. Blueberries and blackberries strewn over lumpy yoghurt, a piece of crispy but bland bread smothered in butter, and an elderberry tea—a breakfast that was supposed to be worthy of Marlenian nobility. Rordan would be eating nothing. My stomach refused to eat because of the thought.

"Two more Elders were found murdered this morning," Bidelia said as she poured the tea.

My eyes flickered up to her face. "Two more since yesterday?"

"Yes."

Bidelia set the cream back on the tray and went about picking up stray articles of clothing off the floor.

"How can you say it like that? Like it's nothing. Like it's normal."

"An Elder has been found dead almost every day for the past week, Kiera. Of course I am concerned. But I must continue doing my part. Just like you."

I set aside the tray, got up, and paced the room. "There's nothing I can do right now. The Advisor is on to me. Alastar's Tome could be anywhere. And Rordan . . ."

"Rordan is doing his part, too." She gestured to the door. "You'd better prepare for court."

Her words were of little comfort.

Rordan's fate and my feelings for Keegan and my fear for my people twisted within me, but my stride was steady as I marched to the throne room. I was met by a lively, festive crowd waving handkerchiefs and flags bearing the Tramore family crest. I squeezed my way into the room, which was packed with nobles and castle servants alike. I found a place next to Lady Milda.

"What's goin' on?" I whispered.

She looked at me like I'd just crawled out of a Freetor tunnel. "The parade. You know . . . when the prince leads his bride into the Grand Square to show the people their new future queen . . ."

My breath caught. "No . . ."

I pushed my way through the cheering nobles and stumbled into the open. Sylvia waddled slowly down the hallway in a giant yellow-and-red dress that lifted her bosom and extended it at least two hands from her waist. She waved at her future subjects and squealed at the attention. Keegan's blue cape billowed behind him as the doors farther down opened, letting in a sharp, cold gust of wind. His curls were swept back behind his ears, but one or two dangled before his eyes. My heart yearned for him. Sylvia was too busy basking in the glory of her prize to see me at first, but Keegan turned his head just as I caught his arm.

"Dominique. What . . . ?"

"Keegan. J'ou know what."

The cheering subsided. Lady Sylvia stared daggers at me and tugged on Keegan's other arm, attempting to pull him further down the hall.

"Tell her to get out of here," Sylvia hissed.

I ignored Sylvia. "Did j'ou . . . I mean, were j'ou able to . . . ?"

The sadness in his eyes told me the answer before his voice. "I'm sorry, Dominique. There was nothing I could do."

"What do j'ou mean?" I exclaimed.

He wrenched free of my grip and started down the corridor. Now he was dragging Sylvia and not the other way around. "Everything has already been arranged. My father could not be swayed."

"But he's my—"

There was no background noise now. You could hear a needle if it dropped, it was so silent. I realized the court probably thought we were talking about our relationship, not Rordan's execution. Everyone had seen us dance at the masquerade and knew that we had left early together. This only made me feel worse.

Keegan showed no sympathy. "I do not wish to discuss this further."

His footsteps echoed as he ventured further down the corridor. Sylvia moved with him, whispering comforting lies in his ear, and I did everything but sink to the floor. I was nothing but a filthy traitor to him now.

My brother was going to die. And Keegan was going to marry Sylvia. And there was nothing I could do to stop either.

I stormed back in the direction I had come from, the nobles' whispers following me. My mind swirled with possible plans, but each one ended with my death or Rordan's. Alastar's Tome—that was what was important, but I couldn't go back to the underground without Rordan. He was all I had.

It was a martyr's death, I told myself. I picked up the pace as I found myself wandering towards the place where I knew I should not go—the dungeons. The southwest part of the castle was colder, damper. Goose prickles sprouted all over my arms.

I had to see him one last time. I owed him that. I owed him everything. He had raised me, taught me everything I knew. If he hadn't been there, I would've been dead a hundred times over. There wouldn't have been a Violet Fox, and my people would've been worse off. My pace slowed as two guards passed and regarded me suspiciously—no noble ventured this way, I knew.

The closer I got to the dungeons, the colder the air was. I walked through a cloud of my own breath. Just one more corner and there would be a gate with at least one guard. I focussed on all the warm thoughts I had: the spot of sunlight in the Great Cavern, the times when Rordan had given me his sleeping blanket when the ground froze, the fire he'd made in our cavern for the neighbours when we'd been gifted a supply of kindling, Keegan's lips on mine . . .

"There she is."

I whirled around to see Advisor Ferguson and five guards. None of them had drawn their weapons, but they looked ready to pounce.

"You created quite a stir with the prince," the Advisor said. "Come, Lady Dominique, allow us to escort you back to your chamber."

He was just trying to keep me from exposing the truth: he had tried to assassinate Prince Keegan. "No!"

Advisor Ferguson nodded to the guards. "Easy, my lady. No one means you any harm. We are just trying to help."

Help kill my people, he meant. Help kill Prince Keegan. I backed away. As I turned to escape, I saw more guards behind me. It wasn't the first time I'd been surrounded by Marlenian guards, though. I still had a chance.

I ducked beneath their arms, but two of them accidentally stepped on my dress, tearing the hem to shreds. I was thrown off balance. Before I could hit the floor, the guards caught me by the arms and held me gently as I kicked and screamed, scratching any who neared. If my heels hadn't been so glued to my feet, I might have lost them and been able to make a getaway. The guards had their iron grip on me now. I closed my eyes and thought, *my face, don't let them take your mask!* before remembering that I wasn't wearing one.

"Set her down!" the Advisor commanded.

The guards gently set me on my feet, but their hands were still around my biceps. Their grip was not as rough as when I was the Violet Fox, but it was their grip nonetheless.

"You are not in your right mind now, my lady," he said, not unkindly. "We will escort you back to your quarters before this reaches the other ladies' ears."

I didn't have a choice. The guards guided me through the castle, but Advisor Ferguson did as he promised. He took an obscure route through the scholars' wing, avoiding the servant passageways. Then he looped around back to the west wing, where my chamber was. He didn't speak the whole time, but he cast glances my way, ensuring that I stayed in line with the marching boots of the Marlenian castle guard. Every corner, every juncture, I calculated an escape plan, but Ferguson's eyes never left me, and the guards' grip tightened at my every thought of running away.

When we reached my chamber, I slowed my walk. The two guards holding me dragged me to the door. I lost my footing again as the Advisor produced a key, unlocked my chamber door—he had a key to my private space!—and threw it open. There were no servants around. No Freetor eyes to see this. Just me, the Advisor, and his muscle.

The guards tossed me into the room. With one swift motion, I tore off my right heel, chucked it at them, and charged the door. They pulled it shut. I tucked on the handle, but seven against one? I was horribly outnumbered. As the lock clicked shut, I noticed that the keyhole on my side of the door had been filled in with some sort of metal. It was still warm to the touch.

"Let me out!" I pounded on the door. "J'ou will pay pour dis!"

"We will let you out tomorrow morning so that you can attend the public burning of the captured Freetor, if that is what you so desire." Ferguson's voice was muffled from behind the door. "But I believe it is best for both you and the other guests if you stay put."

He didn't want me to interfere. He couldn't have me going around the castle as the Violet Fox and saving my brother—if he even knew that Rordan was my brother, and not just another cohort. I ran to the window, but it was glued shut. I threw my other shoe at it but it barely made a dent. I squinted: the glass emitted a faint, blue glow. Freetor magic. Used against me. By a scheming Marlenian.

I was trapped.

I wanted to burst into tears, but I was so angry that I only slammed the door harder, and even when my fists started to bleed and get splinters, I didn't stop. "Please, j'ou have to let me out."

"Your day will come," he said.

I screamed and pounded and shouted some more until I realized there was no point. He was gone.

Rordan was going to die.

\* \* \*

The wooden pole stretched to the sky and, like me, yearned for freedom.

Hay was already stacked beneath the stage, and guards with blank faces added to the pile like worker ants who obeyed no one but their queen. Their future queen was nearby with her entourage, even though the nobles were not required to attend the burning. They had taken the opportunity to dress in fiery orange, as if this were a festive occasion. It filled me with rage that they didn't want to take a stand against the ancient act of cruelty.

Keegan was there, but I couldn't bring myself to look at him. He and the Advisor and the Holy One sat on portable thrones on the steps of the cathedral. I was barely a stone-throw away, standing with the seven other noblewomen and noblemen who had decided to attend.

Advisor Ferguson and his guards—a smaller force than yesterday—had fetched me that morning. I had expected Bidelia and her servants to bring me breakfast, but the Advisor had taken care of that as well. No contact with Freetors, servants, or slaves. Would Bidelia be safe?

The thought of her curmudgeonly face burning after her long years of service to the Marlenians and the Freetor underground made me numb. The Marlenians would kill anyone who defied them.

I chose flat shoes and the darkest dress I had in the wardrobe and then the Advisor's men escorted me to the cathedral square. There had to be someone who could help.

But so far, no one.

The prisoner's carriage moved through the thick crowd. It had no windows, just one door. Even the horses didn't scare the people into budging—soldiers walked before the carriage, waving their swords to split the crowd. It seemed like all of Marlenia City had come to the square to watch my brother burn. The Marlenian people wouldn't miss the burning of a Freetor, and the Marlenian nobility wouldn't miss a chance to promote the burning of a Freetor whom their guards had caught in the castle.

The carriage stopped before the pyre. The guards pushed the peasants out of their way and threw open the carriage door. I strained to see as the crowd pushed back against the carriage, threatening to swallow it whole in its sheer mass. The guards reached in and yanked him from the carriage's belly. The peasants who hadn't been scared away by the guards raked their fingernails across his flesh and shouted profanities at him. He'd only been in the dungeons for a day, but he looked like he'd been there for months. His clothes—what remained of them—were hanging off him in stringy rags and covered in black soot. The wound on his chest looked angrier today than it had on the day I'd sewn it up.

"You don't own me!" he spat.

The crowd laughed at his defiance, and some threw rotten tomatoes at him. The splattering of the fruit on his chest highlighted his scar. Fight back, I wanted to scream. He could fight them. Now was the time for escape.

But he didn't.

Rordan scanned the crowd. Looking for me. A sob caught in my throat. I wondered how many Freetors were in the crowd right now, dressed in dirty merchants' robes, planning their revenge. A flicker of hope swelled into a hopeless desire for the Elders to intervene. They would save him with their magic, wouldn't they? That was what it was for. To protect the Freetors from the evils of the Marlenians.

As they dragged him up the pyre steps, each thunk—the sound of his knees against the hard wood—seemed to throw the crowd into more of a frenzy. Even the nobles around me, as restrained as they were, made jokes about him being dead already and about how there was no point to his passive resistance.

One guard shoved him against the pole, and two others held him in place. Rordan spat in their faces—the crowd cheered and gasped and clambered for his immediate death. Thick rope lay coiled at the guards' feet; one of them picked it up and wrapped it multiple times around Rordan's body. Now is your time to escape, I thought. Now was the time for the Elders to jump from the shadows and rescue him, as I could not. Surely they knew I could not. Surely they cared enough for one man who had served them well . . .

Behind me, Advisor Ferguson helped the Holy One to his feet. The wild crowd hushed to a whisper as his voice boomed over the square.

"This Freetor has confessed to crimes against the divine province of Western Marlenia," the Holy One thundered. "For his crimes, he will burn in Dashiell's holy fire until he is forgiven."

He would burn until he was dead, he meant, but the people didn't care either way. They cheered and started chanting: *Burn him! Burn him! Burn him!*

With only a nod from the Holy One, the "holy fire" was released. The man carrying the special torch exited the cathedral behind me and descended the steps, but not before kneeling before the Holy One to receive his blessing. Two guards, dressed in white and blue, flanked the man with the fire. This time the crowd did move but continued chanting. The Marlenian people might have lost their faith long ago, but they would not dare touch the holy fire that would spark their entertainment for the day.

The fire man ascended the pyre steps. With each step, I prayed for someone to intervene. The Elders. Laoise. I even prayed that I would somehow intervene—that my cloak and mask had been hidden beneath my dress the entire time and I'd rip off my gown and leap from the stairs to save my brother.

But that didn't happen.

Tilting the torch down to the hay, the crowd begged the man to start the fire. Rordan was sweating. I could see it even from where I was. His lips moved. He was muttering something, but what it was, I'd never know.

The flames could hold back no longer. They lashed out at the hay and caught hold, spreading from bushel to bushel around the pole. The flames licked the hay and devoured it hungrily, rising up to engulf my brother's coughing form. Dark smoke encircled him like a snake coiling around its breakfast, squeezing the life out of it. He coughed and sputtered and tried to kneel, but his bonds held him firm. Surely they would cut him down. The Elders would step out at any moment and strip the robes and he would be free to breathe again.

His screams pierced the silence. He called for our mother and father to save him, for the Elders, and even for Laoise.

He screamed my name, too. It was a twisted sound, his last breath escaping his frail body in a swirl of smoke and broken promises. He was supposed to protect me. I was supposed to save him.

Even from where I was standing, the heat was overwhelming. Three tears escaped from my controlled eyes, but they dried the moment they touched my cheeks. To cry meant my life was over. I had to get out of here. I couldn't watch.

No. Lady Dominique wouldn't look away. The Violet Fox would face the flames with bravery and laugh at the heat. I would remain quiet. I would not look away.

# Fourteen

RORDAN'S REMAINS WERE treated like hearth ash from a local tavern. What was left of him was scattered in the streets and on the steps of the cathedral, only to be swept away by Marlenian servants. The rest took to the air with a violent breeze and flew over the wall, or so I desperately hoped. And the Marlenians continued like nothing had happened, as if there wasn't a burnt pole still standing in the Grand Square as a warning to Freetors who dared oppose the Holy One's will.

It was like he had never existed at all.

Inside, I felt hollow. Crippled. I was the only one of my bloodline left. It was my responsibility to carry our family name, our legacy, our struggle against the Marlenians. The one person who had cared for me was gone, and I had stood before the cathedral in the Grand Square and let him die. The Marlenians could pretend that nothing had happened, but that was one thing I couldn't bring myself to pretend. My brother had been murdered.

All because of me.

I sobbed silently all night into my pillow, and when I crawled out of bed at morning's light, my face was swollen and red. I couldn't go out there like this. I had to pretend I didn't care.

I broke down again at the dresser, tearing at my hair and screaming at my reflection. Rordan was gone. Even though I had hated when he told me what to do, at least he had been there, guiding me, stopping me from doing anything rash when I was angry.

Now I only had my wits to stop me from going to the throne room and tearing the Advisor's throat out.

Bidelia brought me breakfast. She set the tray on my bed and hugged me. Her lips trembled but she stayed strong.

"He was a good lad," she whispered.

"It's my fault," I sobbed in her shoulder.

She drew me away to arm's length. "No, Kiera. You mustn't think like that."

"If I hadn't been sneaking around . . ."

Bidelia's look was stern. "Yes, but that was your duty. Rordan understood that, even in death."

"He . . . he died for me. It should've been me." I turned away from Bidelia and wrapped myself around the bedpost. "Maybe I should go confess."

"You want to go tell the Holy One that you're a Freetor?"

I sniffed and nodded. "It's the right thing—"

"Don't be ridiculous!" Bidelia snapped. "Rordan died to keep your cover safe. Do you want his death to mean nothing?"

"I just want to be done with this," I said.

"You can be done. Stop fraternizing with Keegan and find the tome."

It was a low blow, and she knew it. I wanted to crawl back into bed and close my eyes. Maybe I would wake up again in my cavern underground and find that the past two weeks had all been a dream, and Rordan would be there, and I would laugh and tell him how I got to dress up as a princess. He would make a joke about the dress, and then we would go back to stealing apples and bread from the merchants on the surface.

When I didn't say anything, Bidelia moved the breakfast tray from my bed to my dresser. "Eat something, Kiera. I'll be back in ten minutes with servants to help you get dressed. You have a meeting today."

I scoffed. "With who?"

"Elder Erskina."

My eyes snapped to hers. "Erskina? But . . . but . . . how?"

"You'll see. Clean yourself up and eat something, and I'll be back."

She left before I could ask any more questions. Rordan's death and Keegan's choices weighed on me, but I knew Bidelia was right. I had to focus on the mission. Rordan would've wanted me to continue. It hurt to think his name.

I stuffed the breakfast berries in my mouth and forced myself to chew and swallow. I never thought I would have to force myself to eat something and have it taste so bland. It was like there was some other me standing in front of the dresser, especially when Bidelia returned with two Marlenian servants to lace me into my apparel for the day. One of them had suggested a dark pink, but Bidelia dismissed it, probably because it would've brought out my puffed-out cheeks and eyes and nose. She chose instead a dress coloured deep blue. It was straight laced and had no poof at all—at least there was that. I figured this meant I was going somewhere where poof was impractical. I wondered if I would be squeezing through any trap doors.

The person who navigated through the castle corridors and stepped into the waiting carriage in the courtyard was not me. I was there, hovering in the distance, watching this shell of a person with no emotions go through the motions. Even the bouncing carriage ride couldn't shake the feeling that I was holding on by string thinner than a strand of hair. The physical, present part of me wondered where we were headed. Far and away, though, this seemed like a trivial thing to be worried about.

The carriage stopped briefly, and the curtain door fluttered in the wind. I shivered. Maybe we should have taken one of the castle carriages, the ones with doors. For once, I missed the poofy dresses. At least they kept me warm.

"Kiera. You're looking well."

It was like she had been sitting there all along. Elder Erskina's grey wool robe melded into the fabric of the seat like smoke into a cloudy sky. When another breeze whipped the blanket door to do its bidding and sent chills through my arms and legs, the wisps of loose hair in Erskina's bun did not stir.

I didn't know how I was supposed to bow inside the carriage, so I inclined my head. "Elder Erskina. I'm so honoured that you would come to see me. I didn't notice—"

"Our power allows us to travel unnoticed." She smiled thinly, creating more wrinkles on her ancient face. "My condolences on your loss. Rordan died fighting. His service will never be forgotten in the hearts of Freetors everywhere."

"Thank you, Elder," I said quietly.

"You are angry. Confused. That is natural."

I sighed and shook my head. "I just don't know what to do. I feel like Alastar's Tome is within reach, but—"

"I only bring more grave news for you," she interrupted. "One of our envoys has reported that a page travelling with the real Lady Dominique managed to escape our ambush. He's making his way through the wilderness and should be at the castle within days."

My jaw dropped. "How didn't we know this before? This happened like, two weeks ago."

"Sometimes details slip through the cracks. I am displeased, to say the least." Her lip curled. "We have scouts looking for him now. Perhaps it will be nothing to worry about—Northern pages know nothing about the Western landscape and much less about surviving in it."

"But Lady Dominique told me about the harsh weather and terrain in the North. Maybe he's better equipped than we think he is."

"In that case, we must act sooner than we originally planned. Tell me everything you have learned so far."

"Advisor Ferguson definitely has Alastar's Tome. The Holy One said they're allying with the East. I think they're going to trade Freetor magic for troops." I thought of Keegan and Sylvia's looming marriage but quickly pushed it out of my mind. Erskina must not know my feelings about that. "But I haven't been able to get close enough to find Alastar's Tome. Too many guards, and there are even more now that Rordan . . ." I closed my eyes as my grief welled there. There was a lump in my throat that wouldn't go away.

"Your brother was murdered in front of thousands of Marlenians. To try to save him would have been foolish. But now it is our move, and we will show them that the Freetors are not to be trifled with," Erskina said.

"What are we going to do?" I asked.

"There is one solution that will allow us to retrieve Alastar's Tome and exact revenge for your brother. You do want revenge for your brother's death, don't you?"

I looked up at her. "Yes, I do."

Erskina smiled. "A heart for a heart, then. The Holy One has taken away our son, and you will take away his. You will kill Prince Keegan."

My eyes widened. My heart froze in my chest. I could barely breathe. "What?"

"If the tome is with Advisor Ferguson, as you say, and the Crown is going to use it against us by allying with Eastern Marlenia, then we must strike the Holy One where he is vulnerable. A funeral will delay the war and give you more time to search the castle and gain the Advisor's trust."

"The Advisor is the one who suspects me!" I exclaimed. "He knows I'm a Freetor. If Rordan hadn't been caught, I would have burned instead of him! Why can't I kill him?"

Her smile was sickly sweet now. "Do not worry about the Advisor. I have plans for him."

I shook my head. "Elder Erskina. He's dangerous. If we told Keegan about how he's going to take over the throne, I bet—"

Erskina laughed. "You think he has feelings for you, don't you?" I fell silent. "Kiera. I should have known you would fall under his charm. You are young, and free-spirited, but naive of the surface world. No Marlenians, Prince Keegan and the Holy One included, truly love their women. Women are objects to them. Pawns in a game to win more land and more wealth."

"But . . . I don't think that's true."

The Elder's light demeanour vanished as quickly as it had come. The carriage suddenly felt a lot colder. "Are you . . . defending . . . the Marlenian prince, Kiera?"

"Well . . . uh . . . no," I stuttered. "But . . . "

"That would be treason," she continued. "You haven't become the Marlenian you are pretending to be, have you?"

"No, of course not . . ."

"Because that has happened in the past. And we are not forgiving of those Freetors who forget their roots."

The carriage bumped along the dirt road while Erskina's words hung in the air like thick clouds threatening to choke me. I pursed my lips. "What do you want me to do?"

Without taking her penetrating gaze off me, Erskina revealed a hidden fold in her robe and produced a dagger. The edges of the blade were jagged and engraved with glowing magical Freetor runes. I could see my unsure reflection in the blade.

"Take this," she said. "It has been infused with anger in your brother's blood and powered with Freetor magic. It will only harm Prince Keegan."

I could hear my heart pounding. My brother's blood, in this blade? But how? Erskina only smiled. Freetors were everywhere. One of them could've easily clawed blood from him as he'd walked through the crowd up to the pyre where he'd burned. The knife felt heavy in my shaking hands.

"I . . . I don't . . ." I wet my lips. I couldn't lie to her. "I can't do this. I think I love—"

Before I could complete my treason and let out the terrible secret that weighed on my heart, Erskina's hands were around my neck. Agility and strength defied her leathery skin and frail appearance as she practically sat on top of me, squeezing my windpipe shut. I flailed and tried to part the curtain to get the drivers' attention, but the fabric was as stiff as wood.

"Don't." Her voice was as tight as her grip. "You will do your duty or face your brother's fate."

I was seeing dark spots. The more I resisted, the tighter she squeezed. It felt like a snake, not her wiry fingers, was coiling around my neck. Her hands were as hard as stone and just as cold. The magic knife fell from my hands onto the carriage floor.

"Do we have an understanding?" she asked.

I croaked when I tried to speak. She would not let go. "Yes!" I managed.

She released me. I sucked in valuable air, coughing and sputtering as she retrieved the knife from the floor. She dropped it in my lap as if it were no more than a piece of garbage or any other common object. The blade caught on the dress, but it didn't even prick the fabric.

"The collar on your dress should hide the bruises until they disappear," she said.

And with that, she stepped out of the moving carriage, vanishing into a wisp of smoke.

The knife felt heavy on my lap as the carriage wheeled around the city aimlessly, perhaps to confuse me or maybe to give me time to think on Erskina's words. I wrapped my hand around the blade's wooden handle. The Freetor runes vibrated slightly beneath my fingertips. Running the blade across my palm, I found that Erskina was telling the truth about its magic. My skin was not penetrated by its touch. I tucked it unsheathed into my undergarments, beneath my petticoat.

Back at the castle, my feet guided me into my chambers. Bidelia was there. If she knew what had gone on in the carriage, she didn't let on. There were three younger servants with her. I lay on my bed in silent protest.

"My lady," Bidelia said, her voice strained. "Come. We must help you out of those day clothes."

I did not control my body. I did not control my clothes. Somehow I sat up and flopped my legs over the side. My brother was dead. Soon, Keegan would be dead too. And then, once Lady Dominique's page got here, I'd be burnt to a crisp. My insides felt rotten.

The three servant girls helped me to my feet. I stood as still as the wooden pole that my brother had died on as they undid the back laces of my dress. It tumbled to the floor. They left my petticoat on—it was transparent, and the cold magic blade hugged my thigh. The bruises Erskina had given me were easy to see, but neither Bidelia nor the servant girls commented on them. A white chemise passed in front of my face, and suddenly I was in it.

Bidelia was speaking to the Marlenian girls. "You two have kitchen duty tonight. Get down there and ensure that it's made clear that Lady Dominique will not tolerate her steak any more than medium rare. It will probably be chaos down there, so don't lose your heads talking to the kitchen staff."

"But Mother Margaret, I'm not—"

"I did not train you to be insolent. A good servant does what she is told. We cannot have the pre-wedding celebrations be a disaster because one woman would not follow orders."

I turned and sauntered around to the other side of the room and looked out at the gardens. It was an overcast day, and all I wanted to do was hide in the clouds.

"You may stay here and comb the lady's hair and help her dress for dinner," Bidelia was saying to the other servant girl.

"Yes, ma'am."

My ears perked up at the familiar voice, and by the time I turned, the others were gone. I barely recognized Laoise with her cleaned-up face. Her cheeks were rosy, as if she'd spent the day in the cold, and her hair, usually wet and matted, now framed her face—she could pass as a well-groomed daughter of a prominent servant.

She threw her arms around me. "I've missed you so much."

I squeezed her so tightly because if I hadn't, I would have fallen over. My world was fraying at the edges like a worn blanket, but Laoise was my one good thing that had happened today.

"Thank you for coming," I said as we drew apart. "It must have been dangerous, risking your mother's cover . . ."

Laoise shook her head. "They know she has some sort of family. It wasn't hard for my mother to make me part of the staff here. They'll take any low-born Marlenian who cleans up and knows how to speak like them."

My head was spinning. I beckoned to my friend, and she joined me on the bed after grabbing a brush from the vanity. I didn't object when she started working the tangles out of my curls. The unspoken question was heavy in the silence. Over and over again I repeated it in my head until my lips formed the words.

"Were you . . . were you in the square?"

She didn't stop brushing my hair, but her breath became harder behind me. "Yes."

"And . . . other Freetors were there too?"

More silence. "There were too many guards. I . . . I wanted to go up

221

there and stop it, Kiera, I really did . . . but . . ."

I turned my head and the brush caught in my hair. Laoise's quick fingers undid the snarl and the brush fell limply onto the bed. There were fierce tears in her green eyes but she made no sound as she let them roll down her face.

"I wanted to stop it," I whispered.

"So why didn't you?" she countered.

Her question hurt me more than Erskina's grip had. I ran my hand tenderly over my collar that hid the bruises on my neck.

"You know that if I had, I would be dead too. My cover here, which you probably know all about now, would have been blown." I pursed my lips. "He was going to ask you to marry him."

That softened her face. "I . . . I know."

"So he asked you?"

She looked at her feet. "Not . . . no, he didn't ask me that."

I frowned. "What did he ask you, then?"

"I mean . . ." She sighed. "I don't know if you already know, if he'd already told you . . . maybe . . ." She leapt off the bed and crossed the room. "I should go."

I went after her. "Wait. No, please, Laoise. Stay."

Her hand hovered over the door handle, but her body was as still. "I just don't know what to say. He told me not to tell."

"He told me not to tell things too. Maybe he told us the same thing." I remembered the angry scar on his chest and how the flames had licked it clean. "Was it about . . . the man who stole Alastar's Tome?"

Laoise's eyebrows furrowed. "What is Alastar's Tome? What man?"

My insides were made of ice. I'd broken my promise not to tell anyone. Even though he was dead and it didn't matter, it mattered to me.

"Alastar's Tome. All the secrets of Elder magic. Rordan . . . he thought he saw the man who stole it."

"So, what . . . ?" She trailed off. "It doesn't matter. Your mission is between you and the Elders and Rordan. This . . . I'm pretty sure this is different."

"But no less important, it seems. Tell me what he told you."

She was fighting herself. Something was welling within her. "Just . . . don't hate me, okay?"

I took her hands and squeezed all of my fear and affection into them. "You're my best friend. With Rordan gone, you're the only family I have left. Please, Laoise, tell me. I promise, whatever it is, it can't be as bad as you think it is."

Unless it was about murdering Keegan. What if Erskina had told her to kill him if I didn't? That thought made me uneasy.

Her voice was squeaky, tiny, like a mouse trapped in a corner. "He had a plan."

"What kind of plan?" I asked hesitantly.

"He . . . started explaining about how the Freetors mining up in the North had a surplus of some metal, and how he and a couple of other men got a hold of it and transported it down to the Western caverns. He said that when you combine a bit of this metal with sulphur and string and fire, it makes a huge explosion."

I knew where this was going, but my heart wouldn't believe it. "He didn't make explosives, did he? He wasn't . . . planning anything . . . was he?"

Laoise stared at me apologetically, and then after a few tense moments, she nodded.

"Laoise . . ." I shook my head. "What did he do . . . ? What has he done . . . ?"

"He was an Extremist, Kiera!" she exploded.

My ears clouded. My brother believed in killing everyone and everything, just so we could live free again on the surface. Rordan— the man I'd known as my brother—was not who I thought he was. It was like he had died all over again.

The clay in Rordan's bag when the guards caught him. He was stealing the clay to make explosives to murder everyone.

There was a lump in my throat that I couldn't swallow.

She was speaking again. "It's true. He told me himself. He'd pitched the idea of making these explosives to the rest of the Extremists a few weeks ago. He bragged that they were all ready to go and asked if I wanted to join him."

My heart pounded in my ears. "What did you do?"

"Kiera, having Rordan ask me if I wanted to do something with him . . . it was like a dream come true." Laoise buried her face in her hands momentarily, processing the embarrassment and the shame. "At first, I didn't do anything. I went back to my cavern and thought about it. I thought about what we did almost every day on the Marlenian streets. That if Rordan believed in this so much, that it might really make a difference . . .

"In the end, though, I knew I couldn't. I've scratched up a few guards, but I've never killed anyone, Kiera. I just . . . I couldn't imagine myself actually taking a life . . . taking my life . . . setting explosives off in the square and knowing that hundreds of wives and children and Freetor sympathizers were going to die. Knowing that if the buildings collapsed, the tunnels beneath them would probably collapse too and kill innocent Freetors. And knowing that Rordan probably wouldn't survive either." Fresh tears rolled down her face. "Is it . . . is it selfish that I don't want to die to kill the Marlenians?"

I squeezed her hands. "No. No, it's not selfish."

"But we're supposed to hate them!" She sobbed into my shoulder.

"I know," I whispered.

She looked up at me again. "Mother says that . . . that Prince Keegan was showing interest in you."

My cheeks felt hot at the mention of his name. "He did, yes."

Laoise wiped her nose on the back of her hand. "Did you . . . ?"

I couldn't hide my treachery anymore. Not to Laoise. "Nothing serious happened . . . but we kissed. He kissed me."

Her reaction was what I had feared it would be. Laoise's eyes widened in horror as she slapped her hands over her mouth. "No . . ." She curled her fingers into a fist and bit them. "You were gaining his trust, though, right? He may know where Alastar's Tome is . . ."

I looked away. My silence only confirmed her fears.

"Oh . . . Kiera . . ." She pursed her lips.

"I thought there was something there," I said quietly. "I know it's wrong, but I felt like I could trust him. He trusted me. He saved my life."

"What are you going to tell the Elders? Unless they know already!"

"I don't think they know. Erskina visited me today. She . . . she wants me to kill Keegan."

"Kill him? After what happened . . ."

"Yeah." I wiped my eyes. "Maybe she does know what happened, and this is my punishment for betraying my people."

The silence was awkward. Laoise glanced at the door, and when she spoke, her voice quaked. "Maybe you should do as she asks."

I drew in a deep breath. "He tried to stop Rordan's death, Laoise."

"You don't know that. He's a Marlenian noble like the rest of them. Maybe . . . maybe he's charmed you. It's okay, it happens. Remember Aileen, from two caverns down? She and that Marlenian merchant's son—"

"Keegan's different. I know he is."

"But isn't he marrying a lady from the East, and allowing her army to . . . to take our city? If he cared, wouldn't he try to stop it?" Laoise gripped my shoulders with her slender hands and shook me gently. Her face was sweet. Innocent. "I know it hurts. I'm hurting too. But just because his hand wasn't the one on the torch doesn't mean he's innocent. He *killed* your brother, Kiera."

I didn't want to believe it, but Laoise's words sunk deep into me. My mind absorbed them and started churning. He had come to me on that balcony with love and commitment in his eyes, until he mistakenly assumed that my heart was with another. And now his eyes were cold. Was he *punishing* me for asking him to free Rordan by letting his death happen?

He said he had spoken with the Advisor. Of course the Advisor wouldn't let him go, especially if he suspected Keegan was speaking on my behalf.

He could have done something. I could have done something.

I sauntered to the window, steadying myself on the bedpost, and removed the knife from its hiding place.

"Mother and I will check the library again for any other Freetor texts, in case the tome is there. She still has that Freetor book that you took out. It's being passed to the underground. Maybe that will be enough for the Elders," Laoise said. Her voice was teary and sorrowful.

"So, don't worry about that. Focus on Erskina's mission. Then . . . then we can go back and forget that this ever happened. You can go back to being the Violet Fox. You will show them that the Violet Fox is not a Freetor to be trifled with. That they don't kill one of our own without facing the consequences."

My fingers curled around the hilt of the magic knife, and my nails dug into my palm. I knew what had to be done.

\* \* \*

Dinner was a blur of clinking wine glasses, wordy speeches, and empty congratulations. I inhaled my food and tasted nothing. It was like the blade was tight against my brain rather than my leg. Keegan and his bride-to-be sat at a special head table, with the Holy One, the Advisor, and Captain Murdock. Keegan smiled and laughed at the Advisor's words and gave Sylvia his full attention whenever she opened her mouth.

During the dessert course, Keegan managed to get a glob of chocolate beneath his lip. Sylvia noticed and dabbed it with her napkin. Her fingers lingered on his cheek as she examined the scar on his lips. They exchanged soft words that I could not hear, but I knew exactly what he was saying. *This is the scar the Violet Fox gave me.* And Sylvia would say, *You are so brave for facing such a wretched woman.*

The knife should be for her, too, I thought bitterly as our plates were taken away. Laoise and Bidelia hovered near me, going about their duties, but I felt them watching me as I watched Keegan, as if their eyes could will me to do what my heart could not fathom.

Lady Sylvia invited the women of the court to the ladies' drawing room in the east wing for an after-dinner tea so that they could shower her with more compliments and praises for being chosen as Marlenia's queen. It was an open invitation, but I would not go. Not attending would be considered an insult to Lady Sylvia, but if I was going to carry out what I knew I had to do, I had to leave the castle immediately following the act. There would be no more partying, no more rich food and expensive dresses. Tonight,

I would kill the prince, and the Lady Dominique he had adored so much would die with him.

*   *   *

When the castle was asleep, or too drunk with celebration, I prepared myself. I swept my mess of curls away from my face and tied the Violet Fox mask securely around my eyes. The knife was fastened to my belt, but I had a strong urge to carry it in my hands. To feel the steel pierce Keegan's flesh.

I felt sick.

The cape curved around me as I crept from my chamber and went down the maze of corridors. The patrol was thin tonight. I couldn't help but feel that that was Bidelia's doing, or somehow, the knife's doing. The path lay before me. All I had to do was kill Keegan, and I would be free.

*Your brother is dead because of him*, the knife seemed to whisper. *When you came to him for help, he turned away. He would only help one of his own. If he knew you were a Freetor, he would kill you too without thought, just as he signed away your brother's life.*

He felt betrayed, I thought. He thought Rordan was my lover and felt justified in taking Sylvia as his wife.

*He was disgusted with you. No Marlenian would love a Freetor.*

But he cared for me.

*Lies. They were all lies.*

I reached his bedchamber. Unguarded. Maybe the guards had snuck out to join the pre-wedding celebrations. Or maybe, somehow, Elder magic was at play. I didn't hesitate. The door screeched as it stuttered open. Light streamed in a uniform, sharp line that cut across the room and pointed to a slightly ajar window. An escape route. My steps were without sound as I kept with the shadows and crossed the room to where he slept, in a four-poster oak bed, not unlike the one in my chamber.

He groaned and rolled over. I froze. The blankets shifted and revealed his bare chest. The knife hummed in my hand.

I waited a few moments to ensure he was still asleep. His lips were parted, and he snored lightly. Those lips that I had wounded and kissed better again.

*Quickly. Do it now.*

Inhaling sharply, with both hands on the hilt, I raised the blade above my head. Our silhouettes painted a beautiful scene on the wall: me, poised to strike with my back arched and the knife positioned above his heart. Him, lying peacefully in slumber, unaware that he was even a subject in a piece of art.

Killing Marlenians. This would be my new purpose.

On three, I would plunge the knife into his heart, and my revenge would be complete.

*One.*

I took a deep breath. Rordan's face eaten by flames and smoke was all I could see, and this vision fuelled my rage.

*Two.*

This was it. One second to back down.

No, there was no backing down. I was going to do it. Right now.

*Three.*

The knife felt like it weighed a hundred pounds as it suddenly plummeted towards Keegan's chest. The thought of him lying bloodied on the bed, his face white with death . . .

*No. I can't do it.*

Pulling back at the last second, it took all of my strength to counterbalance the knife's power. I stumbled backwards as my grip on the knife loosened. It fell to the wooden floor with a clang.

I sucked in my breath, waiting for him to wake up and discover me.

His chest barely disturbed his blankets as he inhaled and exhaled gently.

Glinting in the moonlight, the edge of the blade pointed to the door.

I drank him in with my eyes one last time as I slid the blade into my sleeve. Erskina might kill me, but at least Keegan would be safe for another day. I would not be her pawn any longer.

I slipped out of his chamber and silently made my way back through the castle to my bedroom. I'd have to escape through the window, through the hedge maze. Maybe I could steal a horse and head into the South. It was warm down there, and maybe I could find a Freetor underground city in dire need of the Violet Fox's help. Erskina might send Freetors after me, or maybe not. She could find some other girl to play dress-up and find the lost tome. Maybe Erskina would be too busy with whatever plots she had going on and wouldn't spare the manpower to chase after one girl. Keegan would be all right.

My stomach panged at the thought of leaving him.

The door to my chamber was slightly ajar. As I stepped over the threshold and felt the sharp breeze whipping through the curtains, the hair on my arms rose. Panic rang in my ears.

I wasn't alone.

A man was poised at the edge of my bed. As I stepped closer, I recognized his profile immediately. The Advisor turned his head, and the moonlight cast half his face in shadow.

I drew the magic knife from my sleeve. It wouldn't hurt either of us, but I prayed he didn't know that. He showed no surprise that I was dressed as the Violet Fox. I dropped Lady Dominique's accent. "Give me a good reason why I shouldn't kill you now."

The Advisor blinked. "I know where your father is."

I had not been expecting that. My infatuation with Keegan had made me soft, though. Bidelia was right. Marlenians lied. "My father is dead."

"He is alive."

"You're lying."

"You still write to him every day."

The journal was on my bedside table, open flat. So he could read Freetor code after all.

"You shouldn't have read that." I slid closer to the bed, ready to strike. If I could get on top of him, hold him down, maybe I could suffocate him with one of the pillows.

"I don't have a choice," he replied. "I promised I would."

"What does that . . . ?"

I trailed off as he drew another, identical book from behind him. He rested it on his palm and the pages flipped by themselves, each covered in painstakingly small, scratchy writing, until they settled in the middle of the book. A thousand blank pages had passed, but the spine was only two fingers thick.

"No . . ."

"Yes, Kiera." He rose to calm me.

"Don't say my name!" I screamed. He didn't deserve to say my real name. Not after what he had done to Rordan. Not after what he had done to both of us.

Because the same man who had ruled over us for so many years was the man who had abandoned me and my brother ten years ago.

Advisor Ferguson was my father.

# Fifteen

EVEN AS I realized this, even as the journal lay exposed on the table and the promise between my father and me hung in the air, I refused to believe it. "No . . . you aren't. You can't be. You've done terrible, horrible things . . ."

His lips twitched. "You were about to do a terrible, horrible thing but listened to your heart in the end. Should I then judge you by your intentions, or your actions?"

"Killing you wouldn't have been so horrible. The number of Freetors you've sent to their deaths . . ."

But the Advisor reached for the knife and ran his fingers along the enchanted edge. "I meant what you were about to do to Keegan."

"How did you know . . . ?"

"I know a great deal about what goes on in this castle," he replied, coaxing the knife from my fingers to study it.

"Because you have the Elders' magic," I said spitefully.

"No, Kiera. Because I am the Advisor to the Holy One. Magic, unfortunately, plays a small role in my existence here."

I didn't know what to say first. Instead, it came out all at once. "I saw you with Freetor magic. The night I arrived. You went to put it in the library. And I took it. Bidelia hid it somewhere. And . . . and . . . you disgust me! You even talk like them." I looked away, squeezing my lips together before anything else could escape me.

"I understand," he said softly. "When you arrived, I barely recognized you. I wanted sorely to believe that you were safe beneath the ground, maybe married and happy. But Erskina sent you here . . ." He paused, and it sounded like he was trying to hold back a sob. Despite myself I glanced at him, and he was sitting on my bed again, his head in his hands.

My lips trembled. I had had no paintings, no traces of his image to remember his face by. I had been so consumed with my hatred of the Marlenians that when my father became one of them, I failed to recognize him as my flesh and blood.

"If you really are my father," I said, choking on the words, "why are you living with the enemy, instead of your family? And if you're here, is my mother still alive too?"

He looked at me as if I had stabbed him and twisted the knife. "No. She died many years ago in a raid—the same raid where I was left for dead. She stepped in front of me as the guard loosed his arrow. It pierced her lung. She died in my arms." He told the story like he was reciting facts from a historical tome, but I could hear the pain beneath his words. "Leaving you was the hardest thing that I ever did. But I do not regret it. I cannot."

"But . . . how did you even become the Advisor? Does the Holy One know you're a Freetor?

"It is a long story. I suppose you deserve to know the truth." He drew a deep breath. "Please understand, Kiera, that I always meant to tell you. I've been practicing for this day. I was hoping to tell you before you left so that you would return to the caverns knowing that your father was safe. That was before the execution."

My hands balled into fists. "You let your son die on the Marlenian streets without even helping him!"

"I did try to help him," he said quietly. "But he wouldn't listen. He was set in his ways."

"Rordan knew you were here? Did you know that he was an Extremist?"

He raised his hand. "Yes. But please, Kiera, let me explain everything. I will get to that, I promise."

I leaned against the bedpost, afraid to sit next to the man who had abandoned me but afraid that if I didn't hear his story, my heart would burst. "Fine. But you have to tell me everything."

He nodded solemnly. "I will tell you what I can."

That wasn't the same as promising to say everything, but I kept quiet as he spoke.

"We were sent to raid a supply shop outside of town. This was before the construction of the wall was finished around the city and commerce was more prosperous between the West and the South. The shop owner spoke out publicly against the Freetors and had even turned in a party that had trusted him to hide them in their basement. Erskina wanted to teach them a lesson.

"Your mother and I and a few others volunteered for the mission. We left you in the care of a family friend."

"Bidelia."

"Was it her? I suppose she would be the one."

"That was the time you gave me the journal," I said softly.

"Yes, it was. I was not sure if I would return."

"Why?"

His eyebrows knitted as he stared at the floor. "I knew it would be a dangerous raid. And I was concerned about your mother coming with me. We hadn't raided together since before you were born. I was afraid we would be a distraction to each other. We argued for days before the mission, but she was stubborn. Like you." The corners of his lips twitched.

"There was a tunnel that ran beneath his shop. It had been filled in after his betrayal, but we dug it back up from our end. In the middle of the night, we burst through his floor. We were sure we were catching him by surprise. But he must have heard us chiselling away at the floor, because when we came up, he was there, waiting for us, along with many Marlenian guards, hiding in the shadows. It was a slaughter."

I swallowed, imagining my mother pierced by a Marlenian arrow. Saving my father. The Advisor. "But you lived."

He nodded slowly. "I did."

"How?"

"I'll get to that. The shopkeeper was caught in the middle of everything—in the dark, one body looks like another. He and his wife were killed. One of the guards stabbed me as I was coming up through the floor. I still have the scar." He laid his hand over his right breast. "I lay barely conscious as your mother and the rest of the raiding party died beside me. I blacked out, and when I came to, it was still night, but the guards were gone. The bodies remained, and I was still alive."

"They didn't . . . clean up?" The thought of my mother dead, a real image of her death, haunted me.

"Not immediately. Because the next day was the first day of the Gathering celebrations, and security was needed in the city, and the matter was forgotten. The bodies sat there for three days before guards came to remove them."

"Three days!" I exclaimed.

"Yes. And I stayed with them. I would not leave your mother. I didn't know what would happen with her remains. I could barely move myself, and I thought I would soon join them. During my unconsciousness, the tunnel was filled in by other Freetors. They had probably heard about the raid and assumed everyone was dead.

"Because it was a shop, however, I was well supplied. For days, I lived off bread, eggs, and water. It was the best I'd eaten in my whole life, at that point. I cleaned myself and dressed in the merchant's clothes and sewed the wound with his supplies. By the time I was strong enough to think about digging up the tunnel, the guards came. They wanted to know what I was doing there. They thought I was a Freetor.

"I did what I did to survive, Kiera, just as you do every day, especially these last few days. So I made up a story. I said that I was from the East, in for the Gathering celebration to sell my wares with my cousin Norman Ferguson, but I came and found his house filled with Freetor bodies. I demanded an explanation from them." He chuckled. "That threw them, for certain."

"But wouldn't they have recognized you?" I asked.

He scoffed. "Of course not. I was clean, I was well-fed, and I was wearing the shopkeeper's best clothes since mine were covered in blood. And, I spoke with such confidence that they didn't question me. And so I became Ivor Ferguson, the wealthy merchant from the East."

Lack of sleep from the night before was starting to catch up with me and my head was pounding, but my eyes were wide awake. "You didn't think of contacting us?"

"I couldn't go near a Freetor without the guards raising their eyebrows, or the Freetors looking at me like I was their next target. I had to play the part of the merchant, until they stopped watching me."

I frowned. "And they never stopped watching you?"

"I'm not finished, Kiera."

"Obviously. A Marlenian merchant is a long way from becoming the Holy One's Advisor."

He gave me a look that suddenly reminded me of Rordan—the *shut up I'm talking* look that I got so often from him when I was little when I was being difficult. I pursed my lips and offered no more snarky comments as he continued.

"You have to believe me when I say that there was nothing I wanted more than to return to you and your brother," he said, casting me a glance. "But I was also awarded a rare opportunity—the ability to live on the surface, as a Marlenian, yes, but to live on the surface without worrying about whether I could give food to my children so that they could live another day . . ." Guilt twisted his face. "I knew Rordan would take care of you, and Bidelia or someone else would take care of Rordan, at least until I could come home. I had hoped to smuggle food underground, to dig up the tunnel and allow others to join me, or to create a more sophisticated smuggling operation.

"I re-opened Norman Ferguson's shop with absolutely no idea how I was going to run it. I was used to stealing money and goods from people, not having them give it to me willingly. I had to deal with out-of-city suppliers, the negative press from the Freetor raid, and cranky customers who were wondering why they couldn't buy two pounds of flour for the price of one. It was thrilling. Exciting. Eye-opening. Suddenly I knew how it felt to have my business be affected by our sabotage. I didn't know whether to cheer because my shipments were late or stolen or to cry because I had lost part of my rent payment for the building. I always left a little something outside the door, hidden in a barrel, just in case a Freetor ran by. Sometimes, one would find it.

"For my first two years on the surface I ran the shop, and each day became a little easier. You know how easy it is to forget how you were hungry when you are always full. I even managed to grow the business. People commented on how much better I was with people compared to my "cousin." This helped me get on several community business boards. And let me tell you, their biggest concern was how Freetor sabotage was hurting their businesses. Some of them were quite jealous and had noticed that in the time I'd been running the shop I'd only been attacked directly once—and that was by a child who'd pickpocketed a few pieces of silver from my side pouch. Word must have gotten around in the underground that I was a Freetor sympathizer, and that word may have reached these businessmen's ears.

"I couldn't do much for the Freetors without being recognized as one of them. But I was trying to help in my own way. So I realized that to divert suspicion, I had to appear to be the most anti-Freetor person in Marlenia. I suppose that's when I really became Mr. Ivor Ferguson, the shopkeeper on Knockatoor Alley. I was the one who put forward the idea to the castle that every shipment coming into and leaving the city be accompanied by at least two guards."

"I vaguely remember that," I said.

"My business saw a twenty percent increase in revenue that year when that idea became law. Others saw just as much, if not more. This caught the attention of the Holy One's council. Because of my "innovation," I was awarded the small sum of two thousand silver pieces, which allowed me to put a down payment on a second business, a bakery, two buildings down."

"And that's how you became the Holy One's Advisor?"

"No. That was only the beginning. For another year and a half, I toiled away in my businesses. I found that I had more money than I knew what to do with. The money that I didn't hide away in places I suspected to be Freetor-trafficked areas, I invested in other businesses—mostly the small market vendors on the main strip. This allowed them to grow, so that when they were hit by the Freetors, they didn't feel so robbed.

"It was by chance that I ended up in the castle." He raised his eyebrows and smiled. "I'm actually surprised you don't know the story."

"Why would I know the story?"

"Well, it was widely told . . ."

"Maybe on the surface. I lived underground for sixteen years. As you seem to have forgotten."

"I know you will never really believe me when I say it, but I never forgot about you and Rordan. Never. But if you will let me continue.

"It was about five or six years ago now. The Holy One and Prince Keegan were riding in a carriage. I don't remember what the occasion was. They were probably going to their country estate fifty leagues south of here. I was discussing business with a fellow merchant on the strip when something fell out of the carriage. I don't remember what it was now . . . a book, or a toy . . . it was something valuable to the young prince, in any case. Keegan was coming into himself, no less awkward than the gangly youths of the Freetor underground or of the Marlenian commoners, and as he leaned out to catch it before the carriage moved away, he fell onto the road.

"This wouldn't have been so bad if there hadn't been another carriage, drawn by four horses, barrelling towards him."

I inhaled sharply. "What happened?"

"The young boy was disoriented and didn't even realize he was in danger. I didn't even think about it. I ran in front of the carriage and pushed him out of the way just before the carriage could turn him into a pancake."

"You saved his life." Things were starting to fall into place. "That was how you got into the castle."

"Quite by accident, yes. I didn't realize until afterwards that it was really the prince I'd saved. I just thought it was some rich noble." He smiled. He was *proud* of this. I felt disgusted all over again. My father had become a Marlenian.

"I was given a medal of honour and an invitation to dine with the Holy One, Prince Keegan, and a few other nobles. Perhaps it was a ploy to make the Holy One seem relatable to the common man, but it was my opportunity to glean how the castle functioned. During that dinner, I charmed the nobles with made-up stories about being from the East. I had gathered enough knowledge from the passing merchants and travellers to create an entire history for Ivor Ferguson. A life before coming to Marlenia City."

"And that was when you knew you were really one of them," I guessed, shaking my head.

"That was when I knew that I was finally in a position to have some influence, to try to really make a difference for the Freetor population."

"But things got *worse* for us!"

"The reputation I had built as an anti-Freetor man preceded me. Not long after that dinner, I was offered a seat on the council, and I accepted. When bills were put forward that put Freetors at a disadvantage—more guards per street, the increased tolerance for slavery—what choice did I have? I couldn't vote against them all without raising suspicion, or having people question my backstory. In time, as I adjusted to my new life with the council, which eventually appointed me Advisor, the rumour that I was ruthless spread far and wide. If I was nothing but that, I was afraid I would be thrown in the dungeons with the rest of the Freetors, and then I would never see you again.

"I could only live and hope that somehow the Elders would send you against me, so I could tell you the truth."

"How did Rordan find out you were here?"

It was hard to say his name, and it was hard for him to hear it, I knew.

"A few months ago, Rordan was on a scouting mission around the castle—counting the guards, the stable hands, the gardeners and gauging whether any of them would be loyal to the Freetor cause or easily kidnapped and replaced. I was on my daily constitutional about the grounds when I saw him." He smiled. "It is true that I make it my business to know everyone who is employed at the castle. Not personally, but I keep a count. I know who is a Freetor, and who is not. And when I saw him . . . I knew it was him. I could barely believe it. My son was alive, after all these years. I knew that if he was alive, you were as well."

"Did . . . did you talk to him?"

"Not at first. He saw me watching him and got out pretty quick. He came back the next day, though."

"Did he know who you were?"

His eyebrows raised, curious. "When you first saw me, did you know me?" When I shook my head, he continued. "Rordan was nine when I left, but even so, he didn't know his father when he saw him again. It only proves that we only see what we want to see—and he saw me then as you see me now—a heartless man who has sent thousands to their deaths because they were born underground.

"When he returned the following day, this time scouting the hedge maze, I followed him. I had had plenty of time to memorize every path in that maze, but Rordan got lost almost immediately. When he came to a dead end, I had him cornered, and when I eventually convinced him that I was his father, he allowed me to tell him what I have told you tonight."

"How did you convince him?"

He chuckled. "Do you remember when you were three, and we took a walk to the river caverns? Trickles of water sliding through mud, they were, but to you and Rordan, they were rivers, and a way to make your clothing filthier than it already was. Your mother . . ." He caught himself as the thought of her hung in the air. He backtracked. "You had just learned to walk, and you waddled into the stream. It wasn't that dangerous, but Rordan thought you were going to be washed away. He grabbed you and threw you to the ground, yelling and screaming your name. Of course, then you started to cry. Well, I thought it was adorable."

So I had a history of falling into rivers? My face grew hot.

He studied me. "Do you remember that day, Kiera?"

"No."

"Really?

"Really, I don't."

"I see. I suppose you were quite young." He frowned and let out a frustrated sigh. "In any case, Rordan did remember. And he embraced me as his father."

That was so ridiculous I laughed. "That's a lie."

"No, Kiera, it's not. He believed me."

"Well he didn't tell me about it."

"No, and that was my idea. He wanted to tell you right away and get you situated in one of my businesses so that you could run one of the smuggling operations I had always dreamed of. It would keep you safe, he said, and away from the Marlenian guards. But when he told me you were behind the Violet Fox escapades . . . well, I thought it was better for you to continue doing that. My daughter, the Violet Fox, the most feared Freetor symbol."

The pride in his voice got under my skin, in a good way. My father was proud of me, like I'd always thought he would be.

But my father was the Advisor, the most-hated man known to Freetors.

And suddenly everything made sense. Rordan had wanted to tell me something. Maybe it was about his Extremist plans, but maybe this was what had been eating away at him—knowing that our father was Advisor Ferguson, hated and feared among our people. I wished he were here. I missed him more in that moment than I had in all the moments since he'd died.

The Advisor continued. "We met every week in different parts of the marketplace, exchanging information and re-establishing our relationship. The Extremist ideas peppered our conversation slowly, and I had hoped that maybe it was just a faze, but what did I know . . ." He shook his head. "He saw my position as an opportunity, but in a different way than I did. He was in over his head. He really was."

My forehead rested on the bedpost. My own brother, believing in radical freedoms, that the way to the surface was paved with the blood of every Marlenian man, woman, and child. "I didn't see it."

"He wanted to keep you safe from it, to save you from any blood-shed he could. But the Extremists were planning something, and there was Freetor magic involved—not just involved, but supporting their plan. Extremist ideas fuelled by Freetor magic—it is an unsettling marriage. I didn't have details, but he was dropping hints that something big was going to happen soon, and that I best leave the castle.

"Explosives," I said, more to myself than to him. "Rordan was making explosives with the Extremists."

And if I had found Alastar's Tome, he might have tried to convince me to give it to him instead of the Elders, I realized. Then he would've had all the secrets of Freetor magic to create more powerful explosives, to kill everyone in the castle.

Nausea swam in my stomach. How far did his plan reach? Maybe Rordan wasn't innocent the day I fell in the river. That arrow had almost killed Keegan. If the Advisor—my father—was eager to keep his position, then Rordan had lied, and loosed the arrow against the Marlenian prince after all. My heart chilled thinking about this side of my brother that I'd never known.

The Advisor chewed bitterly on the information. "I wasn't about to have everything I had worked for destroyed by a dangerous plan concocted by Freetor youths, so to stop him, I went back underground."

"But . . . how? The passwords change—"

"I am the Advisor. I make it my business to know who is and isn't a Freetor. I simply followed suspected Freetors and waited for them to say the password of the day. I dressed in filthy rags—it was easy for me to get in."

"The one time you go back to the underground, and you didn't even come see me."

"Would you have believed me? You barely believe me now."

"I would've believed you more."

"Somehow I doubt that. I didn't even know what cavern you lived in." He paused. "He had had a surveying mission that day, and he said he had to report to the Elders. Discovering a path to the Central Cavern was easy enough, after finding the Great Cavern. When he was alone, away from the Central Cavern, I confronted him and showed him what Freetor magic could do to the uninitiated."

"Then the story Rordan told about catching a Marlenian man underground . . . that was you?" I clutched my heart, remembering the wound that had blazed across his chest. "You wounded him."

"I tried to talk sense into him. I risked my Marlenian identity going down there, but he would not listen. In a twisted way, he believed he was protecting you."

I heard his dying screams in my head once more. "He said that the wound was caused by magic. Was this true? How could you control it if you're not an Elder?"

He looked uncomfortable. "Years and years of study, Kiera. I have collected any Freetor item I could get my hands on, taken it apart, and put it back together again to discover its secrets."

"Then you admit to stealing it." I rose from the bed and gathered my resolve.

"Stealing what, Kiera?"

"No, no. You can't play this game with me anymore. I was sent here to retrieve Alastar's Tome with all the ancient magic written in it. What you stole when you were underground."

He stood defensively. "Kiera, I promise you, I didn't steal Alastar's Tome. Whatever that is."

"Oh, it's only the most important Freetor artefact in existence. And I know you have it somewhere in the castle. The Elders said so. Stop lying to me."

"I've only told you the truth tonight. For the first time in over ten years, I am reunited with you, and I can finally tell you what really happened."

"I didn't come to reunite with you. I was sent here to get Alastar's Tome." I regarded him suspiciously. "You said you studied Freetor magic. Why would you say that Alastar's Tome doesn't exist?"

"Alastar the Hero and all the Elders who came after him wouldn't be so foolish to pen something so powerful," he replied. "And despite all my research, I haven't found any evidence that Alastar the Hero actually compiled any kind of written work. It was too risky, even riskier back then than it would be now.

"Any magical Freetor item has been here for years and is known about by the Holy One. I was in charge of retrieving all of it, and I hoped to recover any piece of my past that would make life here easier. That book you took was a chance find during a Marlenian excavation. They would have thrown it out had I not seen its value. Marlenian mythology as told by a Freetor, an excellent piece of work . . ." He trailed off, as if remembering a pleasant memory, before returning to the present. "The stolen magical tome was a ruse to get you here, to get you close to the prince, so that you could gain his trust."

"And then kill him? But Elder Erskina wouldn't have known that I would kill him."

"With your brother dead, she knew you would have no choice. And don't think she didn't see that coming. Her foresight is unmatched. She would have you believe that it was Keegan's fault, or else she would have used Rordan's death against you so that you would do her bidding."

I swallowed. It was all so obvious now. Not only had Erskina made up a Freetor artefact for me to chase, but she'd sent Rordan with me—I wondered if she knew he was an Extremist, who coveted Freetor magic. Rordan had expanded on Erskina's story about the Southern man stealing the tome because the truth was just as bad, if not worse. "Erskina must have known you were here, though."

"She did," he admitted. "She underestimated me. I have been here a long, long time. It is easy to consider one of your own an enemy when he has been away for so long. Or when you have been in power for so long."

I frowned as his words sat with me. "You think she's planning something big."

"Those are your thoughts, not mine. I have not seen any Elders, at least none that I know of, in a long time."

The more I thought about it, the more it made sense. The missing Elders—the dead ones. Unfortunate accidents . . . or were they? She had sent me here to distract me while she formulated her plan. The Violet Fox was a symbol of hope for the Freetor people. Because I had a reputation of sticking my nose where it didn't belong, I would've been expected to investigate if someone suspected a coup among the Elders. And this was only the beginning. Elder Erskina was going to use her magic to take the Council of Elders by storm. No one hated the Marlenians more than Elder Erskina.

Keegan was in danger.

"The East is not getting Freetor magic in exchange for the troops."

"No. They are merging their bloodline with the most powerful province in all of Marlenia. With the wealth from the West and the population in the East, I suspect that the provinces will merge within the next few years. First the Freetors will be eliminated, and then they will no doubt turn their eye on the rest of Marlenia."

"And if that happens, there will be a war. Exactly the excuse Erskina needs to seize power and attack." My nails dug into my lips as I realized what I had to do. "I have to stop that wedding."

"Kiera, don't." He caught my arm. "This place . . . this world, it's not one you know. They will burn you like they did with your brother. Or worse."

I shook my head. "Keegan has to know the truth."

It wasn't just that I was selfish. The thought of Sylvia at his side overwhelmed me. But it was bigger than that. The Advisor—*my father*—was right about one thing. If the East and the West allied, my people would suffer. And if Erskina was planning on eliminating the other Elders, and she had rallied her forces as strongly as I believed, she would strike soon—especially once she found out that I disobeyed her.

"Don't throw your life away over this," he said. "They will put you in the dungeons the moment they find out you beguiled the prince into having relations with you."

"We didn't have—"

"Regardless, half the castle saw you with him. He spent time with you, alone. You will be a stain on the royal reputation that must be removed."

"But I think I love—"

"You think, but you do not know." His fingers curled around the bedpost. "When I was a Fighter, we made a vow to put the good of the people above our personal needs. Did you make the same vow?"

Meekly, I nodded.

"Are you still a Fighter?" he asked.

I opened my mouth to say yes, but I knew that with one kiss I had betrayed the traditions and values the Freetors upheld.

He saw this in my face. "Now you know how I feel every day."

I shook my head. "Something has to be done. If the East and the West unite, then we will be slaughtered."

"Now you are thinking with your head," he said with a small smile. "Don't think that I want Sylvia to be High Queen, but if you fight for the wrong reason, you will end up dead. In reality, though, I would prefer you not fight at all." The wrinkles around his eyes softened. "I should have listened to Rordan from the beginning. I can set you up in one of the shops I own. No one will question you. You can smuggle people and food in and out of the underground. Maybe you will succeed where I failed."

"It's not enough! The East will still have the throne, and our heads!"

"There is little I can do."

"Keegan said you made the match. You've invited the murder of thousands!"

"It was not just me. Nothing is ever decided by one person. It goes to the council—myself, the Holy One, other nobles with a vested interest and gold in the treasury. We all decide Keegan's future, and the future of Marlenia."

"I can't believe you betrayed me." The words were small, but they felt big in my mouth.

He regarded me thoroughly. "I can see that I'm not going to change your mind. Not about that, at least."

"No," I replied. "So will you help me stop this wedding, or not?"

His lips twisted and his eyes were apologetic. "I'm sorry, Kiera. I can't."

My front teeth gritted and then sank into my tongue. I didn't know why I was so disappointed. Of course he would say no. He wouldn't help Rordan, and now when the fate of the Freetor people was at stake, he wouldn't help me either.

"Fine. Get out of my room."

I expected him to put up a fight, but he went quietly to the doorway. "I really am sorry, Kiera."

"Save your apologies. I've done fine on my own up until now."

He turned the door handle and the door squeaked open, almost hiding his gentle reply. "Your mother would have been proud of you."

And then just as suddenly as he had appeared, my father was gone again. The silence of the night engulfed me, but I refused to be swallowed. The sun would be up in a few hours. As I threw myself upon the mattress and surrendered to sleep, I clasped the magical tome and drew it closer to my body. The hardbound leather with infinite pages to hold infinite wisdom: that was the only father I knew.

\* \* \*

Bidelia yanked the brush through my hair, pulling at the roots, but I didn't scream. "Prince Keegan had his breakfast in his chamber this morning."

"Is that so."

Sighing in frustration, she threw the brush on the vanity. It cracked the mirror when it landed, sending tendrils creeping up my reflection.

"You didn't do it. You disobeyed Elder Erskina—"

"The Advisor is my father. Did you know?"

Bidelia's face was hard and unforgiving. "Of course I knew. I was wondering if he would tell you, or if somehow you would remember, but when you appeared ignorant, I thought it best not to say anything. He could be on a mission for the Elders for all I know, and I would not be the one to interfere with that. You were here to carry out a mission."

"A pointless mission. According to *my father*, Alastar's Tome doesn't exist."

"That's absurd."

"Why?"

"He may be your father, Kiera, but that man is more Marlenian today than the Holy One. Of course he would tell you that Alastar's Tome doesn't exist. He is in charge of any Freetor-related artefact that finds its way into the castle. He wants that magic for himself."

I looked at myself in the mirror. Dark circles cradled my eyes. "I think he was telling the truth about the magic. About his position here."

"Believe what you like, then. Elder Erskina will not be pleased when she discovers you failed to carry out your extra task."

I stood up as Bidelia did up the laces of my corset. She drew them so tight that I felt like a snake was coiling around my body, but I would not let her see me struggle. "I didn't fail. I'm going to stop that wedding."

"Killing him will stop it."

The knife lay innocently on the dresser. I pulled up my dress and slid it into the garter around my thigh. "I won't kill Keegan."

Bidelia considered the knife in my garter, and then my eyes, where she saw the truth. "Then it is as I feared. You have let a dangerous infatuation threaten our lives." She yanked the last corset strings tight, restricting my breathing, and then whirled around. "Laoise will help you with the rest."

She slammed the door behind her while I loosened the corset.

\* \* \*

Dressing and completing my hair took longer than expected, as the servant manpower was devoted to getting Lady Sylvia ready for the ceremony and preparing the large feast that was to follow. I shoved a piece of bread into my mouth and washed it down with a few grapes—if I was going to be a Freetor again, I had to learn to eat like one. I felt like I'd gained weight while at the castle. That weight would disappear soon enough.

My shoes were flat—despite my large dress, I walked to the cathedral. Nobles, anxious to get a seat in the cathedral, fought over the carriages crowding the bailey. The road was congested in both directions, and frustrated ladies threw me resentful looks as I weaved between their carriages. The ceremony was due to start when the sun reached its highest point in the sky. Its rays beat down on me, and I soaked them up bitterly.

The Grand Square was busier than an anthill. It was crawling with merchants, local and otherwise, who had travelled far on short notice. Freetor pickpockets would do well today. Buskers—most Marlenian, but there were probably a few Freetors playing as well—belted out traditional folk songs praising Dashiell, the Tramore family, and the sacred bond between royalty, and the land.

Making my way through the crowd, I climbed the many steps to the cathedral door. Guards dotted the entrance, but they didn't question me as I passed. My clothing marked me as Lady Dominique, daughter of the North.

Soon, that illusion would be shattered, revealing only truth.

The cathedral's ceiling stretched higher than two hundred hands—maybe three hundred. Stained glass windows depicted scenes of the merciful man-god, Dashiell, and Killan Tramore, the man who had declared himself the Holy One because of his triumphant victory over the Freetors. The biggest scene was at the front, before the altar and behind the choir. Captain Killan Tramore, clad in white and holding the Holy One's sceptre, was battling green and red flames with his powerful shining aura. I was sweating just looking at it.

It was already packed. There was no way I'd be able to squeeze my way to the front, not even with Lady Dominique's clothes and demeanour. The aisle down the centre was barely one hand wide, and there were guards around the perimeter, hands wrapped around the hilts of their swords, waiting for the opportunity to lash out at anyone who dared to stop the greatest power-match in the history of Marlenia.

The Advisor—*my father*—dressed in fine Marlenian silks, stood in shadows on the sidelines with Captain Murdock. He smoothed his twisting moustache against his cheek with one finger. I felt him single me out as I tried to hide among the other latecomers. I didn't care. I knew he wouldn't stop me, even if he did have limited command of the Elders' magic.

The musicians played an upbeat march that cued a procession of flower girls strewing rose pedals down the aisle. Their silver and blue dresses fluttered around their knees as they bounced towards the altar.

The pedals rocked gently to the floor, only to be trampled by the girls' dainty shoes.

Sylvia waddled down the aisle. The women *oohed* and *ahhed* at her dress: a flowing gown that hid her fat rolls and highlighted her bosom. A lacy veil hid her face, but I could see her painted blood-red lips beneath. The thought of her kissing Keegan's lips—the lips I had hated and then loved—made my stomach turn and only furthered my courage.

The Holy One himself was performing the ceremony, as was the custom. Being the head of the Church, he had the authority to marry anyone, but because of his frailty, this would likely be his last ceremony. Keegan gripped his father firmly. A flicker of fear marred his face as Sylvia marched ever closer to the altar.

She curtseyed to the Holy One before facing Keegan, her face full of hope and joy. A small squeal of delight escaped her lips as she chanced a glance at the congregation, as if she couldn't believe what was happening. The ladies tittered in response and waved in support. I wrung my dress out like it was a wet rag, trying to control my nerves.

As the music drew gracefully to a close, the Holy One drew a deep, raspy breath. "My children, thank you for gathering here today, to witness the joining of my son, Prince Keegan Tramore, first of his name, to Lady Sylvia of the House Frostfire, daughter of High King Leszek Frostfire of the Eastern province. Today is a momentous day in Marlenia's history, as West and East combine for the first time in over eight hundred years."

The Holy One hacked a nasty cough of death into his sleeve. The Advisor went to aid him, but the Holy One waved him away with his sceptre. Keegan whispered something to his father, but he didn't seem to want to hear that either.

He continued on as if nothing had happened. He led everyone through the traditional prayer, and then the choir sang a song about everlasting love and devotion. Sylvia was living her fondest dream, while Keegan's eyes kept darting to the exits. I wondered if he could see me at the back, but there were hundreds of people crowded in here—to him, I was just another face in the crowd.

But no longer.

Finally, the words I'd been waiting for came after almost twenty minutes of prayer and singing and ceremony.

"If any of you, man or woman, have reason to believe that this couple should not be wed, speak now or forever keep silent."

Some of the nobles let out nervous chuckles as the guards seemed to close in on the congregation. No one in her right mind would object this marriage, not if she wanted to keep her head.

Maybe I wasn't in my right mind, but I was in my right heart.

Being at the back of the cathedral, almost no one noticed when I stood up. The Holy One continued speaking. Keegan's dutiful eyes were locked on Sylvia's.

"Keegan." My voice was a whisper at first, and the people in front of me turned around and frowned in frustration. I cleared my throat and squeezed the Violet Fox mask hidden in my fist. "Keegan!"

This time, the Holy One stopped talking. I took a step forward down the aisle as Keegan turned to look at me. Sylvia looked absolutely disgusted. Murmurs and whispers spread like wildfire, as if they could guess what I was about to do. They would have no idea.

"There's something—"

I was interrupted by the loud squeak of the wooden doors behind me. "*J'ou!*"

I spun around and couldn't believe my eyes.

Elder Erskina had warned me that one of Lady Dominique's pages might arrive at the castle. But I hadn't expected Lady Dominique herself. Being trapped underground for all this time had made her face gaunt and pale. Her dress was reduced to strips of dirty blue fabric hanging off her arms, and the rest of her body was covered in a filthy brown merchant robe. She looked exactly like a Freetor.

We really are no different, I thought.

She saw me and right away, her eyes bugged out of her skull as she pointed an accusatory finger. "Dat's her! Dat's de imposter! Guards, arrest her!"

I opened my mouth to deny it, but paused. Wasn't this what I really wanted? For Keegan to know the truth? But not like this. Not

250

with the real Dominique hovering over me, overshadowing me.

Soldiers were closing in. Some of them were drawing their weapons, ready to strike Dominique at the slightest sign of resistance. Dominique bared her teeth like an animal as they surrounded her.

"No!" My voice echoed in the cathedral and froze the guards in midstep. Keegan was looking at me as if he had just recognized me from somewhere not the castle, as if he was finally figuring out the truth but his mind didn't want to believe it. I savoured that moment, the one just before his innocence shattered, wishing that somehow, we had been born in different places with different skins.

But I knew what I had to do.

"She's telling the truth," I said, pointing to Dominique. "That is the real Lady Dominique Castillo. I am . . . a Freetor."

There was a sudden pause as my confession hit everyone in the room. Then the guards jumped into action, swarming me like birds over a carcass. Lady Dominique smiled smugly as the guards slammed my face to the ground and held it there with their dirt-ridden boots. I didn't struggle. Those in the back row fled their seats and either retreated from the cathedral entirely or crowded the aisle.

Over the confused shuffling and mounting tremors of chaos, my father spoke. "What shall we do with her, Your Grace?"

"On your feet, Freetor," the Holy One declared.

The guards pulled me up again, holding me by my hair and pulling my head back to ensure I would not look away from the Holy One's steely gaze. His weary eyes moved from the real Lady Dominique to me.

"You confess to impersonating this Marlenian noblewoman?" the Holy One asked.

"Your Grace, I will confess that I have suspected this for some time," the Advisor said. "I was gathering evidence—"

"Quiet, Ivor. I wish to hear from the girl."

My mouth felt dry. I swallowed nervously. "I do confess."

"She y'is not just any Freetor, J'our Grace," Dominique continued. "What do j'ou have in j'our hands, *Fox*?"

I'd crumbled my mask into my fist to hide it, but there was no going back. My hands shook as one guard forced the fabric from my grasp and held it up for the Holy One, Keegan, and everyone else to see.

"The Violet Fox," Keegan said. I saw it in his eyes, the moment where everything fell into place. He touched his lip, the scar I'd made. "That was you . . . ?"

"I tried to tell you," I said as the guards tightened their grip on me.

Keegan moved to step off the platform, and I was convinced he was going to come after me, but the Advisor and the Holy One restrained him with a steady hand. "Wait . . ."

"My name is Kiera," I shouted as I was dragged away.

# Sixteen

THE CHAINS WERE tight around my wrists and ankles, but it was so dark that I couldn't have gone anywhere anyway. They rattled as I shivered. My fingers and toes felt numb. They had taken away all of my clothes, except for my undergarments. Even though I'd lived in the dark, damp underground my whole life, the Freetor tunnels were brightly lit compared to the castle dungeon. No sights, no sounds, not even rats dared to tread here. I was alone with my thoughts, probably for eternity.

There was no way to judge the passage of time. Even when the food came, I only knew by the clattering of the plate somewhere in front of me. It seemed to come randomly: sometimes, it felt like days since my last meal, while other times, I swore it had only been an hour or two. They had to be messing with my mind. I ate what I could. Whatever it was, it was slimy and had no smell or taste. Food was not wasted on prisoners.

At least twenty meals after my imprisonment, there was a bright light. It pierced the darkness and seared my eyes. I hid my head in my knees, unable to escape. Maybe this was what dying felt like.

"The Violet Fox," said the voice.

I peered up at him. He had come alone, at least. His hair was combed, slicked back, and held in place by his silver crown. A dark blue cape curled around his body to keep him from the cold. But his eyes spoke another tale. No sleep, they said, and they were cradled in large dark bags. The torch flamed in his hand and cast his face in shadow.

Keegan. He'd come to see me.

"You deceived everyone," he said.

My mouth was dry. It had been forever since I last spoke. My voice was scratchy. "I was trying to save my people."

"You tried to kill me!"

His words stung. How did he know? My father must have told him. "But I didn't."

Keegan was silent. If not for the torch, I would have thought that he had left. But I wouldn't let him have the upper hand. My knees buckled as I struggled to stand. My hands scraped against the dirt-and-stone wall as I tried to support myself. Shadows danced across his face as he regarded me with some kind of emotion that the fire mutated.

"No, you didn't," he said finally. "The guards took away your knife when you were arrested, but it had a flimsy edge."

"It was only supposed to hurt you," I said softly.

"Because of your Freetor magic."

"Because of an Elder who wanted you dead." She wanted to see me dead too. I shouldn't have underestimated Elder Erskina.

"Your Elders speak for your people."

"You and your father speak for the Marlenians, but you don't represent everyone's viewpoints on Freetor freedoms." I gazed up at him, imploring, hoping he would listen. "The man who was burned in the square wasn't my lover. He . . . he . . . was my brother."

"Your brother . . ." He leaned a hand against the scratchy, dirty wall. Regret and sorrow marred his face. "I'm sorry."

"*Sorry*. You don't even . . ." I wanted to go off on an angry tirade. I'd even rehearsed one. Now, staring up at him, it seemed pointless. Rordan was gone forever. It was my people I had to think of now. Rordan would want me to focus on what really mattered, even if he hadn't been right about how it was supposed to be handled. "Why are you here?"

"I thought . . ." He paused. "I thought that there might be something between us."

My insides hurt. Even after all this, he still thought . . . I wanted to resist it. Everything told me to fight what I felt, but I couldn't. There was hope and sarcasm in my voice, even though I tried not to show it. "Aren't you happily married?"

"The wedding is off."

"You . . . called it off? How? I thought . . ."

"Because I realized . . . I don't care if you are a Freetor. I don't even care that you . . . that you are the Violet Fox." He touched his scarred lip. "I care only for *you*."

Heavy words that I'd longed to hear, and finally, he'd spoken them. My heart leapt. Years of distrust between our two people weighed on our shoulders. Keegan was willing to overlook the image our people had created for me. He had come down into the deepest, darkest dungeon in the entire land, risking his position to declare his (could it be?) love for me. I took a deep breath. The words fell out of me.

"But . . . you don't even know who I am."

"I want to. Let me know you, Kiera."

My name. He remembered my name. Hope glimmered within me. "Say it again."

A small smile crept across his face as he drew closer to me. "I want to know you."

I shook my head. "No. My name. Say my name. My real name."

"Kiera." He was grinning now.

"Keegan Tramore." His last name evoked so many tales of hate and oppression, but paired with "Keegan," the weight of "Tramore" was lifted. "Keegan, I care about you, too. That's . . . that's why I wanted to tell you everything. I couldn't let you marry Sylvia thinking that I was someone else."

"I didn't want to believe it. That you weren't from the North, that you really were the Violet Fox, here on some mission. But after you were arrested, your father told me everything."

My father. The Advisor. The association hung darkly in the air. "Everything?"

He ran a hand through his hair. "I didn't believe him at first. Advisor Ferguson is the most upstanding Marlenian in the city. But then he told me about the journal in your room and the identical one he has hidden in his dresser. I was so angry at him. The man whom I had considered family was the enemy."

He still is, I thought, leaning against the wall. The rough edges of the stone dug into my hands and my back, but the pain kept me in the moment.

"Are you going to tell the Holy One?" I asked.

"I . . . don't know," Keegan admitted. "Advisor Ferguson, or whatever his real name is, has been a trusted member of his council for a long time."

"Conal Driscoll," I whispered. The name felt strange and foreign on my tongue. "That's his real name."

Silence, except for our uneven breathing. Keegan's boot scraped against the grainy floor and bit into the quiet. "I . . . really am sorry, Kiera. I can't even imagine not knowing my father."

But I did know him, I desperately wanted to say. He was the one who had listened after each day when there was no one else. I could pour my secrets into the pages and somewhere, somehow, I knew he'd be reading them. I'd imagine the advice he'd give me when I was lost and then act on it. If only I'd known that he was giving his advice to the enemy.

When I didn't say anything, Keegan continued. "If the general public were to discover his true origins—"

"They would push for him to be killed," I finished. "Which would strengthen your father's position as Holy One."

"Maybe." He paused and breathed in the damp, earthy air. From his pocket, Keegan produced a silver key.

My freedom.

"You're . . . letting me go?" I asked as he unlocked the chains that bound my wrists and ankles. They clinked and rattled as they fell to the dirt.

"The guards are gone for the night. If we move fast enough, we may be able to leave the city before dawn."

"Leave the city . . . ?" I rubbed my wrists tenderly as my mind raced. "We can't go. The Freetors need my help. Even the Marlenian people won't be safe if Elder Erskina makes a grab for the throne."

Keegan took my hands in his. "I want us to be together."

I pursed my lips. Was this happening? Was this real?

"I know," I said, my voice raw. "But we have to think about our people. We have to stop Erskina before she destroys your people and mine."

Adoration clouded his eyes, and then he looked away. "You're . . . you're right. We have to think about our people. I was being selfish."

I squeezed his hands. "I almost said yes."

A grin seized his lips. "If we work together on this, no one will be able to stop us. We will get Erskina under control."

"I hope you're right." It was so easy to believe him.

Outside the cell it was still dark, but a torch hung on the stone wall in the distance. My sense of time was confused. I longed for sunlight. My hand dragged along the rough stone, and the other stayed on Keegan's back as he lead us forward towards the lit area.

"I'm curious," I whispered, though there was no need. "What happened to the real Lady Dominique after I was thrown down here?"

Keegan snorted. "She's still here, for the moment. She refused our offer of transport to the North. The servants and the slaves have been tending to Lady Dominique and Lady Sylvia's needs non-stop."

I wondered how she had escaped. Perhaps the murdered Elders had caused such a stir that those minding the Northern lady had forgotten to man their post or had been sent somewhere else. Or maybe she had somehow killed them.

When we reached the torch, I saw a set of narrow stairs that ended at a thick wooden door. We were about to ascend when it flew open. I instinctively drew back into the shadows and held my breath.

"Where is she?" a familiar voice asked.

"Here," Keegan replied.

Laoise rounded the corner—followed by Bidelia, and Advisor Ferguson. *My father.* I was overwhelmed—I'd been in isolation so long, and to be suddenly surrounded by people I knew . . .

"Kiera!" Laoise squeezed me so tightly I could barely breathe. "I was so worried."

"I wasn't down there for long, right?" Part of me didn't want to know how much time I'd spent alone in the dark, but I had to face the truth, no matter how horrible it was.

"Days, Kiera. Didn't anyone tell you?" Her eyes were wide and lined with tears. "It's been awful. So much has changed."

"What happened? What's going on?" I looked to Keegan, but he seemed as confused.

"There've been rumours going around the underground all night," Laoise said, near sobbing. "Fighters are saying that all of the Elders are dead, by Erskina's hand! And that she's going to attack the Holy One at the cathedral!"

"Why there?" I asked.

"The Gathering's final speeches are always held outside the cathedral, in the Grand Square," Advisor Ferguson said. "The Holy One hasn't addressed the people yet about the cancelled wedding, and the nobles and wealthy merchants are demanding an explanation. And we don't know if word has reached the East. They could show up any minute and demand a ceremony, and if not a ceremony, then certain monetary compensation for lost benefits."

I frowned. "You mean that even if Lady Sylvia doesn't get to be queen, because you already announced your intent and have now gone back on your word, you owe them?"

"It is an old custom, one that has not been evoked for several generations, but traditionally, the sum is the bride's weight in silver."

"That could be a lot," I said.

Bidelia cast me a stern glance. "If High King Leszek evokes that right."

"No doubt he will," the Advisor said.

It was dark, and the light was playing tricks on my eyes, but it looked like he was judging me, blaming me for everything that had happened. It was my fault. Everything. But somehow, I had to fix it, so that my people could live in peace, and so that Keegan and I could be together.

I gritted my teeth. "That's not a problem though, right?"

Advisor Ferguson and Keegan exchanged a worried glance. "It's . . . not important right now. Not as important as the Holy One's life," the Advisor said. "We can't let Erskina get to him."

"All of our lives are in danger. Freetor and Marlenian," Keegan said, looking from me to the Advisor to Laoise and Bidelia. "Is there nothing that could stop Erskina's power? Is there nothing stronger?"

"Nothing that we could get before dawn," the Advisor said. "I might know an incantation or two. But I am no match for Erskina and her command of this power."

Bidelia bunched her skirts with her stained hands. "So it is true, then. You can command the Freetor magic."

"I can perform a few small tricks. Nothing in comparison to what Erskina or even the apprentices can do," he replied. "I could distract Erskina. Let her know that I have learned magic without her. That would make her furious."

"And I could rally the castle guard," Keegan said. "But if Freetor magic is as powerful as you say it is . . ."

"Erskina would take one look at all of them and they would fall flat against the earth. And then we'd all be next." I punched the wall, ignoring the pain of the grit that dug into my knuckles. "We can't let her win."

"Isn't there anyone else who could help us?" Laoise squeaked.

"There is no one else. There is only us," I said.

My words were sobering. The Advisor clenched and unclenched his hands, as if considering the magic he yielded. Laoise stared up at the entrance to the dungeon that led to the surface. It was as dark as the underground outside, but soon the sun would pierce the black and Erskina would be upon us.

Keegan nodded. "Together we must warn my father. We will cancel the speech and surround the castle."

"And when the walls start bleeding with Marlenian blood, what will the Holy One do then?" Bidelia challenged. "We know she will strike, and we know nothing will stop her until the Holy One and his line and those who have opposed her are dead. Whom do you think will be next when she is done with you?"

"But out in the open, we are lost. The advantage of the castle—"

"The Elders are the ones who provided me with the castle layout. I was made to memorize it, so I imagine Erskina knows it as well as she knows the Freetor tunnels," I said.

"Then we allow my father to do the speech, in the square, and allow Erskina to descend upon us?" Keegan shook his head and sighed. "It's suicide, Kiera."

"We are all dead anyway if we don't try," I replied.

It was true and they knew it. We had to protect Keegan and his father from Erskina's power—and show the Marlenians who the real threat was.

Laoise reached for my hand and placed something soft in it. Smoothing it out, I felt the worn ridges and threads with my fingertips and knew it as my Violet Fox mask.

"We will follow you," she said.

# Seventeen

IT WAS JUST before dawn.

Laoise wrapped me in a large, dark cloak as the red light of the sun shone through the window. The Freetors always thought the early sun's rays had mystical healing powers, and as I bathed in its light, any hunger or tiredness I'd felt in the dungeons slipped away. Beneath the cloak, I wore my brown leggings and a clean leather dress over a white shirt. In my belt, my dagger was ready to be wielded if necessary, and I'd tucked my Violet Fox mask in there as well—just in case.

"You're sure about this?" Laoise asked.

I nodded. "I want to be there."

"I don't even think Lady Sylvia is going," she said, pulling my hood up. "Too bad. If Erskina accidentally killed her, I wouldn't be too sad about it."

I snorted. "That would be the last thing we need. A war with the East."

"We," Laoise muttered. "It's hard to get used to saying that."

"We will get used to it. We have to. We will be heard."

Laoise averted her eyes. "I wish Rordan were here. I mean, I know he didn't really . . . agree with everything . . . but . . ."

"I miss him too." My voice cracked a little. It was hard to think about him gone. "In the end, we were fighting for the same thing."

She nodded. "Yeah."

Our plan was simple. Keegan and the Holy One would travel by carriage to the Grand Square, just like they always did for the address.

The Advisor had requested a separate carriage. We had little trouble smuggling me in. Most of the guards were down at the square and the cathedral steps already, or were guarding Lady Sylvia and Lady Dominique from any chance Freetor attack. The servants were operating with a skeleton staff, since most of them had snuck down to the square. Laoise shooed those not in the know away and stuffed me in the carriage.

"I'll see you down there," she said.

"You're not coming?" I did *not* want to be alone with my father again.

She shook her head. "Mother and I have a few things to do for the ladies before going. But we will be there. I promise."

"I don't doubt it. Be careful."

"You be careful," she said, and shut the door.

The Advisor showed up a few minutes later. He swung in, tilting the carriage bed. I fell to the other side with a thump.

"Watch it," I snapped.

"Sorry. I wasn't sure if you were in here or not."

"Well, I am."

The carriage jolted forward, but at least I was prepared for that. He eyed me curiously. "This is how you intend to disguise yourself now?"

"It's better than nothing."

"It's better than your mask and cloak, I will give you that."

I gave him a dirty look and stared out the window, watching the winding road pass as we descended into the city proper.

"Kiera," he said my name softly, like it was hard to say. "I know I wasn't there for you or your brother. I thought of you every day. And I wanted you to have this"—he pulled out his journal from his bag— "but I don't know if you or I will be alive past noon today."

I glanced at the journal. The curiosity was killing me. "Did you really write in it every day?"

He nodded. "Every day, as you did."

Silence. I bit my lip.

"Keep it . . . for now," I said finally. "Whatever happens, we'll live."

He slid the journal back into his bag. "Your mother used to say something like that every time we went out on a mission."

I gritted my teeth. "Don't talk like that."

He shrugged. "I'm sorry, Kiera. I've waited so long to talk to you like this."

I wrapped my arms around my knees, curling into a ball on the hard seats. *I know*, I wanted to say. "You could have come and talked to me any time."

"Will you ever forgive me?"

I furrowed my brow to keep my thoughts away from all the nights I'd wished my parents were still alive, all the times Rordan had comforted me when we were alone, and to fight from hearing his dying screams in the square we were about to enter.

He took my silence as an answer.

A few long minutes of awkward silence later, the carriage stopped. I curled further into the corner, hiding myself as he stepped from the carriage into the waiting crowd. I wondered if Erskina was already there, lying in wait like me. I snuck a peek out the window. Keegan and his father were on the pavilion before the cathedral. Safe, for now. My father walked up to join them. I counted my breaths, trying to stay calm and focussed, and waited.

When I couldn't wait any longer, I slipped out of the carriage. No one was watching me. All eyes stared up at the pavilion a few stone-throws away as the Holy One stepped forward and prepared to deliver his statement to the Marlenian people. Guards swarmed the pavilion—a heavy guard for a simple address, but Keegan had of course delivered on his word. I hoped that whatever happened, he would stay safe. There was a round of applause and cheering that quickly quieted as the Holy One opened his mouth to speak.

"My dear people of Marlenia," he began. "Thank you for gathering here today. My news today concerns my son, Prince Keegan, and his marriage that was so . . . unfortunately . . . interrupted three days past."

The crowd held its breath. Nothing was official until the Holy One said it.

"My son, Prince Keegan, will not be marrying Lady Sylvia Frostfire of the Eastern province," the Holy One announced. "The engagement has been dissolved in the eyes of Dashiell, but we are hopeful that my son will find a woman worthy of the throne in the near future."

"Father," Keegan stepped forward. "I would like to say a few words."

The Holy One looked up, startled. "Oh . . . of course, my son."

Gossip flew fast like hummingbirds between the nobles, and the well-dressed young merchant women ruffled up their feathers, wanting to be seen.

"I do regret that my engagement with Lady Sylvia ended. My deepest apologies to the Eastern province," he began graciously. "My father was correct in saying I would find someone. She is, in fact, here today."

Excitement brewed in the air as the ladies common and noble glanced among themselves, eager to know who had stolen the prince's heart. I shrunk behind the carriage's wheel.

The Advisor leaned forward to warn Keegan not to go further, but he waved him away. Keegan looked to my hiding spot and gestured. "Step forward."

This was not part of the plan. I couldn't just go out there and show myself. What if there were archers under Erskina's command, waiting to smite me?

Keegan's eyes beckoned. I had to go.

I didn't think about it. With one swipe I threw off the cloak and revealed myself to the crowd. This didn't have quite the effect I intended. The nobles recognized me instantly—they had seen me in the cathedral, and in the castle. The merchants, the commoners, and the others in the crowd, less so. They knew me another way. That was why I drew the mask from my belt, and placed it over my eyes.

"What charade is this?" the Holy One demanded. "Keegan . . ."

"Father. People of Marlenia." Keegan reached for my hand and led me to the center of the pavilion. "Yes. This is the Violet Fox. The symbol of hope for the Freetor people. The thorn in our side."

He looked into my eyes, past the mask.

"I don't care if you were born underneath a mountain of soil and clay, and I in a mountain of silks and pillows. You hold no lands, you hold no silver, you own nothing because everything you do is for your people. Neither our births nor our titles matter. What matters is our common cause: to prevent harm to our people. To create a peace between us and end this silent war that has lasted almost two hundred years. But it's more than peace that I want." He cast a glance at the Holy One, surveyed his people, and then returned his gaze to mine. "I don't know how I know this, but you are my match. Your strength of conviction, your passion for what is good and right, your love for your people, it is what I hope to have. You are everything to me. And I wasn't sure if I could do this before, but now I know, Kiera. I *know*."

He slid the mask off my face and stuffed it gently in my belt.

"It is my intent to marry Kiera Driscoll, of the Freetor underground, or, as she is known to the Marlenian people, the Violet Fox—if she would have me."

My mouth fell open.

It was like something had snapped within every Marlenian in the crowd. In one second, the Marlenian people moved to the brink of madness.

"Hear me!" Keegan threw his arms into the air, and the power of his father's voice flowed through him. The Marlenians settled uneasily, in fear of words that had never before been spoken. "It is time we ended this war. Almost two hundred years have passed. It's time we started working together against our common enemies—"

"The only enemy we know is that rotten thief!" said a man in the crowd as he pointed at me.

A chorus of agreement roared among the thousands gathered, and some of them started to draw their weapons. If they attacked, there was no way we could hold them off, not unless we had the power of the Freetor Elders on our side.

Which we didn't.

"I may have stolen your bread and your apples and your threads and your fine jewels, but never have I taken a life." My voice rang out louder than Keegan's had, and echoed through the square. "I fought for the freedom of my people, but there were those among us who wanted to destroy you. And still do!"

"Lies!" the crowd yelled.

And then they were calling for my death. "Burn her in the square!" "I won't be ruled over by a filthy Undercity rat!" "Maybe the little prince needs to be taught a lesson!"

As the Marlenians threatened to rise against the monarchy and swallow us like a snake swallows its prey in the tall grass, the air cooled around us, and the sun—which had been peeking from behind the clouds—vanished. A thread of blue and white and violet robes trickled through the crowd in waved lines, worming its way to the centre and front of the mob. Apprentice Elder robes. My heart caught in my throat when I saw who was leading them.

The rumours were true. Erskina's robes were blacker than the darkest night underground, trimmed with a brilliant sky-blue that went around her high collar, which hid her seemingly frail, thin neck. Her eyes pulsed with hatred; bolts of lightning danced between her bony fingers. Those who did not move out of her way were pushed or moved by an invisible force as she floated up the steps. Upon seeing the display of Freetor magic, the Marlenians' cries for revolt diminished to a whisper.

Erskina stopped before us and whipped around to face the crowd. The castle guard drew their swords, ready to strike with the order, but the Holy One was watching her closely. Everyone was. I looked to my father, but his face revealed nothing. My insides felt sick. Soon, we would all be dead.

"Greetings, surface-dwellers," she said with a cruel, condescending smile. "I agree that there needs to be a change in regency." Her head snapped to the Holy One as sparks danced between her fingers. "Hand over the staff, old man. Your days of fine foods and riches are done."

The Freetors in the crowd cheered. They were not afraid to raise their voices against the Marlenians as they stood in Erskina's shadow.

Uncertainty clouded the Holy One's eyes. He took one careful step backwards, cradling the sceptre to his chest. "You cannot take Dashiell's symbol of power."

Marlenians shouted curses at the Freetors. It would be mere moments before chaos erupted between our two peoples. A large man wearing a baker's apron near the front of the crowd spoke up over the noise. "We'll never be ruled by an old Freetor sow like you! Let's kill her and hang—"

But before the dissenter could lead the mob against her, Erskina raised her seemingly frail hands and the man, and at least ten people standing next to him, turned into ash. A sudden violent gust of wind hurled their ashes into the air and swirled them around until the Marlenians' faces were black with soot.

"I will not tolerate troublemakers." Erskina's voice was cold steel. "Is there anyone else who would like to air their grievances regarding having me as your new High Queen?"

The Marlenians quivered with fear, and some shook their heads in disbelief. Those who tried to run out of the Grand Square were caught by Erskina's supporters and pushed back into the crowd.

"What have you done with the other Elders?" I demanded.

"Other Elders? There is only one now," Erskina declared, as if it had been true for a hundred years instead of a day. She spoke to the crowd again. "If you comply with my decrees, you all have nothing to fear."

"And what are your *decrees*?" I sneered.

"Freetors who swear fealty to me will earn lands worked by their ancestors two hundred years ago. Those who do not remember the sun and the lands held by their sires will be assigned new ones, to create new legacies."

The sparkle in the Freetors' eyes was unmistakeable. She was giving them what they wanted. A place in eternal sunshine.

"And you'll force the Marlenians to live beneath the surface? As we once forced you?" Keegan asked.

A bitter laugh escaped her. "Send you to the tunnels that we have worked so hard to build? No. Our hands have shaped them. We would not give what we have created to you so easily."

She raised her hands again, and the ground beneath the Grand Square shook. The sky clouded, and the city was cast in gloom. Bidelia held Laoise close and I reached for Keegan, but he was at his father's side, supporting him as the stones on the pavilion cracked. Like an underground snake, the cracks wormed their way down the stairs and zipped through the square. Marlenians and Freetors alike jumped backwards and forwards out of the way, but in the end, it made no difference. In the centre of the square, a hole started as small as a silver coin and expanded into a gaping, hungry mouth that tunnelled into the darkness. Those on the edge didn't stand a chance. Marlenian merchants, Freetors, and young children with no futures were sucked into the abyss, screaming the names of those who loved them.

The rising wind swept Erskina's dark cloak around her body. "To those who have wronged us: the earth will swallow you whole."

More fell into the darkness, and I could hear Rordan's voice in their cries—like him, they screamed for help that didn't come.

"Stop it!" I yelled, and barrelled towards Erskina.

The Advisor's fire was quicker. A short burst of flame leapt from his hands and seared Erskina's neck. It barely left a burn but it was enough—the hole in the square let out a sigh and stopped rumbling. The crowd skittered away from the edge while Erskina, enraged, turned her murderous glare on him.

"You," she said, her voice full of venom and hate. "Slipperier than your daughter. A traitor to your people. I will put you to rest."

The castle guard advanced, swords drawn, to intercept the powerful Elder. She laughed at them, and with the wave of her hand, she knocked them over like toy soldiers.

"You think steel, a metal that comes from the *earth*, will harm me?" She whipped a blade from inside her cloak and drew it across her leathery skin. The blade had sliced her skin, but she did not bleed.

"Freetor magic does not scare the Marlenian people," the Holy One boomed.

He shrugged off Keegan, who protested as he watched his father hobble towards Erskina. The crowd held its breath. Erskina stared him down like a bug that had to be squashed.

"You wish to fight me?" she asked.

"Death should have come for you long ago, Erskina," said the Holy One.

"Nothing made by man can kill me now," she said.

The Holy One raised and swung the sceptre, but suddenly Erskina was no longer in front of him. She appeared in a whirl of smoke behind the elderly ruler and dug her dagger deep into his back.

The collective gasp of the Marlenian people accompanied the Holy One as he tumbled to the ground. Keegan rushed to his side, but he was thrown backwards by an invisible force. The Advisor's flame, ready to strike at his command, flickered out. Bidelia and Laoise looked to the castle guard, but they were just as useless.

We were being slaughtered.

But I had to try.

I rushed Erskina from behind. She was standing at the edge of the cathedral steps in front of the pavilion, and if I could just push her down, maybe, just maybe . . .

Erskina whirled around as my fingers grazed her cloak. She grabbed my wrist, and her claw-like nails bore into my skin, drawing blood. I struggled, but my throat felt tight, like it had in the carriage when she had asked me to murder Keegan.

"Think about what you're doing, Kiera," she hissed. "Side with them and you will never be free."

Erskina's words grabbed my heart and made me pause, and almost brought me to my knees. She saw the hesitation in my eyes and, disgusted, threw me to the ground. I pushed myself back up and went for her again, but this time she kicked me in the head. My skull struck the hard stone. Erskina was a blur as she crossed the pavilion to where Keegan lay dazed.

"No . . ." I said, but I was in no better shape. My limbs flailed because my mind was mush.

She grabbed Keegan by his hair and held her dagger to his throat. The Holy One's blood dripped from the blade onto Keegan's tunic.

"Freetors, rejoice. The last of the blood that cast us down will now be spilt."

It was like everyone was frozen, unwilling, unable to do anything. Erskina had won. The Holy One was down. His breathing was short and laboured. He wasn't long for this world. His small, beady eyes strained hopefully at the sceptre, lying on the cathedral steps. Within the metal casing, the globe glowed sky-blue colour, pulsing faster and faster like my own thumping heartbeat.

That was no ordinary sceptre.

Only Freetor artefacts glowed a light blue.

I swiped the sceptre from the steps and with both hands, I aimed it at Erskina. It was warm and heavy. "You won't take him alive!"

My words awakened something in the glowing sphere. The sky clouded and hummed loudly as a crack of lightning hit the orb. I tried to let go of the sceptre but my hands were stuck to it. The wind picked up and people screamed as the lightning spun faster and faster around the orb and then released. It bolted for Erskina. The blue lightning struck her in the chest and propelled her backwards. Her head cracked loudly as she landed against the stone steps. Sparks of lightning made her body spasm as her lips quivered her last words.

"The Orb of Dashiell . . ."

Her body shuddered, and then fell limp.

Thousands of eyes stared up at me with fear, and gratitude. My hands were glued to the sceptre. The wood was an extension of myself. It was no longer heavy—it was like it *belonged* to me.

Until it was ripped from my hands.

The Advisor rolled it slowly between his fingers, examining the wood and peering into the orb, keeping it a safe distance from his face as lightning crackled around it.

My eyes narrowed. The mythology book from the library suddenly made sense. "You! You just wanted it for—"

He held it out for me to take. "Oak, with a natural finish. The orb . . . phenomenal power. Most certainly the Orb of Dashiell. How it got into the hands of the Tramore family . . ." He snapped his finger. "Of course. The day Captain Killan Tramore took it from the cathedral to rally his troops to victory against the Freetors. I wonder if he knew what power he had in his hands, power that the Church had protected for centuries . . ."

I stared up at him. "You don't want the throne."

"No, of course not. Kiera, how many times—"

"A lot," I said.

My distrust wounded him, but he nodded.

No one knew what to do. They looked up to us standing on the pavilion, and those standing on the pavilion looked to each other. The sceptre cast a faint blue glow on my skin. I wondered what to say, what to do with this power, when the Holy One hacked up blood chunks on the stone. The Advisor moved to aid him, but the elderly leader waved away anyone who tried to help him.

"Keegan," he said. "And the girl."

Keegan and I exchanged quick glances as we moved to either side of the dying Holy One. We helped him to his feet. His grip was deathly tight around my wrist, and my stomach was in knots.

Each breath was a raspy struggle. Even the wind was silent, waiting for the Holy One to form words.

"My blessing," he managed to say, bringing our hands together and cupping them.

Shocked silence quickly turned into alarm as the Holy One's eyes rolled back into his head and he collapsed. Keegan caught the bulk of his father's weight before his head could hit the steps. A castle guard gently took the Holy One and called for a carriage. Healers standing at the sidelines were finally free to attend him.

"You need to address them together," the Advisor said to us.

"What do we say?" I asked. The sceptre hummed gently in my ear.

Keegan took my hand and squeezed it. "You'll know what to say. I'll start."

Speaking as the Violet Fox, that was easy. I could hide behind the mask and make my words hers. But now the mask was gone. I was Kiera Driscoll, soon-to-be ruler of the entire Marlenian realm. My mouth felt dry. When Keegan gave me a smile, my stomach knots loosened. Together, we would make this right.

"People of Marlenia. Whether you live on the surface or underground, there is nothing to fear. As the prince of Marlenia and heir to its throne, I abolish all penalties and bounties on all Freetor persons found on the surface. Marlenians, you will treat those who have come from beneath the surface with the same respect you would treat your loved ones. Those who fail to uphold and respect the freedoms of either Marlenians or Freetors will be subject to punishment.

"The Freetors will have their land."

But *where*, and *how*, the people cried, and *they can't have mine*, rose from the crowd from the Marlenians, while the Freetors were almost too stunned to speak. Years of hiding underground, and now they were free to roam in the sun. From the mixed emotions displayed on the Freetors' faces, and from my own dual feelings, it was clear that they didn't like seeing a Marlenian—and the Marlenian prince no less—telling them that they could be free. Even abolishing the punishment for being on the surface seemed somehow wrong. We didn't need someone to tell us how or when to do things. That was not the Freetor way. Unless you were an Elder or you carried out the Elders' wishes, it was hard to get Freetors to do anything.

And that was when I realized how hard a task was set before us. Almost two hundred years of prejudice would not melt away in minutes.

Before the Freetors could raise their voices and their arms in protest, I stepped forward. "When we were cast down by the Marlenians, we went like martyrs, because we had the magic to protect us. And we entrusted our Elders to keep the magic for us, for who better than the most learned and wise of our people to keep something sacred? We were all taught this at a young age and have believed it ever since.

"But you have all witnessed what happened today. Anyone can be corrupted. Our Elders have been murdered because a woman wanted nothing but to rule. Freetor or Marlenian, it doesn't matter. Some Marlenians will leave their last loaf of bread on their step for the hungry, starving man, while some Freetors will hoard whatever they have without thought of their neighbours' stomachs. There are good and bad Freetors, just as there are good and bad Marlenians.

"Together we are stronger. Together, we can build a land that is rich and bountiful, so we can trade with our friends, and lay waste to our enemies. Freetors and Marlenians will have an equal say in how the city—and soon, the world—is run."

A rush of power ran over me. I rose the sceptre in the air, in victory. Hundreds of pairs of eyes were staring up at me, and not because I was doing something wicked—it was because my words were invigorating them, making them think about change. Keegan looked at me with such joy that all I wanted to do was kiss him.

"That said," Keegan continued, squeezing my hand, "acting on behalf of my father, the Holy One, I decree that the Freetor slave trade is hereby abolished in the Western province. Freetor slaves in service to Marlenians, you are now free, as of this moment. If any man, woman, or child is found to be in unpaid or unwilling service to a Marlenian, he will face the Holy One's justice."

My heart skipped a beat, and there was a roar of cheers not from the crowd in the square, but from the streets surrounding it. Freetor slaves were told to be unseen, unheard, but now, they flooded into the square, screaming and shouting with victory. There was no reason to hide anymore. They were free. If only Rordan were here to see it.

"Thank you," I whispered.

Keegan cupped my face and kissed me.

As our lips touched, it was as if our words suddenly had meaning. A Marlenian and a Freetor, together, ruling. Another cheer erupted in the square. The musicians behind us burst into a rousing reel, and when Keegan and I pulled apart, I saw the dancing in the square: Marlenian and Freetor, woman and man, child with child—the colours of the clothes and their quality didn't matter.

My heart swelled—this was our moment. We had done it. My people were free of tyranny.

I looked around. Laoise embraced me, tears in her eyes. "I can't believe this. This is really happening, isn't it?"

"I hope so," I said, grinning.

Bidelia squeezed Laoise's shoulders and smiled at me. "You've done a brave thing today."

"What are you going to do now?" I asked her.

"What do you mean?" She looked offended. "I am the head servant to all noblewomen in the castle. A good position, no matter whom I'm serving. I'll be staying right where I am. Where I am needed." And then her smile widened. "I can't wait for those Marlenian brats beneath me to find out they've been taking orders from a Freetor all these years."

The Advisor raised an eyebrow as he sauntered towards us. "Be careful, Bidelia. Just because the prejudice has been erased by decree of the Holy One's son doesn't mean that prejudice in the minds of the people will disappear."

"Oh stop," she said, flustered. "I was just making a wee joke."

He cast his eyes over the celebrating crowd. "This is a victory, to be sure. But we still have much work to do. Have you thought at all about the Elders' magic, and what is to be done with it?"

"All of the Elders are dead," I said. A twinge of sadness fluttered in my chest. "You are probably the only Freetor who knows magic now."

"I wouldn't be so sure of that. Elder apprentices, they may know more than I. And with the Elders dead, they will fill in the Council of Elders. The Freetors are more likely to listen to them, than to you, especially now that you will be adorning a Marlenian crown."

"I will talk to them. I'll make them see that there's no reason for us to fight anymore," I said.

He looked unconvinced. "There is more to running a realm than talking to the opposing side, Kiera. Know that your decrees have consequences. You and Keegan both spoke a lot of words today that may come back to bite you later. The Freetor slave traders. Do you think they will be submissive to your decrees?"

"They will listen," Keegan said firmly. "They must."

"The Freetor slave trade is a business. Many will be out of a job."

It wasn't one of *your* businesses, was it? I almost asked, but I was afraid to know the answer.

"There can't be equality while it stands," Keegan retorted.

"I understand that. But you have yet to understand how to run a realm. You marry a prince, and these are the decisions you are faced with daily." He was not unkind with his words, but there was little empathy on his face. "Welcome to the castle again, Lady Kiera."

My father turned and left me there. My *father*. The man I had written to all these years was a shadow, a lie. I had built him to be someone different than the man who defended us today. Whether or not I could grow to love this stranger was yet to be seen.

The celebrations continued in the square after we left. Guards remained in case the celebrations became a riot, while we went back to the castle. Keegan went to his father's bedside. The healers reported that he had a high fever but that they had stopped the bleeding and bandaged it to prevent infection.

I still held the sceptre. I was afraid to put it down. All this time, a magical artefact, in the hands of the Holy One and his family. Not just any magical artefact, but one of Dashiell's four great artefacts, infused with his blessing and dangerous magic. I couldn't think of a safe place to put it, but I didn't want to carry it around with me—it was too cumbersome. I reluctantly decided to keep it in my chamber—for now, with my Violet Fox cape and mask, and my journal. I locked the windows and assigned three guards to my chamber, just in case.

Sleep threatened to overtake me, but I fought it. There was one more thing I had to tend to before I could sink into bed and not fear for my safety. I found Bidelia in the servants' corridor, heading for the castle kitchen.

"Neither Lady Dominique nor Lady Sylvia have left their chambers since this morning," Bidelia replied when I asked. "I'm about to send someone to check on them now, in case they are hungry. They aren't prisoners, you know."

"I know. But having them in the castle doesn't make me feel any better. I'm going to go talk to them."

"Take someone with you," Bidelia warned with a wave of her finger. "Just because they've been alone all day doesn't mean they haven't cooked up a scheme. You have Keegan, but that doesn't make you immortal. You are the heiress to the Marlenian throne, and even the Violet Fox bleeds."

I nodded and hurried away, wondering absently what I would do with my violet cape and mask. I didn't have to hide anymore. Maybe I could put it on display. Or, maybe someone would create a tapestry to commemorate this historic day. Keegan and I, kissing in front of a large crowd! My stomach felt warm and fluttery, and I was grinning like a fool.

I called Captain Murdock to accompany me to Lady Sylvia's room, and he reluctantly followed. He stayed three paces behind me, which did make me wary. Finally, the Violet Fox so close to his reach, and he dared not touch me—could not touch me—because of the words Keegan had uttered hours ago.

As I entered the corridor containing the ladies' chambers, I heard footfalls bounding towards us. I couldn't shake my first instinct. I whirled around with a hand to where I usually kept my dagger—but it was only Keegan.

"You all right?" he asked, looking from me to Captain Murdock.

I rubbed my eyes and shook my head. "Fine. I just—"

"You should sleep. I can handle the ladies," he said.

"How did you—?"

"You say anything in the servants' corridors and it will reach the ears of the Holy One." He smiled. "Go to bed. We've a busy few days ahead of us."

*We have a busy life ahead of us*, I wanted to say. But I shook my head. "No. We've got to do this together. We have to show them that this is how things will be." I drew a deep breath.

"Well, if you're going to be stubborn about it."

"You gave up that one pretty easily."

"With the Violet Fox, I must choose my battles wisely," he replied, running a finger over his scar.

Lady Sylvia's personal guard was standing outside her door. I stayed behind Keegan as he approached. The guard looked as though he was going to stop us, but Keegan paid him no mind as he knocked once, and then twice, and then called her name.

"Lady Sylvia. It's Prince Keegan. May we have a word?"

Clattering and shuffling came from behind the door. We waited, but no one answered.

"I'm coming in," Keegan announced, and twisted the knob. "Captain, you may remain here."

"Yes, Your Highness," Captain Murdock said gruffly.

Keegan opened the door wide.

Lady Sylvia was straddling the window sill in only her chemise, her petticoat and soft shoes. The bed had been stripped and the sheets tied in knots: one end around the bedpost and the rest trailing out the open window. She was looking down and out the window, her hands gripping the makeshift rope, whimpering. When she saw Keegan and I walk through the door, she leapt from the sill, tripped, and fell backwards onto the wooden floor on her rump, screaming all the way. I suppressed a laugh, but not a grin.

But my smile faded soon enough. Lady Dominique was beside her, also in a loose-fitting chemise and petticoat probably belonging to Lady Sylvia. When she saw Keegan and I, she snatched something tied around her leg. As her fingers curled around it, I recognized what it was: a dagger, fashioned from hard rock mined from the underground. A crude, but common shiv used by Freetors. She crouched, her bare feet awkwardly poised but ready to leap at me nonetheless. I readied to defend myself, but Keegan held up his hand.

"Ladies. Please. Explain to me what is going on here."

"What is going on?" Lady Sylvia's voice was shrill. Desperate. "You. Are. *Marrying*. That . . . creature." She pointed at me as if I were a human-sized slimy bug that she wanted to trample but couldn't. She rubbed her rump tenderly.

"You didn't attend the speech today," Keegan said, eying the both of them with caution. "Lady Dominique, is there any reason you're holding that? Perhaps the captain can help you put that down."

There was a coldness in her eyes that I recognized. It was *my* coldness, how I had looked at the prince when I had been a wanted criminal. That was almost two weeks ago. How quickly things could change. "My *prince*." She rolled her *r*'s and hissed the word like a snake. "Allow me to rid j'ou of dat disease-ridden *filt'* behind j'ou."

"That won't be necessary," Keegan said with a grim smile. "Put the weapon down, my lady. We only want to talk."

"I'm done talkin'," she said. Her knuckles were white with the grip. "She will pay pour her crimes. De Nort' will see to dat."

I wanted to apologize for what she'd been through. Being kidnapped and forced to live underground in the filth and the squalor while I took her name and lived the high life in the Marlenian castle: getting the prince, having the prince fall in love with her name and then, finally, me. But that darkness in her eyes, that hate, present then and now, I wouldn't get past it. She wouldn't listen to reason. Her hate of the Freetors had been present long before all of this, and these events had only strengthened that within her.

"We only want peace," Keegan said.

"J'ou will not get it," Lady Dominique promised.

"No, you won't!" Lady Sylvia declared. She looked around for a weapon, and upon not finding one, raised her finger menacingly. "My father is on his way. And once he finds out that Prince Keegan has denied me my throne, not only will I have my weight in silver, but *all* Freetors in the West and the East shall face the *power* of my father's army—"

"If your father is on his way, why are you sneaking out the window?" I asked.

She stopped, looked to Lady Dominique for an explanation, and then mustered up a forced resolve. "If my father could get here *faster*—"

"You were thinking of running off into the woods? That meeting him there would somehow get you home faster?" I burst into laughter. "You'd be caught by bandits. Marlenian or Freetor, bandits don't care. They'd ransom you to the highest bidder."

"Well we weren't going to stay here another moment!" Lady Sylvia proclaimed. "Were we, Dominique?"

Lady Dominique shook her head very slowly, her eyes still fixed on me.

"You aren't prisoners. You are free to leave," Keegan said.

"Yes, everyone is free today," Lady Sylvia said sarcastically. "But not for long. You will see." She snatched her dress, lying rumpled on the bed, and thrust her thick thighs into it. Wordlessly, Lady Dominique clutched the shiv between her teeth as she helped Sylvia do up the dress. "The East and the North are hereby allied. All past mishaps shall be forgotten. Together, we will crush the West and all of its Freetor-loving scum."

Keegan's expression was grim. "Is that an official declaration of war?"

"Take it as you will," Sylvia said offhandedly. She crossed the room with long strides and pressed Keegan into the wall. I drew my dagger and pointed it at her neck. She flashed me a wicked smile. Her nose and lips were inappropriately close to Keegan's.

"You will be *very* sorry for your choice of bride," Lady Sylvia whispered tenderly.

Ignoring my blade, she stormed out of the room. Lady Dominique eyed me viciously, but she did not say a word. Lady Sylvia's threats I could handle, but the coldness in Dominique's eyes troubled me. I had stolen Lady Sylvia's love, but I had stolen something more precious to Dominique: her name. It was cold to the North, and their life harsh, and I had a feeling that she would be sharing with the West just how cold it could really be. She slunk between us like a dark shadow and disappeared into the hallway behind Lady Sylvia.

"Are we worth this?" I whispered.

Keegan gently pried my dagger from my fingers and tucked it back into my belt. "This, and more."

I stared up at him. "And you meant what you said in the square?"

"I meant every word as much as you did."

"I meant . . ." I bit my lip. "About . . . marrying me."

He pressed his forehead against mine. "Not only that." His hands were warm and strong, and soft against my callouses. "I meant what I said that night of the masquerade. You are . . . you are incredible. I don't care if you are the Violet Fox, and I wouldn't care if you owned all the land there is. If I am to marry to take the crown, I will have you or no other."

"Even if there's a war? The East and the North will crush us. And the South, who knows what will happen . . ."

"Now you're afraid of a little danger?" His voice was gentle and seductive. "Of course it won't be easy. Laws can be changed, though, albeit slowly. The people will adjust. We will have the peace we want. No one will harm you so long as you keep close to me."

I smirked. "I would be gone before they could attack anyway."

"Yes, that's true. So what is your answer, my lady? You never did say yes to my proposal."

"It wasn't much of a question."

"Well then. Kiera Driscoll. Lady of the Underground. The Violet Fox. Would you become my wife and rule by my side as High Queen of Marlenia?"

I grinned. "Yes. Even without the rule, even without the crown, even without the lands and the titles, yes."

"The Violet Fox, she is easy to please."

He kissed me again, cupping my face, sending tingles down my spine. I was going to marry a prince. Me, born from dirt and grime underneath a bustling city, growing up to wed the wealthiest and most powerful man in all of Marlenia. All that didn't matter—our bodies, they were made from the same fabric of life, and the rest had just been sewn in. Together, we would make it work. It shouldn't have been real, but his warm breath on my cheek, his strong hands intertwined with mine, told me otherwise. And the scar that had once separated his lips, now one with mine, had healed.

This feeling, this bliss, made me realize a simple truth.

I had been free all along.

And now, a sneak preview from the next book in the series . . .

*The*

Rule.
That's what the Marlenians are telling me.
But even with this crown on my head,
and my love at my side,
The war is only beginning.

"DASHIELL CAME TO me, in a dream," the Holy One said.

I parted my lips to speak, but he shook his head slowly. "I know your people don't believe. I know that . . . that my ancestors have done violent things in his name. But seeing you . . . in the Grand Square . . ."

He fell into a violent coughing fit. I offered him a white tissue, but it came back red.

He wiped his mouth. "My dream . . . Dashiell, brilliant in white light. He spoke to me. He said, *my messenger will put me back together again*. Do you know what this means?"

I shook my head.

"Your name. Kiera Driscoll." He pronounced the words slowly, carefully. "In the library, in the old texts, it says the Driscolls held land by the Forever Sea, near the western-most tip of this province." He held up a heavy hand and pointed to a pile of tomes on the nightstand. "I have been reading about before the war."

My breath caught. I found my feet and sauntered to the texts. Information about my ancestors, before the Marlenian-Freetor war. Not Rordan, nor my father, had told me anything about what my family had done on the surface. All we'd known, for two hundred years, was hate.

I flipped through the pages. Most of them were faded records and maps of who held what land, who was the eldest son of whom and what daughter had married what other lesser lord. Some of the handwriting was so faded that it was impossible to decipher. But if my family history was in here, then maybe Laoise's was too, and all the other Freetors. We would finally know what lands were really ours.

And so would the Marlenians.

"Most of these books were destroyed during the war," the Holy One said. "No one wanted any record of Freetors holding lands, in case one came to claim them."

My hand passed over the leather-bound covers. "What does this have to do with your dream?"

The Holy One coughed blood again into his tissue. His eyes were creased with wrinkles. I wondered then how old he really was.

"Your name. Driscoll. It means, *the messenger.* Dashiell said, *the messenger will put me back together again.*"

"That's it?" I knew I was being rude, but I couldn't help it.

"The pieces of Dashiell," the Holy One said. "You know them."

I frowned. "I don't know—"

"The pieces." He was more insistent this time. "The artefacts. The orb. The cloth. The slab. The spear." He hacked more blood. "Gifts from our great Lord."

"I'm calling Keegan. You need to rest," I said.

I went for the door when his powerful voice overcame me. "You must find the spear."

I stopped, and turned slowly. "The . . . Silver Spear?"

"Yes. You know the story."

Actually, I didn't. Not really. There was a myth that Alastar the Hero had travelled to the end of the Forever Sea and found a spear encased in ice. It was the most beautiful thing he'd ever seen, and he wanted it, because he could see it was magic. When he tried to break the ice with his own spells, it shattered and marred his face. He lost an eye, some said. I didn't know whether or not he kept the spear, or whether this happened before or during the war.

"It's just a story," I said. But even I could hear the uncertainty in my voice.

"Not a story," said the Holy One. "It *caused* the war between us. And only it can heal the wound between us. Ask Ivor."

I didn't know if I should explain that Ivor Ferguson was really my father, and that his real name was Conal Driscoll. The Holy One was probably too sick to remember. He was already thinking that I was supposed to get some artefact for a man-god that I didn't even believe in.

Still . . .

The Silver Spear was on the Elder's crest. The story about Alastar the Hero probably had some truth to it. And if it was near the Forever Sea, where my ancestors once lived . . .

Maybe the Violet Fox had more adventures in her yet.

# Acknowledgements

Dad, Mom, Jessie, and family. Mom went first in the last acknowledgements so now it's Dad's turn.

Also special thanks to Marie & Joe Farrell, my other family, for letting me turn their basement into my office/living space.

Rachel Small, my editor, for her help in teasing out inconsistencies and general word clean up!

This book would not have been completed without copious amounts of good-tasting energy drinks and support from Twitter friends and book bloggers.

And of course, special thanks to Dave, my partner and cover designer. So many loves.

# CHECK OUT OTHER FICTION AT
# FAERY INK PRESS

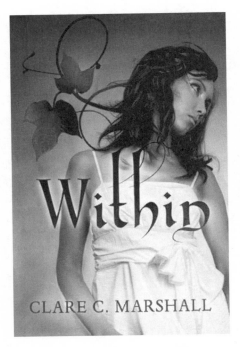

Trinity Hartell's life changed after the accident. Left with irreversible brain damage, she becomes a burden to her mother, a cause for heartbreak for her boyfriend Zack, and a flattened obstacle for her jealous best friend, Ellie.

But then she starts writing. Perhaps it's a coincidence that the psychotic, murderous protagonist of her novel bears a striking similarity to the charming Wiley Dalton, a mayoral candidate in the upcoming election.

Or, perhaps not...

Praise from book bloggers for
WITHIN
by Clare C. Marshall

"This story moved me to tears."

— *Gothic Angel Book Reviews*

"Ms. Marshall has done an exemplary job of writing both sad and emotional scenes, but also weaving together an intricate story line that will capture any reader."

— *Avery Olive, author of A Stiff Kiss*

"Within pours out suspense and developing talent! I'm very curious to see where Clare's work goes in the future. She is definitely one to watch!"

— *Inklings Read*

"Marshall did a great job writing a suspenseful yet heart-breaking plot that kept me reading to the last page."

— *A Written Rhapsody*